MW01240691

What Lies In Truth

Trish Mastel Stricklin

What Lies in Truth

This story is the sole work of

Trish Mastel Stricklin

WHAT LIES IN TRUTH is a novel based on the story of the author's grandparents. Names and identifying details of people and some places in this book have been changed, except for the first names of a few of the author's family members.

All contents are original except for one song now a part of the public domain.

Grateful acknowledgement is made to the Crittenton Home in Helena, Montana for permission to use the name of their foundation in the book.

Dedication:

This book is dedicated to my Aunt Ernestine without whose skepticism, research, and determination, the truth about my grandparents would have never been uncovered.

Prologue

As I grew up, my grandmother was always elusive about my grandfather. Occasionally she gave her children and grandchildren tidbits of information. Some were facts and some were not. Grandmother told us that he'd been a Portuguese aristocrat who had escaped Portugal after fighting a losing battle to keep the Portuguese King on the throne. We learned she'd named my mother after his sister Angelica. That he'd been a traveling salesman and died from influenza on May 28, 1932, in Minneapolis, Minnesota.

She always claimed the pictures she had of him had been destroyed in a flood, so we never knew what he looked like. As a child that seemed believable, but as I got older, it puzzled me because my grandmother had many pictures of herself and her three children growing up.

When I researched my roots after my second son was born, she sent me a picture of my grandfather she'd cut from a group photo. The photo only showed his head; she had an artist draw in a suit. At the same time she told me he'd been born in Soalheira, Portugal, on April 19, 1893, and that they had married on January 10, 1927, a year and eight days before my mother was born. On the rare occasion she spoke of him, she wore a smile, telling us he was very handsome, and he had a beautiful voice that both my mother and my aunt inherited.

After my grandmother's death, we found clues to my grandfather's true identity in the memorabilia she left behind. My Aunt Ernestine, who had long believed her mother had lied about her father, went on a quest to discover the truth. What she found stunned us all.

WHAT LIES IN TRUTH is the novelized story of my grandparents. I drew my inspiration from letters, news articles, photos, documents, and family anecdotes. I have changed all names except for the first names of Henrietta, Angelica, Ernestine, and Robert. The names of towns have also been changed, except for a few Montana cities.

The Crittenton Home that existed in 1928 and still exists today gave me permission to use their actual name in my story.

Trish Mastel Stricklin

Chapter One

Mid-December 1911
A Prison in Lisbon, Portugal

Eighteen-year-old Lieutenant Martim Ferrera stood before the Republican Tribunal, waiting for his trial to begin. His manacled wrists oozed blood and fever ravaged his body. The knife wound festering on his side and the foul bandage wrapped around it added to his misery. None of it mattered. His honor was intact. And nothing they did to him would destroy his loyalty to the Crown.

As he stood between two guards, he imagined he resembled a walking corpse. Months in a dark cell with only watery gruel turned a man into a shadow of his former self. His thoughts wandered to his fellow Royalists, the ones captured with him. Were they still languishing in this hellhole, or had they met their fate? A chill went through him. What had happened to his *papai*? Had he escaped? Could he be rotting away in another barbarous prison? Or was his *papai* dead?

Martim's fellow Royalists had believed whatever befell them would be worth the price if they returned King Manuel II to Portugal's throne. Now they were paying for failure. One thing he knew for sure. Paiva Couceiro, their Royalist leader, had escaped across the border to Spain with nearly 600 of the King's loyal supporters. Martim was sure they plotted another coup. He prayed his *papai* was among them.

A Republican General sat at the bench, pounded a gavel, and Martim's trial began. The General glared at his prisoner as he adjusted the military medals decorating his chest. His gray mustache twitched as his lips curled in a sneer. "Lieutenant Martim Ferrera, you stand accused of treason to the Republic. What say you to these charges?"

Martim glared at the red and green Republican flag hanging at the General's right side. It had replaced the flag of the Monarchy and was a symbol of treachery. Portugal's new Republican government had closed churches, banned teaching religion, and expelled religious orders. He reeled with anger as his mind filled with accusations of his own. With a hostile glare, he rasped, "Outlawing our Church makes you the traitor in the eyes of God."

The General growled. "Don't give me your Catholic babble, Lieutenant. Your Church has crushed the people of Portugal for centuries. Now answer the question. How do you plead to the charge of treason?"

Martim took a deep breath, pain shooting through his side. Determined not to show weakness, he kept his gaze steady on the General. "My effort to restore the rightful king to his throne is not treason. It is the ultimate act of patriotism."

The General's face flushed red. He nodded at one of the guards standing beside the young lieutenant. The man's fist plowed into the prisoner's wounded side. Lights swirled behind Martim's eyes, and agony exploded across his ribs. He groaned and sank to his knees. The guard hauled him to his feet.

The General's nostrils flared when his gavel pounded the bench. "You will not speak to me with insolence, Martim Ferrera. Now answer the charges."

Standing, Martim kept his head high. He responded with silence and a hostile glare. "Very well, traitor," the General said. "We don't need your verbal admission. Your defense of the Church and the Monarchy are verification enough. A ship leaves for our colony in Angola in a few days. You will be on it, exiled for fourteen years of protective custody." He nodded at the two brutes flanking Martim. "Return the prisoner to his cell."

As the guards hauled him down the dank stone passage to the cage where they kept him, Martim's face remained impassive. His mind whirled with the General's words. Fourteen years of protective custody meant hard labor. And in Angola, hard labor was especially cruel.

The guard with the beastly fist shoved him into the cell, spit on him, and then roughed him around to unlock his manacles. As he did so, he leaned into his prisoner and whispered, "Check the mattress. I'll pretend to lock up." The guard slipped the manacles from Martim's wrists, flung him to the floor and gloated, "Enjoy your stay in Angola, scum."

The barred door clanged shut, leaving Martim stunned at this change of fortune. He listened as the key worked in the lock. Had the guard left it undone? The two brutes sauntered away, congratulating one another on giving the prisoner well-deserved treatment.

When the echo of their footsteps disappeared, Martim checked beneath his molding mattress. The straw stuffed pallet was the only furnishing in his cell except for a chamber pot a guard escorted him to empty every few days. He found a pair of ordinary fisherman's britches, a shirt, a gray woolen sweater, and scruffy boots. The well-worn clothes reeked of fish and sweat.

The outfit made for a decent disguise. But what was the plan? He looked through the clothing and checked the mattress again for instructions. Nothing. His heart quickened. There had to be information that told him how to escape and where to go. He fell to his knees and searched every inch of the cell. No luck. Shivering, he slumped against the wall. Was this a perverse joke to trick him into attempting an escape that was impossible?

Heavy boots thudded through the passageway. Sentries. He shoved the disguise under the mattress, wrapped himself in a threadbare blanket, and waited. Keys jangled in a lock nearby. A cell creaked open, and an inmate pleaded for mercy. A loud thump, a cry of agony, and then silence. The door clanged shut and the sound of a body being dragged faded. Martim said a prayer for the unlucky prisoner.

Hearing nothing but the scurrying of rats, he dug back beneath the mattress and searched the disguise again. The trousers' waistband held an object. He picked apart the threads and discovered a small blade, a few coins, and a note. The words caught him by surprise. Neither a fellow officer nor the uprising's leader had penned the letter. It had come from his *papai*. He wasn't dead. He'd escaped to Spain with the other Royalists. Martim's eyes filled with tears as he read his father's words.

Meu Filho,

I paid your passage to Brazil on the Rio Negro, now anchored in the bay on the Rio Tajo estuary. Make haste as the ship sails at dawn. The coins are for bribes, if necessary. When the cathedral bells ring midnight, you'll find your cell unlocked. I paid the guard who delivered your disguise to arrange a distraction for the other guards. He'll be waiting in the north passageway and will lead you from the prison to the streets. Once outside, you're on your own. The sketch below shows the way to the cliffs, down to the bay, and to a dinghy hidden in the boulders marked on the map.

Go with God, meu filho. I am proud of your allegiance to our King and your fight to restore him to his rightful throne.

Papai

The map outlined a passage through the prison, down the steep back alleys of Lisbon to the cliffs that rose above the Rio Tajo's estuary. An X marked the spot where he'd find the boat. Martim knew enough about the city to recognize the route was not the quickest, but likely the safest.

As the hours passed, Martim memorized the map, matching it to his knowledge of Lisbon's streets. He knew nothing of the climb down the cliffs except that it was dangerous. The prison's dim shadows gradually darkened to an inky black. The inmates in the surrounding cells slept fitfully. Their moans and nightmare screams pulsed through the fetid air.

Martim cringed when a bawdy song and stumbling boots reverberated through the cell block. A ghostly glow seeped through the darkness; the lantern of a sentry on his rounds. With one eye half-closed, Martim pretended to sleep. Light threw shadows of the bars across the stone floor. The rancid smell of booze filtered through the stench of his cell. When the drunken jailer staggered to the next cell, Martim fingered the matted bandage on his side. The blow in the courtroom had reopened his wound. Fresh blood ringed the mass of old seepage. He winced as he removed the wrap and then replaced it with strips torn from his prison shirt. He couldn't let blood leak into his disguise. Evidence of a wound could give him away.

He struggled into the fisherman's clothes and then bunched his prison garb under the ragged blanket. The pile gave the impression of a human shape, although one of little substance. He scraped off his scraggly beard with the blade and stuffed the facial hair in his pocket. His stomach churned as he sat and waited, staying alert for unwelcome sounds.

When the cathedral bells rang at midnight, Martim hesitated. Was this a plot to catch him on the run so they could shoot him and save his jailers the effort of sending him to Angola? No. The mines in the colony desperately needed free labor. He'd carefully checked the note earlier, and it was definitely his *papai*'s handwriting. That didn't mean the loyalty of the guard in his father's pay was absolute. But he had to chance it.

"God help me," he prayed as he tied the laces of the worn boots together and slung them over his shoulder. He slipped barefoot down a slimy passage, listening to the moans of his fellow prisoners. He desperately wanted to include them in his escape, but that was beyond his power.

As he approached the place to meet his rescuer, he heard laughter and the slur of garbled conversation. He jumped when a hand touched his shoulder, ready to fight. He relaxed when he recognized the guard. The man put his finger to his lips, peered around the corner, and nodded for Martim to check the situation himself.

Three jailers slumped against the wall in a shadowy alcove. A jug of rum occupied their attention. The heaviest guard took a swig, wiped his jaws with the back of his hand, and handed it to the lanky fellow slouched beside him. A third guard lay on the stones and snored, drool dribbling from the corner of his mouth. A twinge of pity rose in Martim. In the morning, not only would the guards suffer the consequences of their drunken orgy, they'd face serious trouble when they realized he'd escaped.

His rescuer said, "We have to pass by them to get out. You'll be okay. Just follow my lead."

As Martim fought the tremors racking in his body, he pulled his cap farther over his forehead and followed his rescuer into view of the drunken guardsmen. The heaviest man lifted the rum jug and called, "*Amigo*, thanks for the grog."

Martim's liberator chuckled, "You got a reason to celebrate, *meu amigo*. It's not every day a man's first son is born."

A deep scar zigzagged from the big guard's ear to his lip, disfiguring his grin. He nodded at Martim. "Who you got there?"

Martim braced himself for trouble, but his rescuer grabbed the rum and took a swig. He handed Martim the jug and slapped him on the back. "My brother-in-law. He wants to work here. Thinks it'll be easier than fishing."

The big guard's laugh echoed through the chamber. "He's too young to handle the criminals holed up in this cesspool. Tell him to stick to fishing."

Martim took a long swallow of rum, its warmth spreading through him. He took a second swig and let a bit dribble over his sweater. He handed the jug to the drunk and said, "Sound advice, amigo."

His liberator winked at Martim. "Come, let's get you to that bride of yours. I'll bet she's waiting with open arms."

Martim followed his emancipator through the prison service door into a back alley and filled his lungs with fresh air for the first time in months. The cobblestones held puddles from a recent rain. More rain threatened as clouds scudded across the moon. A tangy breeze blew up from the sea, catching Martim's cap. He grabbed it before it got away.

"*Muito obrigado, senhor*." Martim said, thanking his rescuer and shaking his hand. He frowned. "When your mates find me missing, won't they suspect you?"

"Don't worry, *meu amigo*. I'm not on shift. Just brought the rum to help the loudmouth celebrate. Doubtful they'll remember what happened. Besides the blow I busted on your ribs in the courtroom and the roughing up I gave you in your cell are extra insurance."

"Convinced me you weren't a friend," Martim grunted.

His rescuer handed Martim a cloth-wrapped bundle. "Bread and cheese," he said. "Two months on prison rations can leave a man weak."

Martim tucked the bundle under his arm. "I'm forever in your debt, *senhor*."

As the guard put a hand on Martim's shoulder, he whispered, "Go now. Your journey will take hours, and it's a dangerous one. God be with you."

The guard slipped down the street, away from the prison. Martim took off in the other direction with the escape map etched in his mind. He worked through Lisbon's back alleys at a casual pace, not wanting to attract suspicion. After all, he was a poor fisherman returning from the bar to the docks. If anyone stopped him, the rum saturating his sweater and the smell of his breath would confirm his story. He felt his pocket for the coins and the little blade, just in case.

Taking bites of the bread and cheese as he went, Martim stayed in the shadows, a little strength returning. The streets and alleys were empty except for an occasional drunk making his way home. His route took him past the Basilica da Estrela. Anger rushed through him when he saw the magnificent cathedral doors barred by heavy chains. This was Christmas time, for God's sake. For over a hundred years, worshippers had visited the cathedral's famous Nativity Scene, sculpted by Joaquim Machado de Castro. Not this year. Not only had the Republicans exiled their King, they'd shuttered churches, banished priests, and outlawed teaching religion. Somehow, the usurpers had to be driven from power.

A barrage of barking echoed in the alleyway. Heavy footsteps and a gruff command followed. Martim ducked into the covered threshold of a darkened home, slumped against the wall, and held his breath.

Three soldiers prowled by, their shadows stretching in the soft glow of a street lamp. Guns drawn, they searched for whatever had alerted the dog. Could they hear his pounding heart? One soldier grunted, "Nothing here. Let's check the next lane."

As Martim listened to the clomping of their boots fade, he realized if he was going to make it to the ship, he must stay focused. He peered around the doorway. "*Maldito*," he swore as he watched the soldiers disappear into the alley that was his path to Lisbon's cliffs. Now what? Follow the soldiers staying in the shadows? No, too dangerous. He needed to detour. But could he find his way back to his route? He had to. His life depended on it.

He stole away in another direction, down cobblestone lanes, zigzagging between buildings and tall stucco fences. The icy wind bit his face and sliced through his sweater. As the air currents grew stronger, they pushed the rain clouds away. The moon, now nearly full, made it more difficult to stay hidden.

His breath coming in gulps, he neared an intersection that put him back on course. Voices stopped him. He peered around the alley's wall. *Santa Mae de Deus*. The three soldiers stood in the moonlight talking with two police officers.

He froze against the stucco wall and listened. "A damn royalist traitor escaped the prison. Orders are to track him down and bring him back alive if you can but shoot if you have to."

"*Inferno*!" a policeman swore. "How'd he get away?"

A husky voice answered. "The idiot guards got liquored up, so they didn't notice the escape. But a prisoner saw the convict slip by and snitched. No surprise, extra rations always make the rats squeal."

Martim's stomach tightened at the sound of bullets being slipped into a gun chamber. A sneer followed. "Hard to hide in jail garb. He'll stick out like a sore thumb."

A smug grunt followed. "They think he's dressed as a fisherman. Whoever helped the traitor has a price to pay."

Bile burned in Martim's throat as he stole over the stucco fence. Landing in a courtyard, he came face to face with a snarling dog, its hackles raised, its bared teeth glistening in the moonlight. The snarl turned to a vicious bark. Boots raced towards the enclosed patio.

Martim tossed the last of his bread and cheese to the dog and crawled through a laurel hedge, blood pounding in his ears. He slipped over a second wall into an adjacent alley. Out of breath, he pressed his hand against the pain spreading in his side and tore down the steep lanes between the houses. As he raced, he glimpsed moonlight glittering on the bay in the distance, where several ships stood at anchor. Which ship was his?

A breathless shout pierced the air. "Halt, traitor."

Being caught meant execution. He had to escape. Pain didn't matter. Life and liberty did. He smelled freedom in the salty air wafting from the bay. Adrenalin, desperation, and prayer brought him to the cliffs overlooking the estuary.

His chest heaved as fire ripped through his hamstrings. A fierce wind put whitecaps on the waters below. He gave Lisbon one last look. From here, the Castelo de São Jorge, with its ancient towers and crenellations, dominated the skyline. His heart ached. It might be years before he saw his beloved country again. Unless Paiva Couceiro and his Royalist Army stirred the peasants to join the insurrection when they made their next incursion into Portugal.

He scanned the bay's overlook and spotted the clump of trees that marked his route to the beach. He crouched in the shadows. "*Maldito*," he swore to himself. His pursuers sprinted around the last villa, stopped with their weapons drawn, and studied the area. They must not have seen him because they split into two groups and headed in opposite directions.

Martim crawled to the cliff's edge. There was no obvious path through the scrubby vegetation to the beach. Now grateful for the moonlight, he grabbed a branch of stunted Juniper, eased himself over the ledge, and started the steep descent. His sense of urgency grew as he picked his way from foothold to foothold through the stones and brush. Breathless and in pain, he reached the rocky shore. A large outcropping of boulders rose near the tide line twenty meters away. "God please," he prayed, "let the skiff be there."

As he stumbled over the rubble that littered the beach, he made his way towards the mass of rocks. In the darkness, a jumble of fishing net caught his foot and sent him flying onto a jagged rock. He lay there, catching his breath with his hand on his wound. Warm, sticky blood oozed through his sweater. He pushed himself to his knees and crawled the last few meters to the cache of boulders. *Graças a Deus*! His *papai*'s men had hidden the skiff where the map had shown.

The wind coming off the cliff grew stronger, carrying voices from above. A shower of rocks rattled down the hill and landed close by. He looked up. Three soldiers stood silhouetted on the bluff. The shadows cast by the boulders hid him for now. But once he got the dinghy into the water, moonlight would make him an easy target. Should he wait, hoping his pursuers abandoned the hunt? His father's message said the ship sailed at dawn. The sun rose soon. He had to get the skiff into the bay.

He scanned the waters. Ships anchored everywhere. Naval vessels, cargo ships, tugs, and barges. He identified three passenger vessels moored near each other where the harbor met the sea. Which was the Rio Negro? The ships were too far away to tell.

With his feet digging into the stony beach, he pushed the dinghy to the water's edge. The boat's hull scraped as it moved across the rocks. Thankfully, the stiff breeze carried the sound offshore, and it would make rowing easier. He gasped as he waded into the bay, the icy water biting into his wound and chilling him to the bone. He braced himself and plodded beside the skiff until waist deep. His teeth rattled as he eased himself aboard and grabbed the oars. Soldiers remained on the top of the cliff, scanning the beach and the bay. A bank of clouds drifted over the moon. His pursuers disappeared in the darkness, giving him a moment of reprieve.

Barely able to breathe, he set course towards the three passenger ships praying one of them was the Rio Negro. Each pull of the oars, each jolt of the skiff as it bounced on the rough waves, sent pain shooting through him. He gritted his teeth and rowed. He'd rather die on his way to freedom than be held captive again.

When he was halfway to the three ships, the moon slipped from the clouds and sent flickers of light rippling across the whitecaps. The moon's rays revealed the words 'Rio Negro' painted on the hull of a large vessel, and it looked as if it was preparing to get underway.

A hail of bullets tore past him, spraying the water, a few thudding into the skiff. He glanced back. Half a dozen soldiers fired at him from the cliffs. Another round of bullets screamed past his ears. One pinged his oarlock and ricocheted into the prow.

His heart pounded as he shed his boots and slipped into the bay. Panting, he treaded water for a moment. Bullets peppered the surrounding sea. As he set off, the frigid water became another enemy. Over and over, his arms reached for the next wave. He'd always been a confident swimmer, but he'd never faced such treacherous conditions or been challenged by debilitating pain. Doubt whirled in his thoughts. No, he wouldn't let his enemies win.

Fifty meters from the Rio Negro, his energy spent, an undertow sucked him beneath the waves. The sneer on the General's face when Martim stood before him in the courtroom drifted in and out of his consciousness. His eyes gloated, as if Martim's life were worth nothing. The General's judgment was wrong. Martim's lungs burned as he battled to the surface. Gasping, he took a stroke. One more. And then another. "God, help me endure."

The current caught him and carried him near the ship. A safety ring hit the water and bobbed his way. With his strength nearly gone, he grabbed hold of the ring. A towline pulled him to a ladder on the side of the vessel. Minutes later, he lay on the deck, faint with pain and fatigue. A sailor rolled his coat into a pillow and placed it under Martim's head. Someone yelled, "A blanket, a jug of rum. *Pressa*." Martim could feel the vibration of feet running down the deck.

Wrapped in a woolen navy blanket and propped against a lifeboat, his frozen hands gripped a mug of warm rum. Life seeped back into his body as he gazed at the stars. The heavens blazed more brilliantly than ever. He was free, headed to the safety of Brazil. There was Sirius, the Christmas Star. Like the three kings who'd traveled to Bethlehem, he'd found his way. He made the sign of the cross. "Divine Savior, you brought me to safety. I vow to dedicate my life to You in thanksgiving."

Chapter Two

Six years later, March 31, 1918, Easter Sunday
St. Bernard's Church, White Water, Wisconsin
Henrietta Marie Hoffmann

Sunlight poured through the stained-glass windows, sending colors rippling across the pews, dancing through the congregation, and playing on the vaulted ceiling. Incense mingled with the fragrance of lilies that graced the sanctuary. Thirteen-year-old Henrietta had never seen anything so magnificent.

As always, her *vader* had settled his family in a pew near the front where his eight children had an excellent view of the solemn rites. Pride surged through her as pastor Father Verhelst entered the sanctuary and genuflected before the altar, the altar her *vader* had built. She was positive no altar in the entire state of Wisconsin was as lovely. Her *vader* was that good a carpenter. Last week he'd scolded her for bragging about it to her friends. And yesterday he'd told her she'd better admit her sin of pride in confession. Her penance had been easy. Only three prayers of Hail Mary.

As the Mass began, a rustle at the end of her family's pew caught her attention. A young priest she'd never seen before with gold-rimmed glasses and short, dark, curly hair slipped into the end of the pew. His graceful movements and handsome profile sent a thrill through her heart. He genuflected, made the sign of the cross, and joined the congregation in song. His deep voice turned her legs to jelly. She leaned near her sister and whispered, "Greta, who is that priest?"

Greta stretched to see who Henri was eyeing. "I don't know, but he sure is good looking. And oh my, his voice is amazing."

"Amen to that," Henrietta muttered.

Moeder stiffened beside Henrietta. Her fingers paused on her rosary as she flashed a warning to her two middle daughters. *Vader* wasn't so subtle. He reached behind his wife and put a firm hand on Henrietta's shoulder. She wanted to shrug him away but didn't dare. Instead, she bowed her head and pretended to study the missal she'd gotten as first prize in her catechism class, but the corner of her eyes remained on the priest whose voice sounded like heaven itself. When the hymn ended, the impressive priest helped the old lady standing beside him settle into the pew. His kind smile added to the thumps in Henrietta's heart.

Father Verhelst walked to the pulpit and cleared his throat. "Let us welcome Martim Ferrera from Portugal and lately of Brazil, who has joined us as our guest today." The handsome priest stood and nodded at the congregation. Father Verhelst went on. "As a new novitiate, he will study at St. Albert's Abbey and will occasionally visit other local churches. Today, we offer the Mass for an end to the Great War ravaging the countries on the other side of the ocean."

Henrietta murmured to Greta. "He's not a priest yet, but he will be. Maybe when he's ordained, the Abbey will assign him to our church."

Greta put a finger to her lips and tilted a warning look at *Vader*. A deep scowl creased his forehead. Henrietta swallowed her resentment and turned her attention to the altar. Through the entire Mass, the novitiate's rich voice graced every hymn and flowed deeply into Henrietta's soul. When the service ended, she floated with the congregation outside where the Pastor and the novitiate greeted the parishioners.

Out in the sunshine, Henrietta waited impatiently with her family for her turn to be introduced to the handsome man. He stood at the bottom of the stairs beside the Pastor. From the top step, she caught glimpses of him greeting the adults with a handshake, patting the boys on their shoulders, and nodding with a heart throbbing smile at the girls, all of whom giggled like silly goats. She had to stand out from those ninnies and impress him.

But how? A patch of golden daffodils bloomed beneath a cherry tree. They danced in the breeze, swaying in rhythm with the pink cherry blossoms. Flowers! The perfect welcoming gift. She eyed her parents. Good. They chatted in Dutch with another couple from the home country, unaware she planned to help herself to the daffodils. And her five sisters were busy with their friends.

She slipped through the crowd, glad for once she was short for her age. Moments later, she returned to her parents' side with a bouquet hidden behind her back. They hadn't noticed she'd been gone. But her eighteen-year-old brother Fritz, Mr. Goody Two Shoes, had suspicion written all over his face. She smiled innocently at him and turned her attention to the novitiate. Sunlight danced over his handsome face, gilding his hair, and flickering off his glasses.

He shook hands with *Vader* and *Moeder*. And then it was her turn.

Determined not to act like the ridiculous girls before her, she looked up at him with her most charming smile. She knew he wasn't a 'Father' yet. Still she said, "Welcome to our country, Father Ferrera." And then she handed him the daffodils.

His eyes widened as he smiled. "*Obrigado,* thank you." A jolt ran to her heart when he took the daffodils and his hand brushed hers. His accent flowed through her ears like an enchanting melody.

Her brother Fritz hissed in her ear. "Those flowers belong to the Church, Henrietta. You shouldn't have picked them."

She scowled and checked for *Moeder*. She was busy chatting with a neighbor. But *Vader* was watching. The frown on his face meant there would be serious trouble when they got home. Oh well, it was worth it.

She smiled at the handsome priest, who seemed a bit puzzled. Perfect. She hoped his English wasn't good enough to understand the commotion Fritz was making. And Pastor Verhelst's attention was on an elderly couple, so he wasn't aware of the little flap going on right beside him.

Father Ferrera said, "*Senhorita*, your name is?"

"Henrietta Marie Hoffmann," she answered in her most mature voice.

Pastor Verhelst interrupted with a hand on Father Ferrera's shoulder. "We need to go, Martim. The next Mass begins in ten minutes."

"Pleased to meet you, Miss Henrietta Marie Hoffmann," Father Ferrera said, his accent melting through her. He looked at the daffodils in his hand and bowed. "*Muito lindo*. Very lovely." He turned and followed Father Verhelst into the church.

She watched until the doors closed behind him. She hoped she'd see him again. Soon.

Chapter Three

Six Years Later
Palm Sunday, April 13, 1924.
St. Albert's Abbey,
Glade Harbor, Wisconsin

Henrietta held on to her hat as a chilly breeze whipped through St. Albert Abbey's college campus. Spring was taking its time to unfold. Tiny bits of green had just showed on the birch and cherry trees. Daffodils remained closed, waiting for warmer weather. But the heady scent of hyacinths blooming in beds along the cobbled walkway promised spring was ready to rise.

Morning shadows stretched in front of the congregation as they strolled towards the campus chapel. Most students and community members still wore winter coats. A few optimistic souls like Henrietta wore lighter jackets, hoping wearing them would nudge spring to get on with its business.

Henrietta noticed none of these signs of spring. Her mind was on Easter Sunday six years ago when a young novitiate with an amazing voice had captured her heart. Other novitiates had come and gone from St. Bernard's since, but none had moved her in the way Father Ferrera had. He'd never returned to her family's church. Greta said he'd been ordained four months ago and now taught Engineering and Theology here at the Abbey's college.

Tomorrow was Henrietta's first day as an Abbey servant working in the kitchen, serving meals, and helping with the laundry. Without a doubt, she'd come into contact with Father Ferrera often. She laughed to herself, remembering the giddy pleasure she'd experienced in his presence when she was thirteen. Did her delight still linger, or had her infatuation been a young girl's crush? She leaned into her sister, walking beside her. "Greta, who's celebrating the Mass this morning?"

Greta shrugged. "You never know. It could be any of a dozen priests." Greta had been a servant at St. Albert's for two years. When *Vader* learned about an opening at the boardinghouse where Greta stayed, he'd insisted

Henrietta was now old enough to work at the Abbey and earn her own way. *Moeder* had added the experience would help prepare their willful daughter to settle down with a good man and become a wife and mother, hopefully soon.

Henrietta and Greta entered St. Albert's chapel, took a palm frond from the linen-covered table, and made their way to a pew near the altar. Henrietta surveyed the sanctuary. Like all Catholic Churches around the world today, purple cloth shrouded the crucifix above the altar and the statues of Mary and Joseph. The shrouds would remain until Easter Sunday. Kneeling, she thumbed through her missal, but her mind refused to focus on her prayers.

A slow, sorrowful melody hummed from the organ and interrupted her thoughts. A priest dressed in purple vestments entered the sanctuary, swinging a vessel of burning incense. Henrietta's heart jolted. She leaned into Greta and whispered, "It's him."

Greta gave Henrietta a flabbergasted stare. "Yes, it's Father Ferrera. Don't tell me, you're still smitten?"

She huffed, "Of course not, Greta. Don't be silly. That was ages ago." But her eyes remained on Father Ferrera. Her heart suggested she wasn't being honest.

Greta nudged her sister. "Me thinks thou doth protest too much. The glow on your face tells me you're hiding some unholy feelings."

"Fiddlesticks. My feelings are nothing more than admiration for a fine priest." She paused. "I admit, he's a good-looking man, but I realize he's off limits."

"Saying he's off limits is fine and dandy. But you don't fool me, Henrietta. You've always gone after what you want. The consequences be damned." Greta put a finger to her lips and turned her attention to the altar.

Henrietta shrugged and continued watching Father Ferrera. He moved from the sanctuary and down the main aisle, swinging the incense vessel over the congregation as he sang the Palm Sunday opening hymn. The spicy smoke enveloped her as he passed by. And just as it had six years ago, his deep voice melted into her soul. She felt Greta's elbow prodding her side. She turned and mouthed, "What?"

Greta hissed. "I can read you like a book, Henrietta. He's a priest. He's not available. Besides, there's Ike, and he's crazy about you."

"Yes, there's Ike." She sighed and turned her eyes back to Father Ferrera. Throughout the service, Henrietta struggled to keep her mind on her prayers. When Mass was over, the congregation slowly paraded from the Church, each person stopping to greet Father Ferrera outside the chapel. As the pews emptied, Greta nudged Henrietta towards the aisle. Henrietta shook her head. "Not yet."

"Why not? Don't you want to say hello to the priest you've been ogling?"

"Don't be ridiculous. You're imagining things. Of course I want to say hello. But if we're last, we can talk longer." Greta was right. She needed time to pull herself together, so she didn't make a fool of herself. After all, he was a priest, and she had a serious suitor. Her heart shouldn't be atwitter over a man who was forbidden.

They dawdled until only one person was ahead of them. Midway through Father's conversation with the young man, he caught Henrietta's eye. His brows rose in surprise. Did he recognize her? He turned back to the young man, shook his hand, and said, "I'll see you in class tomorrow, James." His accent wasn't as pronounced as it had been before. Still, the musical lilt in his words added to the commotion in her heart.

He turned to Henrietta and searched her face. "You look familiar."

She couldn't help it. Her smile turned flirtatious. "A few years ago, Easter Sunday. You were at St. Bernard's. Father Verhelst said you'd just arrived at St. Albert's."

His face lit up. "Ah, yes. You were the girl with the daffodils."

She tilted her head and laughed. "Right. I'm Henrietta Hoffmann and this is my sister Greta."

"What brings you to St. Albert's?" His tone had a hint of amusement.

"I start work tomorrow in the kitchen and the laundry."

His eyes crinkled. "The College can use a worker with your spunk, Miss Henrietta Hoffman."

The way he said her name caused a flutter of guilty emotion. All she could do was smile. He looked at Greta. "I imagine it'll be nice having your sister here to work with you."

"Today's my last day, Father. I have a new job as a housekeeper for my cousin, Father Cornelius Hoffmann."

"Father Hoffmann. We're acquainted. He's a good man." He looked at his watch and frowned. "Ladies, I wish I could stay and talk, but my next service starts shortly." He stepped back. "I'm sure I'll see you later, Miss Hoffmann." He turned and jaunted up the chapel steps.

Henrietta watched as a new flock of churchgoers followed him inside. With a hand on her chest she said, "I can't believe he remembered me."

"You're not easily forgotten, Henrietta. After all, who steals daffodils from a Churchyard and doesn't care if she gets in trouble?" Greta shook her head and laughed. "Who tricks the boys in her class to eat worms and then tells everyone it was their idea. And what thirteen-year-old girl sends away for cigarette samples pretending she's a grownup and almost sets the barn on fire when she tries them out?"

An impish grin grew on Henri's face. She shrugged. "So?"

Greta shook her head. "You're a piece of work, Henrietta. Come. I'll give you a tour of the grounds. Someone told me when Father Ferrera first arrived at St. Albert's, he helped plant the trees you see all around you. And the priest he worked with taught him English."

***

A week later

Late Easter Sunday, the clock at Henrietta's bedside ticked towards midnight. She lay awake in her boardinghouse bedroom. Moonlight worked its way through the chintz curtains and flickered off a bottle of rose water sitting on the dresser. Her back ached from the long hours she'd spent in the Abbey's kitchen this past week. She turned over and stretched, trying to ease her sore muscles. But the pain had set up camp and refused to leave. She resigned herself to the lumps in the mattress and pulled her quilt tighter around her shoulders.

Thoughts of the day rolled through in her mind. She'd been up early to attend the first Easter service and then spent the day helping prepare the holiday meals for the Abbey residents. With the meals done, she'd worked at the sink for hours scrubbing pots and pans. At least she got tomorrow off as compensation.

She smiled, remembering this morning's Easter Mass. As she had hoped, Father Ferrera had officiated. There was something about him that gave the service a deeper, more spiritual quality. Was it his rich voice, his tantalizing accent, or the aura of kindness that glowed around him? A shiver of pleasure ran through her. Maybe the specialness she found in the service was something else. Something that was forbidden.

Whatever it was, Father was constantly on her mind these days. She'd seen him in the dining room throughout the week, surrounded by students. All seemed in awe of him. Several times she'd glimpsed him hurrying to a class he taught, deep in thought. Yesterday, she'd worked in the Abbey's laundry. The head laundress had assigned her to deliver clean sheets to the small table located outside the room of each resident priest. When she'd heard a beautiful voice singing in the room at the end of the hall on the third floor, she realized the room was Father Ferrera's. Although it was strictly forbidden, she'd knocked on his door and offered to make his bed. He hadn't objected. In fact, he'd welcomed her in and thanked her.

She wondered if he'd be officiating again at the early Mass next Sunday, the one she'd attend in order to be on time in the kitchen. She hoped so. Her heart slumped. Next Sunday brought an issue she didn't relish facing. Ike planned to visit that afternoon when she had time off. What was she going to do about him? Everyone thought he was her beau, except Henrietta herself. He was likable enough, steady, and *Moeder* and *Vader* thought he'd make a suitable husband. Unfortunately, she had no romantic feelings for him.

She got up, padded across the wooden floor, and opened the window. The breath of spring drifted in. Stars sprinkled the sky. Moonlight glittered on newly forming leaves in the yard below. The Abbey's grounds beckoned from across the street. She hadn't found time yet to walk beneath the trees Greta said Father Ferrera had helped to plant. She couldn't sleep, and she loved the night. So why not go now?

Mrs. Phillips's boarding house had a strict curfew for the ladies living under her roof. She didn't allow women boarders out after nine o'clock. The rule didn't apply to young men. Mrs. Phillips allowed them to come and go as they pleased. Ridiculous. Sure, safety was important. But sometimes the reason for this kind of rule seemed exaggerated to restrict women's freedom. Nothing she'd seen or heard this past week suggested the Abbey grounds were unsafe.

She slipped into her shoes and coat that covered her nightgown. Her boarding house key went into her pocket as she crept from her room, down the stairs, and out the front door. Her heart settled into a peaceful rhythm. No one to watch her. No one to hold her back. No one to tell her what to do. She headed up a path on the Abbey grounds and into the trees. Moonlight painted lacy shadows of the tree branches on the ground.

She found a bench beneath a cherry tree facing the Abbey. The cool damp from the stone seat oozed through her coat. It didn't matter. Though it was around midnight, a few lights still glowed in the windows of the three-storied abbey. One of them was the last room on the third floor. Father Ferrera's room. Was he awake preparing for tomorrow's classes? Or writing a sermon for next Sunday? Or maybe a letter to his family in Portugal? Was he a night owl like she was? When his light winked out, she got up and wandered down the path through the trees to a pond she'd been told was there. Lily pads floated on the moonlit water, a few already budding. Last autumn's cattails had gone to seed. Their fluff exploded like white hair gone wild. She settled on a large flat rock and watched the dance of night. Somewhere in the distance, an owl hooted. A frog jumped from a log into the water, forming ripples on the pond. And bats swooped through the air, catching newly hatched insects.

She startled at footsteps behind her and turned. Her heart seized as a man strolled towards her. "Oh, Father Ferrera, it's you," she said. Her heart settled.

"And it's you," he said, his voice full of concern. "What are you doing out here alone in the middle of the night?"

"I couldn't sleep, and it seems so safe."

He nodded. "I understand. I love the night air and when the moon is bright, I come here to clear my mind." His voice became stern. "Nevertheless, Miss Hoffmann…."

She interrupted him. "Please call me Henrietta."

"Henrietta it is." Though his face was in shadow, she could see a deep frown creasing his brow. "Doesn't Mrs. Phillips have a strict curfew?"

"She does." Henrietta tilted her head, looked up at him, and smirked. "Are you hearing confessions next Saturday, Father?"

"I am."

"Then I shall confess to a priest who understands my transgression and can forgive."

He gave half a laugh. "Henrietta, it is not up to me to understand. It's the Lord who understands and forgives." He sat beside her. "The Abbey's grounds are safe, but you should be worried. The Lord will forgive you for being out past curfew. But Mrs. Phillips will not. She's thrown out boarders before who don't follow her rules."

His closeness took Henrietta's breath away. She shivered. It wasn't from the cold or from fear of being caught. Feelings blazed through her, feelings she should have for Ike. Not for a Catholic priest. She wanted to linger beside him. But she had to go before she said or did something she shouldn't. "It's good to know someone shares my love of the night, Father. But you're right. I should go. I don't want to be forced to leave."

***

Martim

Father watched her disappear into the shadows. Her smell lingered, hinting of rose water and mingled with the perfume of spring. Who was this woman who loved the night? Her appearance at Mass last Sunday had sent an emotional quake rumbling through him. Throughout the past week, he'd gotten glimpses of her in the dining hall, on the Abbey grounds, and she'd been in his room to make his bed. She stirred him in ways he recognized were wrong. How could a woman he'd met only a week ago move him so deeply?

His mind flew to the treatise he'd read when he'd worked on the Brazilian Railroad in the Amazon before he immigrated to America to become a priest. The treatise had a long title, but it was one he'd never forget.*The Demonstrations of the Necessity of Abolishing a Constrained Clerical Celibacy; Exhibiting the Evils of that Institution and the Remedy.* The treatise spoke of the need to abolish the required celibacy of the priesthood. Was the Brazilian bishop and senator who authored the treatise right? The bishop certainly had plausible arguments in favor of allowing priests to marry. But it didn't matter. For now, the Church considered it wrong. And he'd taken a vow of chastity.

Perhaps Henrietta had been placed in his life as a test. Though he barely knew her, she seemed an intelligent and unconventional woman with a passion for life and a mind of her own. He laughed. She was also a bit of a rogue. Still, that didn't excuse his immoral feelings. He would confess as soon as possible. But he would never reveal who had brought his sinful desire. He didn't want his superiors to have a reason to send her away.

Chapter Four

Sunday, April 27, 1924
St. Albert's Abbey
Henrietta

Henrietta fretted through the week trying to figure out what to do about Ike. Her efforts had been fruitless. Father Ferrera kept hijacking her thoughts. Maybe she should just marry Ike and be done with it. But she longed for a career, to be something more than a wife and mother. Her parents had pulled her out of school after eighth grade, so both teaching and nursing colleges were out of the question. But business school was an option. They accepted students without high school diplomas. But would Ike want a wife who worked outside the home? She'd bring up the idea about attending the Glade Harbor School of Vocational Training when he came to visit on Sunday. See what he thought. Let him know she would save as much of her salary from the Abbey as possible and pay the tuition herself.

Sunday afternoon found her wandering the campus waiting for Ike, hoping he'd support her plan for business school. The day was glorious. Bees danced through the cherry blossoms. Robins flitted through the branches, making nests for their little ones. She found a spot in view of the Abbey where she'd told Ike to find her. She hummed to herself as she brushed away a cluster of pink petals that sprinkled the stone bench and settled down with her composition book. All day she had an urge to write a song that kept playing in her head. She opened her notebook and began.

Let the Rest of the World Go By
By E.R. Ball and J. Keirn

Is the struggle and strife
We find in this life
Really worthwhile after all?
I've been wishing today

I could just run away
Out where the west winds call.

Chorus

With someone like you, a pal good and true,
I'd like to leave it all behind, and go and find
Some place that's known to God alone,
Just a spot to call our own.
We'll find perfect peace,
Where joys never cease,
Out there, beneath a kindly sky.
We'll build a sweet little nest somewhere in the west.
And let the rest of the world go by.

She put her pencil down, annoyed with herself. Someone had invaded her thoughts as she'd written, and it wasn't Ike.

As she closed her book, a shadow passed over her. And there was Ike, dressed in his tweed jacket and tie with a fedora covering his reddish- brown hair. One hand held a picnic basket, the other a bouquet of daffodils. He handed them to her. "For my blue-eyed beauty," he said, his voice sick with love.

She composed herself and took the flowers. She might like Ike better if he didn't seem so eager. But it wasn't his fault. He assumed this was the way to win her heart. She sighed, "They're lovely, Ike."

He grinned. "You ready for a picnic?" His face hinted of a secret. He took her hand and helped her up. "Your letter said there was a pond nearby."

"About a quarter mile through the trees," she said, hoping today she'd find something to love in Ike. His hand, smooth and clammy, did nothing to spark desire. It spoke of a comfortable life, of an accountant who made good money. Her parents had two criteria for a suitable match. First, the man she married had to be Catholic and attend church faithfully, which he did; the second, he had to earn a good living. Money was necessary, but it wasn't nearly as important as a husband who saw her as an equal, a difficult standard when the church didn't recognize women as equal to men.

She watched Ike spread a blanket beside a large rock, the rock where she'd sat in the moonlight with Father Ferrera a week ago and had learned he enjoyed the night as much as she. Did Ike share any of her passions? If she were to say 'yes' to the marriage proposal she was sure he planned, she had to find a few things they had in common other than both being Catholic.

Today, the sun glittered on the pond. Swallows, not bats, swooped over the surface, snatching bugs in mid-flight. Her interest peeked when she saw a pair of ducks skittering among the reeds, gathering bits of cattail fluff. "Oh my gosh, Ike." She pointed. "Check it out. I think a momma and poppa duck are building a nest in the sedges."

Ike glanced, muttered something about spring, and returned his attention to the picnic basket. He laid out a china plate of finger sandwiches, a Wedgwood bowl of peeled boiled eggs, a jar of pickled beans, and two cherry tarts. He handed her a napkin with a hopeful grin. "Shall we eat, sweetheart?"

Henrietta tucked her skirt beneath her legs and arranged herself opposite Ike with a magnificent view of the pond. She reached for one of the dainty sandwiches, saying, "The meal looks wonderful, Ike. Who put it together?" She hoped somehow he'd helped with its preparation.

"My mum. She knows what pleases the ladies."

"What about you?"

"What do you mean?"

"Did you help your mum put it together?"

"Me?" He gave her a puzzled stare.

She sighed. "Never mind." The ham salad sandwiches were tasty and the cherry tart exceptionally good. But she would've preferred a lunch Ike had made himself, even if it had been ordinary peanut butter and jelly sandwiches. She wanted a man who could and would work in the kitchen and put together a meal when necessary. As she ate, Ike babbled on about the raise he'd gotten and how he'd taken over a big account at his firm. She watched the ducks moving about the pond.

They finished the lunch, and she began packing things back into the basket. Ike touched her hand and grinned. "I'll do that, sweetheart. Just sit there and be your pretty self." At last, a good sign.

As he cleaned up, she took off her shoes and stockings. With fingers crossed, she said, "When everything's put away, let's wade in the pond. I want to find that duck nest and see if it has any eggs."

"You go ahead," he said, shuddering. "I hate the feel of muck on my feet."

"Really? I love mud squishing between my toes." She shrugged. "I guess I'll explore by myself."

Ankle deep, Henrietta waded through the water along the shore, careful not to scare the ducks. As she got closer to a clump of cattails, the female skittered away, squawking. "It's okay, Momma duck. I won't hurt anything. I promise." Parting the reeds, she discovered a clutch of five pale green eggs. She signaled for Ike to come see. He shook his head, his hands signaling a firm 'no way'.

Frowning at his squeamishness, Henri turned and moved closer to the nest, hoping for a better look. Momma duck squawked at the intrusion, letting Henri know she was too close. Reluctantly, she returned to shore.

Back on the blanket, she dried her feet as Ike fretted. "Are you sure the Abbey doesn't mind you being in their pond?"

"No one ever said not to," she answered, trying to keep from showing her frustration. "As they say, 'sometimes it's easier to ask forgiveness than for permission'."

Ike laughed. "Sometimes I think that's your motto, Henrietta. You push boundaries until you find a roadblock you can't get around." He scratched the back of his neck. "You are more adventurous than any other woman I know."

She grinned. "I enjoy trying new things." She paused and gave him a serious look. "There's one adventure I feel compelled to take."

He took her hand. "Is it something I can help with?"

"No. But you need to know, I want to go to business school and become a stenographer."

He gasped. "Why?"

"I don't want to be a servant all my life. I want a career. And being a stenographer could be a stepping-stone to something bigger, something challenging."

He looked perplexed. "You won't be a servant forever, sweetheart. And you won't need to worry about money." He pulled a ring from his jacket. "Marry me, Henrietta Marie Hoffmann. I'll take care of you and do everything I can to make you happy." He took her hand and slipped the ring on her finger. His face was eager and full of hope.

Her heart seized. Words froze on her tongue. She had suspected a proposal was coming, but not this soon. She'd hoped to figure out her own heart before it happened, and then gently let him down.

When she didn't answer, he went on. "Your parents gave me their blessing."

"It's not my parents marrying you, Ike. And I'm not sure I can."

"But I love you, Henrietta."

She tucked her skirt tighter over her knees and looked at the ring again. A diamond glittered, surrounded by five tiny rubies. It was elegant and beautiful. Her girlfriends would ogle it and tell her how lucky she was. But luck wasn't what she wanted. She yearned for a man she could love in return. She sighed and looked at him. "Ike, you're a decent man, and I know you love me. But I don't have the same feelings for you."

His voice became emotional. "I'm sure you could learn to love me, Henrietta. Many marriages start that way." He paused, waiting for an answer. When all he got was silence, he sighed. "At least wear the ring a while and think about it."

"I can't Ike. It'll give you false hope. You deserve a woman who will love you in return. That woman isn't me." She stared at the ring again. It was more gorgeous than any she imagined she'd ever wear. But the love it should symbolize wasn't in her heart.

Today, she'd hoped she'd find something in what he said or did that would kindle her love for him. Instead, her doubts had grown. All the little things that happened this afternoon only pointed out the reason their marriage wouldn't work. He wanted a traditional wife. That's not who she was. Feeling hollow inside, she took the ring from her finger, opened his hand, and laid it on his palm. "I'm sorry, Ike." She stood and walked away grateful he didn't follow. Her parents' probable disappointment in her decision didn't matter. She'd save money and prove to them a woman could be more than a housewife.

Chapter Five

Two years later, April 30, 1926
White Water, Wisconsin
Henrietta

Late Friday afternoon, Henrietta ducked under the fence and took a shortcut through the pasture to her family's farmhouse. The milk cows watched as she plodded by, their mouths brimming with spring grass, their tails swishing away the flies. Their contentment was contagious. As she worked her way around the cow pies, the strain of her secretarial courses and her part-time job cleaning for an invalid woman melted away. It wasn't just the thought of a weekend with her folks, but she'd learned Father Ferrera would officiate Sunday's Mass at St. Bernard's, where he'd taken over the ministerial duties while the regular pastor was away.

Henrietta hadn't seen Father since she'd enrolled in Glade Harbor's Technical School almost a year ago. She missed him more than was morally right. She missed their day-to-day contact in the dining hall and seeing him on campus. Most of all, she missed their chance encounters at the Abbey's pond. It seemed they could discuss anything; relationships, church matters, political issues, the natural world. He'd become her friend and her spiritual advisor. His being at St. Bernard's meant they'd be able to chat after Sunday's service. The conversation would probably be brief, but it was better than nothing.

She walked into the kitchen with an airy heart. *Moeder* stood at the stove, lid in hand, stirring a steaming pot. The smell of ham and boiled cabbage permeated the air. Henrietta hung her coat on a hook by the back door and set her suitcase on the floor. "Mm, smells good, *Moeder*. Are Greta and Father Cornelius coming to supper?"

Moeder glanced up with a smile. "Greta is coming, but *Vader* Cornelius is away giving the Last Rites to one of his old parishioners."

She kissed *Moeder*'s cheek. "Give me a minute to say hello to *Vader*, then I'll be back to help with dinner." She found him in the parlor, relaxing in his chair, a pipe between his lips, pouring over a Dutch newspaper.

"Ah, *dochter*, it is good to have you home. You are making good progress at school?"

"Absolutely, *Vader*. I graduate in June. Then it's time for a job hunt."

"Well, I hope you get a good one using those fancy skills you learned, or all that tuition money is for naught." He folded the paper onto his lap. "Should we be expecting Leonard for supper?"

Oh Lord, here it comes. After she'd turned down Ike's proposal, she'd been seeing Leonard to get Ike to leave her alone. Henrietta forced a smile. "He's busy and won't be coming."

Vader scowled. "What does a single man do on a Friday night that's so important he can't come to dinner with his beau and her family?"

Henrietta hesitated. *Vader* would disapprove of her answer. But he'd find out, eventually. So she spat out the truth. "I told Leonard I couldn't see him anymore."

"What? This man, he is the second suitor you turn down. Why?"

How could she explain to a father who held on to the old ways? She shook her head and plunged into reasons she knew would never satisfy him. "Leonard believes he knows everything, and that women have sawdust for brains. He pretends kindness when I'm around, but I've seen another side of him when he thinks I'm not paying attention. I can't marry someone who is arrogant and often downright mean."

Vader unleashed his usual arguments. "Your last beau, Ike, he is kind."

"He is, but he has no sense of adventure. And he thought I needed to be taken care of. I don't need to be managed or protected. I want the man I marry to treat me as an equal, not as a subservient housewife." She glanced at the kitchen. Had *Moeder* overheard? Mother had spent her whole married life submitting to her husband.

"Bah. The Bible says, 'Wives must submit themselves to their husbands, as it is fit with the Lord.'"

She choked back her anger, answering as calmly as she could. "There's another Bible passage that says, 'Husbands and wives should submit themselves to one another in fear of the Lord.' Leonard would never submit himself to me or allow me to be his equal." She snorted. "There is no way I'd marry him. And he decided I'd never be the wife he wanted. So we ended the courtship. It's the one thing we agreed on."

"Pish posh. What Leonard didn't like is your strong will." He took a deep breath and let it go. "I suppose sometimes it is good to be strong minded. But if you plan to marry, it would be best to tone down your opinions with the men who come courting. You are too picky. If you aren't careful, you will end up an old spinster. Is that what you want?"

Henrietta felt blood rush to her cheeks. "Better a spinster than a servant."

Vader glared. *Moeder* appeared in the kitchen doorway, wiping her hands on her apron. Her soft voice broke the tension. "Husband, leave her be. She is this way because of you. You taught her to think for herself. Not be swayed by opinions of others." She turned to Henrietta. "And *dochter*, your *vader* and I, we are equal in our love for one another. I am in charge of matters in the home. He is in charge of matters in the world. It is good for us." She gave *Vader* a pointed look and returned her gaze to Henrietta. "Still, I understand the way your *vader* and I live together may not be right for you."

A slow smile spread on Henrietta's face. "*Dank je, Moeder.*"

The back door creaked open and clapped shut. A moment later, Greta stood in the parlor doorway with brows raised and a hint of amusement in her eyes. "Good heavens. I hope I'm not interrupting anything."

Henrietta took a deep breath. With her eyes on *Vader*, she said, "We've all had our say. *Moeder*, let's get dinner on the table. I imagine *Vader* is hungry."

Vader grunted, got up and followed his women into the kitchen. He settled with his newspaper at the table, waiting for his supper.

Henrietta sliced bread for the meal. She imagined what life would be like with Leonard wielding the knife with unnecessary energy. She saw herself in a stuffy kitchen stirring a pot of stew. Leonard would come in smelling of cigarettes and of a world she wasn't part of. He'd expect her to do his laundry, press his shirts, clean up after him, and take it all for granted. And God forbid she'd have to let his pompous hands touch her. There was nothing inside of her for him.

Greta broke through her thoughts. "I have news that might interest you, Henrietta," she said, placing plates around the table. "You must have heard Father Ferrera is the temporary pastor at St. Bernard's while Father Verhelst is out of town. Unfortunately, the rectory's housekeeper had to leave to care for her ill sister. Now the rectory has no one to cook or clean. Father Cornelius suggested you fill in for the weekend."

Two days keeping house for Father Ferrera? A very interesting proposal. "I'd be glad to help," she said, hiding the commotion in her heart.

"Yes, *dochter,* that is a good thing you do," *Vader* said, closing his paper. "A little housekeeping for the priest will make you humble. You will see how housework is a fine way for a woman to live and serve the Lord."

"In this instance, *Vader*, it is." Her mind whirled with the thought of working for Father Ferrera. She bowed her head as *Vader* began the mealtime prayer.

***

Early Sunday evening, sunlight streamed through the dining-room window of St. Bernard's rectory. Henrietta bunched lilacs into a vase, thinking of how much she'd relished these last two days. Working for Father Ferrera had brought her a new appreciation for housework. Yesterday, she'd cooked and cleaned as he heard confessions and prepared his sermon. Between his duties, he'd chatted with her over tea. And after each meal, he helped clean up the dishes. Quite extraordinary for a man.

As she worked with the lilacs, she listened to Father sing "Crucifixus" with Enrico Caruso, whose recording played on the Victrola in the parlor. As always, Father's voice flooded into her heart and drowned her in its beauty. She closed her eyes and let the smell of lilacs mingle with the splendor of the song.

She set the flowers in the middle of the table and stepped back to admire them. The bouquet complemented the rectory's china set for dinner on a fine white linen tablecloth. Thankfully, she'd been able to scrub away yesterday's wine stain. She chuckled for a moment at the absurdity of Prohibition. Despite the ban on alcohol, the use of sacramental wine was allowed in churches. The clergy, including Father Ferrera and her cousin, Father Cornelius, often took advantage of the loophole.

The last notes of "Crucifixus" faded. Father Ferrera and Enrico began her favorite, "Domine Deus". Today it made her more giddy than usual. Suddenly, Enrico was singing solo. She turned to see Father standing in the dining room doorway, watching her. "The table looks lovely, Henri. And your fricasseed chicken smells *muito delicioso*."

Henrietta loved the way he called her 'Henri.' He'd used that name for her at St. Albert's College whenever they'd found themselves alone. She missed those times. This weekend was ending too soon. Tomorrow, she'd be back in school.

"When this temporary assignment is over, Father, will you go back to Saint Albert's?" she asked, hoping she wouldn't lose contact with him.

His face became pensive. "No. I'm sailing to Portugal in a few days to visit *minha mae*."

"Your mother?"

He nodded.

A knock interrupted their conversation. Greta called from the kitchen. "We're here, Henrietta."

Father Cornelius's voice rumbled after Greta's. "Martim, I brought wine to test for next Sunday's Mass."

Father Ferrera grabbed goblets from the sideboard and called to the kitchen. "Bring it here, Corn. We'll sample it while the ladies finish preparing the meal."

"Dinner won't take much longer," Henri said, and headed to the kitchen. She found Greta grinning with a covered dessert in her hands. She peeked beneath the cloth. "Cream puffs, Greta. You shouldn't have."

"Seemed perfect to go with your chicken," Greta said, putting the pastries in the icebox. "You know, Henrietta, the best part of this little weekend job of yours is you'll be able to add it to your resume when you finish your secretarial training. It'll help when you look for a job."

As she spread egg whites on her risen dinner rolls, Henrietta said, "Though I loved helping in the rectory these last two days, my heart is set on a secretarial job, work that could lead to a more challenging position. And I have to prove to *Vader* school was worth the expense."

"Ah yes, *Vader*. Still Henrietta, there's no shame in housekeeping. I find keeping house for Father Cornelius very satisfying. It's much better than working as a servant at St. Albert's. I feel needed. Father is good to me, and mostly, I'm my own boss."

Henrietta snorted. "*Vader* and *Moeder* want us to get married like our two older sisters." She stoked the embers in the stove's fire chamber and put in a small chunk of wood. "I have nothing against marriage, Greta. But Ike, Leonard, and every other man who courted me never treated me as an equal. It's wrong." She scowled as she opened the oven door. Heat roiled around her face as she popped the rolls inside. She banged the door shut and took the boiling potatoes from the stove.

Greta pulled the butter crock from the icebox and filled a dish. She laughed. "Your problem, Henrietta, is you don't like anyone telling you what to do."

Henrietta added a dollop of butter to the potatoes, picked up the masher, and beat them furiously. "Of course I don't. The man I marry deserves my love. But I can't cherish a man who believes it's his duty to run my life and treats me as if I'm incapable of making my own decisions."

Greta gave her a side-ways glance. "I'll bet you'd marry Reverend Ferrera in a heartbeat if he weren't a reverend."

"Greta," she gasped. The potato masher picked up speed. "He's a priest. And that's the end of that." Her face flamed. Was Greta right? Had her feelings for Father moved beyond friendship? No, the Church didn't allow anything more intimate. He was her confessor, a man of God. Anything else was wrong.

A half hour later the two sisters sat at the table with the two Fathers, their heads bowed for the blessing. With a hearty 'amen', Father Ferrera served himself chicken and passed the platter to Father Cornelius. "*Minha mae* never prepared chicken this way, Miss Hoffmann, but I think she'd find it to her liking."

"How would your mother cook an old hen?" Henrietta asked, glowing at the compliment.

A smile curled on corners of his mouth. "The Portuguese usually cook meat in a pot together with vegetables and potatoes or with rice." His voice became wistful. "I'll be in Portugal in a week. When I see *minha mae*, she'll probably make *Bacalhau a bras.* It's one of my favorites, salted cod sautéed with onions, potatoes, and eggs, splashed with wine, and then topped with olives and parsley."

"It sounds interesting. If I get the chance to cook for you again, and you bring me your mother's recipe, I promise, I'll make it for you."

"It's a deal," he said, grinning.

Henrietta cut a bite of chicken. "You must be looking forward to seeing her."

His face clouded. "I left Portugal fifteen years ago. Since then there has been coup after coup. There was a new attempt to restore the King to the throne in February. Like all the others, it failed. Now rumors suggest another upheaval is in the works."

Father Cornelius's brows rose. "And you're still going?"

"I have to Corn. I want to be sure *minha mae* is safe."

"But what about you, Martim? Will you be safe?" Father Cornelius said, putting down his fork full of potatoes.

"I don't know. I may still be a hunted man."

Henri's eyes widened. "A hunted man?"

His face turned grim. "I didn't just leave Portugal, Henri. Insurgents captured me when I took part in an attempt to restore the King to the throne. My captors sentenced me to fourteen years of hard labor in

Angola. I escaped. The political situation is as bad now as ever. And there may be those who want me back in prison."

Henrietta shivered. He could be in danger. "How long will you be gone?"

"Two months, perhaps longer depending on what's happening."

Father Cornelius's face flushed with worry. "If there's a coup while you're there, will you join?"

His voice quieted, "I'm not sure, Corn. It all depends on the situation."

Henrietta sucked in a deep breath and let it go. What if something terrible happened to him in Portugal? Dear God, please keep him safe.

Hours later, she lay in the housekeeper's bed listening to the clock tick minute by minute, hour after hour. Her heart twisted with worry and with feelings she didn't want to admit. She got up, pulled a heavy sweater over her nightgown, put on her slippers, and padded to the back door. Careful not to make a sound, she moved onto the porch and settled in the swing hanging from the rafters. She watched the clouds scud across the moon, praying for Father's safe return and wondering what her future held. Would she ever find a man to love, a man who'd love and respect her in return, a man free to marry?

She pulled a picture of Father Ferrera from her sweater pocket and pressed it to her heart. He'd given it to her when she left St. Albert's last year. The photo was of his ordination three years ago. He stood in front of St. Albert's College in the snow wearing his white habit; handsome, dignified, a man with all the qualities she could love, a man completely unattainable. Tomorrow he left to face danger halfway around the world.

The screen door creaked. Father Ferrera stepped onto the porch. "Henri? What are you doing out here?"

She held back a gasp. His long johns peeked beneath his dark bathrobe, and his feet were bare, his hair wild. Even in the shadows and under his robe, his body was fit and alluring. He padded across the porch and sat beside her. His nearness nearly drowned her with a longing she tried to shut down.

She swallowed, trying to keep emotion from her voice. "I couldn't sleep, Martim." She put her hand to her mouth. "I'm sorry. I shouldn't call you by your first name."

"Martim is fine when we're alone, Henri." He looked out across the moonlit yard and laughed. "Here we are again, together under the stars. So, what brought you out this time?"

She sighed. "The situation in Portugal sounds dangerous."

"It is," he said, his voice troubled. "But I've waited a long time to return, and Portugal may never be completely safe. *Minha mai* is in her early seventies. If I don't see her now, it might be too late. There is a silver lining, however. I just became an American citizen, and that gives me a level of safety I didn't have before. If something happens and I'm detained by the authorities, I can contact the American Consulate for help." He took her hand and squeezed it. "Still, it will help if you pray for me, for my mother, and for Portugal."

Oh my God, he's holding my hand. Is it meant to comfort me as a friend, or is it reassurance from my minister? Whatever the reason, she felt a spasm race through her body. She wanted to keep her hand in his, to sit beside him forever, but that led to forbidden thoughts. She tucked her hand in her pocket. "While you're gone, I'll trust in the power of prayer to keep you safe." She closed her eyes and breathed slowly for a moment. "I'm curious. What are your plans when you return?"

Martim's voice took a lighter tone. "I'll continue teaching engineering and theology at St. Albert's, but not for long. The Abbot spoke to me last week and said he'll assign me to my own parish next year."

Henrietta's hand flew to her cheek. "That's wonderful. Will it be nearby?"

"That would please me. But the Abbot says there is a great need for priests in Montana, so perhaps there." He reached into his pocket, took her hand again, and placed a rosary in her palm. "Thank you for helping me these last two days. You're an amazing woman. I hope wherever I'm assigned I find a housekeeper half as capable and gracious as you." He squeezed her hand and walked inside.

"Stay safe," she muttered, as the door closed behind him.

Chapter Six

May 17,1926
Portugal
Martim

Martim stood on the deck of the passenger ship, a chilly breeze ruffling his hair. Shivering, he choked with emotion as he watched the sunrise over Lisbon. The city's long shadows stretched far into the waters of the bay. People bustled around the run-down buildings that lined the waterfront. Shabby fishing boats, manned by hopeful *pescadors,* bobbed against the city's aging wharves. Derelict ships rusted at anchor. Even the Navy's vessels told of years of neglect. Progress had left his country behind.

He gazed at Lisbon's bluffs rising strong and vigilant against the winds and restless sea. He'd escaped down those very cliffs fifteen years ago and swam the bay under a hail of bullets. The clerical collar he now wore fulfilled the sacred promise he had made when he'd reached safety.

His nerves were on edge. He realized from the letters he'd received from his *mamãe* and from his cousin Francisco that the political situation in Portugal continued to be turbulent. The parliamentary system set up by the Republicans was crumbling. Plots, counterplots, riots, and intrigue roiled the country. There was one silver lining. The Catholic Church was regaining influence and respect. In some ways it had become a symbol of resistance.

He felt for the passport tucked in his inner pocket. The document brought him a measure of safety. He wasn't sure if he would join an insurrection if one arose. If Francisco persuaded him that his help was crucial to bring stability to his homeland, he might become involved. If he joined and the opposition captured him, his American citizenship would give him a measure of protection. His citizenship might also help if the powers that had sentenced him to the mines in Angola found him and still consider him a fugitive.

He turned to see the Portuguese deckhand he'd befriended light up a cigarette. He nodded at the weathered man. "*Bom Dia, Manuel.*"

Manuel inhaled deeply on his cigarette. "*Bom Dia, Padre.* Today you are home. I hope the chaos threatening our country won't interfere with your journey to Soalheira."

"My desire, as well *meu amigo*."

The deckhand leaned in and spoke in a hushed tone. "Things are a-foot, *Padre*. Everyone knows the army is plotting another coup. This time several factions, that at one time were enemies, are working together including the Church." He moved closer. "Truth is, most people hope it happens. We all hunger for order. Many believe only the army can restore it."

Martim kept his eyes on the Castle de Sao Jorge, silhouetted on Lisbon's skyline. It was the last sight he'd seen when he'd escaped from Portugal. Wondering what the ordinary man was aware of, he muttered, "Does the plot include restoring the monarchy?"

The deckhand looked around before he whispered. "There are some who hope it does. But they don't speak of it. Rumors are the monarchists are actually one faction in thick with the conspirators."

Martim nodded. "I've been told that many of those loyal to Manuel II feel restoring him to the throne is a hopeless cause. And that the King himself has urged his supporters to no longer conspire on his behalf."

The deckhand shrugged. "It is true." He tossed the last of his cigarette into the bay and nodded at a craft pulling alongside the ship. "I better get back to work. The Customs Officials board soon. Have a safe journey, Padre."

***

Martim stood on the ship's deck near the end of a long line of passengers waiting to pass through customs. Officials questioned every traveler and checked their passports against a thick list of names. So far, the agents had returned all passports and allowed the passengers to disembark.

Martim's eye caught sight of a tall, thin man several persons ahead of him dressed in shabby clothes. The fellow lit a cigarette. His hands shaking as he scanned the crowd. When the stranger's turn came to be checked through customs, he dropped the cigarette and ground it out on the deck. Shoulders slumped, he handed the officials his documents.

The creaking of the ship and the bustle on deck and the wharves below kept Martim from hearing the young man's interview. But the facial expressions on both the officials told him things weren't going well. The interrogation lasted much longer than it had for the other passengers. The bloke straightened with a defiant look. Guards flanked him and escorted him down the gangplank. He disappeared into a *policia* wagon.

Blood pounded in Martim's ears. In a few minutes, that might be his fate. He prayed. God, help that young man through whatever lies ahead for him, and help me pass safely into my country. Someone nudged him from behind. He was next. He squared his shoulders, handed the official his passport, and waited. Barely breathing, he waited as the official checked a thick stack of paper. The agent turned to Martim and scowled. "I see you are now an American citizen, Lieutenant Martim Ferrera. And I see you joined the priesthood. You may go but watch your step."

Martim took his passport and sauntered down the gangplank fighting an urge to hurry. He looked past the poverty and reveled in the beauty of his country. The sun danced on the ripples swelling on the bay. Gulls screeched overhead, soaring on the salty breeze. The old ships and ocean liners groaned against their moorings, and the tang of the creosoted pilings hung in the air. He paused halfway to the docks and basked in the brilliance of the city's red-tiled roofs.

Despite the gorgeous day, tension radiated everywhere. Passengers, dockhands, and even the officials kept their heads down. They hurried through their work with little of the usual chatter that characterized his fellow countrymen. Their eyes sent furtive glances through the crowd, as if they realized trouble could erupt at any moment. The mood magnified Martim's anxiety.

"Martim, *estamos aqui*."

He turned. "Angelica!" He gathered his sister in his arms, and all apprehension swept away. He stepped back, his hands on her shoulders, and studied her face. The sun haloed her chestnut hair. A curl had escaped from the elaborate twist fashioned on her head and swirled around her neck. Not a trace of makeup showed on her creamy skin. But her lips had a hint of color.

He faced Angelica's husband, Luis, a short, stocky man with a full mustache that capped a generous smile. The two men hugged and slapped each other's backs. Luis stepped back and said, "We worried Customs might detain you."

"The possibility concerned me, too. But they let me through

because of my American Passport. They know more about me than I would like."

A barrage of swearing peppered the air. The three turned to see an aproned shopkeeper standing in front of a fish market pointing a pistol at two ruffians. The shopkeeper shot into the air and screamed. "*Você pedaço de merde de vaca*. Take your politics and get out of my market, you piece of cow shit. And don't come back." The troublemakers retreated, swearing they would return with their compatriots.

As the agitators drifted away, whispering to each other with angry looks, Martim stiffened. "Don't look, Luis. The guard who just hauled away an unfortunate passenger is lurking in the alley by the fish market. He's talking with a burly man who seems familiar to me. But I'm not sure why. I think they're watching me."

Luis shouldered Martim's bag. "Come. Regardless of whether you're being watched, we need to go now. Plots are brewing, and I don't want to be caught here if trouble breaks out." He gestured at an old warehouse. "My Renault is parked over there."

Martim studied the burly man now limping into the fish market. He'd seen that face before, but where?

As they drove throughout the city, Martim kept a careful watch. For a while, it seemed a dilapidated auto followed Luis's Renault. But then it disappeared. Once in the countryside, he relaxed and turned to Angelica, who sat behind him. "How is *Mamãe*?"

Angelica leaned forward. "As quick witted and spirited as ever. She misses *papai,* and she's eager to see you. I think having you home will ease her pain."

Several years ago, *Mamãe* had sent news of his father's fatal heart attack. *Papai* had been working with the Monarchists in Spain when it happened. Grief had clung to Martim ever since. "I want to visit *Papai*'s grave while I'm here."

Angelica put a hand on his shoulder. "*Mamãe* didn't tell you? They buried him in Spain. She could never put together enough money to have his body brought home."

The sun disappeared behind the clouds, shadowing his mood. Ever since his escape, Martim had regretted never being able to say goodbye to *Papai* or to thank him for making his escape possible. Throughout this trip, he'd been buoyed by the thought of visiting the grave and telling him how grateful he'd been for his love and his wisdom. Now the visit would never happen.

They drove in silence through olive groves and vineyards, passing ancient villages tucked in the valleys. Martim's mind turned to the days ahead, when he would reconnect with his cousin Francisco. He suspected Francisco was with a group plotting a movement against the government in power. Curious about his mother's awareness of the political situation, he asked, "How is *Mamãe* taking the political turmoil that's still afoot?"

"It pains her that the group in power is only interested in personal advantage instead of what is best for the people of Portugal." Angelica crossed herself. "May God have mercy on us." She leaned over the seat and kissed Luis's cheek. "*Amor,* let's detour to Fatima, show Martim the grotto where the Virgin appeared, and pray for our poor country."

Luis frowned. "A detour will add hours to our trip. Your mamãe has her hands full watching our children, and she's eager to see Martim. She'll worry if we show up late."

"*Absurdo Luis,*" Angelica said, her voice flirty. "You know perfectly well *Mamãe* is happy to have her grandchildren spend the day."

Martim grinned. Angelica hadn't changed. She still used her charms to get her way.

Luis shifted to low gear as they headed up a hill and sighed. "You're right, *Querida*. But danger is everywhere. And we don't know when it will erupt. We need to get home before dark. The Holy Mother will answer our pleas whether we are in Fatima or in our own chapel at home. We'll take Martim to Fatima some other time."

Martim spoke up. "Angelica, Luis is right. I want to visit Fatima. But I can go later."

"Who knows what the future holds? Later, the trip could be more difficult. So please, let's go now."

Luis resigned with a shrug. "*Certo, meu amor.* We shall go." As Luis turned the Renault west towards Fatima, he grinned at Martim. "Your sister is an enchanter and can convince me of anything."

As Martim watched Angelica melt her husband's heart, Henri flamed into his thoughts. Though he'd fought it tooth and nail, Henri's charm had the same effect on him. She inspired his kindness, understanding, and compassion. An unsettling truth had surfaced the night they'd sat in the moonlight on the rectory's porch. Her presence challenged his vow of celibacy. Even now, thousands of miles away, thoughts of her sent desire surging through him. He would marry her if he hadn't become a priest.

Two hours later, Martim strolled with Luis and Angelica through an ancient grove of oak and olive trees. An aura of otherworldliness permeated the grounds. Throngs of worshippers knelt on the ground outside a small stone chapel built on the site where many believed the Virgin Mary had appeared nine years ago. Most in the gathering prayed the rosary. Some begged the Holy Mother to cure their physical or mental afflictions. Others prayed for peace.

Inside the chapel, believers knelt around a statue of the Holy Mother. Vases of roses, lilies, and baby's breath perfumed the air. Martim knelt with his sister and Luis and began his own appeal. "Holy Mother, help me find the right path while I am in Portugal and bless me with the courage to follow it."

Henri's face floated into his thoughts again. He wished she were here with him to share this beautiful experience. Would he see her when he returned to the Abbey? It might be best if he didn't. He added to his prayer. "And most of all, Holy Mother, give me the strength to keep my mind and my body worthy of your love." A sense of peace filtered through his soul as he prayed.

The sun had passed its zenith when the threesome made their way back through the crowds to Luis's Renault. As they scattered a flock of pigeons pecking at breadcrumbs on the fringes of the crowd, Angelica nudged Martim. "I just saw the man who was talking with the Custom agent at the fish market."

Martim stiffened, but kept his outward demeanor relaxed. "Where?"

"I see him too," Luis said. "He's skulking in the olive grove by that outcropping of rocks, and he has that scar running down his cheek from his ear to his lips.

"We don't want him to realize we're aware of him," Martim muttered. "I still haven't figured out why he seems so familiar."

Angelica put her arm through Luis's as if nothing were amiss. "Let's get to the car and see what happens."

For ten kilometers, twelve, and then fifteen, an old auto followed, keeping its distance as if to say it was no threat. Five kilometers later, Luis said. "Hang onto your hats. I'm convinced we're being followed. We have to get far enough ahead so we can disappear onto a rarely used side road. It will take us home in a round-about way." He picked up speed and shifted into top gear. Dust enveloped the car. Martim braced himself as the Renault jolted over ruts and spun around hairpin turns.

They passed through a stand of trees a few kilometers down the road. Luis screeched to a halt. He backed up and made a sharp left turn around an enormous boulder crowded by trees and brush. The maneuver took them into a seldom-used lane. Hidden from the regular road, Luis turned off the ignition. "Now we wait until we see the dust of our pursuer pass by. Hopefully, he doesn't know this little byway."

Minutes later a car rattled by. Clouds of dust filtered through the brush and trees. They listened as their pursuer continued down the main road. The ruse had worked.

The sun touched the hills and painted the sky with reds and purples by the time they reached the city of Fundão. Memories of Martim's youth flowed through him as they drove through familiar streets to the parish of Soalheira, where Martim's family villa nestled among ancient cherry and wine wood trees. A tiny woman in a long black dress and a lacy shawl stood in the arched stone gateway. A smile spread across her face. Except for the silver flecking her dark chestnut hair, *Mamãe* was just as he remembered.

She wrapped her arms around him and choked out the words, "*Voce esta em casa, meu filho*."

His voice extra husky, he said, "Yes, *Mamãe*. I'm home."

***

Martim sat on an outdoor balcony enjoying *Mamãe's* fabulous *Bacalhua a Bras*. Usually, *Mamãe* served the cod and potato dish splashed with wine at Christmas. But today she'd made it to celebrate his homecoming. He had devoted his first few days home to her, Angelica, Luis, and their children. Now two friends who had been fellow officers in the coup attempt of 1911 enjoyed a late lunch with him. Marco put down his wineglass and grinned. "It's hard to believe you joined the priesthood, Martim. I remember you as a man who wanted a wife, children, and a family."

Martim shrugged. "The longing is still there," he said, thinking of Henri.

Picking a bone from his fish, Filipe said, "We learned about your escape from prison. It seemed a miracle."

"It was. So when I made it to freedom, I promised to dedicate my life to God."

"That explains your Roman collar. But someone told me you didn't join the priesthood right away."

"I didn't. I spend six years in Brazil designing a railroad and almost died of malaria. God saved me again. I finally realized the best way to honor my vow was to become a priest." He gazed through the trees shading the villa. Henri wouldn't leave his thoughts. But his vow gave him only one honorable path. He put on a smile. "When I return to America and am assigned a parish, my parishioners will be my family."

Filipe sipped his cherry liquor. "Remember Padre Alfonso? He kept a mistress and had two children. Everyone knew. But no one spoke of it. We all thought it quite normal. The bishop must have known but looked the other way."

Martim watched a gecko scamper up a tree thinking of the path that had led him to the priesthood. His life had been spared on those two miraculous occasions, but there had been other influences. He fingered his Roman collar and returned his gaze to his friends. "There were two priests who played a big role in my decision. Padre Alfonso was one of them. He showed me the power of empathy and compassion in everyday acts. The other was the priest who made daily rounds through the prison in Lisbon. His encouragement helped me keep hope alive through all the desolation of that cesspool. I pray to follow the example of those two blessed men."

Marco nodded. "I always thought Padre Alfonso was one of the best. It's possible having a woman and his own children helped him better understand issues that arise in families." He scowled. "And he didn't go after young boys like some priests."

Filipe grunted. "I wonder when the Church will recognize the downside of required celibacy."

"I'm familiar with the debate," Martim said, shaking his head. "It's one I frequently have with myself. When I lived in Brazil, I came across a treatise written by a bishop who was also a Brazilian senator. The treatise advocated the abolishment of clerical celibacy. The logic made sense to me. Perhaps I could be a better priest if I had my own family. But the Church doesn't see it that way."

A car sped through the villa's gate, interrupting the conversation. A man who could almost be Martim's twin bolted from behind the wheel. Martim stood and called from the balcony. "Francisco, it's about time you showed up."

The car still running, Francisco rushed towards the house shouting, "Come, Martim. Filipe, Marco, you too. Anarchists from Lisbon are threatening shops in Fundão. The town folk need our help."

Martim bolted up, wine swirling sourly in his stomach. Marco and

Filipe raced with him down the stairs. Rushing out the door, Martim grabbed Francisco in a quick hug. "It's been a long time, cousin."

"Too long, Martim. Quick, to my car. We'll catch up later."

Martim raced to the auto, his heart in full gear. "Times are desperate, Francisco. We do what we must."

Ten minutes later, Francisco roared to a stop outside a Fundão print shop. A man wearing an ink-filled apron and a visor stood in front of a small band of terrified locals. The little group faced a crowd of red-scarved anarchists flaunting clubs and pistols. A large thug in black trousers and a threadbare jacket had a middle-aged man in a chokehold. Blood poured from the hostage's nose.

"We're outnumbered," Martim said as the four friends climbed from the car. "But if we remain calm, maybe we can reason with them."

"Agreed," Francisco muttered. "We'll let you do the talking, Martim. Most Portuguese, including the Red Scarves, still respect a man of the cloth."

The printer's face filled with relief when he saw Martim. "Francisco, thank God you brought a priest."

With an eye on the rabble rousers, Martim asked the printer, "What's happening, *Senhor*?"

The man clutched his apron and said, "*Padre,* those hoodlums followed my brother from Lisbon, and now they've seized him. I beg you, persuade them to let him go."

Bile inched its way into Martim's throat. He nodded. "I'll do my best." He approached the thugs and let his gaze rest on those who dared to meet his eyes. His voice rose above their angry mutterings. "*Amigos,* what is your quarrel with this man?"

The leader's face matched the deep red of the scarf circling his neck. He breathed in ferocious gulps and tightened his arm hold on his captive's neck. "This scum claims he's innocent. He is not. He's an enemy of The Brotherhood. The league he is part of sent our comrades to slave in Angola's mines." The angry man sneered at the shop owner. "Your brother belongs to us. We take him, and we leave your town in peace."

Shouts of protest and pleas for mercy erupted from the townsfolk.

Martim felt for the rosary in his pocket. "What would you do to this man you think is your enemy?"

"We do to him what he did to our brothers. Make him slave on one of the Brotherhood's ships."

The printer gasped. "My God. They're shanghaiing him."

Martim nodded at the enraged ruffian. "I understand your anger, *Senhor.* A few years ago, the regime in power sentenced me to Angola. Fortunately, I escaped."

The thug scanned his followers as if to check their mood. Some nodded, others looked away. He turned to Martim. "So what? They sent priests into exile often enough back then. That's got nothing to do with this."

"I wasn't a priest when I was given that sentence."

The man tightened his grip on the prisoner. "What he did to our brothers was unjust."

"Perhaps what happened to your comrades was wrong. But is this man truly the one responsible for their exile in the mines?"

"There are plenty of rumors he's the one."

"You want justice, but there is no justice if you become judge and jury based on rumors."

Hesitation materialized on the faces of a few anarchists. The man who stood beside the leader mumbled, "Osvaldo, we should listen to the priest." A few mutters of agreement circled the mob.

Osvaldo elbowed the dissenter away, gripped the hostage tighter, and sneered. "There is no justice left in Portugal. Those who run our country are corrupt. So, it leaves justice to us."

The foul mood on the burly leader's face deepened.

Martim chose his words carefully. "You have a legitimate complaint, *Senhor*. And many agree with you. But if we fight among ourselves and punish those with little power, we achieve nothing but more injustice. Fight the real enemy, the corrupt government in Lisbon. That's the only path to positive change."

The crowd's angry mutterings dwindled. Some agitators lowered their weapons and exchanged looks. A voice from somewhere in the mob called out. "He's right, Osvaldo. Let's take our fight to Lisbon."

The leader's jaw twitched as he scorched his comrades with an angry look. By now, his hostage's face had gone deadly gray as he struggled to loosen Osvaldo's grip. Many of the brute's backers mumbled among themselves. As he watched a few of them slip away, his voice turned to bravado and bluster. "Okay, Padre. But if this coup fails like all the others, we take justice into our own hands." His arms opened. His captive dropped to the ground where he lay with his hand at this throat, gasping for air. The printer and a few of his friends hurried his brother into the shop.

As the tension dispersed with the crowd, Martim stiffened when he noticed a man among the anarchists staring at him. A scar ran from his ear, down his cheek to the corner of his mouth. He could hear the blood rushing in and out of his heart. The fellow was the man Martim had seen talking to the Customs police in Lisbon. The man he'd seen at Fatima, the one who had chased Luis's Renault for miles. When Martim caught his stalker's eye, he turned and limped away. Martim hurried through the departing troublemakers, hoping to confront the man. Though the bloke wore no red scarf, he disappeared into a vehicle with some of the Brotherhood.

Francisco came up beside him as he watched the car speed away. "What was that about?"

"Someone I thought I recognized, but I'm not sure who. I wanted to talk to him. No matter. Maybe I'll catch up with him another time." Or, he thought, it's possible he'll catch up with me.

Back in Francisco's car, the four friends headed to Martim's family home, preoccupied with their own thoughts, until Francisco broke the silence. "Martim, the trouble we saw back there is the kind of confrontation happening everywhere. There are plans afoot to stop all this chaos. And I'm in the thick of the movement, helping to organize a plan of action."

Marco lifted a brow. "Come on, Francisco. There've been hundreds of plots for years."

"He's right," Filipe said. "And nothing good has ever come from them."

Francisco kept his eyes on the road. "I understand your skepticism. But this plot could bring positive change. I'm working with General Gomes da Costa and a few others on a framework for a new government. In the next few days, we plan to overthrow the corrupt regime in Lisbon. At this very moment the General is sending telegrams to all military units encouraging them to join us. Over sixty percent have already pledged support."

Filipe's hand rasped against the stubble on his face. "General Gomes da Costa and a majority of the army? It might work."

Marco weighed in. "Sounds promising, Francisco. This may be the movement we've needed for years. Any other major players involved?"

Francisco nodded. "General Carmona is on board. He's set up a breakfast meeting with as many monarchist supporters and officers as possible." He patted Martim's shoulder. "When the General learned you were back in Portugal, Martim, he specifically asked me to invite you. Many of your fellow officers and colleagues plan to attend. Filipe and Marco, you are both included in the request. The General will share the basic ideas and the rationale behind our plans at the breakfast. He hopes many of you will sign on. If not, at least remain neutral."

Red flags waved through Martim's thoughts. "General Da Costa? General Carmona? Unless things have changed, neither are advocates for democracy."

Francisco glanced at Martim. "True. And I've long weighed the implications. But our parliamentary system, supposedly a democracy, has completely failed to bring social justice or to support the working class." A frown broke across his brow. "I've said enough for now. General Carmona will explain the rest at the breakfast."

Martim rubbed the back of his neck. He'd come home to visit his mother, to make sure she was safe. Now his cousin had invited him to take part in another coup. Its goal differed from the movement he'd been in fifteen years ago. Would this new rebellion bring positive changes to Portugal? If he joined, what would he be asked to do?

Filipe leaned forward from the backseat. "Like you, Martim, I supported the return of the King in the past. But so much has changed since then. I believe a monarchy, even a parliamentary one, is no longer in the best interest of Portugal."

Questions raced through Martim. What kind of government did the army generals intend to set up? Would they allow the Church to resume its original functions? He didn't ask his cousin these questions assuming he'd learn more in the days to come.

Francisco drove through the villa's gate and stopped the car. "So, gentlemen, will you be at the breakfast meeting?"

Both Filipe and Marco pledged to go.

Francisco caught his cousin's eyes. "And you, Martim?"

"I'll come and listen to what General Carmona has to say. I imagine there'll be a role for a priest in the struggles ahead. If nothing else, I'll be pleased to see my old friends."

"Then I'll meet you in three days in Porto at the Villa da Floresta," Francisco said. "The future of our country hangs in the balance."

"Dear God," Martim prayed to himself. "Help me serve your will in the hard days ahead."

Chapter Seven

May to October 1926
Portugal
Martim

Francisco led Martim to a lush garden courtyard in the Villa da Floresta, where Filipe and Marco waited. The smell of gardenias drifted through the air. Tables covered in fine linen and set for breakfast were spread out on a tiled terrace and were sheltered from the sun by a large white canopy.

As the courtyard filled, old classmates and fellow officers greeted Martim with enthusiasm. Their conversations told the details of the past fifteen years of their lives.

As if on cue, the guests quieted. All eyes turned to the head table. General Carmona had arrived. He stood tall and straight with his hands behind his back, his white hair and mustache impeccably trimmed. Epaulettes nested on his shoulders, and a wide red sash crossed his chest. A single gold eight-pointed star rested over his heart.

He cleared his throat and began. "Thank you for joining me this morning. We will begin with a blessing." He glanced at Martim. "Today an old friend and fellow officer, Lieutenant Martim Ferrera, now Reverendo Ferrera, honors us with his presence." The General nodded at Martim. "*Reverendo,* would you lead us in prayer?"

Martim stood, his cheeks warming. "Thank you for the honor, General." Facing the group, he bowed his head, made the sign of the cross, and prayed. "Lord, Savior of the World, Personification of Peace, we implore you to forgive our shortcomings as a nation. Purify our hearts, enabling us to know and love the truth. Bless our leaders with wisdom. And keep our nation in your care during these troubled times." He swallowed to clear the catch in his throat. "And thank you Lord for our food today, for the opportunity to reunite with close companions, and for the family who graciously opened their home to us."

The gathering chimed, "Amen."

The General nodded approval. "A fine blessing, *Reverendo.* Gentlemen, please be seated. Before we get down to business, let's enjoy the meal."

Chairs clattered on the tiles as everyone settled at their tables. Conversations erupted, filled with theories about the political situation, speculation about the General's plans, and worry about the outcome of yet another coup everyone knew was coming. As the discussions unfolded, the guests helped themselves to the platters of ham, cheeses, pastries, and fresh fruit. When Francisco joined Martim, Marco, and Filipe at their table, he patted Martim's back. "Cousin, a fine prayer. You have a gift you could bring to the cause."

"*Obrigado*, Francisco," Martim shivered at the thought of so many who could lose their lives in the days ahead.

When a few slices of cheese and some pastries remained on the platters, a young woman appeared in the courtyard. Martim watched her move gracefully from table to table, refilling coffee cups, flirting with the men, and impishly offering her point of view. She was so like Henri, witty, energetic, and full of charm, it nearly took his breath away. The ache he'd been fighting since he left the States flared again.

A uniformed man hurried through the courtyard and handed the General a telegram. The General's brows rose as he read it to himself. He stuffed the telegram in his pocket and clinked a fork against his glass. The gathering grew quiet. "Gentlemen, we have just received word that Commander Cabecadas is making a move to set himself up as President in the Capitol. The Commander opposes the restoration of the Monarchy but wants to keep the government a Constitutional Republic. We do not believe this is the best path for our country."

Clouds covered the sun, casting shadows over the Courtyard, adding to the gloom seeping through Martim. The best path for Portugal was not a Republic? What kind of government did the General have in mind? Martim studied the faces of his old friends. Most eyed one another with approval. A few wore grim scowls.

The General smoothed his mustache, tightening its curl before he continued. He chose his words carefully. "At one time, many of you believed in restoring the monarchy as a republic. Events have changed some minds. A few of you may still harbor hope of bringing King Manuel back to his throne." He cleared his throat. "We are a nation with a proud history. But with so many factions vying for power for so many years, it's been impossible for Portugal to prosper and regain the respect of the world. It's time to bring our people together again with common goals that lead to advancement and peace. As our nation stands today, there is no path to a monarchy. I'm asking you to consider an alternative, one that will avoid a great deal of bloodshed and loss of life. We must bring order to the chaos. Only a united army can assure that outcome."

There was a long pause. The General surveyed the crowd as if to read its mood. He must have sensed acceptance, because he nodded and spoke again. "Most army garrisons have already joined our cause. There are some holdouts in Lisbon, but we now have enough units to establish order and maintain it. In the next few days, we plan to send troops to surround Lisbon. The military will take control of the government. It's the only way to make the reforms necessary for our country and to allow the Catholic Church back into our lives."

Martim's mind eased at hearing this part of the General's plan. Restoring the role of the Church was more important than restoring the monarchy. Someone mumbled, "This could lead to civil war." The words, full of truth, reignited Martim's fears.

The comment didn't seem to reach the General's ears because he continued. "I'm inviting you to join our cause or, if you're unsure, remain neutral until you see what we achieve. Thank you for coming. I won't be able to stay as I have much to accomplish before we make our move in the next few days." The General nodded at Martim's cousin. "Your colleague, Francisco Rolao Preto, has worked with General da Costa and me. He will remain to answer questions. I leave you to consider your decision." With that, he hurried from the courtyard, his staff hustling behind him.

The crowd lingered, hashing through the options. Tempers flared. A few men left angrily. But most came to agree with the General's plan. The group gradually dispersed, but Martim remained ambling through the garden, deep in thought. The General's words hinted that if the coup succeeded, the new government might not have a democratic constitution. What did he plan instead? There had been many failed coups attempting to return the king to his throne, so he understood why a monarchy was no longer an option. But no democratic constitution? That was hard to accept.

He felt Francisco walk up beside him. They paused at a fountain. As they watched the water gurgle over three elaborate basins, his cousin spoke. "Our country is at a crossroad, Martim. What have you decided?"

"The course your group plans seems to lead to a military dictatorship, Francisco. Much like the one Mussolini has already established in Italy. That's hard to swallow. A democratic republic works well in America. I would love to see Portugal with that form of government."

"This isn't America," Francisco said, passionately. "As you know, for many years Portugal has tried to set up a functioning Republic. Our efforts have only brought chaos. A military dictatorship with the Catholic Church playing a central role is the only workable solution."

Martim took a long breath. His worries were real. They were planning a military dictatorship. He squared his eyes with his cousin's. "I can't agree with this, Francisco. But I leave in a few months. It's the people who remain in Portugal who must decide how they will be governed, not me."

"I understand, Martim. We all have hard choices to make. I leave you to your decision." His cousin squeezed his shoulder and hurried off, leaving Martim alone with his thoughts.

He'd take *Mamãe* to stay with Louis and Angelica in Alpedrinha, where she'd be safe. He couldn't be part of a movement that would end in a dictatorship even it was one that supported the Church. But he could join a garrison in need of a chaplain, offer daily Mass, hear confessions, give counsel, and God forbid, if necessary, perform the last rites. With his decision made, he crossed the courtyard to the gate.

As he wove around the tables, he passed the serving woman he'd seen earlier. She sang to herself as she carried a stack of dirty dishes towards the villa's kitchen. Her shapely figure and the wisps of hair wiggling from the scarf tied around her head brought Henri into his thoughts again. The young woman stopped, set the dishes down on a table, and retied her apron.

"May I help, *senhorita*?"

Though her eyes weren't blue like Henri's, they held the same warmth and humor. She laughed. "Heavens no, Padre. My employer would have fits if I let a guest do my job." She waved him away with a grin.

He left the villa and headed to Porto's Church, where he and Francisco had agreed to meet. Henri refused to leave his thoughts. For God's sake, he told himself she was a friend, a good friend. That was all. He smiled. She would make an excellent housekeeper when he returned to the States and was assigned a parish.

As he walked through a stand of trees on the Church grounds, deep in thought, someone grabbed him from behind. A musty cloth bag plunged over his head. His arms wrenched behind him. A pistol jammed in his back. A deep voice muttered, "Don't say a word, Lieutenant Ferrera, or you'll find a bullet in your back."

"Who are you? What do you want?"

The pistol deepened in his ribs. "I said not a word."

Martim's mind whirled as his captor dragged him to a car and threw him inside. The car drove a short distance, bumping over ruts, and stopped. Jerked from the car, powerful hands pushed him through what felt like tall grass and weeds. Thrown to the ground, a heavy boot exploded on his ribs. The bag was ripped from his head. He gulped in air, looking into bloodshot eyes inches from his own. Salt and pepper stubble flecked his captor's face. The sour smell of rum hung in the man's breath. His captor was the burly, scar-faced man who had stalked him since he'd entered Portugal. But Martim still couldn't place the familiar face.

The drunk's glazed eyes glared at Martim. Words sloshed from his lips "You monarchist scum. I lost my job because of you."

Holy Mother. One of the plastered prison guards he'd encountered when he'd escaped from prison. Just as he'd believed, the prison bosses had fired the man. "I'm sorry, *senhor.* I worried that might happen."

A blow slammed his cheek. "Shut up. 'Sorry' don't make up for the trouble you caused me. Only work I can find is shoveling horseshit." He leered. "Waited fifteen years to get back at you."

Martim took a deep breath. "How can I make it up to you?"

"Make it up? Ain't no way. Can you get me my job back? No." He slumped beside Martim and stared through the graveyard. His stubbly chin dropped to his chest. He sat for a while, picking at dirt in his cracked fingernails. He covered his face with his hands and moaned. "What's the use? It's wrong, so wrong. God'll send me to hell if I hurt a priest," he mumbled with half a sob. "Padre, do you think I'll ever get another chance?"

"A chance at what, *senhor*?"

The man pressed his palms to his temples. "Who am I fooling? Ain't nobody gonna hire an old sot like me. Even if they did, I'd have to lay off the booze. Can't do that."

Martim leaned against a headstone. The pain from the guard's boot brought back memories of the abuse he'd received when he was in prison. This man had his own wounds. They weren't so much physical as spiritual. He nudged his captor. "What's your name?"

"Raul."

"Prayer has the power to fight many demons, Raul, even alcohol. Have you talked with your confessor about your troubles?"

The man shook his head. "Ain't been to Church since they shut 'em years ago."

"They reopened churches a while ago."

The man stared at his hands. "So I heard. Something's kept me away. Could be stubbornness. Maybe fear."

They both froze as the sound of boots thudded through the cemetery. Francisco and a man in a military uniform raced toward Martim with pistols drawn. Francisco pointed his pistol at the drunken man and yelled, "Freeze."

The military trooper hauled the old prison guard to his feet, cuffed the man's hands behind his back, and snarled, "The days of taking priests hostage are over."

Francisco helped his cousin up and untied the ropes binding his hands. "Are you all right, Martim?"

Martim rubbed his side. "Except for a few bruises, I'm fine. I was apprehensive at first. But I realize this happened for a reason."

"A reason?"

"Injustice inflamed the old sot, an injustice for which I may be partially responsible." As the trooper prodded the culprit to move, Martim called, "Wait. Where are you taking him?"

"To spend a few days in lockup. Give him some time away from the bottle to clear his head."

"No. Take him to the Church. Find a priest he can talk to. I believe he's ready to find a better way to live than to drown his anger in rum." He put a hand on the old guard's shoulder. "Am I right, Raul?"

The man nodded, his eyes downcast. "Forgive me, Padre."

Martim gave the old drunk a blessing. "Go in Christ."

Raul stumbled a few steps, then stopped and turned to Martim. "When you broke out, they fired two other guards. They plan to kill ya, too."

Martim inhaled. "*Obrigado, Senhor*. Thank you for telling me."

***

Four months later,
Friday, September 17, 1926

As Martim stood at the ship-rail, watching Lisbon fade in the distance, disillusionment dug in. The events of the last few months had unfolded fast and furiously. His planned departure for the end of June had come and gone. Since that breakfast meeting with General Carmona, he'd joined an army unit serving as their chaplain. Miraculously, the coup had been bloodless. He never had to perform the Last Rites.

Three different Portuguese presidents, including General Gomes da Costa, had risen to power after several coups. On July 9th, General Carmona had been named premier and minister of war. There was another coup attempt yesterday, and more coups could be in the works. Despite the recurring plots, it seemed General Carmona had the support of the military and was firmly in control. Few of Portugal's ordinary citizens seemed aware the army would run their country as a dictatorship. Democracy might not be in Portugal's future for many years to come.

Through all the chaos of the revolution, he had kept his eye out for the vengeful guards Raul had warned him about. Frequently, he'd sensed he was being stalked, but no one confronted him. If they had a deep desire for revenge, they could follow him to America. But that was unlikely. He doubted they had the means.

When the Castle de Sao Jorge was no longer visible, he returned to his cabin. Mementos his *mamãe* had given him lay spread on his berth. His fingers traced the outline of her face in the small photo of her she'd given him. Her courage, strength, wisdom, and unwavering love were qualities he aspired to emulate. He might never see *Mamãe* again, but he had some things to remind him of her, of his heritage, and of his homeland.

He put the photo aside and picked up his grandmother's silver ring. Inscribed inside the band were the words, "Faith, Hope, and Love". Martim choked, remembering *Mamãe* placing it in his hand, her arthritic fingers closing his fist around it and insisting he take it. She'd told him his grandmother would have been proud to have an ordained priest in her family. He'd argued with *Mamãe* that the ring didn't fit his fingers and should belong to Angelica.

But *Mamãe* had argued. "Angelica and her children will inherit everything of your grandmother's. The ring may not fit your finger, *meu filho*, but it fits who you are. 'Faith, Hope and Love' will remind you of your mission as a priest." *Mamãe* was right. He put the ring back in its velvet pouch, praying to always live with those virtues in his heart.

He steadied himself as the ship pitched and rolled on the sea. The three photos on his stack of mementos caught his eye. The solemn face of a young lad in an ornate chair stared back at him. A noble dog sat guard beside the boy who didn't realize someday he would become King Manuel II, or that as a young king, some of his subjects would trap him in a web of deceit, dethrone and banish him. A web Martim had become caught in when he fought to restore Manuel to his throne. He and

Manuel had become friends when they were lads, spending hours together learning from the same maestro.

The two other photos were of himself in his teens. He'd never have children of his own, so he wasn't sure who would want them when he died. But the Lord would sort that out.

Finally, there was a card with the directions for *Bacalhau a bras*. Henri had promised to make the dish if he brought her the recipe. When the Abbot assigned him to his first parish, he'd ask her to be his housekeeper. He wasn't sure she'd accept. She had set her hopes on being a stenographer. But he would try.

Chapter Eight

Seven Months Later, April 2, 1927
Sage Prairie, Montana
Martim

Martim shivered at his desk, starring at a blank piece of paper. He fastened the last few buttons of his sweater and breathed on his icy fingers. The wood stove did little to heat the drafty old parsonage. Outside, last night's dusting of snow still lay on the ground, but spring was undeterred. Daffodils and tulips were well on their way to blooming.

An internal debate had raged for hours as he considered whether to write this letter to Henri, and if he did, how to keep his feelings for her hidden. A sense of propriety had always kept him from showing how much he cared. As cautious as he'd been, he suspected Henri was aware of how he felt. And there was evidence she cared as deeply for him.

Her portrait lay on the table before him. She'd sent it with a note congratulating him on his appointment as pastor to several churches in northern Montana. The letter had also given him the details of her dual job as a stenographer for a printing business and as a housekeeper for the owner's wife.

He studied her photo. Beneath her smoldering eyes and beguiling smile was a passionate soul. He'd never met a woman like her—so full of life, tenacious, open-minded, and willing to challenge traditions. He missed her vivacity and her questioning mind. She was a woman who complemented his ideals. It seemed when he was with her, he felt complete.

He got up, stoked the fire, and paced until overwhelmed by the desire to have her come. Knowing it would be best to keep things on a semi-professional level, he picked up his pen and began. His letter would be warm but discrete.

Dearest Henri,
I can't tell you how much your letter meant to me.

He stopped, looked at his words, crumpled the paper, and began again.

Dear Henri,

I enjoyed your newsy letter and appreciated your photo. It completely captures your indomitable spirit.

Having weekends free from your job sounds wonderful. I imagine your moeder is grateful for your help when you're able to spend weekends at home.

My new assignment in Sage Prairie has kept me busy. When I arrived in February, the bishop asked me to help to dedicate the new Catholic Church in Billings and to conduct a three-day mission while I was there. Currently, I'm helping to create a Bible study syllabus for high school students at the request of Montana's State Board of Education.

I travel a great deal, as my multiple parishes are miles apart. I find my far-flung flocks personable and supportive of the Church but in need of guidance, counseling, and religious instruction.

With all my duties, I am grateful the Diocese has recognized my need for a housekeeper and has given me permission to hire someone in this capacity.

He put his pen down and scooted closer to the stove's crackling fire. His conscience warred with itself. Maybe he shouldn't ask her. But there were reasons she'd be perfect for the job. Her warmth and infectious charm would inspire the young ladies in his parishes to be more involved in Church activities. She was an excellent cook and would manage his rectory efficiently.

By now the chill had left his body's front. He turned to warm his back. Henri's efficiency and buoyant spirit would enliven his congregations. But, if he were honest, there was another side to this coin. She would test his resolve to honor his vow of celibacy. But that temptation wasn't anything prayer couldn't handle.

She was a catch for some young man. And out here in this rugged country there was a definite possibility she'd find a husband that suited her spirit. If that happened, and it likely would, she wouldn't be his housekeeper for long. Probably for only a year. So why not bring her here, help him establish programs for young women, and benefit from her housekeeping skills? He'd put it in the hands of the Lord. It would be a challenge. But God gave no one a burden they couldn't handle. He dipped his pen in ink and returned to his letter.

With that in mind, I'm wondering if your work in Mr. Parker's business and his household is satisfying and if you feel committed to remaining in his employ, or if you would consider coming to Sage Prairie to be my housekeeper.

The parsonage at Our Lady of the Prairie Church could use someone like you who is an excellent cook, with great organizational skills and efficient work habits. I need a housekeeper with a sense of humor who can carry on an interesting conversation. I fondly remember our walks at St. Albert's College. They always left me with something to think about.

Please write and let me know if you will come. Though my little parsonage's facilities are small and outdated, the Diocese has given me permission to develop plans and build a modern rectory next year.

If you agree to take the job, I will ask your cousin, Father Cornelius, to approach your parents with the idea.

Blessings,

Father Martim Ferrera

P.S. I have minha mamae's recipe for Bacalhau a bras. I'd be very happy if you made it for me.

Martim stared at the letter. Was he making a mistake asking her to come? He bowed his head and prayed. "Dear Jesus, I beg of you, give me strength to remain pure of heart so that my body serves my soul and together they serve Thee."

He slipped the letter in an envelope and sealed it. He'd mail it in Havre tomorrow.

Chapter Nine

Wednesday, April 25, 1927
Glade Harbor, Wisconsin
Henrietta

Henri sat on her boss's back porch, marveling at the intricate shadows created by the late afternoon sun, its rays weaving through the budding trees. Her eyes wandered to the printing shop across the yard from her boss's home and watched him work in the window of his business. She'd assumed she'd spend most of her time working in his business when she'd interviewed with Mr. Parker for the part-time secretary, part-time housekeeper position. Turned out she was wrong. Mr. Parker's wife was a semi-invalid and rather demanding. So the cooking, cleaning, and laundry took up most of Henri's time. Mr. Parker was a decent enough boss, but like most men his age, he probably wouldn't change. It was like working for her father, but with no mother to soften his chauvinistic attitudes.

Her mind returned to the letter in her hands. Father Ferrera had offered her a job, and she'd accepted with no hesitation. Excitement grew as she thought of life ahead. Tomorrow she would board a train to Sage Prairie. A job away from her parents would bring her the freedom she longed for. And maybe, just maybe, she'd find a forward-thinking man she could love and marry.

If that didn't happen, at least she'd be working for someone with an open mind, someone who was easy to talk to, and someone she admired. She had deep feelings for Father as a friend, so deep she often thought of him as Martim instead of Father Ferrera. Her chest tightened. Her fondness for him had edged to the point of being improper.

The battle to suppress her feelings had gotten easier when he'd left to visit his mother in Portugal. She'd written him a note of congratulations when she learned the Abbot had assigned him as pastor to the Catholic missions in northern Montana, and then she'd buried her desire, recognizing she wouldn't see him for a long time, if ever. His letter had reignited her affections. She read his note again. Was she imagining his words expressed his own deep feelings for her? No. It couldn't be. It was wrong. She was reading too much into his words

She jumped when the gate on the side of the house creaked open. Her favorite sister came around the corner.

"Greta, what a surprise."

Greta settled beside her. "I know we said our goodbyes yesterday, sis, but I'm going to miss you so much. It might be a long time before we see each other again."

Henri put her arm through Greta's and laid her head on Greta's shoulder. "I'll miss you, too. And all our talks and adventures."

Greta's eyes clouded as she handed Henri a small box.

"What's this?"

"I know they serve meals on the train, but I thought you might like some cookies to snack on."

Henri's throat tightened. Tears threatened. "You're the best sister ever, Greta."

"You too, Henrietta." She wiped the corners of her eyes with the back of her hand. "Is everything ready for big brother Fritz to take you to the train tomorrow?"

It took a moment for Henri's words to loosen from her tongue. "Everything's ready but my heart. As much as I'm happy to no longer be under *Vader*'s and *Moeder*'s thumbs, I'm going to miss them terribly, and you, Father Cornelius, Marta, our whole family, and especially our little niece Lillie."

Greta sniffled. "Everyone will miss you too. Still *Moeder* and *Vader* are relieved their headstrong daughter will be under the watchful eye of a good Catholic priest."

Henri nodded. "I'm well aware of how they feel." She mimicked *Vader*'s words when he'd approved of her taking the job. "It is good, *dochter*. You will serve a man of the cloth. And God willing, *Vader* Ferrera will help you find a man who is to your liking so you can settle down and have *kinderen*." Henri stared out across the yard. "Seriously, Greta. I want to have children. But I have to find the right man to marry first."

Greta squeezed Henri's hand. "That's the usual protocol, Henrietta. I pray it works out."

***

Friday, April 27, 1927
Great Northern Train to Willow Grove, Montana

Henri gazed out the train window at a herd of antelope grazing on the spring prairie. Their shadows stretched away from the setting sun. They looked up, unperturbed by the clacking of the train, and returned to their evening meal. Despite the train's plush seats, her body had grown stiff from hours of travel. She shook the tingles from her sleeping foot and sighed. She shouldn't be having romantic thoughts of Martim. No. Not 'Martim' he was Father Ferrera, her employer. And it was best to think of him that way. Sure, she hoped to find someone to marry who had many of his qualities. But for God's sake, it wouldn't be him.

Banishing her troubling thoughts, Henrietta turned her attention to a little girl sitting across from her. The girl's mother was reading *The Tale of Jemima Puddle-Duck* to her. Suddenly the child squealed, "Oh Momma, don't let that mean man eat Jemima."

Henrietta clapped a hand over her mouth to keep from laughing.

The mother gave her daughter a gentle squeeze. "Don't worry, Hannah. Jemima has a friend who will help her stay out of the oven."

The girl nestled closer to her mother, clutching two more Beatrix Potter books on her lap. Hannah's mother continued with the story, reading it three more times. Finally, she closed the book and rasped, "That's all for tonight, Hannah. My voice needs a rest." She reached for a rag doll that had fallen on the floor. "Here, sweetie, I think Emmy Lou is very tired and needs a nap."

Hannah cradled the doll in her arms and began sweetly singing 'Rock a Bye Baby'. Her eyes drooped. Soon she was asleep. Her wispy blond hair and cherub cheeks reminded Henrietta of her little niece Lillie, whose innocent smile and sweet giggles oozed into Henrietta's heart every time they were together and deepened her longing for children of her own.

Henrietta turned her thoughts back to her journey. Tomorrow afternoon she would arrive in Willow Grove, Montana. Father Ferrera would pick her up at the station. She would help him with the mission he was conducting at St. Peters. A few days later they would head to Our Lady of the Prairie's rectory in Sage Prairie, where keeping her thoughts of Martim to ones approved by heaven would be hellishly difficult. Still, it was a difficulty she relished facing. She reached into her dress pocket and felt for the rosary he had given her a year ago.

***

Saturday, April 30, 1927

A long whistle announced the train's arrival at the Great Northern Depot in Willow Grove. Henrietta closed *The Tail of Peter Rabbit*_and gave the book to Hannah. Henrietta had taken over entertaining the little girl when her mother's voice had worn to a whisper. She gave Hannah a sad look and said, "I have to go now."

"No," Hannah begged, "Read it again. Please." Her sweet face tugged at Henrietta's heart.

Henrietta laughed. "You've heard that story so many times. I'll bet you could read it yourself now."

Hannah's frown turned to a smile. She opened the book and began. "Once upon a time there lived four little rabbits, Flopsy, Mopsy, Cottontail, and Peter." She turned the page.

Hannah's mother whispered, "Thanks for entertaining her. You helped to make our long journey easier."

"It was my pleasure," Henrietta said with wistful look at the little girl. She picked up her valise and headed down the aisle to the door.

As the train whooshed to a stop, she surveyed the small crowd. She saw him. His glasses glinting in the sun gave him a distinguished air. Trim dark curly hair framed his handsome face. Feelings bloomed in her heart. Maybe it was infatuation. But it seemed more like love. Love for a friend was okay, but never romantic love. She took a deep breath and followed a line of passengers down the train's steps into the sunshine. She deliberately slowed her pace as she wove her way through the throng towards him.

When Martim—. No! When Father Ferrera saw her, his face brightened. Her heart lit up. "Good grief," she scolded herself. Of course, he was glad to see his new housekeeper. She'd cook his meals, clean his house, do his laundry, and make the rectory a home. It was nothing more than that. Yet joy fluttered in her stomach as he hurried across the wooden planks towards her.

He grabbed her valise and said, "It's good to see you, Miss Hoffmann. You've made it in time for the last two days of my mission."

Henrietta frowned. Miss Hoffmann? He'd called her Henri since her early days at the Abbey. But then she noticed two boys standing beside him. Of course. He would have to address her formally in public, especially around his parishioners. She smiled. "Is your mission going well, Father?"

"Wonderfully. Almost a hundred and fifty people are in attendance. Some are returning to the church after being away for years, some are new to the church, and some are among the faithful who want to deepen their connection to the Lord." He handed her a card. "For you. It commemorates the mission."

Henrietta glanced at the crucified Christ on the front and turned the card over. Her eyes focused on the words, "Only One Thing is Necessary. SAVE YOUR SOUL". Life as his housekeeper might make that difficult. But prayer would help her stay on the straight and narrow. She swallowed and slipped the card into her pocketbook. "I see my luggage. It's just been unloaded."

Father Ferrera motioned for the boys beside him to follow. "Come lads, let's get Miss Hoffmann's trunk to my car." He turned to Henrietta. "I've arranged for you to spend the next two nights at Mrs. Morgan's. Her home is near the church. We have to hurry and get you settled there so I can get back to St. Peters in time to prepare for the evening service."

Henri's giddiness grew as they worked their way around the baggage scattered on the landing. Father smiled at her. "Since tomorrow begins the special month for our Blessed Mother, I planned a living rosary this evening in her honor. If you're not too tired, I saved a bead for you."

"What an honor. I wouldn't miss it for the world."

"Perfect," he said, a warm smile filling his face. Over the noise of the crowd and the rumble of the train's engine, she heard him say, "I'm glad you're here." Again, her heart moved where it shouldn't go. He picked up her suitcase and motioned for the boys to get her trunk. She grabbed a small tote that held memories of home; hollyhock seeds, iris roots, and rhubarb plants from her mother's garden. She'd plant them right away, so they'd be ready to enjoy next spring.

They worked their way through muddy ruts around to the back of the mercantile. By the time they reached a small row of automobiles and a few horse-drawn wagons parked behind the store, muck coated Henrietta's shoes.

They came to a halt beside a marine blue sedan, top half shiny, bottom splattered with grime. Father grinned. "My new Chevrolet." He opened the back door and set her suitcase on the seat.

"It's gorgeous," Henrietta said, ignoring the muddy half. "Definitely the cat's meow. I'll bet it quickly gets you around to your many parishes."

He patted the hood and grinned. "Absolutely. She gets me back and forth at 30 miles an hour. And she already has an amazing number of miles on her." He loaded Henri's trunk and handed each of his helpers a shiny dime. The boys gave Father Ferrera and his new sedan an admiring look and scampered into the mercantile.

Father opened the passenger door. "Hop in, Miss Hoffmann. Saint Peters Church is at the edge of town."

Henri hesitated, looking at the muck on her shoes. Father laughed, "Don't worry, Henri. Plenty of mud has already christened the floor. Just wipe your feet on the running board."

"How very accommodating," she grinned, glad to hear him call her Henri now that they were alone. Still, it might be better if he kept to a professional 'Miss Hoffmann'. As the car pulled away from the mercantile, she redirected her thoughts. "How was your mother when you saw her?"

His face became reflective. "When I arrived in Portugal, I caught wind of another coup. I took *minha mae* to stay with my sister Angelica and her husband where she will be safe." He half laughed. "Incredibly, the coup was bloodless." He frowned and shook his head. "But there is still some danger."

"Your mother must have been relieved to have you there."

He shifted into gear and turned onto the road. "And I was glad to spend time with her. She's an amazing woman. Getting old, but still beautiful and sings like an angel." He glanced at Henri, smiling wistfully. "As I told you in my letter, she gave me the recipe for *Bacalhau a bras*. Now you have to keep your promise and make it for me."

Henri tilted her head with a flirty grin. "I hope I can do it justice."

"I'm sure you will." He patted her hand sending her heart a twitter.

The car stopped beside a small white steepled church. He nodded at a tent set up in a field nearby. "That's where I'm holding my mission. St. Peters Church is too small for all the people who came."

The tent was huge, evidence of his ability to inspire. One more reason she admired him. He pointed at a farmhouse nestled in the fenced pasture next to the church property. "That's Mrs. Morgan's place where you will be staying. As soon as we unload my supplies, I'll take you over."

***

Dark clouds gathered on the horizon as Henri walked from the farmhouse to the open-air tent where Father Ferrera was holding the living rosary. Mrs. Morgan had left earlier to settle into her role as the organist. A stiff breeze threatened to sweep Henri's hat from her head. She tightened her sweater over her royal blue Sunday dress and followed a crowd into the tent. She dipped her fingers in a silver bowl of holy water and made the sign of the cross. Worshippers already filled most of the wooden benches. A temporary altar occupied the back of the canvas church. A simple crucifix rose behind it, with statues of Mary and Joseph on either side. Quiet conversations hummed below the hymn Mrs. Morgan played on the organ.

"You look lovely this evening, Miss Hoffmann," Father Ferrera whispered. Fire flamed across her cheeks as he went on. "Your place in the rosary is over here."

The 'living rosary' surrounded the faithful seated on the benches, ready for the service to begin. He led her to a spot in a circle of people, each person a bead, and stationed her beside a young woman with curly bobbed hair peeking from beneath a deep pink flowered hat. Father handed Henri a candle. "You two should become acquainted as you will probably see a lot of each other over the next few months." Then he hurried away.

"Hi, I'm Etta Kroft," the young woman murmured. She leaned over and lit Henrietta's candle with the flame glowing on her own taper. "You must be Henrietta, Father Ferrera's new housekeeper."

"Call me Henri." Etta's friendly face prompted Henri to ask, "What about you? Do you have a job?"

Etta grinned. "Not yet. I still have two years of high school. Then I plan to attend a secretarial school until I find the right man." Etta kept her voice low. "Ma and Pa spend a lot of time volunteering for the church. Pa even hunts with Father Ferrera. My folks are on the front bench with my grandparents, my two brothers, and my little sister."

Henri inched closer to Etta. "Just like my parents. They always made sure we sat down front."

Etta nodded. "I have two other sisters. They're part of the rosary."

Shh," came with a scowl from an older woman standing on the other side of Etta.

Etta put a hand to her mouth to suppress a smirk. She put on an angelic expression and cupped her hand around the flame of her candle to shelter it from the breeze flitting through the tent.

Guarding her own flame, Henri scanned the growing crowd. A little girl wiggled on a nearby bench. She caught the youngster's eye and winked. With a cute smile, the girl tried to wink back but ended up blinking instead, scrunching her face in a way that melted Henri's heart. Someday, she'd be a mother herself. She wished for a child half as dear as the sweet little pumpkin flirting back at her.

The organ pumped out the first notes of Ave Maria, interrupting Henri's thoughts. Father Ferrera entered the tent with another priest. Etta leaned in close to Henri. "That's Father Jansen. He's the resident priest at St. Peters."

But Henri's eyes were on Martim as he walked towards the altar and joined the congregation in song, his robes rippling in the breeze. A rumble of distance thunder fringed the song. As she watched her candle flicker she begged, "Holy Mother, help me drive away my sinful thoughts."

Chapter Ten

Willow Grove, Montana
Saturday Evening April 30, 1927
Henrietta

The prayers echoed through the congregation as they moved from bead to bead through the first two decades of the rosary. And now it was Henri's turn. The glow of the candle warmed her face as she finished saying her prayer. "*Holy Mother of God, pray for us sinners, now and at the hour of our death, Amen.*" She glanced at the altar. Father Ferrera's eyes were on her. He smiled and gave her an imperceptible nod. She looked away, hoping he couldn't read her heart.

As Etta began her Hail Mary, a young man hurried down the side aisle to the organ and whispered in Mrs. Morgan's ear. The older woman clutched her chest and beamed. Flushed with excitement, she followed the man down the aisle and worked her way around the living rosary until she came to Henrietta. "My daughter is having her baby. I need to go. Make yourself at home. If I'm not back by tomorrow morning, could you milk Prissy and collect the eggs?"

Henrietta whispered, "I'd be happy to. And thanks for letting me stay." Mrs. Morgan patted her arm and hurried away with the young man out into the darkening sky.

Occasional plops of rain sounded on the canvas above. The rumble of thunder grew closer. The crowd seemed restless but continued praying bead after bead as the rosary moved around the congregation to its end.

Soon, the last prayer echoed through the tent. "Glory be to the Father, and to the Son, and to the Holy..." There was a flash of lightning so bright it lit every face in the makeshift church. A deafening clap of thunder drowned the final words. A moment of stillness, and then rain pummeled canvas. Father Ferrera's voice rose above the roar. "Remember, tomorrow we crown our Blessed Mother. May she help us grow in love with one another and live in peace." With that, the crowd threw coats and jackets over their heads and rushed into the storm to their cars.

Etta squeezed Henri's arm and grinned. "What an ending to the service, like heaven itself has spoken!"

"When a rainbow comes after a storm, I've always believed it is a sign of God's forgiveness and a promise for a better tomorrow."

"It'll rain pitchforks tonight," Etta said. "And I'm sure there'll be a rainbow in the morning. Montana rainbows are magnificent. Sometimes two arcs stretch across the sky from horizon to horizon."

"Etta," a man called from the tent's opening. "Your brothers and I are helping Father Ferrera secure the tent. Your ma is inside St. Peters with your sisters getting flowers ready for tomorrow's service. She needs your help."

"Okay, Pa. I'll be right there."

Henri sensed Father Ferrera beside her, his arm brushing lightly against hers. "Miss Hoffmann, could you lend Mrs. Kroft a hand? I happen to know you're good with flower arrangements."

Henri nodded, not trusting herself to speak. Even his smallest compliment caused her heart to flutter.

A powerful gust of wind whipped through the tent, nearly lifting it from its anchors. Father rushed to the nearest stake. "Fred, we'd better get our canvas church battened down before it takes off."

An hour later, thunder still ripped across the prairie, rattling the windows in St. Peters. Henrietta tucked the last of the tulips into a mass of lilacs and placed the vase with the others to be used in the morning service. The church door banged open. Mr. Kroft hurried in and removed his dripping hat. Father Ferrera wore no hat. Though the rain had soaked him to the skin and water streamed down his face, his tight curly hair seemed impervious to the downpour. He studied the bouquets. "Ladies, my compliments. The arrangements are lovely."

Mr. Kroft took his wife's arm. "Come, Elizabeth. The kids are waiting in the car." He paused. "Miss Hoffmann, it's awfully wet and much too dark to walk to Mrs. Morgan's. We can squeeze you into our Ford, if you'd like."

"Don't worry, Fred," Father Ferrera said. "You've got a crowded car already. I'll drive Miss Hoffmann next door before I head to St. Peters' rectory." As the Kroft family left, Father picked up a pearly rosary that had fallen between two vases. "I recognize these. I believe they're yours, Miss Hoffmann." He placed them gently in her hand.

Strangely, his icy fingers sparked a fire burning through her veins. "Thank you," was all she could say, keeping her eyes on the beads.

Father Ferrera's sedan slipped through the ruts to Mrs. Morgan's house, the road barely visible in the headlights, and the wiper blades working overtime in the onslaught of rain. When the auto skidded to a halt near the front porch, Henri sighed. "It's so dark, I'm not sure I'll be able to find my way to the steps." She reached for the car door handle.

"Wait, Henri. I'll help you until you get a light on in the house." He grabbed a lantern from the back seat.

Henri pulled her sweater over her head and sloshed behind Father. As they reached the covered porch, the banging of a barn door broke through the pounding rain. She turned to see lightning sizzle in the pasture, illuminating a cow standing near the fence. Darkness enveloped them again, followed by a long rumble of thunder, and then came the cow's frightened moo. "Oh, for crying out loud. That's Mrs. Morgan's cow."

Father stepped off the porch, his lantern glittering in the rain. "I'd better get her to the barn, or she'll be off her milk in the morning."

"I'll help," Henri said, fastening the top two buttons on her sweater.

"No Henri, you'll get soaked and catch cold."

"Can't be helped. Prissy is frightened. It'll probably take both of us to convince her to go back inside." Henri stepped back into the rain.

"Stubborn woman," he said as he slipped one arm out of his mackinaw and wrapped the freed half over Henri. His closeness took her breath away. They trudged to the barn in silence. Father found a rope, and Henri stuffed oats into her sweater pocket. Back outside, they slogged through the pasture.

Occasional flashes of lightning showed the cow standing anchored against the fence, mooing loudly, her ears flattened to her head. Her eyes bulged, and she shied away when Father reached for her tether.

Rain ran in rivulets down Henri's face as she pulled a handful of grain from her pocket. "It's okay, Prissy," she soothed. "Wouldn't you like to cozy up in the barn? See, I have a treat for you, big girl." Henri slipped from under Father's mackinaw. She slowly swayed back and forth as she offered Prissy the grain. Prissy looked curiously at Henri and studied the oats but didn't budge.

Father stepped towards the cow. Her eyes ballooned and she cowered back.

"Don't move, Father. Just keep the lantern steady so she doesn't see me as a threat." Henri's shoes oozed with mud as she inched her way towards the cow with the oats in her hand. Prissy's ears twitched. She lost some of her frightened look and took a hesitant step towards Henri.

"That's right, Prissy. Mrs. Morgan said you'd do anything for a bit of oats." Henri waited patiently, rain soaking her clothes. As Henri gently swayed side to side standing still, Prissy plodded closer and sniffed the treat. Henri reached out and scratched her between her eyes. The cow's big slobbery tongue licked up the grain. Henri took hold of her halter, allowing Father to slip the rope through the tether and tie it.

Father brought the mackinaw back around Henri as they led the cow to the barn. "That was amazing, Henri."

Henri nodded, his closeness suppressing her tongue.

With Prissy sheltered in her stall and happy with plenty of hay, her two rescuers huddled back beneath Father's coat and trudged to Mrs. Morgan's. The thunder and lightning had stopped, and only a few drops fell from the sky as they plodded through the darkness. The clouds opened, revealing the moon and liberating the stars. Father paused halfway to the house and lifted his face to the heavens. "Beautiful, isn't it, Henri?"

The stars cast a dreamy spell over the night. She shivered wildly but wanted to linger beside him. She wrapped her arms tightly around herself and surveyed the boundless stars. "That God created the universe from nothing completely amazes me."

"It is a marvel, Henri. I could watch the night sky for hours." He paused and looked down at her. "But you're well beyond cold, and it's been a long day. We'd better get you to the house so you can warm up and get some rest."

She hated to give in to common sense, but he was shivering as much as she. "You're exhausted, too."

He tightened the coat around them, and they turned towards the farmhouse. The lantern had gone dim. Neither of them saw the prairie dog hole until it was too late. She tripped. Pain screamed through her ankle as she fell.

"Are you alright?" Father asked, helping her up.

She winced at her first step. "It's not too bad," she said, biting her lip. A second step sent pain exploding up her leg. She gasped. "But I better not put too much weight on it."

"Let me help." He draped her arm around his neck, put his arm about her waist, and helped her hobble to the porch.

Agony mixed with the commotion in her heart. His closeness was so overwhelming, she was almost relieved when she was finally out of his arms and seated on a kitchen chair. He knelt before her, removed her shoe, and sat back on his heels. "You'll have to remove your own stocking, Henri."

Fire blazed on her cheeks. "Yes, Martim. I should do that myself."

He turned away.

As she unfastened the stocking at her thigh and rolled it over her ankle, she realized she'd called him 'Martim'. The name had slipped from her mouth as naturally as breathing. She stuffed the hose in her pocket. "I'm ready, Martim."

His eyes caught hers, and then he looked down. "Let's see how bad it is."

He gently probed the area, already hot and swelling. The rest of her still shivered uncontrollably. Water dripped from her hair and rolled down her bare leg. She flinched at a painful prod. He looked up, his eyes filled with tenderness. "Sorry! My hands are so icy."

"Actually, the cold feels good."

He gently massaged her injury. "Such a lovely ankle," he murmured. "Too bad it's sprained." He stood. "Stay there. I'll be right back."

She half laughed and pointed at her ankle. "No chance I'm going anywhere." She listened to his footsteps hurry across the porch. As she waited, her mind spun with the strangeness of it—that she could feel wonderful and be in so much pain at the same time.

She jumped when the door clicked open. He hustled in with a brown woolen blanket and a black medical bag. He helped her remove her rain- soaked sweater and snugged the blanket around her. His every touch surged through her heart.

He rummaged through the bag, coming up with a container of horse liniment and a bottle of aspirin. He knelt at her feet and gently massaged the salve into her injury, the pungent odor permeating the air. He grinned. "Don't worry Henri, liniment isn't just good for horses. It works on humans as well."

"I sure hope so," Henri said as his hands worked their magic on her ankle and the liniment warmed her foot. She nodded at his medical bag. "You travel prepared."

"I have to," he said and wrapped a long strip of bandaging around her ankle. "I'm often called on to give medical treatment when I visit my parishes."

He got up and went to the sink. She watched him work the hand pump and wash his hands. He was incredible. Not only did he minister to people's souls but also to their bodies. He dried his hands and hung the towel over the sink, his movements fluid and graceful. Everything about him would attract the attention of most women. She blushed again and scolded herself. "Remember, Henri, he's a priest, my employer, and nothing more."

He handed her a dipper of water along with two aspirin. As she drank and swallowed the pills, he stood back and studied her. What was he thinking? Were his feelings like hers?

Worry wrinkled his brow. "You're still shivering and probably hypothermic. You need to get warm, or you'll catch a cold to go along with that sprain." He lifted her into his arms. "I'll take you to your room. Then I'll be on my way."

She swallowed. "Martim, really. My ankle isn't that bad. I can walk."

"I'm not taking chances with my new housekeeper. Tell me, where has Mrs. Morgan put you up for the night?"

With his face so close to hers, she had to look away, fearing he would see the desire in her eyes. She breathed in slowly and let it go. "Up the stairs in the garret."

She heard him swallow. There was a catch in his voice when he spoke. "You shouldn't be negotiating steps with your ankle." A roller coaster of emotion spiraled through her as they started up the stairs. He nudged the door open with his foot. Moonlight filtered through the curtains as he laid her on the bed. "You're still shaking," he said, tucking a quilt around her.

She couldn't tell him her shivers weren't just from the cold. "I'll be fine, Martim."

Spreading another blanket over her, he leaned down and lightly kissed her forehead. He straightened and backed away, buttoning his coat. In the dim light, she couldn't read his expression. His voice low and soft, he said, "Get some sleep, Henri. I'll be back in the morning to pick you up for services."

She watched him disappear out the door, his kiss scorching her skin. What did it mean? Was it a brother's kiss, like the one Fritz had planted on her cheek when he'd said goodbye at the train station? Was it a fatherly kiss? Or the kiss some foreigners give one another to say hello or goodbye? Whatever it meant, the clamor in her heart was overwhelming. Were her feelings simple infatuation or affection for a friend? Because that's what he was. But the tumult in her heart argued he was something more.

Chapter Eleven

Willow Grove, Montana
May 1, 1927
Henrietta

Sunday dawned fresh and clear. Henri limped into the early sunshine with a tin pail in her hand, wincing at every step. Mrs. Morgan hadn't returned, and Prissy needed milking. She paused for a moment, distracted by yesterday's storm clouds disappearing on the horizon. Etta had been right. A double rainbow arched across the sky. Did it show forgiveness of her dishonorable feelings for Father Ferrera?

As steamy streams of milk pinged into the bucket, she ignored the pain in her ankle. Her thoughts riveted on what had happened last night. Martim's chivalry when they'd rescued Prissy and his skill when he'd tended her sprain had been kind and almost loving. Then there'd been that kiss. It must have been a kiss of brotherly affection. Was it a sin to think it more?

By the time she placed the milk in the icebox, her ankle hurt too much to collect the eggs. They'd have to wait until Mrs. Morgan got home. She hobbled up the stairs to get ready for church.

Dressed in her blue satin dress and cloche hat, she sat on Mrs. Morgan's front steps and waited for Martim to pick her up. A dark sedan turned off the road, into the gate, and bounced up the driveway. Her pulse quickened. Martim. She'd know soon enough if that kiss had changed things between them.

As the car drew near, she could see it was not his blue Chevy. Was Mrs. Morgan finally returning? As the auto pulled up in front of the farmhouse, she recognized Mr. Kroft in the driver's seat and Etta beside him.

Etta helped Henri into the back seat and scooted in beside her. "Father Ferrera told us about your adventure with Prissy last night. He asked us to pick you up."

Henri adjusted her leg until the pain eased a bit. "I was lucky

Father was there to dress my ankle. I re-wrapped it this morning. The bruise has gotten uglier, but it feels better than last night." She eyed the bulge in her stocking, remembering Martim's gentle touch. Why hadn't he come himself? Was he avoiding her because he realized he shouldn't have kissed her?

"Father Ferrera is amazing," Etta said, gripping the seat as the auto bounced over the ruts. "He's been in Sage Prairie for only three months, and he's already known for his medical expertise." She reached into her handbag and handed Henri two white pills and a small flask. "Water to wash the aspirin down. Doctor's orders."

Henri swallowed the tablets, staring out the window. Last night's rain still glistened on the prairie grass. She told herself the aspirin, in this case, was a sign he cared for her the way he should, as a patient. Still, the kiss befuddled her. What did it mean? She couldn't imagine he kissed his other patients, brotherly, fatherly, or otherwise.

Etta gently elbowed Henri. "You seem to have something on your mind. What is it?"

She smiled and shook her head. "I'm just taking everything in. It's all so new."

Etta nodded as they turned down the lane to the church. A tide of people dressed in their Sunday best flooded into the tent, now drying in the morning sun. Boys in knickers and scratchy dress-up shirts tugged at their bow ties, their hair slicked to their heads with pomade. Girls flounced around, spruced up in flour-sack dresses adorned with sashes and lacy collars, their heads haloed in flowered garlands.

"The girls are adorable," Henri said as Etta helped her out of the car. "When I was little, I loved being a flower girl in Mary's May Day procession."

"Me too," Etta said, supporting Henri as she hobbled towards the tent. "Today Father asked me to organize the girls on the front benches. He told me you'd want to help but made it clear I'm to make sure you stay off your feet."

"No argument there." Henri banged her ankle as she slumped onto a bench. She gasped and reached down to massage the throbbing sprain.

Etta mouthed, "Are you alright?"

Henri caught her breath and nodded. As she waited for the pain to subside, she scanned the tent for Father Ferrera. No sign of him, but that wasn't unusual. On Sunday mornings, priests rarely appeared until Mass started.

A gloved hand landed on her shoulder. Henri turned to a beaming Mrs. Morgan. "Henrietta, thanks for milking Prissy this morning. Knowing you were there to take care of her gave me extra time to be with my daughter and new grandson."

Henri patted the older woman's arm and smiled.

"It looks like the flower girls are ready," Mrs. Morgan said, removing her gloves. She hurried to the organ and began pumping the opening hymn, "Hail Mary Pearl of Grace."

Everyone rose. Father Ferrera and two altar boys stood in the sunshine at the tent's entrance. He moved down the aisle to the altar singing with the congregation. She tried to catch his eye. But he didn't seem to notice. Maybe because she was partially hidden by the taller folks around her.

As the mass unfolded, she hoped he would give her a nod of recognition, a smile, a quick glance. Something that would help her understand what had happened last night. But by the time he stood at the pulpit to begin his sermon, their eyes still hadn't met.

Five minutes into his sermon on the Virgin Mary, Father Ferrera's words connected to a question that was constantly on her mind.

"Every day of her life, the Blessed Mother did what mothers have done since time began. They make sacrifices as they look after their families. Raise their children and make their dwellings a home. Mary sanctified these ordinary everyday acts."

What was her future? Would she be a mother with a home to care for and a husband to love? If she married, she wanted a man who recognized her worth beyond being a cook and a housemaid. Her throat tightened as she caught herself again considering Martim as the perfect husband and father. She had to stop thinking of him that way. He was a priest. The irony was they would never have met if he hadn't been ordained. Was she falling in love with him? If she was, should she go back home? Thoughts and questions plagued her through the rest of the Mass, through the crowning of the Blessed Mother, through the congregation's potluck picnic. She debated the right path through the evening and into the night. Her dreams were full of him and of things that should never happen.

By morning, turmoil and indecision tore her apart. Her heart told her to stay as his housekeeper. Her conscience told her to return to Glade Harbor.

Chapter Twelve

Monday, May 2, 1927
Willow Grove, Montana
Martim

Martim breathed in the crisp morning air. Yellow-breasted meadowlarks perched on the fence posts along the grasslands bordering the church, and the birds serenaded him as he packed the car for the return trip to Sage Prairie. His leather satchel carrying the last of the hosts, his vestments, the missal, and his silver chalice went into the back seat. He stashed the half bottle of leftover wine in the trunk and checked the engine oil. Then, shielding his eyes from the sun, he headed to Mrs. Morgan's with Henri on his mind.

He'd watched her limp through yesterday's services, appalled with himself. The kiss on her forehead had been impulsive, unplanned, instinctive. He knew why he had done it, and the reason wasn't moral. She must wonder what it meant. How could he explain it to her?

Mixed with the predicament of the kiss, he'd worried about her sprain. He'd given Etta orders to make sure she didn't overdo it. But just like Henri, she'd ignored his advice. As the rituals had unfolded, through the crowning of the Blessed Mother, the picnic luncheon, and the last of the service, it seemed she'd been on her feet way too much. There'd been so many activities that needed his attention; he hadn't been able to make sure she kept off her feet. He'd introduced her to a few parishioners but had left the rest of the introductions to Etta. What if she felt slighted because he hadn't found a chance to talk with her?

Throughout the day, he'd caught sight of her limping around, being her charming, friendly self. But too often she'd stood apart from the crowd as if musing about something. Maybe she missed her family or speculated about her new life ahead. But if he were honest, his impulsive kiss had probably caused her to brood. On the bright side, several parishioners had told him he'd made an excellent choice hiring her. Even better, several of the young ladies already seemed connected to her.

The muddy ruts to Mrs. Morgan's house had started to crust over when he drove up her lane. The elderly woman met him at the door, wiping her hands on her apron. "Come in, Father. Breakfast is almost ready. Can't have you two heading off without a proper meal." The aroma of coffee and bacon teased him as he followed Mrs. Morgan to the kitchen. She called upstairs as she poured pancake batter on a griddle. "Henrietta, Father is here. Come join us for breakfast."

Henri called from the garret. "I have a bit more to pack, then I'll be down."

Martim moved to the stairs. "Miss Hoffmann, wait there. I'm coming up to fetch your luggage."

"Thank you, Father," she called back. "But I'm quite capable of carrying my suitcase." Her voice had a sharp edge to it. Was the pain in her ankle bothering her more than she wanted to admit?

He ignored her refusal, climbed the stairs, and knocked on the door. "I know you're capable, Miss Hoffmann. But you shouldn't carry anything heavy until we're sure your ankle can bear the weight, especially down a flight of stairs."

She opened the door with a determined expression, her suitcase in her hand.

"Please don't be stubborn, Miss Hoffmann. Let me take it. Your sprain will heal faster if you don't overuse it."

She huffed with exasperation but handed him her luggage. "I guess you're the doctor."

He followed her as she hung onto the rail and descended one step at a time.

Mrs. Morgan beamed when Henri joined her in the kitchen. "Ah, there she is," she said, setting down her pancake turner and pulling Henri to her side. "Father, you've hired a gem. Not only is she charming, she's capable in the kitchen and around the farm even with a sprained ankle."

He grinned. "She came highly recommended."

Henri settled on a chair, put a napkin on her lap, and spoke, "Thanks for breakfast, Mrs. Morgan. It smells yummy."

"Wait till you see what I packed for your lunch," she said, gesturing at a picnic basket on the sideboard.

"You're spoiling us," Martim said, sitting across from Henri.

Savoring the last bite of pancake, Martim put his fork on his plate. "Very delicious, Mrs. Morgan." He turned to Henri. "You've been quiet this morning, Miss Hoffmann. Is your ankle bothering you?"

She gave him a wan smile. "Some, but that's to be expected."

"I want to check it before we go."

"I checked it myself this morning, Father. It looks uglier than ever, but it's healing."

"Still, it will heal faster with a fresh coat of liniment."

"Thank you, Father. But I'm fine for now." Was he imagining coolness in her voice?

Mrs. Morgan added her two cents. "Are you sure, Miss Hoffmann? Father excels at that sort of thing."

Henri half laughed. "I'll be fine."

Mrs. Morgan patted Henri's hand. "I'm sure you're right, dear."

With Henri settled in the car beside Martim and her luggage on the back seat, the car turned out of Mrs. Morgan's driveway and headed down the road to Sage Prairie. She stared out the window with the picnic basket on her lap. He eyed her and said, "Mrs. Morgan outdid herself preparing lunch for us."

Henri nodded, her eyes remaining on the scenery flowing by.

"Are you nervous about the job?"

She shrugged. "Not really."

"You have any questions?"

She shook her head. The miles passed without a word. Her silence unnerved him. From the moment he'd picked her up at the train station on Saturday until he'd left her at Mrs. Morgan's Saturday night, she'd been her usual gregarious self. Now, clearly something bothered her, and it wasn't just her ankle. Without a shadow of doubt, he knew it was the kiss. He wasn't ready to bring it up, and he wasn't sure he should.

It was well past noon when he found the turn he'd been searching for. He bumped off the road onto a path in the prairie grass towards a stretch of budding cottonwoods and willow trees. Henri straightened. "Where are we going?"

Martim grinned. She'd finally spoken. "There's a magnificent spot by Willow Creek where we can have our picnic lunch, and you can soak your ankle. The spot reminds me a bit of the pond at St. Albert's." She glanced at him, a smile hinting on her lips.

He turned off the engine and helped her from the car. With his arm through hers, he guided her through the trees to a burbling stream. She stood beside him without a word, seemingly entranced by the loveliness of the day. Though warm and sunny, an occasional chilly breeze rustled through newly formed chokecherry leaves. Bees burrowed in the blossoms opening on the shrubs that lined the creek. Ants swarmed up and down the cottonwoods, collecting the red and yellow resin oozing from their buds. Across the stream, a red-winged blackbird plucked feathery tufts that had erupted from the cattails during the winter.

She put her hand to her cheek and inhaled deeply, slowly letting it go. “You’re right. It’s lovely.”

“Like a bit of paradise.” With Henri now happy beside him, the day had become perfect. He spread the woolen blanket he’d wrapped around her Saturday night on a patch of sand near the bank and laid out the picnic. With lunch ready, he helped her settle on the ground. She ran her hand across the tightly woven wool. “It’s still damp,” she said, her voice a million miles away.

As Martim relaxed beside her, her stomach growled. She giggled, putting both hands on her waist. “I’m famished,” she said, surveying the slices of bread and butter, cold chicken, boiled eggs, pickled beans, and two slices of cherry pie. As she peeled an egg, she looked at him, her face serious. “I’ve been thinking about…” She put the peeled egg on her plate and let her gaze wander through the trees.

The kiss. It had to be on her mind. Should he bring it up, or leave it buried? If he spoke of it, how could he explain why it had happened without admitting the emotions he’d resolved to keep under control? If she knew how much she tempted him, she might feel compelled to go back home. Unless she brought it up, he’d let the incident lie for now. He picked up a slice of bread and buttered it. “You seem far away, Henri. What are you thinking?”

Still staring in the distance, she took a deep breath and hesitated. “Your sermon, I guess.” She gazed at him. “The one about the Blessed Mother. You shared how she inspires women around the world. Do you think fathers ever feel slighted?”

“What do you mean?”

“Saint Joseph must inspire fathers. But he doesn’t have an entire month dedicated to him. If we spend a month honoring the Holy Virgin and the mothers of the world, shouldn’t we honor fathers for their sacrifices and for the support they give their families?”

Martim blinked, taken aback by her insight. “You’re right, Henri. Mary’s month has just begun. There are plenty of days ahead to include the role of fathers in our celebrations.” He squeezed her hand. “This is the reason I need you as my housekeeper. You give me perspectives I’m not aware of.”

She stared at her hands. “You need me? Because right now I think

I'm a distraction."

She was a distraction. But she was also a catalyst that made him more compassionate, more understanding. She was the trial he'd been given. He couldn't tell her that. Instead he said, "You open my mind to new ideas, things that don't enter my thoughts. You are an inspiration."

She straightened. "An inspiration?"

"Yes. I'm doubly blessed. Not only will your work in my rectory give me time to spend with my far-flung flock; you open my eyes to new ideas. You already have a positive effect on the girls and the ladies in my congregation." He placed the leftover picnic items in the basket and closed the lid.

She sat, studying her hands. Finally, she met his eyes. "Then I'll stay."

The knots in his stomach eased. "You'll stay?"

Her frown disappeared, and a smile hinted on her lips. "As long as I'm not a distraction."

He stopped himself before he patted her ankle and stood. "Let's get that sprain soaking in the creek."

Her nose wrinkled. "And get rid of that awful smelling liniment."

"Smelly or not, we're putting it back on after the soak."

She laughed. "You're cruel, Doctor Ferrera."

"You'll thank me later."

He helped her to her feet and settled her on a massive sun-bleached log lying across the stream. They sat together, absorbing the tangy scent of spring as she dangled her feet in the icy water. Her closeness nearly overpowered him. He wanted to fold her in his arms. Hold her close. Instead, he sat on his hands, kicked through the water, and prayed.

Henri interrupted the long silence. "I think my toes have turned to prunes." She brought her foot onto the log and laughed. "See? Practically raisins."

He teased. "They're almost as purple as your ankle."

Back on the picnic blanket, he opened the jar of liniment and propped her foot on his satchel. Touching her was intoxicating and a torment. Had he made a mistake asking her to come, encouraging her to stay? No. She was exactly what his parishioners needed. She was an amiable companion, and he needed her. Her presence was a test of faith he would face with prayer and sacrifice.

As he massaged a generous dose of ointment into her ankle, she waved away the odor. "Not too much, Martim." Her cheeks flushed. "I shouldn't call you that. You're Father Ferrera."

"I like being called Martim when we're alone. I'm not above you. We're partners on a mission to serve my congregations."

Her brows bunched into a frown. "*Martim* slips off my tongue too easily. I'd better stick to Father Ferrera."

She was right. And he'd better stick to Miss Hoffmann.

Chapter Thirteen

Friday, May 5, 1927
Sage Prairie, Montana
Henrietta

Henri looked around the rectory kitchen with a sense of satisfaction. She'd accomplished a lot her first week in Sage Prairie. She'd scrubbed the soot from the curtains and starched and ironed them to perky perfection. Now they framed the windows she'd shined so even with rain streaking down the glass in the darkness, they appeared much brighter. The big, enameled sink no longer flaunted rust, and a cheerful gingham curtain hid the ugly pipes below it. Martim had said she'd performed a miracle creating a homey place to relax, enjoy a meal, and entertain his parishioners.

She sighed. Her plan to think of him as 'Father Ferrera' had been an utter failure. Thankfully, she'd never let 'Martim' slip when others were around. Martim hadn't been able to stick to Miss Hoffmann, either. She finally admitted to herself that her feelings for him had grown beyond friendship and constantly debated whether to go home. But how do you leave someone you care for so deeply? And going home meant dealing with her parents and their relentless push for her to settle down with a man who lacked the qualities she could love.

With a cup of chamomile tea warming her hands, she noticed rain no longer dripped into the pot on the kitchen floor. The drenching squalls that had rolled across the prairie all day had stopped. Thank heavens Martim was heading to Willow Grove tomorrow for supplies to patch up the leak. Every time it rained, the water in the pan inched higher than the previous storm. Tonight, it was nearly full. She stepped outside and poured the water in the laundry tub sitting by the back steps. Stars and a crescent moon gave her hope Saturday would be dry enough to hang the wash outdoors.

She yawned, wandered to her tiny bedroom, and got ready for bed. Back in the kitchen to finish her tea, a soft knock fell on the door. "Henri, it's me."

Surprised he returned, she slipped her bathrobe over her flannel nightgown. They'd said goodnight an hour earlier, and he'd gone to his study in the Church sacristy where he'd set up a bed for himself, leaving the rectory's only bedroom to her.

She tightened her robe and opened the door.

Martim stood sheepishly on the porch with a lantern in his hand. Mud covered his boots and spattered his breeches. His eyes widened. "Oh, you're ready for bed. I saw the kitchen light on, so I thought it'd be okay."

She laughed. "No problem. What do you need?"

His brow puckered. "I hate to ask, but my Chevy is stuck in the mud. I have to free it tonight so I can leave early tomorrow to get the roofing supplies and be back in time for confessions. I checked next door to see if Ben could help, but he's at his brother's farm. And Big Mike isn't home either. All I need is someone to gun the car's engine while I push. You think you can do it?"

"I've driven a tractor but never a car."

"It's pretty much the same thing."

He looked so desperate, her reluctance disappeared. "Okay, but you'll have to give me instructions. Let me change into my overalls, get my galoshes, and I'll be right out."

"Thank you, Henri. You're a lifesaver."

"Don't thank me yet. You never know what might happen."

Boots on, sweater buttoned, and her nightgown tucked into bib overalls, Henri settled behind the steering wheel and propped a pillow beneath her so she could see over the dashboard. The car's headlights beamed on the side of the Church.

Martim leaned in the passenger window. "Put it in first gear like you would a tractor and keep your foot on the clutch. When I say 'go' ease off the clutch and give it as much gas as you can."

"You make it sound easy," Henri said, seeing all the things that could go wrong.

"You'll be fine, Henri."

She put her foot on the clutch and wrestled it into gear. "Okay, let's do it."

Martim disappeared into the darkness. She heard him call from behind the Chevy. "I'm ready, Henri. Go."

She bore down on the gas and eased off the clutch. She heard the tires slurp as they spun. The auto inched forward and then slipped back. Martim called from behind. "More gas, Henri. Give it more gas."

Though she practically stood on the gas pedal, the tires spun wildly, and the Chevy didn't budge. She could hear mud flying everywhere. Suddenly, the sedan lurched forward. The side of the church rushed towards her in the headlights. Oh my God. She was going to hit the building. She let go of the gas, and the car jerked to a stop.

Martim came around to the door. Mud streaked from his boots to the top of his head. "You almost got it, Henri. One more time and I think she'll be free."

"The car might get free, but she's way too close to the church. Look, she could smash up in the process."

Martim held up his kerosene lamp and gaged the Chevy's distance to the building. "There's plenty of room, Henri."

"Doesn't seem like it to me. What if I gun it too hard?"

He exhaled. "Trust me. Turn the steering wheel hard to the left, and you'll have plenty of room to stop."

"No way," she said and climbed out of the Chevy. "You drive. I'll push."

He shone the lantern on himself. "You want to end up like this?"

"So? I'll need to clean up. Much better than wrecking your car and damaging the church."

"What makes you think you can push hard enough?"

"You said she's almost free. It won't take much if you gun it like you say. If you smash into the building, it's on you, not me."

"Henrietta Marie Hoffmann, you're hardheaded, but okay." He climbed into the driver's seat. "Let me know when you're ready."

With her galoshes deep in the muck, she positioned herself against the back of the car and called, "Ready." The tires whirled. Mud spewed up her body and splattered her face and into her hair. Moments later the auto lurched forward and came to a stop inches from the chapel siding, finally free.

"Told you I could do the pushing," she said, slopping through the mud to drier ground near the car.

Martim climbed from the sedan, held up the lantern, and laughed. "You should see yourself."

She giggled, wiping mud from her face. "Can't be any worse than you."

"Come on," he said, laughing harder and heading to the rectory. "I'd better clean up in the kitchen. The water jug in my study doesn't hold enough for all this muck."

"And I don't want those muddy boots or those britches on your study floor," she said, catching her breath between giggles. "Or I'll be hauling buckets over there to clean up the mess."

They stopped on the rectory porch and, between fits of laughter, slipped out of their boots and muddy coats. Just inside the kitchen door Henri said, "Stop on that mat, Mister. You're not messing up my kitchen. Get a pair of dirty britches from laundry tub right there by the door. Then off with those grungy socks and trousers and leave them piled on the porch."

His trousers fell in a heap on the floor. He stood there in his long johns and gazed at Henri, the humor now gone from his eyes. He spoke, his tone soft and intoxicating. "Your turn, Miss Hoffmann. What's fair is fair."

Her hands shaking, her eyes held captive by his, she reached for an overall strap. He stopped her, covering her hand with his, and unhooked the clasps. Her britches dropped, exposing her nightgown. She closed her eyes and drew in a deep breath. He pulled her to the sink, lifted her chin until their eyes met, and wiped the mud from her face bit by bit, kissing the clean places as he went.

"My turn," she whispered, aroused beyond caring. She rinsed the cloth and slowly washed his ears, his cheeks, and finally his alluring lips. When she finished, he lifted her in his arms, carried her to the bedroom, and undid her gown one button at a time. He removed his shirt and lay beside her. As the cool night air stirred across her skin and the warmth of his hands played over her body, she buried her face in the hollow of his neck, drunk on the musky smell of his skin.

"Henri, my sweet roguish Henri. You are my strength and my weakness." His lips brushed hers; a touch so soft she wondered if it had happened, except for the fire blazing in her body. Yesterday and tomorrow no longer mattered. They were lost in the now, taking steps from which there was no return.

Too soon, time became tangible. He brushed the hair from her face. "I'm so sorry, Henri. I didn't mean for this to happen."

"It wasn't my plan, either. But it was wonderful beyond what I ever imagined."

He sat on the edge of the bed with his head in his hands. He turned to her, his face full of guilt. "It was an expression of how I feel, and that's a dilemma for both of us. I am the man, a servant of God. No matter my feelings, I should have stopped."

She lay, still floating in exhilaration, and listened as he plodded to the kitchen. He returned dressed in a pair of slacks he'd dug from the laundry and kissed her forehead. "I care for you so deeply, Henri. But we can never let this happen again."

The kitchen door closed with a soft click. The warmth of his body left, and a chill set in. She was no longer a virgin. Now alone, guilt and fear replaced her euphoria.

***

Martim

He entered the church sacristy through the door from his studio bedroom. Remorse weighed on him as he knelt at the altar and prayed. "God, how do I atone for breaking my vow, for violating Henri's trust, for endangering her reputation? Forgive my arrogance in believing I could resist temptation, knowing full well I love her. I should have never asked her to come. The temptation was too much. Should I send her home? But what if my sin leads to pregnancy? If that happens, she'll need my support through a very compromising situation."

He had another dilemma. Though the Church allowed him to perform the sacraments with this mortal sin on his soul, he would be a hypocrite until he confessed. But to whom could he bare his soul without damaging Henri's reputation? In order for his sin to be forgiven, he would have to promise to avoid the near occasion of sin. If she agreed to stay until they found out if she was in a family way, they would have to remove themselves in every possible way from the temptation of each other.

Chapter Fourteen

Three weeks later - Thursday, May 26, 1927
Sage Prairie, Montana
Henrietta

As Henri patted the soil around the iris roots she'd brought from *Moeder*'s garden, losing her virginity was forefront on her mind. The experience had been beautiful, but unsettling. She knew it took only once to become pregnant. If a new life were growing inside her, the months ahead would be filled with hard decisions and terrible consequences. But if she were granted a reprieve, it would be best to leave Sage Prairie.

Every morning since she and Martim had expressed their love so intimately, she'd studied herself in her bedroom mirror. And each morning she found the person staring back no longer had the aura of an innocent young lady. Now she had the eyes of a knowing woman. Would others notice her transformation and understand the cause? A married woman might. *Moeder* would. And God knew what happened. She had a mortal sin on her soul. Whether or not she was pregnant, she had to confess. But to whom?

Getting up from her newly planted garden, she plodded to the pump for a bucket of water. She and Martim had agreed to limit the time they spent together. Now they only shared breakfast to talk about church affairs that involved her. She packed him a lunch and brought dinners to his room in the sacristy where he ate alone. Unless there were guests. Then they shared a meal in the rectory with the company. The arrangements were far from satisfactory. But keeping their distance was the right thing to do. Their souls were jeopardized when they spent time alone together. They'd discussed whether she should go home and had agreed she should stay for now.

A screech pierced the air. Henri glanced up to see ten-year-old Caleb racing towards the church. He frantically beat on the sacristy door. "Father, Father Ferrera. Come quick."

Henri made a beeline to the church. By the time she reached the sacristy, Martim was already on the stoop.

Gasping, Caleb barely got the words out. "It's Billy. His face..." His lip quivered. Tears streaked down his cheeks. "He's caught in a roll of barbed wire. And he's bleedin' like a stuck pig."

Martim put a hand on the boy's shoulder. "Calm down, Caleb. Tell me where."

"By the grain silo."

"Where the railroad is putting up fencing?"

Caleb nodded, his body shaking.

Martim grabbed his medical bag and a pair of pliers from his Chevy. He turned to Henri. "With no doctor within fifty miles, I have to take care of this. I'll bring the lad to the rectory. Get me the vinegar, a bottle of altar wine, and plenty of towels. Heat a pan of water and make a paste of sugar and honey." He grabbed Caleb's hand and hurried with him towards the silo.

Blood pounded in Henri's ears as she rushed back to the rectory. By the time Martim walked in with Billy moaning in his arms, the requested supplies lay on a table by the sofa, and water steamed on the stove.

Blood soaked the cloth covering Billy's face, and Martim's shirtsleeves were a gory mess. He turned to Caleb. "Get your folks, lad."

Caleb swallowed his sobs and wiped his eyes with the back of his hands. "They're gonna be so mad. I was s'posed to watch him."

"Don't blame yourself, Caleb. Now go," He laid Billy on the sofa and turned to Henri. "Bring the water, and I'll get started."

Martim handed the bottle of wine to the boy, his freckled skin ghostly pale between the smears of blood. "Take a good swig, Billy. I have to stitch your laceration. It'll hurt like the dickens, and I have no anesthetic. The wine will help you be brave."

Billy's lips quivered. "But I'm only eight, and Ma told me only priests can drink this stuff."

"Your ma is right, Billy. But in this case, it's not wine, it's medicine."

"Okay." Fighting back a sob, he took a few gulps. He wiped his mouth with his hand and handed the bottle to Martim. "Cross my heart, Father. I'm gonna be brave," he said, his voice shaky but determined.

"You're a gutsy guy. No doubt, you'll get through this with your honor intact." He glanced at Henri with a grim face. "Miss Hoffmann, hold Billy's head as still as possible."

With the patient's head in her lap, Henri shuddered as Martim removed the bloody cloth, exposing a jagged laceration. As she'd grown up, she'd seen a few serious cuts *Vader* had gotten in his carpentry shop. They'd never made her squeamish. But then she'd never been the nurse. Right now, she could use a glass of that wine. But she wasn't the one wounded, and she would soldier through without it.

Spasms rolled through the little guy as Martim cleaned the wound and doused it with vinegar. The stitching began. He screamed and tried to pull away. She gripped him tighter, whispering. "It's okay, Billy. Father will make you good as new."

Martim reached into his medical bag and came up with a piece of tightly braided leather. "Bite on this, lad. It'll give you grit."

Through tears and heartbreaking sobs, Billy clamped the leather in his teeth.

As Henri watched the needle pierce his skin again and again, nausea washed through her. Her throat lumped. The poor kid was in serious pain.

Finished with the third suture, Martim took a moment to stroke Billy's hair. "Only two more stitches, and we're done. Your folks will be so proud of how brave you are." He looked at Henri and mouthed, "You okay?"

She nodded. Though she felt light-headed and queasy, her eyes remained riveted on Martim's hands. They were skillful and tender, and his soothing words calmed Billy through his ordeal. How could she not love a man so capable and caring?

Finished, the black thread traveled neatly down a raw red line on Billy's cheek. She rose to get the paste of sugar and honey. Her legs were like jelly on the way to the kitchen. As she watched Martim apply the mixture to Billy's wound, she inhaled slowly and gradually let it go, trying to pretend she was under control. When Caleb arrived with his folks, Billy sat on the sofa licking a spoonful of the leftover sugar and honey.

A fog settled over her as Billy's parents thanked Father and praised his medical skills. She felt miles away as Martim gave them directions on how to clean the wound and apply the sugar and honey paste every day to ward off infection. Somewhere in the conversation, Martim told them he couldn't have done it without Miss Hoffmann's help. Had she managed to smile when the parents took her hand and thanked her?

The back door closed with a click. The whirlwind inside her hadn't eased since she'd seen Caleb running towards the Church. Weighed by the ordeal, she slumped to the sofa, and the calm she'd been faking broke. She put her face in her hands and let the tears fall.

Martim settled beside her and took her hand. "It's over, Henri."

Her voice faltered. "I know, Martim. But I'm not cut out to be a nurse." They sat in silence, their hands entwined. The fog lifted, replaced by a flurry in her heart. She studied his long, supple fingers. "You have a gift for healing, Martim."

Somehow, their thighs were touching when he spoke. "Gift or not, I'm grateful you were here. I couldn't have helped Billy as well without you."

When she met his eyes, she saw tenderness pooled with love. "You're amazing, Martim," she said and kissed him. It was supposed to be a quick kiss, a grateful kiss, but her lips lingered. His lips responded. Pressed in his arms, she welcomed his hands exploring her body. The stress and trauma of the day disappeared. Guilt and resolve melted away.

Afterwards, they lay in silence on the sofa, awash in their own thoughts. She curled in his arms with her back to him, his breath fluttering her hair.

The shadows of the trees dancing on the parlor wall disappeared. Clouds darkened the room. He took her hand and kissed it saying, "The Church teaches what we've done is wrong. But there's a part of my heart that tells me it's right."

"My heart feels the same, Martim. So why do I feel guilty? Now I have two mortal sins on my soul. The Church says I have to confess, and I can't receive the sacraments until I do. But to whom do I confess?"

"You could to me."

She bolted up. "What do you mean? You're as guilty as I am."

"True, but the Church teaches that if a priest has a mortal sin on his soul, he can still administer the Sacraments."

She scowled. "That doesn't seem right."

"The Church says it is. No matter my sins, when I administer the sacraments, Christ still works through me."

She stared at the blood-soaked cloths scattered on the floor. "But is that true when a sinful person confesses to her accomplice?"

"I'm wrestling with that dilemma, too. We are taught when we confess, we must promise to stay away from the near occasion of sin." He grimaced. "That's me."

She gave a rueful laugh. "As I am to you."

"Have you changed your mind about going home?"

"I can't. Depending on what happens, living with my parents would make it worse. I need to stay in Sage Prairie, at least for now."

He nodded with a relieved smile. "Then we pray, Henri. We ask God to help us find the right path and the courage to follow it."

She fought tears as she watched him go. Her weeks of begging God for courage and grace had done nothing to keep her from sinning again. Once more, her heart had overwhelmed her conscience. She had succumbed to passion, despite her determination to remain chaste. All her prayers had been for naught. What if God wasn't listening? What if He had abandoned her? Or what if God had answered her prayers, and she had turned away?

She plodded to the kitchen. A breeze whipped through the open window. A dusky gloom filled the air. She closed the window and sat at the table with pen and ink. Words rose from heart and unfolded on paper.

Dear Jesus, relentless Lover of my soul,
Sometimes I feel it is all quite useless to make another effort.
I have tried and tried again, and what does it all amount to?
I know it is all too wrong to forget Your changeless love,
The very worst sin I can commit is to lose my confidence in You.
Yet at times I all but lose it. Dear Jesus, never let that be.
Just grant that however discouraged I may become,
However sinful I may have been,
However far I may have strayed from You,
That when Your grace comes knocking at my heart,
I may never cry, "Too late."

As she read her words over and over, an undeniable truth exploded into her thoughts. Her ever-reliable monthly courses were ten days late.

Chapter Fifteen

Saturday, July 2, 1927
Sage Prairie, Montana
Henrietta

Though it was early summer, the grass stretching for miles around Sage Prairie was already turning brown. Henri missed the trees and all the shades of green in Wisconsin. And she missed *Moeder* and Greta even more. She hauled two buckets of rinse water from the laundry tub to the iris and hollyhocks she'd planted under the rectory windows. Neither would bloom this season. Next year, whoever lived in the rectory would appreciate them. Henri's heart stumbled. It wouldn't be her.

It was almost noon, and the train was due anytime now. If the wind's direction changed, and she didn't get the wash off the line before it clacked by, her laundry would be covered in soot. She hurried to the clothesline. Unclipping the bed sheets, she inhaled their fresh scent and dropped them into the basket. The costume needed for the heroine in tonight's community play "A Cheerful Liar" wasn't quite dry, but the dampness would make it easier to iron. She unclipped it and laid it on top of the sheets. All the roles Martim played in Sage Prairie amazed her, making her love him all the more. He was a priest, a doctor, a farm advisor, and a choir director. Now he was a drama coach.

She pressed her arms against the soreness in her breasts, one more reminder of the child growing inside her and of the unsettling future ahead. A bit of loneliness crept in as she plodded to Martim's bedroom with the clean linens. As hard as it had been, they had remained chaste since the day Martim had stitched up Billy. Though he knew of the possibility, Martim wasn't yet aware she was pregnant. She'd tell him tomorrow when the play was over, and the news wouldn't distract him from his work.

The irony of her dilemma made her laugh. Knowing she could get pregnant hadn't kept her from sinning, but her pregnancy had. And now she questioned herself over and over. Should she go home, stay here, move to another town? It all led to shame, and to a baby that society would label illegitimate. She shuddered; a baby she might not be able to keep.

As she neared the door to Martim's quarters in the back of the church with clean sheets for his bed, Billy raced up with a tin pail. "Miss Hoffmann, my ma said to bring you some peas. She promised Father Ferrera the first batch from her garden cuz he mended me so good." He touched a red scar now fading on his cheek and grinned. "See, it's turning out real good."

"So it is." Henri smiled, amazed again at Martim's ability to stand in as Sage Prairie's doctor. "I hope you're being more careful, now."

"Yes, ma'am. I am," he said, handing her the peas.

She picked out a pod, snapped it open, and popped the green gems into her mouth. "Tell your mother thank you. Father is fond of fresh garden peas. I'll serve them tomorrow with a Portuguese dish I'm making." She watched Billy pick up a stick and run off, pretending to shoot some wild beast. She put her hand to her belly. Soon she'd have her own child to love and care for. Anxiety squeezed in her chest. She prayed. Holy Mother, What I've done is wrong, but I beg of you, help me find a way to keep my baby, a baby I've always wanted.

Inside Martim's study-turned-bedroom, Henri set the peas on his desk and the laundry basket on the floor. As she straightened, her head spun, and nausea rolled through her. Sitting on the bed, she held her hand to her stomach and grimaced. She'd make herself peppermint tea when she got back to the rectory.

She forced herself up and made the bed while listening to the cast practice their lines in the church. Martim had turned it into a theater for the evening. She wanted to peek in the sanctuary but decided to stay out of sight.

As she smoothed the wrinkles from the quilt, the door to the sanctuary opened. "There you are," Martim said, surveying the room. He grinned at the bouquet of wildflowers arranged in a mason jar on his desk. "Where did these come from?"

"They were growing against the fence by the clothesline. I thought they were lovely."

"You spoil me, Henri." The pail of peas caught his eye. "And what Good Samaritan brought these?" he asked, helping himself to a few pods.

"They're a thank you from Billy's mother. I'll serve them with tomorrow's *Bacalhau a bras*."

He grabbed a few more peas. "We're lucky Maguire's store could get the salted cod. It's been a long time since I've had a taste of Portugal."

He wrapped her in his arms.

For a moment Henri melted into him, then pulled away.

He put up his hands. "Avoiding one another is difficult, but you're right, Henri. I shouldn't have done that." He studied her for a moment. "You look tired. Lie down and rest," he said, gesturing at the newly made bed.

Henri snapped. "Absolutely not."

"Don't worry, I won't join you. The set still needs work."

"It doesn't matter. If I need rest, I'll do it on my own bed."

He scoffed. "I know you, Henri. You won't relax when you're back in the rectory. If you're here, I can keep an eye on you. Besides, it's safe right now. Everyone has gone home for a few hours to relax before tonight's performance."

"It's never safe, Martim. There are always unexpected visitors." Her thoughts diverted to the unexpected life growing inside her. She forced a smile. "Is everything ready for this evening?"

"Mostly." His voice had a hint of exasperation. "Except for the squabble between my leading lady and her understudy. They're like two cats over the same mouse."

"I thought you tamed them with the sermon you gave last Sunday on petty jealousies and how they lead to failure."

"Apparently my efforts were a temporary fix. My leading lady, Mrs. Latimer, is losing her voice. Miss Mercer thinks they should switch roles since her part has much less dialogue and because as the understudy, she knows the leading role so well. Of course, Mrs. Latimer insists with a little honey and lemon in some tea she will be fine by evening."

"Is Miss Mercer right?"

"Perhaps, but I'll wait until curtain time to decide. Sometimes I think it would have been better to cast you as Charlotte."

"Pish posh, Martim. I'd have loved a part but being in your play would have put us under scrutiny. And I'm not sure we could have kept our interactions platonic." Besides, she thought, a role in the play would bring her in constant contact with gossipy women always on the lookout for signs of pregnancy.

"You're right, Henri. But if you had the leading role, I wouldn't be dealing with jealousy between the prima donna and her understudy."

Henri lifted the laundered costume from the basket and shook it out. "Well, Charlotte's dress is clean for whoever plays the part. It took extra scrubbing, but I got the stains out. Now it needs an iron." She picked up the basket and moved to the door.

He held her back with a questioning look. “You don’t look well, Henri. Promise you’ll rest.”

The concern on his face touched her. She bit her tongue to keep from blurting the truth. Tonight, he needed to focus on the play. Tomorrow was soon enough. She forced a smile and said, “I promise. After I iron the dress.”

He frowned. “I’m worried about you.”

Did he guess? Perhaps. But the discussion would have to wait. “I’ll be back later with your dinner. If you need to, you can eat while you work. I have fresh bread, cold ham, and pickled beans. I’ll whip some cream to serve with the cherry pie.”

“Sounds wonderful. Bring enough for both of us. We can eat together for once.”

She shook her head. “I’m not hungry. But I’ll have a cup of tea and keep you company while you eat.”

He tilted his head with a questioning gaze. “Not hungry?”

“It’s nothing. Anyway, I better get the wrinkles out of this dress.” She left, trying to hide her queasiness. She’d make that peppermint tea while she waited for the iron to heat.

***

Henri arrived at the little white church well before the play would begin. She tucked a purple aster into the band of her hat as she climbed the steps to the double doors. Before entering, she took a moment to adjust the sash at the hips of her rose-colored dress. Hopefully, it hid the weight she’d gained. Pulling off her white gloves and tucking them into her handbag, she made her way to a pew near the front. As she squirmed to get comfortable on the hard wooden bench, she surveyed the church’s transformation into a little theater.

Martim and his stage crew had turned the space below the sanctuary into a stage. A backdrop painted with the walls of a parlor hid the altar from the audience. They’d set the scene with an old-fashioned gas lamp glowing beside a cozy settee and a roll-top desk with a wooden chair nearby.

As she watched the audience fill the pews, she chewed a piece of ginger root. The sweet spicy tang settled her stomach. Etta’s family appeared in the doorway and headed down the aisle. They took the pew behind her, except for Etta. She slipped beside Henri. As she squeezed Henri's hand, she whispered, "Everyone's so excited. We haven't had a play in Sage Prairie for years."

Henri leaned in to Etta. "Father loves the performing arts."

Etta surveyed the audience. "A lot of folks here are from out of town, and they appreciate Father too."

A grizzled farmer trudged his way to their pew and eased onto the spot beside Henri and nodded at the two ladies. With his hat on his knee, he leaned in and mumbled. "Hope you don't mind me settin here, ma'am. Can't hear worth a gosh darn these days."

Henri nodded with a weak smile and tried not to breathe. The reek of sweat and farm animals was almost unbearable.

Etta brought her hankie to her nose and moved close to Henri. "His wife passed away nine months ago. I don't think he's had a bath since." Henri put her hand to her mouth and gagged. Etta's eyes met Henri's. "You look positively gray, Henri. Are you alright?"

"I'll be fine." Henri swallowed the bile rising from her stomach and found her own hankie.

"You want to sit somewhere else?"

"I think it'd be rude to move," she said, glad the old farmer seemed hard of hearing.

As Etta sighed, the lights in the church winked out and the stage lights blinked on. Martim strolled onto the set, handsome as ever in his black shirt and slacks, and tugged on his clerical collar. "Ladies and Gentlemen, welcome to Sage Prairie's Drama Club presentation, A Cheerful Liar. I'm pleased so many have come to enjoy the hard work of our cast and crew."

Henri settled in, determined to let the two-hour play take her mind off her troubles.

***

Back at the rectory, her distraction over, her dilemma surged back into her thoughts and wreaked havoc on her stomach. She winced as she lit a fire under the teakettle. "A cheerful liar" indeed. Such irony. She'd be forced to tell many lies in the months ahead, and they wouldn't be cheerful. She desperately wanted to keep her baby, and falsehoods would be the only way to protect her child from the awful label of illegitimacy.

As she waited for the water to a boil, she plodded to the bedroom and pulled the card from her missal with the prayer she'd written five weeks ago.

Through two cups of tea, she read her prayer over and over, asking God for the grace to face Martim with the truth of her pregnancy. Not only did he deserve to be told, but she also needed his help in the months ahead. He said he'd stop by the rectory for the last piece of cherry pie after he finished dismantling the set and got the church ready for tomorrow's services. She had to tell him. He knew of the possibility, but what would he do now that her pregnancy was a fact? She was sure he loved her. But a Catholic priest fathering a child would be an enormous scandal. Would the Church force him out of the priesthood? Or would he resign on his own? Would she want him to? Would leaving his ministry make things better or worse for their child?

She had come nowhere near figuring it out when she heard his footsteps on the back porch. With a soft rap, the door opened. He walked in and stopped mid-step with a worried look. "Henri? You say you're alright, but you don't look well."

She waved away his concern. "I'm just tired after a long day."

"Are you sure?"

She nodded. Maybe she should tell him now. The words froze in her throat. She patted the chair. "Sit. I'll get you that pie."

His face remained doubtful, but he took a seat. "What did you think of our production?"

Henri faked a cheerful smile. "It was completely ducky, and the audience loved it. I especially enjoyed the way Mrs. Latimer drank her lemon and honey tea while she used her hoarse voice to fit her character." Henri set the pie and a bowl of whipped cream in front of Martim. "All that laughter must have given the audience a break from their problems."

"Then it was a success," Martim said, piling his pie with whipped cream. As he chatted about the behind-the-scenes snafus, Henri watched him eat. She loved the glow of satisfaction on his face. But how long would it last?

She got up, put the leftover whipped cream in the icebox, and pulled out the salted cod she'd been soaking all day so it would be ready to cook for tomorrow's dinner. She'd learned the trick to making good *Bacalhau a bras* was to remove some of the salt from the cod. With her back to Martim, she drained the water from the fish and pumped fresh water over it, all the while swallowing gag after gag brought on by the fishy smell.

Behind her Martim asked, "Will there be enough *Bacalhau a bras* to invite Father Jansen for dinner? He seemed very interested in the dish when I told him about it."

A new gag erupted in Henri's throat. This one was not going back down. She fled the kitchen, stumbled outside, around to the side of the rectory. Everything she'd eaten all day covered the ground. Trembling, she sucked in a breath, let it go, and heaved again.

And then Martim was beside her with a damp cloth. As he wiped the mess from her face, she looked up at him. As awful as she must appear, there was love in his eyes.

"There's something you've been keeping from me, Henri." His voice said he knew.

She stared at the contents of her stomach, now spattered on her dress. As she wiped it away, she met his eyes again. Words worked their way past the knot in her throat. "I'm going to… No, we're going to have a baby." Hot tears spilled from her eyes. "And I refuse to think of our child as punishment for our sins."

He wiped the tears from her cheeks and folded her in his arms. As she sobbed against his chest, he muttered, "I'm so sorry I put you in this situation, *meu amor.* Maybe God is forcing me to make a decision."

She looked up at him. "A decision?"

He kissed her forehead. "We'll talk about it later. For now, you need to rest."

Chapter Sixteen

Monday, July 11, 1927
Sage Prairie
Martim

Martim sat on a rise on the outskirts of the little town he'd grown to love. The people he served depended on him for his spiritual guidance, for his medical expertise, and for so much more. But others could fill those roles. Giving up the priesthood was a long and arduous process and involved the Pope. But as problematic as it was, it could be done. Maybe he should. Maybe he must. He loved Henri. Right now, she needed him more profoundly than any of his churches.

It was wrong to think he could have both her and his congregations. He'd broken his vow of celibacy. Confession would remove that mortal sin from his soul. Penitent, he could continue his ministry. He'd taken another vow, one to dedicate his life to serving God as a priest. Should he break that vow as well? If he left the priesthood, it would be the most difficult thing he'd ever done.

He turned to the evening sky, awash in brilliant purples, reds, and yellows, and prayed for courage, strength, and wisdom. He jumped at footsteps in the crisp grass behind him.

Henri frowned down on him. "You've been avoiding me, Martim."

He patted the ground beside him. "Not avoiding you, *meu amor.* Just contemplating what to do about our baby."

She slumped beside him. "I'm terrified, Martim."

"I'm afraid, too, but I know it's much harder for you. I promise, I won't abandon you or our little one." He picked up a rock, weighed it in his hand, and heaved it across the prairie. He pulled his knees to his chest. "We love one another, Henri, and despite what the Church teaches, a part of me believes we're married in the eyes of God."

Henri ran her hand down her cheek, her fist resting under her chin. She glanced at him. "You really believe that?"

"I do, Henri. And my conviction grows stronger the more I'm with you." He paused. "I also believe that sometime in the future, the Church will change their rule on celibacy and allow priests to marry."

She half laughed. "That's not an option right now, and in the meantime, there aren't many alternatives."

"I imagine you've ruled out going home."

"Of course." Exasperation tinged her voice. "The last thing I need are my parents telling me that Ike or Leo or another suitor is available for the holy sacrament of matrimony. Ike, for one, would marry me in a heartbeat, pregnant by another man or not."

He tilted his head and turned to her with a quick laugh. "There it is again, Henri. That indomitable spirit I admire so much." He felt relieved she had no desire for another man. And there were plenty of suitors, not just Ike, who would find her appealing despite her condition. He'd overheard a few young men in his parishes discussing what a fine catch she'd be. If she found someone acceptable, any gossip caused by a quick marriage would soon fade. But there would be a big scandal if he left the priesthood and married her, and it could linger for a lifetime.

She plucked a blade of grass and rolled it between her fingers. "I don't need a moony-eyed man or a husband who feels superior to women. I need a safe place to have our baby, and where I'm allowed to keep it."

Of course, she'd say that. It was foolish to think otherwise. There was another option that made him shudder. He was sure of her answer, but he had to ask. "Would you give our baby up for adoption or for fostering after it's born?"

She folded her hands around her belly. "This child is a part of us, Martim, created by our love. No matter how hard it will be, I will never give it up."

"I'm glad you feel that way," he said, his heart returning to normal.

"So how do I keep our baby, Martim? Where do I have it? How do I support it? And how do I protect it from gossip?"

Her questions and the worry in her voice tore at his conscience. "The baby is mine, Henri. I'll support you and the baby. And I'll do whatever I can to help you figure out the rest."

"I knew you would, but it's good to hear you say it out loud. One thing is clear, I can't stay here for long."

He wanted to pull her close, fold her in his arms, but they were too near town. Someone might be watching. As the sun disappeared, he said, "There's a home in Helena that takes in unwed mothers. I understand their mission is to help women in your situation create a future for themselves, one that includes their babies."

"Really?" she asked, astonished. "The only homes for unwed mothers I've ever heard of, shame the poor women and take their babies away."

"The Crittenton Home is different. If you agree, I'll go to Helena and check into it. If it's as wonderful as they say, I'll arrange for you to stay there." Guilt ripped his heart. How could he offer her a home for unwed mothers as a solution? It was the easy way out for him, but not for her.

Henri relaxed beside him, leaning back and propping herself up on her elbows. They sat in silence until the night enveloped them. As a sliver of moon replaced the sun, Martim prayed for the courage to take the honorable course.

Henri straightened. "We'd better go, Martim. Before it gets too dark to see the gopher holes. The last thing I need is another sprained ankle."

He laughed. As she moved to get up, he tugged her back down, his heart beating wildly. He couldn't let her go until he shared the one option he knew was right. "You know there's an alternative to the Crittenton home."

She turned to him, her voice perplexed and suspicious. "And that is?"

"What if a man you got along with very well, wanted to marry you? Would you consider his proposal?"

She scoffed. "Who would that be?"

"Me, Henri."

She gasped. "And leave the priesthood? I can't ask you to do that."

"But I'd give it up, Henri. That's how much I love you."

"And I love you too deeply to agree to such a thing. Too many people depend on you as their priest, their doctor, and for all the roles you play in the community."

"Regardless, Henri. You and our baby are my responsibility."

She gave an exasperated sigh. "I admit there have been many times I dreamed of being your wife. But I never prayed for it. It doesn't feel right to take you away from the Church. You help so many people with your kindness, your wisdom, your talent for healing. Not just bodies, but souls as well. I could never ask you to leave a role you love and are so incredibly capable of doing."

"Perhaps my role isn't to be Father Ferrera. Maybe it's to live as a father to my child."

"You are the child's father."

"You know what I mean, Henri." He stood and helped her up. "Just think about it."

"I will. But you leaving the priesthood? I see a million complications." She sighed, studying her hands. "For now, Martim, see if the Crittenton Home is the best place for me and our baby."

***

Thursday, July 14, 1927
Martim

Martim drove south as the morning sun blazed through the car window, the heat saturating his black shirt. His mind reeled with the dilemma he'd put himself and Henri in. Now there was an innocent child caught up in his sin. As much as he wanted to believe Heaven blessed his union with Henri, here on Earth the Church didn't approve. He'd taken a sacred vow of celibacy. But hadn't he'd also given Henri an implicit vow the moment they'd fulfilled their love? If he kept one vow, it meant breaking the other. Both his heart and his conscience told him Henri and his child came first. Before he'd left this morning, he'd asked her again to marry him. But she continued to insist marriage wasn't the right solution.

Now he traveled to Helena to do what Henri wanted; arrange a place out of the public's eye where she could stay during the last months of pregnancy and for the birth of their baby. So far, she'd hidden her condition. But it wouldn't be long before the truth became obvious.

Henri's refusal to accept his proposal did nothing to lessen his guilt. And she was right. There would be serious complications if he left the priesthood. First, his superiors would probe his motives. Eventually, his petition would be sent to the Pope. Only the Holy Father could authorize the removal of his priestly vows.

If the Pope released him, he'd have to support Henrietta and the baby. Catholic institutions would never allow him to teach in their schools. Perhaps he could teach elsewhere. And he had other talents to rely on. The most troublesome part of leaving the priesthood would be informing the congregations he'd grown to care for and with whom Henri also had a relationship. Some would understand. Many would be appalled and want nothing to do with him or Henri. Even worse, Henri would face the censure of her family, perhaps even ostracism. But wouldn't his love and

Henri's overcome those obstacles?

He rolled down the window and welcomed the breeze ruffling his hair. Henri knew the reason for his trip. But he'd told everyone else he had business with the bishop in Great Falls. It was true. Yesterday he'd stopped to visit His Excellency at St. Ann's Cathedral, discussed plans for the new parsonage in Sage Prairie, and spent the night at the bishop's residence. The modern conveniences of the cathedral rectory gave him ideas for his own new rectory already in the planning stage. A rectory he'd probably never share with Henri. One, he might never live in himself if he gave up the priesthood. In the meantime, he'd oversee the rectory's construction.

Hours later, he topped the Big Belt Mountains and pulled to the side of the road for lunch. From here he could see the spires of the newly built St. Helena's Cathedral looming near the outskirts of Montana's Capitol. Somewhere down there was an old mansion converted into a home for unwed mothers. The Crittenton Home, with its room for fifty women and thirty children, would be a haven for Henri until late January when their baby was due. The Home would also allow her to stay as long as necessary after the baby was born.

Grabbing the canister from the back of the car, he replensished his gas tank. He scrubbed his hands in a nearby creek. As he planned the specifics of the tale he'd tell the home's director, he nibbled the ham sandwich the bishop's housekeeper had made for him.

He found the Home easily, and what a blessing. It was near St. Helena's Cathedral and to St. John's Hospital. He parked and walked across the vast grounds to the gabled brick mansion. His anxiety built as he climbed the stairs to the door. This was a home for unwed mothers. They must have been told every hard-luck story imaginable. What could he tell the director to convince her Henri wasn't any ordinary wayward woman?

He rang the bell and waited. The bitter taste of bile coated his tongue. A few minutes later, he was escorted to the director's office, a cozy room with oriental rugs, a fireplace, and homey furnishings. A small sprightly middle-aged woman with kind eyes and a generous smile sat at an ornate desk and stood when he entered. Martim offered his hand. "Thank you for seeing me on such short notice, Mrs. Cullum."

She shook his hand and gestured at a comfortable couch. "Please be seated, Father." She settled back into her chair and folded her hands on her desktop. "I understand you know a young woman who would benefit from a stay at our home."

"Yes. Miss Henrietta Hoffmann is the cousin of a friend of mine. She's gotten herself in a family way." He hoped his voice didn't show the emotion he felt.

Mrs. Cullum nodded. "Do you know the baby's father?"

He looked out the window. Guilt surfaced again. People called him 'Father' all the time, but could he ever be a true father to his own child? He hid his feelings behind his minister's mask. "She's kept his name secret but assures me they deeply love one another. Unfortunately, marriage is out of the question."

The director nodded with a sad smile. "Unfortunate indeed, and so often true in these cases. Does her family know of or suspect the pregnancy?"

"They live in Wisconsin and are unaware of her condition. Naturally, she worries they will condemn her. She plans to confide in her closest sister. With Henrietta's permission, I shared the news with her cousin who is a fellow priest."

A frown stretched across Mrs. Cullum's forehead. "Families can be very harsh, but they can also be supportive. What takes her away from her family?"

"She's employed as a housekeeper in Sage Prairie."

"Is her employer aware of the situation?"

Martim swallowed and managed a shrug. "She's been able to hide her condition quite well to this point."

"I'm glad she had you to confide in, Father," Mrs. Cullum said, pulling a leather-bound notebook from a desk drawer and opening it to the middle. She reached for a pen and a bottle of ink. "We need some information if Henrietta stays with us."

"Understandable." Whatever he told her had to be believable. God forgive him if he had to lie. He crossed his legs and tried to appear relaxed.

For a while, Mrs. Cullum asked about Henri's general health and took notes on the progress of her pregnancy. She fanned the page with a blotter until the ink dried, filled her pen from the bottle, and continued. "Has Henrietta spoken with you about whether she wants to keep the baby? It's something we always encourage. If so, she can stay here with her baby until she can arrange a secure future."

"I understand that's your policy, and I've shared it with Miss Hoffmann. She desperately wants to raise the child herself."

A broad smile spread across Mrs. Cullum's face. "Excellent. Scandal almost always happens to a woman in her situation. That she's willing to face disgrace and humiliation to keep her child is admirable."

"Your support and understanding will be a tremendous gift to her and the child." And to me, he added silently. He'd be heartbroken if their little boy or girl disappeared from his and Henri's lives forever.

Mrs. Cullum fingered a locket gracing her chest as she said, "Someone very dear to me was in the same predicament. An old spinster hid her through her pregnancy, but neither the young lady nor the old woman had the means to keep the baby. The mother had to give up the wee one to an orphanage. It broke her heart, and she never saw her child again."

"What a dreadful burden to carry through life."

The director nodded. A faint smiled played on her lips. "It's why I'm here helping these women keep their babies." She re-inked her pen. "Though we refuse no one, Father, we always ask if anyone can pay the twenty-five dollars for her stay and the delivery of the baby."

"I'll cover the expenses," he blurted.

Mrs. Cullum straightened and studied Martim. He wasn't sure how to read her curious expression. Connecting unwed mothers to the Home was not unusual for a minister. But he wondered if she sensed the actual relationship he had with Henri. Sweat beaded on his brow. He forced himself not to look away.

Mrs. Cullum's brow arched, and then she smiled. "She's blessed to have your support, Father. You must feel responsible for her with all you are doing."

Though nothing he'd told the director had been a lie, part of him ached to reveal the whole truth. But Henri had insisted he not implicate himself. She'd said doing so could make the problem worse. Even if she were right, he'd gladly face the consequences if she agreed he leave the priesthood. It was the honorable thing to do. He nodded. "My purpose in life is to support those in need. And this young lady is definitely in need."

"I understand. One last question, Father. Young women usually begin their time with us when they are five or six months along. Knowing that, when should we expect Henrietta?"

He did some mental calculations and said, "Sometime in October would be best."

Mrs. Cullum put the stopper on the inkbottle and closed her notebook. "Tell Henrietta she'll be assigned to help in the laundry during her stay, and in that way contribute to the upkeep of the home."

"Work in the laundry would suit Miss Hoffmann well," Martim said, remembering how she'd charmed him by defying the rules and put fresh linens on his bed early in her job at St. Albert's.

"That's wonderful. Mrs. Parker, our laundress, has a great heart and a wonderful relationship with the women under her charge." She handed Martim a card. "My phone number. When you know the exact date of her arrival, please give me a ring or send a telegram. We'll have a place ready for her. She'll share a dormitory room with other mothers to be."

As Martim got up to leave, Mrs. Cullum added, "We will keep Henrietta, her child, and the anonymous father in our prayers."

Not trusting to keep emotion from his voice, Martim bowed with a smile and left. As he walked to his car, he hoped he wouldn't always be anonymous.

Chapter Seventeen

Friday, July 29, 1927
Sage Prairie, Montana
Henri

Heat hung heavy in the rectory's little parlor. The day had been a scorcher, and Henri had kept a fire going in the wood stove the whole day, baking bread, apple tarts, and the evening meal. It all added to the swelter. She didn't dare open the windows. There were no screens to keep the flies from invading Father's dinner party with Mr. and Mrs. Kroft; a thank you for everything they'd done for the Church.

Mrs. Kroft put her fork down and studied Martim. "Something bothering you, Father? You're not your usual self."

Henri froze. Maybe they shouldn't have invited the Krofts for dinner. They knew Martim so well. Father mopped the sweat from his brow and put on a smile. "I'm okay, Betty. It just the heat."

She put her hand on his. "You sure?"

"Absolutely."

"Betty, leave the man alone," Fred scolded. "Priests have a lot on their minds. Stuff we ain't privy to." He sat back and rested his hands on his belly. "Henrietta, that's the best trout I've had in a long time. Crisp on the outside. Flaky on the inside. And your fried potatoes and onions were top notch." He patted Martim's shoulder. "So much first-rate grub is putting weight on you, Father. You're gonna have some dang good insulation when we go elk hunting this winter."

"Not too much, I hope," Martim said, patting his own stomach.

Henri put down her napkin. "Father keeps himself extremely busy. He burns off the calories as fast as he puts them on. I doubt he'll ever be a portly man."

Mrs. Kroft squeezed Henri's hand. "Before you arrived, the good Father was practically skin and bones. Now look at him. Filled out so nicely." She gave Henri an affectionate smile. "And you too, dear. You seem to thrive on your own cooking. And a little meat on your bones is quite becoming."

Fire rose in Henri's cheeks. This was the fourth reference to her weight gain in the last three days. Her nausea had disappeared, replaced by an enormous appetite, swelling breasts, and extra padding on her hips. The comments were meant as compliments, but soon everyone would put two and two together.

The decision to accept or refuse Martim's marriage proposal pressed on her. Too many people depended on him for so much, and it weighed on her conscience almost as much as the mortal sin on her soul. There had to be another way. Perhaps she could conjure up an absent husband. But then everyone would wonder why she'd never talked about him. Why he was never around. And why she referred to herself as a 'Miss'. She hadn't figured out a way to make such a story plausible. At least she had a place to stay where her baby could be born away from prying eyes. She stood, smiled through gritted teeth, and gathered the empty plates. "Everybody ready for dessert?"

"Ah, yes," Martim grinned. He flashed Henri an understanding look and turned to his guests. "The smell of her apple tarts has teased me ever since she pulled them from the oven."

Fred patted his belly again. "Can hardly wait."

A few minutes later Henri sent a plate of the flakey popovers around the table but didn't take one herself. "None for you, dear?" Betty Kroft asked.

Henri shook her head. "No, I'd better not. I sampled one before you came," which wasn't true. As the conversation continued around her, Henri thought of Etta. She was glad the invitation to dinner had just included Fred and Betty instead of their entire clan. Etta had been one of those to comment on her weight gain. The two of them were becoming close friends. If Etta figured out she was carrying a baby out of wedlock, their growing friendship could easily end.

A fly hovered over the last of the apple tarts. Henri broke out of her reverie and swatted it away.

Mr. Kroft was saying, "Tell me, Father, you ever castrate piglets?"

Martim shook his head. "Back in Portugal, *meu papai* taught me to dress the game after our hunts, but our farmhands always took care of neutering the livestock. Still, I often watched the process and admired the surgical precision it required."

Fred chuckled. "Well, tomorrow's your lucky day. Got me a passel of piglets and could use a hand with the job. With your skill dressing game, it won't take long to get the hang of it. And then when them piglets are full grown; I'll supply you with ham and sausage for the winter."

"An excellent proposal," Martim said with a worried glance at Henri. "But Miss Hoffmann is making preserves tomorrow. I promised to tend the fire and keep it at the right temperature while she focused on keeping the preserves from burning."

Betty's hand flew to her chest. "Oh my! Of course she shouldn't make jam by herself. I'll tell you what, Father. You help Fred, and I'll send Etta to help Henrietta."

"Heavens, no," almost escaped from Henri's lips. Proximity with Etta for hours? What if her friend figured out she was pregnant? Don't be ridiculous, she told herself. You enjoy her company. Just wear your full-length apron. Her worry receded. "I'd love to have her help, Betty."

Martim ran his hand through his hair. "An excellent solution, Elizabeth. The outdated equipment in our old parsonage makes everything difficult for Miss Hoffmann. But in a year or so, we'll have a new rectory with all the modern conveniences."

It will be wonderful, Henri thought. But too late for me.

***

Saturday afternoon Henri and Etta stood side-by-side admiring their strawberry rhubarb preserves. The jars were sealed with wax and rested on the pantry shelves beside the peas and green beans Henri had canned earlier in the week. Gingham fabric tied to the tops of the preserves gave them a cheerful appearance.

Etta wiped her hands on her apron. "With all the canning you're doing, Henri, you and Father will be set for winter."

"That's my goal," Henri said. She wouldn't share the bounty, but she wanted to stock the pantry for the months ahead when Martim wouldn't have a housekeeper. She took off her apron, now splattered with preserves, and grabbed a loaf of bread from the breadbox. "Let's sample the fruits of our labor," she smirked.

Etta laughed. "Ha, ha, very punny."

The two ladies rested at the table, drinking tea and savoring thick slices of bread lavished with butter and newly made jam. "So delicious," Etta said, swallowing a bite. Suddenly she giggled.

Henri looked around. "What, Etta?"

"Your blouse, Henri. Look."

"Oh my," Henri gasped. Two buttons in the middle of her chest were undone, exposing her underwear. She quickly fastened them, but they popped out again. Her face burning, she managed a laugh. "I'm almost twenty-one. Guess a bigger bosom comes from being a full-fledged woman."

Etta glanced at her own barely perceptible breasts and sighed. "Flat chested is the fashion these days, but I hope I end up with more than what I have now."

"You're only seventeen. You have plenty of time."

A rap sounded on the back door, saving Henri from further conversation. She grabbed her bibbed apron to hide the telltale gap in her blouse. As she pulled it over her head, the threads on a button gave way. It fell to the floor and rolled under the table. A second knock clacked more insistently than the first. She tied her apron and opened the door to bright sunshine. A tall man about her age stood on the steps. Sweat trickled from his mop of short wavy brown hair, grease streaked his shirtsleeves rolled to his elbows, and dust covered his shoes and khaki brown britches.

His face lit up when he looked at Henri. He removed his cap and said, "Well, hello ma'am. Harry Eismann here. And you're?" he asked with a hint of shy flirtiness.

Henri grinned, took his offered hand, and shook it. "Henrietta Hoffmann. I'm the housekeeper here for Our Lady of the Prairie's pastor."

"Father Ferrera, right?" Harry's grin grew bigger.

"Yes, but he's not here," Henri said, feeling guilty for the attraction building in her. Etta stood without a word beside her and gave her a nudge.

Harry asked, "Will Father be back soon?"

Still smiling, Henri answered. "Yes, in about an hour. Could I help?"

The young man sighed. "Unfortunately, it's not a job for the ladies. My brother's car had a breakdown a few miles east of town. We can't figure what's wrong. My brother is still out there working on it. I heard Father Ferrera is a crackerjack with car problems."

Henri adjusted the bib of her apron to be sure it hid the lost button. "He's an expert in many things, and I'm sure he'd be glad to help." Etta nudged her again. Getting the hint, Henri glanced at Etta and said, "This is my friend, Etta."

"You've come to the right place," Etta said, mischief hinting in her voice.

What's she up to? Henri thought as she moved out of the doorway and beckoned Harry inside. "Come in and rest while you wait for Father.

You must be hungry. We have tea, bread, and fresh preserves."

"Much obliged," Harry said, showing his greasy hands. "I should clean up first."

Henri nodded. "There's a pump, a washtub, and a bar of soap outside around the corner."

As the door shut, Etta whispered, "I'll stall him. You go freshen up and put on a dress that'll stay buttoned."

"I'll just leave my apron on," Henri said, knowing she had the same problem with most of her dresses.

"No, you won't. The apron's too dirty. Now go change. You've invited him to eat, and they say the way to a man's heart is through his stomach. Who knows? Harry might end up being the man for you." Etta grinned as she grabbed a towel and scooted out the door.

"Bossy, bossy," Henri called after her. She wanted to add, "Martim is my man." But Etta was right. To be a gracious hostess, she should make herself presentable. She hurried to fix her hair and changed into a flapper-style dress, the only one she could still comfortably wear.

A while later, the two ladies sat with Harry while he enjoyed a meal of bread and butter, preserves, fresh radishes, and cold trout left over from last night's dinner. As he picked bones from the fish, he explained the escapade that led to the auto's breakdown.

"My brother, his wife, and I have been traveling in his old Ford looking for decent paying jobs. Our family has scraped by on our homestead longer than most. Europe has slapped so many tariffs on our wheat, we can't make a go of it any longer. The land isn't worth much. We sold the livestock and the farm equipment to have some money to live on for a while. Ma and Pa moved in with our sister and her husband. What makes the situation more difficult are the painful memories my sister-in-law left behind." Harry stared out the window. "Poor Dottie has buried three babies in the last few years, all born too early."

Henri's hand slid to her belly. "Oh, my gosh. That's terrible," she said, choking up at the thought of losing her own baby. Many unmarried women in her situation would be happy to miscarry. Not Henri. She had a long episode of spotting last week. Thankfully, it stopped, but a miscarriage could still happen.

Harry nodded. "It's been hard on Dottie. We're trying to have some fun along the way to take her mind off her troubles. While we searched for jobs, we took in a rodeo, watched a few car races, and attended a couple of fairs. We picked up a few odd jobs to keep us going, but so far nothing permanent. This morning we checked with a rancher to see if he needed more help, but he has all the hands he needs. The drive back to the road was pretty rough. We had to cross a stream with a passel of big rocks. That's what did the old Ford in." He laughed. "Now we're up a creek without a paddle."

Etta snickered.

Henri grinned and forced her hand away from her growing baby. "Where will you go once your Ford is running again?"

"Dottie wants to visit her brother in Havre. She hasn't seen him for a while. He has an amazing racecar. My brother Vic thinks we can talk him into letting us try it out." Harry wiped his hands on his napkin, helped himself to the last piece of trout, and continued. "While we're in Havre, we'll check into jobs with the railroad. If nothing pans out, we'll head to Missoula. See if we can find a job in the flour mills. If not, we'll take a break and head to Glacier and camp awhile. Do some hunting, fishing. Then we'll head to Helena and search for jobs there."

"Helena," Henri said, reflecting on the life she'd soon have there. "I've heard Helena's new cathedral is beautiful and that the capitol building's massive rotunda is better than the cat's meow. I'd love to see them both."

Harry's face lit up. "Would you consider…" He stopped. "Nah. It probably wouldn't work."

Henri looked at him quizzically. "What wouldn't work?"

Harry shrugged. "Dottie could use female companionship. You know someone to talk to besides men. There's room in the Ford for another passenger." He frowned. "But I imagine Father needs you here."

Henri asked herself, could it work? She and Martim had talked about her slipping away quietly at the end of September. But if she continued to gain so much weight, this fall might be too late. In fact, considering the comments these last few days and the button incident with Etta, she needed to leave very soon.

In the distance, the train whistle blew, followed by the click-clack of its wheels. Harry picked at a callous on his hand. Etta looked between the two of them and said, "Ma and Pa took my entire family to Helena last year. The capitol has so many unforgettable sights."

Harry's eyes twinkled when his gaze returned to Henri. "Seems like there are some unforgettable sights right here in Sage Prairie." He blushed and reached to fetch the napkin fallen on the floor. When he straightened, he held two pearly buttons. "These yours, Henrietta?"

Henri bit her lip. Two buttons? She'd lost two buttons? She held out her palm for the fasteners. "Thanks, Harry. I have some sewing to do."

Etta muttered, "Another one?"

Henri avoided Etta's eyes, wondering if her friend was guessing the truth. There was no doubt now she'd have to leave earlier than September. But how? And what reason could she give for her departure? As she contemplated the dilemma, she heard Martim's Chevy pull up. Relieved, she stood. "That's Father right now, Harry. Come. I'll introduce you. He'll have you on the road in no time."

***

'No time' took longer than Henri thought. Sunday evening, she loaded the sink with dinner dishes and looked out the window at the old Ford. A hauling trailer loaded with camping equipment was hitched to the back. Yesterday, after Martim had used his car to pull the disabled vehicle to the rectory, he and the two men had worked late into the night. Today he'd gotten under the hood again after he'd finished Sunday services. Right now, he poked at the engine while Harry and his brother Vic peppered him with advice. A tent was pitched a few yards away, where the two men had slept last night.

Vic's wife, Dottie, pumped water over a dishrag and rung it out. As she wiped crumbs from the dinner table, she said, "You've been so gracious, Henrietta. Last night, the warm bath you prepared for me was the first I've had in weeks. And you were wonderful to share your bed."

Pouring boiling water into the sink, Henri said, "I didn't mind. You brought back memories of my sister Greta sleeping next to me for years." She put the kettle back on the stove and started scrubbing plates.

Dottie picked up a towel to do the drying. "Father Ferrera has been wonderful too, not just helping Harry and Vic fix our car. After Mass this morning, he prayed with me. I feel so much better." She pulled a card from her pocket. "See, he even wrote a prayer to say when I get depressed."

Henri wiped her hands on her apron and took the card filled with Martim's handwriting.

Dear God, losing my babies has broken my heart. I place my pain in Your hands. Please rescue me from despair. Through Your love, I will not let my grief overwhelm me. Give me strength so I may share Your solace with others. Amen.

"It's beautiful, Dottie," she said, returning the card. She turned back to the sink, hiding the tears building in her eyes. Here was another reason she could never ask Martim to leave the priesthood. He healed the heart as well as the body and soul.

Outside, Vic sat in his Ford and tried to start it as Harry and Martim stood by. It sputtered a moment and then died. The three men returned under the hood.

***

Well past midnight, Henri lay with her mind churning as Dottie slept soundly beside her. She rose, buttoned a sweater over her nightgown, and tiptoed out the kitchen door. Snores came from the nearby tent. The dirt felt cool beneath her bare feet as she took the path to the church.

Covering her head with a scarf, she entered, dipped her fingers in the holy water, and made the sign of the cross. Votive candles flickering in dimness lit her way to a front pew where she knelt below the statue of the Blessed Mother. Tears salted her lips as she prayed to find a path to keep her child and to protect it from scandal. Her fingers moved across her rosary beads, filling her with a sense of peace and easing her fears. She'd find a way so Martim could continue to serve the people who needed him.

As she tucked the rosary into her sweater pocket, Martim came through the sacristy door into the sanctuary. Not noticing her, he knelt before the altar and bowed his head in prayer. He stretched his arms towards the cross above the altar and began singing 'How Great Thou Art'.

Henri sat and listened to the father of her child. Boy or girl, what would it be? Would he or she be blessed with Martim's beautiful voice, blessed with his rich brown hair, and dark brown eyes? Would the child have his charm and his thoughtful ways with people? She smiled at the possibilities. His voice brought a swell of love and the chorus misted her eyes.

Then sings my soul, my Savior God, to Thee
How great Thou art, how great Thou art

The song ended. He made the sign of the cross and stood. As he headed back to the sacristy, he noticed her. With a curious expression, he stepped from the altar and slipped into the pew beside her.

"I couldn't sleep either," he said, taking her hand.

Tenderness spilled through the rough warmth of his hand. She laid her head on his shoulder, his closeness overwhelming her. "Martim, I have to go soon. It won't be long before my pregnancy becomes obvious. The longer I delay, the greater the chance someone will put two and two together."

"I wish you'd reconsider my marriage proposal."

"It's on my mind all the time. But today, watching you help Harry and Vic, reminded me again how much you do for the community. The encouragement you gave Dottie was especially healing. It's like she's been transformed. I'd feel selfish taking you from all you do for so many people."

He wrapped his arm around her and kissed her cheek. "I can find other paths to do those same things."

"Maybe. But I don't believe another path would be as powerful. There has to be a better way. I'm praying to find it. In the meantime, I have to go."

"I don't want you to leave. Not yet."

"I don't want to go, either. I'm prepared to live with the consequences of my pregnancy. But I'm not prepared for a scandal that harms you."

They sat in silence. Finally, he said, "You're only three months along. Mrs. Cullum said women usually begin their stay in the Home around their sixth month."

"There's a way I could leave now," she said, facing him.

His arm fell from her shoulder. "And that is?"

"Harry told me Dottie could use female companionship as they travel. He invited me to join them."

Martim picked up her hand again, his fingers rubbing her palm. "How would traveling with them make you safer?"

"It's not the best of circumstance, Martim, but it is a way to escape prying eyes. I think it'll be easier to hide my pregnancy from three strangers who haven't been watching me gain weight these last few months."

"You may be right. Still, I don't like it. I imagined you with me two more months, then driving you to Helena myself, or at least taking you to Havre and putting you on the train." His hands rasped across his unshaven face. He heaved a sigh. "If you think it's the best option, then you should go."

Relief swept through her. "I've saved nearly my entire salary since

I arrived in Sage Prairie, so I won't be a financial burden to two men looking for a job. And I'd be company for Dottie."

In the dim light, she saw a smile grow on his face. "Practical, frugal, kind. You're quite the lady, *meu amor.* I'll cover your expenses and make sure you have enough money to buy a dress or two that will help you keep your secret as long as possible. And don't worry about clothes for the baby. The home will provide what you need."

He pulled her close and cradled her head on his shoulder. Soon the rhythm of their breathing fell in with one another's. She watched the candle flames flicker across the statue of the Blessed Mother and said, "I've been thinking of names."

"Names haven't crossed my mind. I guess that's a mother thing. Do you have any ideas?"

"I was thinking of Martim for a boy."

"Would that be wise? Wouldn't the gossips wonder about a connection?"

"It's common for people to name their children after family friends and those they admire."

"In that case, I'd be proud to have our boy carry my name."

"If it's a girl, I want to name her after someone in your family."

"I've always loved my sister's name, Angelica."

Henri straightened. "Angelica. A lovely name for a little girl."

He placed his hand on her swelling belly. "I'll miss you when you go, *pequeno bebê*, and I'll miss your *mamãe* even more."

***

Early Monday afternoon, the Ford was running. The men loaded their trailer with the tent, the camping supplies, and Henri's trunk and hitched it to the car. Vic, Harry, Dottie, and Henri headed to Havre to visit Dottie's brother and to look for work. If they found nothing in the towns along the way, they'd travel to Helena late in September. Henri told her fellow travelers when they arrived at the capitol, she'd stay there for a while with friends.

As the car bumped onto the road, Henri watched Martim standing on the steps of the Mother of the Prairie Church until he was out of sight. She steeled herself against the loneliness she already felt and wondered how he'd explain her unexpected departure. A stab of guilt added to her sorrow. It didn't seem right to have left without saying goodbye to Etta.

Chapter Eighteen

Thursday, October 20, 1927
Helena, Montana
Henrietta

Gusts sent crispy brown leaves swirling through the crowd congregated on the station's loading platform in Helena. Clouds of steam billowed around the train's gigantic wheels. Henri pulled her winter coat around her body and shivered, grateful the weather had turned cold so early. It gave her a reason to wear her heavy coat. Without the help of her coat and the drop waist dresses that were the style, Dottie would have realized she was pregnant.

She stood back and watched as Vic shook Harry's hand saying, "I'll miss you, brother. Good luck finding a job in California."

Harry's usual optimism flashed with a grin. "There's a good chance I will. Standard Oil is hiring, and they promise decent wages. Who knows, I might even earn enough to buy a home." His smile disappeared. "I wish you and Dottie were coming with me, Vic."

Vic wrapped an arm around his wife and pulled her to his side. "I couldn't pass up our brother-in-law's offer to race his car at Helena's track. I got a chance of winning a big purse. But if the racing circuit doesn't work out, we'll join you in California." The two brothers hugged, slapping each other's backs.

Harry picked up his rucksack and turned to Henri. "It was wonderful traveling with you, Henrietta. I'm going to miss you."

A twinge of loneliness struck Henri. Though she'd make friends with other mothers-to-be at the Crittenton home, she'd miss her traveling companions. She missed her family back home, even her strict parents. And she missed Martim even more. As she stared at her hands, she forced a smile and looked at Harry. "Exploring Montana with you three was wonderful. Whoever hires you, Harry, will be lucky."

Harry paused as if he had something important to say, but seemed to change his mind, and handed her an envelope. "A few photos of our travels so you can remember the good times we had."

Henri stared at the envelope for a moment and then tucked it in her coat pocket. "You're so thoughtful, Harry." An urge to stretch up and kiss his cheek swept through her, but then a sharp kick thwacked her ribs. She sucked in a breath as her hand flew to her side. Grimacing, she pushed the baby's foot back into place.

"Are you alright?" Harry asked.

She waved away his concern. "It's nothing, Harry. Just something I ate."

Harry's grin was back. "Enjoy the stay with your friends, Henrietta. And when you see Father Ferrera again, tell him he has my deepest gratitude for the help he gave Vic and me."

Cries of "All aboard," ended the moment. Dottie hugged her brother-in-law goodbye, and Harry disappeared up the steps into the passenger car.

Vic turned to Henri. "Well Henrietta, I suppose we should get you to St. Vincent's Academy so you can meet up with your friend."

Henri nodded as she clutched her purse to her chest. This was a turning point in her life, one mixed with fear of the future and the joy of knowing she'd soon be a mother.

When the Academy came into view, she noticed a tall woman in a dark wool coat and a cloche hat standing at the bottom of the steps. "There's Mrs. Parker, now." The worry plaguing her since they'd left the train station disappeared. Thank heavens Martim had arranged for her to meet Mrs. Parker at the Academy instead of at the Home. Now Vic and Dottie would never know she was staying in a place for unwed mothers. Henri waved and the woman who would support her through the months ahead ambled down the walk.

As Vic unloaded Henri's trunk, Mrs. Parker smiled. "It's good to see you, Henrietta." She introduced herself to Vic and Dottie and added, "Thanks for bringing Henrietta to Helena. We've been looking forward to her visit. Don't worry about her trunk, Vic." She flashed a knowing look at Henri. "We ladies can carry her luggage ourselves."

"Are you sure?" Vic asked.

"Absolutely sure." Henri said, grinning.

"I guess it's goodbye, Henrietta," Dottie said, giving her a hug. "It's been wonderful having you in my life. You've helped me weather some tough times."

Thinking of her own difficult future, Henri swallowed the lump clawing at her throat. "You, Vic, and Harry have been a blessing to me too." She patted the pocket holding the photos Harry had given her. "I'll never forget our adventures."

A few minutes later, she and Mrs. Parker watched the old Ford disappear around the corner. Mrs. Parker picked up a trunk handle and Henri grabbed the other as her eyes explored the neat city streets and the tidy homes with landscaped yards. "How far is the Home?" she asked.

"Just two blocks," Mrs. Parker said, her voice gravelly but kind. "After we settle you in the dorm, I'll give you a tour of the Crittenton Home and the grounds. It's a lovely place to spend your time-in-waiting." She grinned. "And after the tour, I'll show you the laundry room where you'll be helping with piles of dirty diapers and linens. It'll give you a taste of motherhood for sure."

Henri laughed. "I've had experience with my nieces and nephews back home, Mrs. Parker. But not to this extent."

"Call me Mimi. Mrs. Parker is much too formal."

A young woman with a plain face and thin brown hair appeared beside them. "May I help?" she asked.

"Mildred. What a surprise," Mimi said. "I wasn't expecting you."

Mildred took the handle of the trunk from Mimi and said, "Ruth volunteered to watch my two little ones while they napped." She gave Henri a shy smile. "Hi, Henrietta. I'm Mildred Blakely. Everyone calls me Toots."

Henrietta grinned, "Call me Henri."

"You have the bed next to mine, and I'm assigned to the laundry, like you," Toots said. "I wanted to meet you without the hubbub of my babies."

"That's very kind," Henri said, feeling as if she already belonged.

Toots pointed down the street. "See that enormous manor at the end of the road? That's the Crittenton Home. You'll be safe and welcome there."

Henri gasped. "It's beautiful." Just as Martim had described, the home was an impressive three-story Victorian Mansion built of brick and stone. Though the building had a few signs of wear, Henri never imagined she would live in such a grand place.

Her amazement grew as she and Toots carried her trunk through a modern kitchen, a large dining room, into an immense parlor covered with thick carpets, and then up a double staircase that curved to the landing above. Breathing hard, Henri continued with Toots up to the third floor and into a dormitory. Light filtered through a bounty of muslin-curtained windows. Rows of beds lined each side of the room. A few women napped, their babies beside them or in small cribs at the foot of their beds.

Toots whispered, "Your bed is at the other end next to mine." Henri crept with Toots down the aisle and set the trunk in front of a small dresser stationed between two beds. Mimi appeared beside them with a camera and signaled Henri and Toots to follow her. As they headed down the stairs, Mimi said, "First, we'll stop in the office on the main floor so I can introduce you to Mrs. Cullum, our director, then we'll explore outside and take a few pictures."

Toots leaned into Henri and murmured, "You'll love what she's planning, Henri. It's part of the welcoming ritual."

Gusts of wind whistled through the nearly barren trees as Henri ambled with Mimi and Toots over the mansion grounds. Orange and yellow leaves cluttered flowerbeds now gone to seed. The spruce trees didn't care winter was coming. Their dark green needles would survive the cold. Wistful thoughts of picnics with her family scurried through Henri's mind. She bit her lip and said, "It's as lovely as any park back home."

Mimi gazed at Henri. "Speaking of home, Henrietta, does anyone in your family know you 're expecting?"

"No." Henri sighed. "I can't tell them, not yet, except for my sister, Greta. I've started a letter to tell her a dozen times. Though I'm close to her, I haven't found the right words."

"No one knows except Father Ferrera?"

"Only Father and now you." She stopped for a moment and gave a little laugh. "Well, and of course, the baby's father. Others will know soon enough."

Mimi gave her a sympathetic look. "I know it's difficult, but I imagine you'll want your baby baptized so you need godparents. Close family members are often the best to take on that role. Write to your sister, Greta. If she's as close as you say, she'll understand."

Henri bit her lip. "I've been praying for the courage. So far I haven't found it."

Toots took Henri's hand. "I'll pray for you, too, Henri."

Mimi put an arm around her shoulder and gave it a gentle squeeze. Her voice took on a lighter tone. "Let's take some pictures. You can send them with your letter. If we do the photos right, your sister will be able to share them with your family and no one will suspect you're pregnant." Her voice turned serious. "You must believe, Henrietta, you're a woman with a future. There's a path where your baby can be a part of your life. That's the mission of the Crittenton Home. But only if it's a path you choose."

A fierce scowl flushed Henri's face. "There is nothing I want more, and I will make it happen." A jab jolted her ribs as if the baby were saying, "Get things rolling, Mother. I'm on my way." Henri gasped and pressed at the bulge pushing against her abdomen.

"Your baby?" Toots asked with a grin.

Henri nodded, letting her breath escape. "The baby is so active, like it's dancing all the time." She prodded the foot back into place. Sharing the joy of her baby's movements instead of pretending they were something she'd eaten sent gratitude racing through her heart.

Mimi laughed. "Active is a healthy sign." She pointed to a spruce tree with branches spreading over the grass and handed Toots the camera. "Here's an excellent spot for the photo, Henrietta. Let's do one of us together and one of you alone." Mimi sat on the lawn in front of the tree, wrapped her coat around her, and tucked her legs beneath her.

As she folded herself beside Mimi, Henri noticed fluffy white dandelion seed pods sprinkled through the grass. Remembering her little niece Lillie's delight last spring when she'd blown the fluff to the wind, Henri plucked a tuft and sent the seeds swirling through the air. By this time next year, she'd be sharing this joy with her own child.

Chapter Nineteen

Christmas Eve, 1927
The Crittenton Home
Henrietta

Sunlight filtered through the frost on the dormitory window and dazzled the snow glittering on the rooftops, the trees, and the gardens below. Henri watched Toots trudge across the grounds, pulling her little Sonny and baby Robert on a sled, their breath coming out in puffy clouds. "Silent Night" drifted up from the piano in the parlor, bringing a wave of nostalgia. This was her first Christmas away from her family. If she hadn't given in to passion, she'd be sharing Christmas and all its pageantry with Martim right now. She smiled faintly. If she hadn't done such a terrible wrong, she'd never have experienced the depth of her love. Or be expecting a child she already cherished.

She pulled away from the window, propped herself up on her bed, and browsed through the photos she'd pasted in her Rogue's Gallery. She smiled at the pictures Harry had given her and at those of Toots and her boys. The ones her sister Callie had sent of her family and friends back home tugged most at her heart. Her favorite was of little Lillie, taken just before she'd left home to be Martim's housekeeper. Would she have agreed to take the job had she known about the future? She cupped her hands around the little one growing inside her. Yes, she would have come without a doubt.

She studied the only photo she had of Martim, the one he'd given her of his ordination day. Should she paste it in her Rogue's Gallery? No. Its appearance in her album could give the wrong impression to the suspicion minded. Undoubtedly, there were already a few people in Sage Prairie who harbored doubts about her mysterious disappearance. She tucked the photo in her missal, a natural place for a picture of her pastor. She closed the album, pulled Greta's letter from her pocket, and read it for the third time.

Dearest Henri,
The news of your pregnancy shocked me only a little. Maybe

it's sacrilegious, but I like to think heaven blesses the love you and Father Ferrera share. Looking back at all the suitors you had, how you flirted with them and dangled your heart for them to grab, but never let them capture your love. That was something only Martim could do.

I imagine you're scared to death. The world will condemn you for sure. Vader and Moeder will be fit to be tied when and if they find out about the baby. It would upset them even more if they knew who the father was.

Despite the hard times ahead, I'm happy you're keeping the baby, and that the director at the home will help you create a future with your little one. Have you come up with a plan yet, one that keeps the baby's illegitimacy secret?

Your letter is in ashes and your secret safe with Father Cornelius and me. We both understand what happened between you two. We'd be honored to be the baby's godparents, though we won't be able to come for the ceremony. You wrote about the marvelous Mimi Parker. Perhaps she'd fill in as a proxy.

You, Martim, and the baby are in our prayers. I look forward to meeting my new niece or nephew.

Much love,

Greta

P.S. Cornelius already knew about the baby. Martim confessed to him a month ago. On another note, I'm crocheting a baptismal outfit for my Godchild. I'll send it as soon as it's finished.

Henri lay back on her pillow and closed her eyes. The term "illegitimate" taunted her, growing in big red letters and pressing into her brain. Was there any way she could keep that awful label from her baby's birth certificate? Beyond that, how would she create a respectable life for herself and her baby? Vague possibilities popped up one by one. No concrete ideas appeared.

"Henrietta?"

She bolted up. Mimi settled on the edge of the bed and nodded at Greta's letter, still in Henri's hand. "What did your sister have to say?"

Henri unfolded the letter and stared at the words. "Greta is a wonderful sister. No judgment. Just understanding. She and my cousin, Father Cornelius, agreed to be the baby's godparents, but they can't come for the baptism." She caught Mimi's eyes. "Would you stand in as proxy?"

"I'm honored, Henrietta." Mimi's smile faded. "The medical staff that comes to the Home to deliver your baby will know you're an unwed mother. So, they won't ask for a father's name when they fill out the birth certificate. But you'll want one for the baptismal certificate. Do you have one ready?"

Henri's face grew warm. "I'm working on it."

Mimi continued. "Father Ferrera told Mrs. Cullum you and the baby's father love one another, but circumstances don't allow you to marry right now."

Words lumped in Henri's throat. She gazed out the window at a squirrel scampering across a snow-covered limb, jumping to a nearby spruce, and sending clumps of snow to the ground. Mimi wrapped an arm around her "If marriage is possible in the future, perhaps you could use his name at the baptism."

Henri stared at her hands, cracked and raw from her work in the laundry. She'd put lotion on them later, but nothing could soothe the rawness in her heart. "Actually, he asked me to marry him."

Mimi looked at her, shocked. "That's the honorable thing to do. So why isn't it happening?"

"He belongs to someone else. He'd have to leave…" She turned away. "Every time I consider his proposal, I can't get past the fact that it would be wrong for him to break the vows he's taken and for me to make him do so. Our marriage would ruin him without making my life or the baby's any better."

Mimi's brows rose. "I see. So, he's already married. Well, if you can't use his name on the Baptismal certificate, what will you do?"

Henri ignored Mimi's mistaken supposition. "I've thought about fabricating a fictional husband. But then I'd have to explain why he never shows up."

Mimi took Henri's hand. "A fictional husband could work. And you're right. The dilemma of making him real but keeping him invisible is ticklish. Perhaps your sister or even Father Ferrera could help you figure that out."

She bit her lip. "I'll write to Father and ask for his ideas."

"You're little one is due in four weeks, so the sooner the better."

***

Early Christmas morning, snowdrifts caught the moonlight and glittered as if sprinkled with a thousand tiny gems. Stars still studded the skies like the whole universe were celebrating the birthday of Jesus.

The morning's magic comforted Henri as she trudged along a shoveled walk, holding little Sonny's mittened hand. Toots plodded beside her with baby Robert cuddled in her arms. They followed three other mothers-to-be towards St. Helena's Cathedral. Light from inside the cathedral poured through the stained-glass windows as if the five young women were approaching the Gates of Heaven.

Halfway up the granite stairs, Henri stopped to catch her breath. Her baby drained her energy, and once again was dancing on her ribs. Toots took her elbow, and Sonny's eager tugs urged her up the last few steps to massive wooden doors. Inside, an organ played. The soft notes of "Lo How a Rose Ere Blooming" filled the cathedral. Henri took off her gloves, dipped her fingers in the marble font, and made the sign of the cross. She breathed a sigh of relief when she saw only a few congregants kneeling in the pews, waiting for Mass to begin. Arriving this early meant there were fewer disapproving eyes staring at her swollen belly.

Three women from the Home seated themselves in the shadows of the last pew, knelt, and began their prayers. Henri and Toots braved their way down a side aisle, their footsteps echoing on the marble floor. They stopped at a life-sized manger arranged in an alcove near the altar. Henri took a deep breath, inhaling the smell of fir needles and candle wax. A forest of evergreens clustered around the Nativity scene, twinkling with electric-colored lights. Last year Henri had seen this new type of Christmas light decorating the bigger stores in Glade Harbor, but not in such grand profusion. Their soft glow gave the Holy Family and the stable a radiant air that warmed her spirits.

She and Sonny stood for a while with Toots and the baby, letting their souls soak up the serenity of the scene. A woman in a luxurious coat lavished with a thick sable collar joined them. A girl of about eight years, wearing a fancy fur-lined bonnet and muff, stood beside her mother. Henri sensed their eyes inspecting Sonny, Toots, the baby, and then herself. Though Henri was sure neither the woman nor the girl could know the truth of her pregnancy, she pulled her coat tighter around her bulging belly.

The girl nudged her mother and hissed, "Mama, there's that lady I saw pulling a sled yesterday at that place you said bad women live."

The mother's eyes flitted over Toots, the boys, and then stabbed into Henri. She snorted, "They shouldn't be allowed in here where there are impressionable children."

Tears swelled in Toot's eyes as she hugged Robert. Sonny clutched Henri's knees and looked up at her anxiously.

Henri glared at the woman. In a hushed voice she snarled, "For heaven's sake. It's the birthday of our Savior. What did he say about casting stones?"

The woman grabbed her daughter's hand and said, "Come, darling. We'll visit the baby Jesus when those strumpets leave with their misbegotten." The mother and daughter paraded away, genuflected in front of the altar, and then settled in a pew on the other side of the Cathedral.

Fury burned on Henri's cheeks as she helped little Sonny move closer to the manger. "Look," she said. "That's Baby Jesus. He was born to save us all no matter what our sins." The Blessed Mother herself had been condemned for carrying a baby without an earthly father. She must have been afraid, worried Joseph wouldn't marry her, and that her child would carry the stigma of illegitimacy throughout its life.

A bank of votive candles flickered near the manger. Henri took a deep breath, gave Sonny a penny to put in the slot for offerings, and helped him light a candle. As she knelt before the manger, she opened her missal, stopping for a moment to gaze at Martim's photo. She then turned to the prayer she'd inscribed on the inside cover dedicated to her new friend Toots, and read the words.

Our Lady of Good Success, pray for us. In the name of Jesus, thy only son, we beg of thee to take our cause into thy hands and grant us the courage, strength, and wisdom to make a good life for our children and to keep them safe from scandal. Amen.

Just as Mary had done, she would put her trust in God to help her and her baby through the years ahead.

The woman's disdainful words weighed on Henri as the day unfolded. They pressed like a millstone while the toddlers dug into their stockings to find the candy canes and oranges Santa left, through a breakfast of hot chocolate, slices of fried ham, and holiday buns, and through the singing of carols in the glow of the Christmas tree. She and her child might face worse judgment in the years ahead. Even if she relented and married Martim, there'd be plenty of condemnation.

The thoughts still plagued her as she drained the water from the sink. She was untying her apron when Mimi appeared beside her with her camera. "Come, Henri. Get your coat and hat. You and I have important business outside before the snow turns serious again."

They trudged through the snow-covered grounds, flakes fluttering from the sky. Mimi squeezed Henri's hand. "I heard what happened at the Cathedral this morning. You'll never be able to hide your situation completely from everyone. But you can create the illusion that your life meets with society's approval. I'll show you what I mean." She handed Henri the camera and plodded to an enormous tree, bare of leaves. She peeked from behind its massive trunk, revealing only her hat-covered head, her face and warm smile, and her shoulder. "See what I mean?" she said. "Your picture will show you celebrating Christmas as if everything is above board and proper. Send the photo to anyone, and no one will be the wiser."

Henri took Mimi's picture but hesitated when it was her turn for Mimi to take hers. A moment of bitterness held her back. Why should she be forced to hide her pregnancy and her love for Martim? But she relented. If she had to weave a web of deceit to protect her child and Martim, then so be it.

Chapter Twenty

Friday, December 30, 1927
Sage Prairie, Montana
Martim

Martim perched on a stool in the back room of Maguire's Mercantile, examining the mangled mess on the young store clerk's left hand. A potbellied stove blazed nearby. Martim's medical bag lay open on the floor beside him. "You're lucky you didn't blow your head off, Sam," Martim scolded as he handed a bottle of bootleg whiskey to the young man. "Take a good swallow. If it hurts now, it will be excruciating when I put those little finger bones back in place."

A fiery blush burned across Sam's cheeks. "Aye, Father. Me Da warned me about a loaded gun. Don't know what got into me head." He lifted the bottle and guzzled until he came up sputtering.

Mr. Maguire glowered above Sam, his arms crossed, his grizzled brows wedged together in a serious frown. "I told him over and over to check the breech for ammunition before you go messing with a rifle." He handed his clerk a chunk of leather. "Bite on this, lad. Keep you from screaming and embarrassing yourself. And I'm holding your arm and hand like you're stuck in a vise, so Father can do his work."

"First things first," Father said. He crossed himself and prayed. "Lord, give me a steady hand and Sam the moxie to get through this."

With a muffled "Amen" from Sam and the store's owner, Martim tuned out the young man's moans and began the delicate task of putting three pieces of his little finger bone back in place. As Martim splinted the finger, wrapping it with a long strip of white linen, he said, "You'll have a scar, and your finger will be stiff and crooked until the day you die. Let it be a reminder every time you pick up a rifle."

Sam held up his bandaged hand and studied it with a grimace. "A bent finger's better than a missing finger. One thing for sure, it'll help me get it through me thick skull there's better places to do target practice than on me self." His face turned solemn. "I owe you a debt of gratitude, Father."

"You can pay that debt by being safe."

Mr. Maguire shook his balding head and eyed his clerk. "Father, will Sam be fit to work soon? Or should I give him a few days off for his foolishness?"

Martim examined his patient's pupils and turned to the store owner. "Despite Sam's display of bravado, he's in a bit of shock." Martim nodded at a small cot Mr. Maguire kept in the back of his store. "He should rest a couple of hours with his feet propped. Keep the fire going so he stays warm. If he feels like working later, let him. But keep an eye on him and see that he doesn't overdo it. If he vomits, get me right away."

Mr. Maguire wagged a finger at Sam. "You ain't immortal, lad. And I don't want to lose the best clerk I ever had."

Sam grinned sheepishly as he lay back on the cot, his pained face ghostly white. Martim put a twenty-pound bag of potatoes under his legs and covered him with the woolen blanket he always carried with him.

The chatter of customers in the store's front faded, and the mercantile door tinkled open and then closed. Mrs. Maguire appeared in the storeroom and handed Martim a package wrapped in brown paper, tied with string. "Some bacon, Father, for all your help."

"That's very generous."

"Least we could do," she said, tucking a loose bit of gray hair back into her bun. "How's the patient doing?"

Sam mumbled from the cot. "No worries, Mrs. Maguire. I ain't aiming to die for a long time."

"Good news, Mr. Hotshot," she said and tucked the blanket tighter under Sam's chin.

Mr. Maguire put a hand on Martim's shoulder. "I don't know what we'd do without you, Father. No actual doctor within a fifty-mile radius and here you are, doing just about everything he would do."

The front door bells tinkled again. Mrs. Maguire sighed. "More customers. Better get back to work." She stopped halfway to the door, turned, her eyebrows raised. "By the way, Father. Have you heard of how Miss Hoffmann is doing? All the ladies are wondering when she'll be back."

Martim's stomach tightened. In early August, not long after Henri had left, he'd put a notice in Sage Prairie's weekly paper letting the community know that Miss Hoffman had left for a hospital in Helena where she would receive medical attention. He forced a weak smile. "I hear she's improving. I'm not sure when or if she'll return. That's in the Lord's hands." And in Henri's hands, he added to himself.

"Well, we all miss her." Mrs. Maguire cocked her head and faced Martim. "She's been gone a long time. Is her, um, medical condition something serious?"

Mr. Maguire gasped. "Woman, that's none of our business. If Henrietta wanted us to know, she'd have told us."

A smug look appeared in the older woman's eyes. She harrumphed. "Whatever is wrong, we're praying for her recovery."

Back in the rectory, as Martim cooked himself a dinner of eggs and the bacon Mrs. Maguire had given him, Sam's incident played over and over in his mind. If Henri ever relented and married him, he couldn't perform the sacraments ministering to people's souls. But he could work in other jobs and serve as a type of physician when necessary. Probably not in Sage Prairie, but he could use his skills wherever he and Henri set up home. It would have to be in a town where no one knew their history. First, he had to convince her marriage was the best option.

As the eggs sputtered in the bacon grease, his eyes drifted to the bedroom. Dirty laundry spilled from a basket beside the dresser. The quilt Henri had brought from White Water lay rumpled on her bed. He'd begun sleeping there when the weather turned icy, as the heat was nearly nonexistent in his room in the sacristy. Being in her bed had brought dreams of her sleeping beside him. Then he'd wake to the ache of loneliness.

He missed Henri's cooking. He missed clean laundry and pressed shirts, and all the things she did around the rectory. Though it wasn't always pretty, he managed those things himself. But his life was empty without her laughter, her quick wit, and her dauntless personality. What good were his ideas without her to challenge them? She always told him what she thought, even when it opposed what he believed. Her point of view often jarred him from his self-assurance, and he'd come away with a clearer outlook on the issue.

Just thinking of her sent a hunger through his body. Remembering the smell of her hair, the curl of her lips, the sparkle in her eyes stirred a longing to take her in his arms and love her.

He splashed cold water over his face and sat down to dinner. As he ate, he read Henri's letter again. Thank God, the mail had come through on Saturday's train despite the heavy snow.

He reread what had happened at the Cathedral on Christmas Day. If only he'd been there to protect her from suspicion. He skimmed over the news of her visit with the physician. She was experiencing early contractions, and the doctor predicted the baby would arrive around the third week of January. He imagined holding the baby in his arms, exploring his son or daughter's face. Would the child have Henri's beautiful eyes? His hairline? Her smile? His nose? Would he see his *mamãe* or his *papai* looking back at him? However God made the child, he would love the *bebê*. He looked at the calendar. If only he could arrive in Helena without arousing suspicion.

Suspicion. It ran rampant here in Sage Prairie. When questions arose concerning Henri's sudden departure in August, he'd deflected the queries with a nod, a shrug, and a smile. Printing the notice in the community paper did little to ward off conjecture. Instead, it fueled rumors about her being in a family way. After all, she'd been the picture of health before she disappeared. So what else could it be, the whisperers said.

He felt guilty that the mutterings didn't involve him. The gossipers assumed she'd been pregnant when she'd arrived in Sage Prairie. He had written a long article on "Falsehood" in November for the newspaper. He'd even preached a Sunday sermon on the eighth commandment; Thou shalt not bear false witness. Since then, the rumors had gone underground. But they still occasionally reared their ugly head as shown by Mrs. Maguire's comment today.

He sopped up the last of the egg with a scrap of toast, pushed the plate aside, and reached for his pen, bottle of ink, and paper.

Dearest Henri,

I'm pleased to hear you and our baby are healthy. But it breaks my heart to hear you are already suffering the humiliation of bearing a child that will be branded illegitimate. The use of such a label is cruel, archaic, and unchristian.

In your letter, you suggested creating a fictitious husband and father for our child.

He got up and paced, plagued with guilt. A fictitious husband? A fictitious father? He was not fictitious. Was he condemned to live his life in the role of a mysterious ghost? The thought was painful. He'd try again to convince her that leaving the priesthood and marrying her was best. He sat back down to his letter.

A fictitious husband wouldn't be necessary if you agreed to marry me. Being released from my vows would be long and arduous, and The Pope himself would have to authorize it. Though there would be scandal, perhaps a great deal, leaving the priesthood is an ordeal I'm willing to go through. You already face judgment. I should go through it with you.

You're right. I do find tremendous satisfaction in serving my parishioners, as I attend to their spiritual and physical needs. But Henri, I love you more.

You said you worry about how I could earn a living. I taught at St. Albert's College before they assigned me to my parishes. I can teach again. The Church wouldn't allow me to be an instructor in one of their institutions. But I believe most secular schools would. Or I could use my skills as a medical practitioner. And I'm trained as a structural engineer. If jobs in those professions aren't available, I'd do anything, labor as a farm hand, work as a store clerk or a janitor, dig ditches just to be a family with you.

It will grieve me deeply if you refuse my proposal again, meu amor. But if you turn me down once more, then you're right. You need a fictitious husband and a reason he wasn't in your life while you lived here in Sage Prairie. Your spouse will need a name. Though it will be a small consolation, I like the idea of the fictitious identity of our bebê's father having a connection to me. How about Rollão or perhaps Rollado? Rollão is part of my mother's maiden name.

No matter what you decide, I will send money to support you and our child. I miss you and wish I could be there to share the burden.

You asked about Etta and the Krofts and what they know about your situation. They're aware of what I had printed in the newspaper, that you're in Helena for medical attention. They may wonder what has caused your medical issues, but they've been too polite to ask.

You and our bebê are in my heart and my prayers.

Martim

He wouldn't tell her about the gossip and the innuendos. Her burden was already too great. He got up and poured himself the last of the coffee, now burnt and bitter. The escaped grounds swirled as he stirred in cream. All this subterfuge would be unnecessary if Henri agreed to marry him. His heart told him God intended them to be together.

Chapter Twenty-One

Late afternoon, January 18th, 1928
The Crittenton Home
Henrietta

Henri sat in the dim lamplight at Mrs. Cullum's desk. The drapes were closed to keep the heat in and the cold out. Shadows flickered across the room as the fire blazed in the hearth. Henri gripped the telephone handset, grateful the director allowed the ladies to make long-distance calls if they paid for them. And Mrs. Cullum gave them their privacy for their conversations. Still, Henri whispered when someone picked up on the other end. "Greta, is that you?"

There was a gasp. "Henri, it's you. Did the baby come?"

"Not yet. But soon. I've had contractions off and on for days now. The doctor said it'll be sometime this week."

"So why the call?"

"I need someone to talk to."

"You know I'm always here."

Henri paused, squirming to move the baby off her bladder. "Martim offered to leave the priesthood and marry me."

Greta gasped. "Oh my gosh. Will you accept?"

"I'm so mixed up, Greta. Part of me wants to marry him. Another part tells me it's completely wrong."

"Why? I thought you loved him."

"I do. But then I think of the people who need and admire him. If he left the priesthood, how many of them would despise him instead? I couldn't bear for that to happen."

"Did you tell him that?"

"I did. But he says it doesn't matter. He said he'd despise himself if he didn't do what was right."

"If that's how he feels, why haven't you said yes?"

Henri bit her lip. "I think it's selfish to ask him to leave something he loves doing so much. Something he's so good at it. People depend on him for all his talents. Besides, his leaving the priesthood for me would expose us to gossip and all kinds of disgrace. And how do I know he wouldn't end up resenting me?"

"Does he know what you're thinking?"

"Of course, but he has his arguments," she said, staring at the words in Martim's letter. "He's convinced there are many ways to serve others if he isn't a priest. Though he wouldn't be able to heal souls, he says he could heal bodies. It's true. But he helps so many people spiritually. If he renounced his vows, would people consider his past guidance invalid? And wouldn't they question whether it was right for him to break a sacred vow?"

"Well, he did break a vow."

"That's not the same as permanently giving up on a promise. It's complicated, Greta. I finally found a man I can love. I can't be the reason he stops doing the things I admire about him."

"That is a dilemma, Henri. And I don't have an answer. You're the one who has to decide."

"You're right. It just seems life would be less complicated if I faked a marriage."

"A fake marriage, Henrietta? For God's sake, that seems complicated to me."

"Maybe. But if I do it right, it'll minimize the scandal, maybe even avoid one." She paused, her fingers rolling the corner of Martim's letter. "The truth is, I've already decided. I'm creating a fictitious husband, Jack Rollado. He'll be a traveling salesman, a job that gives a perfectly logical reason he's never around."

"How in God's name do you fake a husband?"

Henri's heart raced. Should she ask? Yes, she had to at least try. The baby depended on it. And so did Martim. She braced herself and said, "I need a favor—a big one to make it easier."

"Like what?"

A contraction squeezed her abdomen and took her breath away. When the pain subsided and her lungs worked again, she said, "I need a marriage certificate, Greta."

"Where on Earth will you get a marriage certificate?" Greta's voice hinted of suspicion.

The room had become extra warm. Moisture oozed across her forehead, in her underarms, and soaked her body. "Martim says he confessed to Father Cornelius, and Cornelius seems to understand. Do you think he'd fill out a Church document for me? One that has me married to Jack Rollado?"

Silence followed.

Finally, Greta said, "Henri, that's asking a lot."

"I know. But it's the best way to protect my baby and Martim."

A long sigh came over the phone. "Henri, you and Martim have a huge predicament. Both Father Cornelius and I understand what's happened. And we don't judge. So, I'll ask him. If he agrees, I'll send it as soon as I can."

A knock rapped on the door. Mrs. Cullum peeked in and pointed at the grandfather clock ticking beside a wall of bookshelves.

"I have to go, Greta. The Home's director just signaled my time is up."

"I'll do my best to convince Cornelius. If he agrees, I'll send the certificate right away. It'll take about a week to arrive. Hopefully, it comes before the baby. I love you, Henri."

"I love you too, Greta." She put the handset back on the hook and breathed a sigh of relief.

On her way out of the office, Henri stopped to toss Martim's letter in the fire. As she watched it burn, Mrs. Cullum came beside her and squeezed her shoulder. Another contraction ripped through Henri. Water soaked her stockings and puddled on the floor.

The Director rushed to her desk, picked up the phone, and asked the operator to ring the doctor. Minutes later, she nodded with a deep frown. "I see."

Henri moaned as she doubled over, feeling as if she were being split in two. Mrs. Cullum hung up the phone, hurried to Henri, and led her to the door. "The doctor and our usual mid-wife are both out on other calls. Your baby has to be delivered in the hospital."

Chapter Twenty-Two

Thursday, January 19, 1928–7:30 a.m.
St. John's Hospital, Helena, Montana
Henrietta

In the dim light of early morning, a strange haze fogged Henri's brain. She lay in the hospital ward studying her beautiful baby girl, born sometime yesterday evening. At least that's what the nurse told her. Henri remembered nothing of the labor or the delivery, only that the doctor had injected her with a drug called Twilight Sleep when her contractions were five minutes apart. She had no memory after that. Except for those few moments in Mrs. Cullum's office, it was as if she'd never experienced hard labor or the pains of birth.

The doctor had told her Twilight Sleep was a miracle drug and that it would relax her uterus so he wouldn't have to use forceps. Interesting. She felt as light and as carefree as the doctor had promised. He told her she'd have this sensation for a day or two. Shaking her head to clear her thoughts, she noticed bruises around her wrists. Strange. She'd have to ask the nurse what happened. Had she told the nurse her baby's name was Angelica Greta? A wonderful name Martim had suggested, after his sister and her own.

Henri traced her finger over Angelica's perfect mouth, a miniature of Martim's. The hint of a widow's peak in the baby's fine blond hairline came from her father as well. She kissed her daughter's forehead, inhaling her sweet baby smell. She couldn't believe she held a life that had begun with the love she shared with Martim. Their little angel slept, her breath like a whisper of joy.

The squeak of wheels echoed down the hall. A nurse wheeled a gurney into the ward. Henri smiled. Another new mother and her baby. The nurse looked like she'd arrived from heaven in her starched white uniform and her veil fluttering around her face. All she needed was wings.

Uneasy thoughts broke through Henri's euphoria when the new mother moaned. Oh my! They tied her wrists to the side rails, and she's thrashing about, trying to get loose. She lifted her hands and stared at the bruises on her wrists. Was I tied to the bed, too? Did I try to break free? Angelica stirred in her arms, snuggling against her breasts. Her worry floated away.

The nurse leaned over the new mother on the gurney and stroked her hair. "Shh, it's okay. Everything is fine. You have a beautiful baby boy. We'll bring him to you in a few hours." The nurse wheeled the woman into a cubicle next to Henri's, closed the curtain separating the beds, and came around to Henri. She smiled. "It's time your little darling went back to the nursery, Henrietta. You need to rest." She scooped Angelica out of Henri's arms and said, "When we bring her back, we'll help you start nursing the baby."

Reality burst through Henri's fog. Her throat tightened as the nurse whisked her baby away. Nurse her baby? She'd already decided she couldn't nurse. She had to return to Sage Prairie and put rumors to rest as soon as possible. It would break her heart to leave Angelica at the Home. But she had to, at least for a while. The Home would take good care of her. She had to figure out how to spread the news about this fake husband. And give herself time to set up a life away from Martim. And away from her parents. The haze oozed back in. She drifted into sleep.

A voice broke through a troubled dream as a hand gently shook her shoulder. "Henrietta?" Her eyes opened to the nurse standing above her. A short, balding man with gold-rimmed glasses stood beside the nurse, his hand resting on a shiny typewriter parked on a rolling cart.

The nurse smiled at Henri, her eyes full of sympathy. "The registrar from the State's Bureau of Vital Statistics is here to record your baby's birth." She turned to the registrar. "Mr. James, this is Henrietta Hoffmann."

The registrar eyed Henri, his thin lips pressed in disapproval. "That's Miss Hoffmann, I presume." The word 'Miss' sneered across his lips. "You're from the Crittenton Home, aren't you?" he said and rolled a form into the typewriter.

The contempt in his voice removed the last of her twilight fog. The way he had said 'Miss' had been especially insulting. She sat up, propped a pillow behind her, and glared. "I am, Mr. James. So let's just get on with the registration." The words snapped off her tongue.

"The Baby's name?" His voice dripped with condescension.

"Angelica Greta."

"And the child has no last name?" he said, his fingers tapping away.

"She has a last name. It's Rollado. Her father is Jack Rollado."

The registrar looked up from his typing. Surprise mingled with the disdain on his face. "Is this alleged Jack Rollado here to declare the child as his?"

Her voice turned to steel. "He couldn't be here." Oh God, why hadn't she asked Greta and Father Cornelius for the marriage certificate sooner? But even if the document had come, this obscene man would've been suspicious. After all, she was from the Crittenton Home.

"Couldn't be here? How convenient, Miss Hoffmann. But the law is straightforward with this type of birth. I'm not allowed to place a father's name on the birth certificate unless he comes to declare himself. Will he be showing up anytime soon?"

She sat erect and met the registrar's eyes with an icy glare. "No. He's a traveling salesman, and circumstances don't allow him to be here. But I assure you; he loves our child as much as I do."

"Again, how convenient," the registrar muttered and tabbed the typewriter carriage to the next space. "Legitimate?" Without waiting for her to answer, he smirked, "No," and then pounded the two letters onto the form. He moved the carriage to a new line and continued. "Since there is no father of record, we leave this section blank," he said and tabbed to the middle of the page.

She didn't have proof. Not until she got a marriage certificate. Still, she'd try. A hiss steamed across Henri's lips. "She has a father."

"Regardless, the space for the father's name remains blank. Your residence, Miss Hoffmann?" His words were so smug, Henri wanted to rip the form from the typewriter and shred it to pieces. Instead, she snarled, "Sage Prairie, Montana." As her rage grew, she vowed to do everything possible to make sure her daughter's birth certificate never saw the light of day. If only the doctor who ordinarily delivered the Crittenton babies in the Home's clinic hadn't been away on another call, she wouldn't be here answering this wretched man. She'd be safe with those who understood. Or if a mid-wife had been available when her water broke. That would have been fine, too. The law didn't require midwives to register babies.

"Miss Hoffmann, I've asked your age twice now."

She wanted to say, none of your business. "Twenty-one."

The registrar studied her. "I'm presuming the child is white. Unless of course the father is a colored man."

"He is not."

He tapped away. "Your birthplace?"

"White Water, Wisconsin."

"Occupation?"

She couldn't say, 'housekeeper'. The churlish man would ask who she kept house for. She snapped, "Stenographer."

He peered at her over the rim of his glasses. "Very interesting. Sage Prairie doesn't seem to be a place that would have much need for stenographers."

Henri responded with a hostile glare.

The man shrugged. "Okay. My last question. How many children have been born to you, dead or alive, including the present birth?"

"One."

The man stood. "That is all, Miss Hoffmann. We'll get this information into the official record. If you ever need a copy of your daughter's birth certificate, contact the Montana State Bureau of Vital Statistics."

Mimi Parker came in as the registrar wheeled his typewriter out of the ward. She stood by Henri's bed, her eyes filled with sympathy. "If you'd given birth at the Home, this nasty process would have been avoided."

The tears Henri had been holding back brimmed in her eyes. She swallowed the bite in her throat. "He wouldn't list Jack Rollado as Angelica's father."

"I heard." Mimi took a deep breath. "I saw most of that exchange, Henri. I'm glad you stood your ground and didn't let him walk all over you. But don't worry. When she's baptized, they can list Jack Rollado as her father, and you can substitute a birth certificate with a baptismal document for almost everything." She grinned. "I've already arranged for her baptism at the Cathedral next Sunday."

As Henri let her guard down, tears poured down her cheeks. "Could you send Father Ferrera a telegram for me and sign it from you? Tell him, 'God's miracle happened Thursday evening.' He knows the baby's father and will pass on the news."

A knowing look appeared in Mimi's eyes. She leaned in and whispered. "Tell me truthfully, Henrietta. Is Father Ferrera the baby's father?"

Henri gasped. "How did you know?"

"Experience from the many years I've had helping young women in your situation. I see love in your eyes when you talk about him. And Mrs. Cullum introduced him to me when he came to arrange your stay. There was love in his eyes as well." Mimi's sadness gave way to an impish grin. "I'll get the news to Father and sign the telegram from me. One never knows when a telegraph operator might let slip some confidential information."

***

Sunday, January 29, 1928

The afternoon sun streamed through St. Helena Cathedral's stained glassed windows, splashing the massive marble columns with color. As Henri journeyed with Mimi to an immense octagonal baptismal font in the center of a grand side aisle, their footsteps echoed through the church. The priest and two other families with their newborns were already gathered at the baptismal font. One mother hummed a hushed lullaby, soothing her colicky baby. The anxious father wrapped his arm around his wife as their little girl hugged his leg with a thumb in her mouth.

Angelica nestled in Henri's arms, her blue-grey eyes exploring the glittering basilica above her. A bit of milk pooled in the corner of the baby's mouth. Henri dabbed it away and smoothed a wrinkle in the lovely gown Greta had crocheted.

Mimi leaned in and whispered, "She looks like an angel."

Henri nodded, a storm brewing in her heart. Soon she'd be leaving her little angel with the staff at the Crittenton home to return to Sage Prairie. As heart wrenching as it was to abandon her baby temporarily, she was convinced it was the best way to stave off gossip. To ease her guilt, she vowed to visit Angelica as often as possible.

The huge wooden entry doors groaned open behind them. Henri turned. Had Martim slipped away to witness his daughter's baptism? She knew he had Sunday services to perform in several of his parishes, so it was next to impossible he would appear. But perhaps he'd found a way. There'd been a Chinook this past week, and all the snow had disappeared. And miracles happened. Her hopes plummeted when another family entered, their entourage heading to the font.

A few minutes later the priest, dressed in white silk vestments elaborately embroidered with gold thread, cleared his throat and said, "I believe all of our families are here." He opened a thick black leather-bound book and began the baptismal rites.

The priest christened the babies one by one until it was Angelica's turn. As Henri handed her infant to Mimi, a now familiar ache flooded through her breasts. She flinched and pressed her arms against them. The pain had camped there since Angelica's birth but had diminished the last few days as her milk began to dry up. But sometimes they still filled enough to warrant the clean hankies she'd stuffed in her bodice to catch the leaks.

The priest turned to Henri and asked, "What name do you give your child?"

"Angelica Greta Rollado." Henri smiled. The name 'Rollado' already felt natural on her tongue.

"What do you ask of God's Church for Angelica?"

"That original sin is washed from her soul, so that she may have eternal life."

"Do you promise to bring her up to follow the teachings of Christ?"

"I do."

"I understand that Angelica's father could not be present. Does he so promise?"

"He does." The intensity in Henri's voice startled Angelica. Her lip quivered, ready to fuss.

Mimi rocked the baby "Shh, shh. You're fine, little angel."

Henri caressed her daughter's cheek. "It's okay, sweet baby. Your father loves you and would be here if he could."

The priest continued with the ceremony. "Mrs. Parker, as proxy you may answer for Angelica's official Godparents. Are they ready to help Angelica's parents raise this child in the tenants of the Catholic Faith?"

Mimi answered with her eyes on Angelica. "They are."

Elation and apprehension mingled in Henri's emotions as the baptismal ritual continued. Guilt took over when the priest sprinkled Angelica with the Holy Water that washed away the Original Sin Adam had brought to all mankind when he disobeyed God. What about the sin she and Martim had committed? Their sin would remain on her birth certificate forever and could never be washed away. She hoped love and careful planning would keep her child's illegitimacy hidden, and that the document would never be seen.

As for her sin? It still stained her soul. Confession might expose Martim. She couldn't risk anyone finding out, not even a priest in the confidentiality of the confessional, unless it was to her cousin Father Cornelius Hoffmann back home in White Water, Wisconsin.

When the ceremony was over, Henri watched the priest sign Angelica's official baptismal certificate, her heart warmed by the sight of Jack Rollado listed as Angelica's father.

Chapter Twenty-Three

February 1, 1928
Havre to Sage Prairie, Montana
Henrietta

Henri held tightly to the rail as she stepped from the train onto an icy platform. She pressed her arms against the ache still lingering in her breasts and searched the throng for the face she longed to see. There he was. Apprehension scrambled with love as she walked towards him. He stood beside a young woman dressed in a loose-fitting coat and a knitted hat, her hands buried in a furry muff. Martim had written an article for the *Sage Prairie Weekly* announcing his new housekeeper would arrive today from Minneapolis and had included a statement about Miss Hoffmann's return to Sage Prairie to train the new housekeeper.

As she struggled to hide her giddiness, she made her way to him, the slushy snow soaking her shoes. Love filled his eyes when he spotted her, but his voice was neutral, as if their only relationship was former employer and employee, priest and parishioner. "Miss Hoffmann, it's good to see you again. This is Caddy Rogers, my new housekeeper."

The young woman extended her hand and smiled shyly. "I appreciate you coming, Miss Hoffman. There's so much to learn."

Henri shook Caddy's hand. "Please call me Henri. I'm glad to help."

She sensed Martim's eyes on her as he picked up her bag. She wanted to hug him, hold him close, and link her arm through his. More than anything, she longed to share Angelica's loveliness, and how much she looked like him. But that would have to wait for later.

"Come ladies," Martim said. "Mrs. Gimbal is waiting in the car."

What a wise move, Henri thought. Mrs. Gimbal never pried, making her the perfect safety net to protect Martim, herself, and maybe even Caddy from gossip.

On the ride to Sage Prairie, Caddy chatted with Henrietta in the back seat. In the front, Martim and Mrs. Gimbal gabbed about the details of the last hunting trip Martim had gone on with Mrs. Gimbal's husband. It was evening by the time they dropped Mrs. Gimbal at her home and then drove to the rectory. After a light supper, Martim formally bid them good night and disappeared to his room in the sacristy.

Henri lay awake in her own bed for the first time in six months, weary from the day's trip and from pretending her relationship with Martim was proper and ordinary. Caddy tossed and turned beside her. Having shared a bed with one sister or another her whole life, Henri was used to restless bedmates, but tonight she was desperate for sleep. For the past two weeks, she'd slept in fits and starts with Angelica beside her. The lack of sleep had been worth the hardship, knowing she might not hold her daughter again for what already seemed like an eternity. She would endure the vast emptiness, for Angelica's sake.

Caddy shifted again, pulling the quilt they shared from Henri's shoulder. A muffled sob shuddered beneath the blankets. Henri opened her eyes and listened. The ticking of the clock punctuated the silence that followed. And then came another soft snivel. Henri rolled and faced Caddy's back. "Caddy, are you alright?"

"I'm sorry, Henri," Caddy said. She turned on her back and stared at the ceiling. "I didn't mean to wake you."

"It's okay. I couldn't sleep either."

Caddy lay motionless, her profile etched in the moonlight seeping through the curtains. Finally, she murmured, "I miss him."

"Miss who?"

Caddy's answer came through a choked sob.

Henri sat up and brought her knees to her chest. Had she heard right? Had Caddy said my baby? "Who was that again?" she asked.

"It doesn't matter, Henri. He's gone now."

"Who's gone?"

"I can't say." Her answer seemed wrung from her heart.

Henri hesitated and took a chance. "Is it a baby you miss? Your baby?"

Caddy nodded, moonlight catching on Caddy's wet cheeks. "I came here to start new, where no one knows about my baby boy except Father Ferrera and my aunt and uncle Rogers."

Henri's eyes widened as she clutched the top of her nightgown. "Where is he?"

Caddy propped herself up on her pillow, her voice shaking through her tears. "He's with some couple back home. They're fostering him. I know nothing about them except my mother said they're from our church. When I gave him up, I had to promise to stay out of his life. It's for the best, but it hurts so much."

Henri's throat tightened as she wrapped an arm around the woman beside her. "I understand how you feel, Caddy. Truth is, I just left my new baby daughter at a home in Helena."

"Holy Mother. You have a baby too?"

"I do. My marriage is a secret. But if people knew about my baby, everyone would assume she's illegitimate. Right now, she's with people who are helping me set up a future where we can live as a family without suspicion."

"You are so blessed, Henri."

"I am." As hard as her situation was, no one had forced her to give up Angelica. It was more than a blessing. It was a miracle. She wanted to ask Caddy about her baby's father but knew it would bring up questions about Angelica's.

The two sat in silence as Caddy's sobs subsided. She wiped her eyes on the cuff of her nightgown. "Thanks for understanding, Henri. It really helps to know someone else suffering with a problem almost like mine." She plumped up her pillow and lay down with a sigh.

Henri squeezed the new housekeeper's hand. "Hang in there, Caddy. I'm here anytime you need to talk."

An hour later, Henri listened to Caddy softly breathing beside her. Though exhausted, Henri couldn't sleep as she laid thinking about Martim. Would he press her again to marry him? Would the time with him in the months ahead, watching how his parishioners needed him, how he loved his work, convince her to change her mind? She doubted it. But maybe it would. If she could banish her misgivings, Angelica would have her father in her life.

She ached to be in Martim's arms and share the details of their little girl. Did she dare slip over to the sacristy? She watched Caddy's body rise and fall as she breathed.

"Caddy? Are you awake?"

The only answer was another soft breath. She got up, slipped into her shoes and coat. As she tiptoed to the bedroom door, she heard the bedsprings creak.

"Henri? Where are you going?"

She jumped and turned to see Caddy sitting up in bed. "Just to the church. I want to light a candle to our Blessed Mother."

"I'll come too," Caddy said and reached for her shoes.

***

Friday, February 3, 1928

The sun had long set by the time Martim's new Buick rumbled up to the rectory. He was back from the Krofts, where he'd dropped off Caddy with a basket of laundry. She would spend the night there. In the morning, Mrs. Kroft would teach her how to use the Kroft's new wringer washing machine, saving her from the tedious task of doing laundry in a big tub the old-fashioned way. Caddy's lesson meant Henri and Martim would have time to themselves.

Henri hurried to the porch and waited as he made his way through the darkness. He took her hand, walked into the light, and closed the door.

"*Meu amor*," he said, enveloping her in his arms. He kissed her forehead, her eyes, her ears, taking the long way to her lips. The familiar tang of the outdoors permeated everything about him. The feel of his body, his breath upon her cheeks, even the stubble on his face filled her with heady intoxication.

His arms slipped away. He stepped back and let out a long breath.

"Martim?" she asked.

He took her hands again. "I want to keep you in my arms forever, Henri. But it's too tempting. It's best to just sit and talk."

She nodded, relieved. "You're right."

He helped her settle in a chair. "Sit and rest, Henri. I'll make us some tea."

She watched him putter around the kitchen, putting the teakettle on to heat, sprinkling chamomile leaves into their cups, and setting a tin of butter cookies on the table. The conflict between her heart and her conscience flared back into her thoughts. The Church taught what she had done was a deadly sin. But how could the love that brought Angelica into this world be so wrong?

The tea ready, Martim sat down and scooped a bit of honey into Henri's cup and then into his own. He held his steaming cup in his hands as he gazed at Henri. "I was desperate to come to Helena, to hold my daughter and let her know I am her *papai*. But it seemed too risky. Births and baptisms are always emotional occasions, especially when it's your child and the woman you love. I worried others would see through my facade, pretending I'm only your pastor and family friend."

She swallowed, fighting the tightness in her throat. "I wanted you there too, Martim, especially for her baptism. But you're right. It was safer you didn't come."

He put his head in his hands, drew a deep breath, and let it go. He looked up, his eyes filled with anguish. "It rips me apart that we have to lie to protect our daughter. We should be shouting our joy to the world. Instead, we're skulking around hiding her existence while we create a mythical husband to make her birth respectable."

The bitterness in his words tore through Henri. "I'm so sorry, Martim. I love you all the more for letting me choose my own path."

"I hope someday I'll be part of that path as your husband and Angelica's father. Until then, it's unfair that most of the burden falls on you."

"I don't like all the pretense either, Martim. Not for a moment." Her voice turned hard. "But it's what I have to do. What I think is best. At least for now."

A smile played on his lips. "You've never outright refused to marry me, Henri. That tells me there's hope."

She couldn't stand the grief in his eyes, so she told him what he wanted to hear. "Maybe things will change and marriage will seem right. Until then, thank you for standing by me."

"If we don't marry, what will you do?"

"I'm working that out." She looked at her hands, picked at her nails, and turned to him again. "I have the marriage document Father Cornelius made for me. It arrived in time to put Jack Rollado on her baptismal certificate. When I find a job to support myself and Angelica, I'll set up life in another town where no one knows anything about me except what I tell them."

"And what will you tell everyone about this Jack Rollado?"

"That he's a traveling salesman. It'll be the reason he's never around."

He ran his hands over his face and through his hair before he looked at her again. "Sounds like you've thought this through. It might take a long time to put your plans in place. Until then, stay here. Caddy can use your help, and I will be grateful for your company."

A lump caught in her throat. "Your help and understanding means so much. You're right. She smiled wistfully. "Angelica is so beautiful, Martim. She resembles you in so many ways. I wanted to bring a photo of her, but the light in the Home isn't right for taking pictures. And outside was too cold for a newborn."

His voice cracked. "I can't wait to meet her."

She reached for a cookie and dipped it in her tea. "It was wise of you to bring Mrs. Gimbal when you picked up Caddy and me," she said, and pushed the cookies towards him.

He held up his hand and shook his head. "I'm not hungry." He shrugged. "They say discretion is the better part of valor. We need to be vigilant. There are rumors. Not widespread, but enough to cause concern."

Her stomach knotted. "Protecting us and our baby from gossip is so exhausting."

He touched her cheek. "I know. We've talked enough for now, *meu amor*. It's time for bed."

She yawned, weary to the bone. "It's been a long six months. And I'm so glad to be home."

"Before I leave for the night, I have something for you." He fished in his pocket, took her hand, and placed a silver band in her palm. "Consider it a promise ring. A promise to marry you if that's what you decide. Or a promise to honor your decision if you choose to be married to the elusive Jack Rollado."

She studied the ring. Subtle coiling tendrils etched around the band in interlocking loops. "It's beautiful, Martim." The words barely escaped the tightness in her throat.

"It was my grandmother's. There's an engraving on the inside."

She held the ring to the light. Her eyes misted as she read, "Faith, Hope, Love."

He took the ring and slipped it on her finger. "Faith, hope, love: the way we must live our lives despite the difficulties we face. Regardless of whether you marry me, Henrietta Marie Hoffmann, you and Angelica will always be my family."

Chapter Twenty-Four

February 4, 1928
Sage Prairie
Henrietta

Late Saturday afternoon, Henri plodded through the slush to Our Lady of the Prairie Church. She lit a votive candle and knelt beneath the statue of the Blessed Mother, squirming from the soreness that lingered from Angelica's birth. Decisions had to be made, and prayer might bring some answers. She pulled out her rosary.

A whispered "Henri" startled her.

Henri put a hand to her cheek and gasped. "Etta. It's you." The two fell into a hug. Henri murmured, "I wasn't expecting you."

Etta nodded. "Pa brought Caddy and the laundry back. I just couldn't wait to see you. It's been so long. Let's talk." She took Henri's hand and led her to the nearest pew. "I heard you were in the hospital, Henri. I worried, especially when you didn't write."

Henri sat in silence, not sure how to explain. "I'm sorry, Etta, truly sorry."

Etta's eyes bored into Henri's. "I heard gossip you were in a family way. But I don't believe it."

Henri's fear made it almost impossible to breathe. She whispered, "What they said is true, Etta. I do have a baby." She hesitated. Should she tell Etta the whole truth? Not yet. Maybe when they got to know each other better. She swallowed her guilt and started the story she'd prepared. "No one here knows I'm married except Father Ferrera." She pulled out the ring Martim had given her the night before, now hanging around her neck on a black silk ribbon.

Etta stared at the ring in disbelief, and then at Henri. "Oh, my gosh. What's his name? When did it happen?"

Henri bit her lip, her head spinning with the lies developing in her thoughts. They almost caught on her tongue but slipped out when she thought of Angelica. "He's Jack Rollado, a traveling salesman. About a year and a half ago, he walked into the printing business in Glade Harbor where I worked. He introduced himself and asked to see the owner so he could have some small posters printed promoting the sugar he sells." She absently rolled her rosary beads between her fingers as she figured out a way to make it all believable.

Etta's eyes were full of questions. Ignoring the shame for deceiving her friend, Henri continued. "We were attracted to each other instantly. Jack was everything I wanted in a man, kind, intelligent, with a wonderful sense of humor. He felt the same about me. He stayed in the Glade Harbor area for a few months as he worked his sales route. In the evenings, we spent our free time together. I never thought people could fall in love so quickly."

"You must have been head over heels." Etta said, entranced.

"We were." Henri's story now unfolded more easily. "A couple months after we met, Jack and I drove to Minneapolis and got married by a Justice of the Peace."

"A Justice of the Peace? He isn't Catholic?"

Henri's mind whirled as she planned the next part of her story. "Oh, he is. But the Church wouldn't marry us because he's divorced. His first wife ran off with another man. You know, because he was away on his sales route so often. He had to return to his job a few days after we married, but it didn't matter. The times we had together made up for all the times we were apart." Henri smiled, her fable now feeling almost real. "Anyway, I accepted the job with Father Ferrera to get away from prying eyes. Jack was back in Glade Harbor a week before I boarded the train to Sage Prairie." She looked down, her conscience pricking at her. "I'd been in Sage Prairie a month when I realized I was pregnant."

"That's so romantic, Henri. You should just tell people. That would end all the gossip."

She swallowed. Her story had a glitch. "I can't, Etta. Not even my family knows about Jack. Except for my sister Greta and my cousin Father Cornelius."

Etta's face flushed with confusion. "Why not? It can't be because a Justice of the Peace married you. His wife left him. He can get an annulment. Then you could marry in the Church, and everything would be hunky-dory."

Henri felt heat rush up her neck and flood her cheeks. Her mind raced, testing one idea after another. It landed on something she'd read in the weekly paper about a new sanitarium in Galen. She took a breath and plunged in, her tongue tripping over her lies. "There's another reason. Jack's dad and his sister are in a tuberculosis sanitarium. He doesn't have it, but that won't matter to my folks. It's so contagious, they'll be deathly afraid one of us could catch it and pass it on to someone in my family."

Etta's eyes widened. "That's a tough one, Henri. But still..." She shrugged. "There are ways to keep safe."

Henri bit her lip, groaning inwardly. What would it take to satisfy Etta's curiosity? She had to make the risk of discovery more serious. Martim had told her of the possibility of real danger stemming from his life in Portugal. It would be easy to elaborate on it; make it seem more menacing. She patted Etta's hand. "I promised Jack I'd tell no one, but I trust you, Etta. I know you'll keep it a secret. It's hard to explain."

"At least try," Etta said, her eyes wrinkled with worry. "You can trust me, Henri. I'd never share with anyone, not even my parents."

Henri took a deep breath and plunged in. "Jack was part of a failed attempt to restore Portugal's King to his throne. The revolutionaries assassinated the King and captured many of the King's supporters, including Jack. He escaped, but the revolutionaries now in power could still be searching for him. If they find him, they might kill him, and maybe even me and our baby." Shame flooded through her. What was she doing? Twisted truths were actually lies, and the lies were piling up.

Etta put her arm around Henri and pulled her close. "Such a beautiful story. But sad and frightening at the same time. Does Father Ferrera know about Jack?"

"He does, and he's very understanding."

Etta straightened with a puzzled look. "So where is your baby?"

Finally, she could tell the truth. "Friends in Helena are caring for her right now.

"A girl! You have a little girl." Etta's eyes bubbled with excitement. "Tell me about her."

Chapter Twenty-five

Six months later - August 1928
White Water, Wisconsin.
Henrietta

Henri rode in Father Cornelius's car in the back seat feeling more relaxed than she'd been in a long time. Cornelius and Greta had picked her up at the Minneapolis train station hours ago. As they drove to the family home in White Water, Henri filled her sister and her cousin in on all that had happened these last few months. It felt wonderful to speak openly to people who knew the truth about her daughter and Martim.

Greta studied Henri's photos of Angelica. "Corn, take a peek at our beautiful goddaughter. I'd love to snuggle with her and kiss those chubby cheeks."

Father Cornelius glanced at the pictures and grinned. "I'm not an expert on babies, but she looks a lot like her father."

Henri smiled; feeling a rush of love she never knew existed until Angelica was born. "She definitely resembles Martim, so much more than me, though her hair is lighter and less curly." A twist tore through her heart. She wished her little girl could be with her now; to show her off to the family, let her begin a relationship with her grandparents, her aunts and uncles and cousins. It had been extra hard leaving her at the Crittenton Home.

She'd debated for months whether it was better to show up with her baby, let the shock sink in, and then spin the tale of her marriage, or break the news of her fantasy husband before telling them about Angelica. Either way, there'd be fireworks and lots of them. The news would upset *Moeder*. But a granddaughter in her arms would instantly melt her heart. What she couldn't face was *Vader*'s fury or his coldness. Worse, his anger would hold him back from Angelica, not wanting to fall in love with her. It was best to tell him about the pretend marriage first. Once he knew about Jack Rollado, she'd send pictures and news of Angelica as often as possible. Eventually *Vader* would get used to the idea. In a year or two, she'd return to White Water with her little girl, and *Vader* would meet his new granddaughter. Like the wonderful grandfather he was, his heart would open to her.

As they headed up a long hill, Father Cornelius glanced back at Henri. "When Martim visited me in June, we talked about your situation. Are you sure your friend Etta won't tell anyone about Angelica and your supposed marriage?"

"I'm positive, Corn. I trust her completely, but I feel terrible not telling her the truth."

Greta handed the photos back to Henri. "When do you plan to tell *Vader* and *Moeder* and the family?"

Henri's chest tightened. "There will definitely be an uproar whenever they find out. If I tell them right away, I'll be wretched the whole time I'm home. *Vader* will be especially difficult. He'll want to know why I kept my marriage and Angelica secret. I haven't figured out how to answer those questions."

"That's a tough one. You probably should wait until just before you leave to go back to Sage Prairie."

"That's my plan, unless the perfect time shows up earlier. I'm worried *Moeder* and *Vader* will figure something's up before I spill the news. Somehow they always seem to ferret out the truth no matter how well it's hidden."

"They have other things on their minds right now. Remember I wrote you about little Joey Jameson, the baby *Moeder* and *Vader* are fostering? He's a big distraction, especially for *Moeder*." Greta grew somber as she stared out the window. "His mother is unwed, and she couldn't conjure up a pseudo-marriage like yours."

"A baby in *Moeder* arms will sidetrack her. But *Vader* is another story. And when he gets past his anger, he and *Moeder* will want to meet Jack. How in the world am I supposed to make that happen?"

"You'll have to make up excuses along the way. But it'll be easier since you made him a traveling salesman." She turned and faced Henri. "I've been wondering. How do you plan to support yourself and Angelica since this husband of yours is non-existent?"

"Martim is helping."

Greta nodded. "You're lucky. He's a blessing most unwed mothers don't have."

"I know, Greta. But I can't count on that blessing forever. I'll find someone to care for Angelica and get a job as a stenographer. It won't pay much, but it'll help, so I don't have to depend completely on Martim. Collection plate money should go for his churches and his own living expenses, not for his secret family." The last two words tasted bitter on her tongue.

Greta met Henri's eyes. "If you accepted Martim's proposal, it wouldn't have to be a secret family."

Before Henri could answer, Father Cornelius spoke up. "Leaving the priesthood is possible, but very problematic. But if your love is strong enough to face tough issues, marriage might be worth considering."

Henri bit her lip. "As much as I love him, it's the harsh consequences I can't bear to impose on Martim or on Angelica."

Father Cornelius shifted into lower gear as they approached a hill. "That's noble of you, Henrietta. But when Martim visited in June, he told me he loves you enough to deal with any repercussion."

Henri scowled. "Maybe he could handle it. But I can't bear the thought of him facing the fallout. I detest the thought of taking him from the people he serves. It would devastate many of them to lose his gifts as a priest, his medical expertise, and his talents as a leader."

Greta spoke up. "Sounds as if you're carrying a load of guilt, Henri."

Henri swallowed the bile burning her throat. "The bible says there is a time and a season for every purpose under heaven. I've prayed and prayed. Maybe there'll come a time when it's right to marry Martim." Tears welled in her eyes. "My heart tells me this isn't the time for that to happen."

Greta interrupted. "You know if you announce a fake marriage now, there may be no turning back."

"If I become convinced marrying him is the best path, I'll find a way. Until then, I can't ask him to abandon his vows."

Greta snorted. "You've always been gutsy and independent and had your own way of thinking. I can't help but feel you're being too hardheaded about this."

Henri straightened, her fingers tapping her leg. "I prefer to think of myself as pragmatic, Greta. Right now, a pretend marriage is the best option, for him, for me, and especially for our baby."

The two sisters and their cousin rode deep in their own thoughts until the Ford turned into the long driveway to the Hoffmann farmhouse. The cows in the pasture looked up with wads of grass dangling from their mouths, their tails chasing away the flies. Henri's brother Fritz, on leave from the Navy, stood atop a horse-drawn wagon full of hay. Cornelius honked the horn. Fritz waved and urged the horses faster to the barn.

As they approached the family home, Henri saw *Moeder* slip on to the porch holding her foster baby. *Vader* came out and stood beside her. Then the entire family flooded out the door. Sister Anna Marie in her black habit, Callie, little brother James, Julia and Marta with their husbands and little ones. Her heart danced seeing everyone waiting for her.

As Henri climbed from the Ford, little Lillie escaped her father's arms and raced towards her. "*Tante* Henrietta, I tot you never come." Henri scooped her in her arms and covered her with kisses. Tears threatened as the sweet scent of Lillie stirred a longing for Angelica. Lillie's tiny hands turned Henri's face to her own. Her eyes sparkled as she said, "I have a widdle bruder, and *Oma* has baby Joey, too. Come on," she said, hopping down and pulling Henri to the waiting crowd.

The family surrounded Henri with hugs, and then Lillie tugged her to the backyard where a picnic supper was spread out under the apple trees. Henri led the line past a table full of food and filled her plate with favorites; fricasseed chicken, potato salad, corn on the cob, and fresh green beans. The welcome would have been different had she shown up with Angelica.

***

As the trees sent long shadows dappling across the grass, Henri sat on a wooden lawn chair, holding baby Joey, hushing him as he fussed. It was strange. Little Joey kindled loneliness for Angelica and eased it at the same time.

Vader came and sat on the empty chair beside her. She watched him fill his pipe, aware he had something on his mind. "You've gained weight, *dochter*," he said, his accent was as strong as ever. Henri held her breath, waiting for what he would say next. He lit the pipe, took a puff, and blew it out in rings. Turning, he studied her face, his steely blue eyes penetrating to her soul. "You're cooking must be good. Has *Vader* Ferrera gained so much weight like you?"

Henri managed a laugh. "No. His parishes keep him too busy. He could eat like a horse and never gain a pound."

"Humph. So all this weight is left for you. This is good. Men like a woman with a matronly figure. Have you found a man yet, a rancher, a farmer? Someone who is looking for a good cook? A man who can provide for a family?" He nodded at little Joey. "Someone to have babies with?"

Henri struggled to stay calm as *Vader* sat back and enjoyed his pipe, waiting for her answer. She placed the baby on her shoulder and began patting his back. Was now the time to tell him about Jack Rollado and Angelica? She opened her mouth to respond but couldn't bear the thought of causing a scene with her family enjoying each other's company. And she wasn't ready with answers to the questions they'd throw at her.

Before she could figure how to respond, five-year-old Roger bounced up and rested his elbows on his *opa's* knees. Roger looked at him with admiration and said, "*Opa*, make your pipe do circles again."

Vader tousled his grandson's hair, blew a few more rings, and said, "Come Roger, I will show you our new calf."

As he took Roger's hand, Lillie raced up, grabbed *Vader*'s other hand, and giggled. "Me too, *Opa*." *Vader* grinned down at her and tousled her hair.

He was a stern *Vader*, but a dotting *Opa*. She hoped someday he would look at Angelica with those same adoring eyes.

As the three ambled to the barn, Marta took the seat beside Henri. She bounced little Gerald on her knee and smiled. "Look at you, Henrietta, so good with Joey. You'll make a wonderful mother. Hopefully, you'll find the right man soon."

Not Marta, too. The tightness was back in Henri's throat. She faked a smile and tried to keep her voice light. "For now, I'm happy to practice with my nieces and nephews and with this little guy."

Wasps filled the silence, buzzing around the bruised apples on the ground. Marta said, "I know you felt Ike was too fawning, but whatever happened with Leon? *Moeder* and *Vader* approved of him. He seemed ideal, and I know he proposed."

Knots snarled in Henri's stomach. She scowled. "He was like so many other men, Marta, eager to tell me what to do and when to do it. He has a mediocre mind and thinks he's an expert at everything. That's not my idea of an ideal man. I want someone who treats me as an equal."

Marta shook her head and frowned. "Goodness, Henrietta, even Callie will marry soon, and she's younger than you. Your problem is, you're too picky. Is it ideal to keep house for someone else, or do you want a home of your own?"

Heat rose in Henri's cheeks. "I don't need a man to have my own home."

Suddenly, Greta stood beside her sisters. "There's nothing wrong with keeping house for someone, Marta. I'm happy working for Father Cornelius. I have companionship, respectability, a salary, and more freedom than if I married. Besides, marriage isn't for everyone. Look at Anna. She's found the perfect life as Sister Anna Marie."

"True, Greta," Marta said with a hint of sadness in her voice. "But I always thought you and Henrietta wanted children of your own."

"Like Henrietta, I'm satisfied with my nieces and nephews and little Joey here," Greta said, lifting Joey from Henri's arms and kissing him. "He may be a foster child, but I'm sure he'll be with us forever. At least I hope so."

"I hope so too," Marta said. "I feel bad for the poor woman who had to give him up. But it was probably for the best."

Anger ripped through Henri. For the best? Marta didn't know what she was talking about. To keep from lashing out, she stiffened and said, "Joey needs a diaper change, Greta, and I'll be glad to do it." She gathered up the baby and headed towards the house, hoping to escape.

A moment later, Marta hurried up beside her. "Gerald needs a change, too. I'll come with you and show you where Joey's diapers are."

Biting her lip, she followed Marta to her parents' bedroom, where *Moeder* had set up a nursery in the corner. The sisters lay the babies on the double bed *Vader* had built when the Hoffmann family first arrived from Holland twenty-six years ago. A bed where she and her younger siblings had been conceived. A bed that was a private sanctuary for her parents. The kind of bed she would never have with Martim night after night for all of their lives. As she fought her bitterness, she unpinned Joey's diaper.

Marta interrupted her thoughts. "I didn't mean to upset you, Henrietta. I know Greta enjoys working as Corn's housekeeper. But I wonder. Are you satisfied keeping house for Father Ferrera?"

Though Caddy Rogers was now Martim's official housekeeper, Henri had stayed on as her mentor for much longer than she'd planned. For once, she could answer truthfully. "Father is a good employer. He's highly respected and admired by the people he serves. For me, it's a wonderful adventure, seeing new places, getting away from home and out from under *Vader* and *Moeder*'s watchful eyes. I've become my own person."

"I used to feel stifled by our parents, too," Marta responded. "But now that I have children of my own, I appreciate them differently." Marta took a moment to smother Gerald with kisses until he squealed with laughter. As she began removing his diaper, she prattled on. "Henrietta, I always envisioned you being something other than a domestic. Perhaps one of those modern women who has a career and a family."

"I don't plan on being Father Ferrera's housekeeper forever, Marta. In a few months, I intend to enroll in a commercial college in Great Falls to extend the training I got at the Vocational School in Glade Harbor. If there's a way to be a professional woman and a mother, I will find it." She grabbed the baby powder and shook an overabundance over Joey's diaper area.

Marta pinned Gerald's clean diaper and pulled his gown over his chubby legs. "That's a hard path, Henrietta, and very unconventional, even in this day and age. For your plan to work, you have to find a man who'd allow his wife to work outside the home."

"There are ways to make it happen, Marta," she said, thinking she had already started down that path.

Marta put an arm around her sister and pulled her to her side. "You're right, Henrietta. If anyone can do it, it's definitely you."

Moeder appeared in the doorway. "Ah, Henrietta. You're the one who has stolen my little guy," she said, her accent as thick as *Vader*'s. She took Joey and kissed him. "He's lucky to have so many mamas in his life."

***

The scent of drying hay filtered through the window of Henri's childhood bedroom. She folded her Sunday dress and smoothed it into her suitcase, hoping to keep it from getting too wrinkled. She'd be leaving to return to Sage Prairie right after lunch. For three weeks, she'd doted on her nieces and nephews, enjoyed family get-togethers and outings at the lake with her old friends.

Now time was up. The pseudo marriage and the baby she'd been hiding ate at her insides. She had to break the news before she left for the train. Every moment of every day since she'd arrived, she'd tried to convince herself it would be best to spin her tale in a letter when she got back to Sage Prairie and save herself the confrontation. But as hard as it would be, *Vader* would respect her for telling him face to face. He always said it was cowardly to share difficult news in a letter unless there were no other options.

She set her luggage by the front door and wandered to the kitchen, her stomach a mess as she plotted the best way to begin. She found him sitting at the table reading his weekly Dutch paper, smoking his pipe. *Moeder* fussed over the sausage and pea soup she was making for lunch.

As Henri bustled around slicing bread and setting the table, she kept an eye on *Vader*, trying to gage his mood. The tightness in her jaw loosened when Greta and Father Cornelius walked in. They'd both agreed to be here to give her support when she set off the bombshell.

Vader was enjoying a second bowl of soup when he frowned at Henri. "*Dochter*, you are not eating."

She forced a smile. "I'm not hungry."

One bushy brow rose. "Seems like you have something on your mind, Henrietta."

Henri glanced at Greta. Her sister nodded encouragement. Henri put her napkin down and braced herself. "I do, *Vader*. It's something I've needed to tell you and *Moeder* for a while." She pulled her arms to her side to curb the sweat pooling under her arms. "I have news that's difficult to share." She avoided *Vader*'s eyes and turned to *Moeder*. The words pushed past the tightness in her throat. "I'm married."

Moeder gasped, clutching the front of her dress. *Vader* bolted up. His fists pounded the table, rattling the dishes, sloshing the tea from Henri's cup. She watched his face flush deep red. He shouted, "*Getrowd*?"

Greta sucked in her breath. Cornelius put a gentle hand on *Moeder*'s arm. Henri inched her chair from the table. She refused to look away from the fury in *Vader*'s eyes. "Yes, *Vader*. *Getrowd*. I am married. Isn't that what you always wanted?"

"Not this way. Not hiding it like some kind of dirty secret." His face grew darker. "What kind of man is he you never bring him to meet your *moeder* and me?"

She'd rehearsed her answer over and over. Still, the words were hard to shake loose. "He's Jack Rollado, a wonderful man."

"Wonderful isn't skulking around like a man with no honor, never asking permission to marry my *dochter*."

She almost blurted he was the most honorable man she'd ever known. But then she'd have to explain why.

"What else have you to say for yourself?" *Vader* impatiently motioned for more details, his scowl growing deeper.

Greta reached under the table and took Henri's hand, giving her the strength to go on. "We married last year, January tenth in Minneapolis."

Moeder's eyes filled with tears. "For heaven's sake, Henrietta, why didn't you tell us?"

"You wouldn't have approved."

Vader's face grew redder. "Not approved?"

"We were married by a Justice of the Peace."

His glare intensified. "Not in the Church? What about your faith?"

Blood pounded in her temples. Don't back down now, she told herself. She swallowed and went on. "He's a Catholic and very devout. But he's divorced. You know that means the Church wouldn't marry us." The lies mixed with partial truths were piling up, but it had to be done.

"For good reason," *Vader* spat. "Marriage is supposed to be until death do you part."

"I know, *Vader*. But his wife disappeared with another man. He wants to do the honorable thing: find her and get an annulment. Then we can marry in the Church."

Vader snorted. "If this Jack Rollado is so honorable, why isn't he here with you?"

"He wanted to come. He really did. But he's a traveling salesman for a sugar company. His route at this moment is in New England. He couldn't get away."

Moeder's face stewed with confusion. "So you still work for Father Ferrera? You don't live with the man you married?"

"It's not uncommon for traveling salesmen and their wives to live apart. Right now, we can't afford to set up our own household. Until then, I'll work at Our Lady of the Prairie's rectory. Father Ferrera understands."

Moeder's face relaxed. "Father knows about the marriage?"

"He does, but no one else except Greta, Cornelius, and a good friend of mine back in Sage Prairie. And now you." She pulled the ring hidden on a ribbon from around her neck and handed it to *Moeder*. "My wedding band."

Moeder inspected the ring. "Faith, Hope, Love. Such wonderful qualities to bring to marriage."

Vader stood with his hands gripping the back of his chair. "Faith? What about having faith in us, *Dochter,* faith to understand? You finally find a man who suits you, but you keep him secret? It is no way to start a good marriage. Better to be open and honest." Disappointment mingled with the anger in *Vader*'s voice.

Moeder handed the ring back to Henrietta. "When will we meet this Jack Rollado? So we see what kind of man has captured your heart?"

The glitch that worried her. How would she stall a meeting forever? "I don't know, but we'll do our best. It depends on his sales route and if he can get time away."

Vader's face softened. "At least you had the spunk to look me in the eye. For that, I give you credit. Now, get him here so we can meet him."

She swallowed and turned to *Moeder*. "There's one more thing. Jack and I have a baby girl."

Moeder's eyes widened. "A *kleindocter*? We have another kleindocter?"

Henri lifted her chin. "Yes, another granddaughter. Angelica Greta Rollado was born January 18."

A smile lit up *Moeder*'s face. "Angelica. A lovely name."

Henri sighed wistfully, thinking of her daughter. "She was baptized at St. Helena's Cathedral in Montana. Right now, she's with friends in Helena."

Vader sank back into his chair. The hurt in his eyes was harder to bear than his anger. "Why did you not bring her?"

"I couldn't bear the thought of your reaction. I want your anger gone and your heart open the moment you meet her."

"Keeping my *kleindocter* secret? That's harder to forgive than a secret marriage." He turned to Greta, his face now ashen. "You know about this?"

"I do, *Vader*. But it was Henrietta's news to share."

"And you, Cornelius?"

Father Cornelius looked at Henri, sympathy in his eyes. "I did. But a priest never shares what someone confides in confession." He smiled. "Greta and I are Angelica's godparents."

Vader got up and plodded out the door. Henri watched from the window as he stumbled across the pasture, slumped onto an old stump, and put his head in his hands. Smoke spiraled from the pipe still lying on his saucer. The pain of knowing she had deeply hurt her parents was part of her penance for what she had done.

***

Henri stared at the forest of Sugar Maples as her train home rolled through northern Minnesota. She rehashed over and over her conversation with *Moeder* and *Vader* about her marriage and her baby and the hurt her news had caused. Their reaction was what she had expected. She wished there'd been a less painful way. What if she had told them Father Ferrera was Angelica's father and that he was leaving the priesthood to marry her? She imagined their reaction would have been far worse.

Her eyes settled on the document in her hand. The document she'd always carried in her handbag since the day it had arrived in the mail just before Angelica's baptism. There it was, in black and white. She married Jack Rollado one year and eight days before her daughter was born. The document stated Father Cornelius Hoffmann had officiated and Greta had been the witness. It contradicted what she had told her parents about a Justice of the Peace. But so be it. She didn't want to implicate her sister and her cousin any more than she already had. And her parents never needed to see the marriage certificate.

She winced as she slipped the document back in its envelope and tucked it into her handbag. She kept it handy these days, never knowing when she would need it. The sharp ache in her breasts was back. It had first appeared four days ago when she'd been swimming with her friends in White Water Lake. She'd thought the coldness of the water had caused the ache. But there was no coldness now. In fact, the overwhelming heat in the train nauseated her.

Her mind flashed to a night a few weeks before she left for Wisconsin. Her resolve not to sin after Angelica was born had worn away during the months of living so close to Martim. All that time, her conscience had fought with her heart. It had become more and more difficult as her body healed from her pregnancy and the birth. One night when they'd found themselves alone under the stars, passion had taken over. Now she understood the ache in her breasts, her growing nausea, and the bloat she'd felt the last few days. She was pregnant again.

Chapter Twenty-Six

Friday, September 14, 1928
The Road to Sage Prairie
Martim

Martim drove across the prairie towards Sage Prairie, with Henri sitting quietly beside him. Too quietly. She stared out the window, her hands folded tightly on her lap. Since they'd left Havre's train station where he'd picked her up, he'd wanted to stop at every grove of trees they'd passed and kiss her. But she seemed preoccupied. He'd try one more time to get her to talk. "Henri, you've barely said a word since you got off the train. Did something happen when you were with your folks to upset you?"

She looked at her hands and muttered, "No. I had a wonderful time."

"What is it then?"

She turned to him, avoiding his eyes. "It's just…" She shook her head and returned her gaze to the monotonous prairie.

He wouldn't press her. Whatever it was, she'd tell him in time. But mile after mile, her silence grew more troublesome. When she ran her hands down her face and heaved a sigh, he couldn't stand it anymore. As he kept one eye on the road, he reached over and squeezed her hand. "Whatever is troubling you, *meu amor*, you know I'll help."

She turned to him, her eyes full of worry, but no tears. "I know, Martim. You've always been there when I've needed you." She folded her hands across her belly. "We're going to have another baby."

His heart reeled. Another child? But of course. What had he expected? When Henri had refused his proposal, he'd done his best to remain celibate, to focus on his mission as a priest finding fulfillment in his work. But he'd failed. A few weeks before she'd left to visit her family, they'd walked beneath the stars watching for meteors. Her closeness and the beauty of the night had been seductive. A comet had streaked the sky and in a moment of wonder they'd given in to love. Another baby coming might be an omen, a message that he needed to try harder to convince Henri to marry him. He turned off the road, rattling over the rough ground, kicking up clouds of dust, and stopping beside a tangle of tumbleweeds.

"Martim? What are we doing here?"

He looked at her with half a smile. Complications lay ahead, including the blessing of another child. He helped her from the car. As he led her through the prairie grass, swarms of grasshoppers exploded from the brush, chirruping around them. Without a word, he settled her on an outcropping of rocks and sat beside her. He took her hand and gazed out across the expanse. "We have to sort through this new challenge."

She took her hand from him.

"I'm so sorry. I knew better, but I let it happen. The fault is mine, Henri. I've put you in another precarious situation."

"I'm not innocent either. No matter how hard I try, I can never do what is right. I should have said 'no'. I didn't." Her voice was full of self-loathing.

"And I should have stopped but didn't. I'm the man, the one who is supposed to be strong. And for God's sake, I'm an ordained priest who's taken a vow of celibacy. If there is blame, it is mine." He ran his hands through his hair, now sweaty from the noontime heat. "Truthfully, except for the trouble our relationship causes you, I still don't completely believe the expression of our love is wrong."

"Wrong or not, Martim, the Church says it is. The world thinks it is." She paused, a pained expression on her face. "I'm scared, Martim."

"I am too," he said, his heart beating wildly. "And with a new child on the way, I feel even more strongly I should leave the priesthood and marry you."

She took his hand and stroked her thumb across his calloused palm. "I've considered marrying you over and over, Martim. Maybe I should, now that another baby is on the way. But it's become more complicated. Before I realized I was pregnant again, I broke the news to my parents about Angelica. They think I'm already married." She pulled a paper from her handbag, unfolded it, and handed it to him. "Proof of my marriage to Jack Rollado." She clasped her hands in her lap. "At least the ugly 'illegitimate' label won't taint this new baby's birth certificate."

He took the document and studied it. He'd known about the certificate but hadn't seen it. There it was, in black and white. Henrietta Marie Hoffmann married to Jack Rollado. That space should hold his name instead of this imposter. As he beat back the torment, he handed the document to her. "I'm glad you have proof that protects you." He stared across the prairie. "How did your parents react to the news?"

Her voice grew steely. "I didn't show them the marriage certificate. It would have implicated Greta and Cornelius. I told them a Justice of the Peace married Jack and me a few months before I moved to Sage Prairie. They bought the story, but it outraged *Vader* and hurt him immensely. *Moeder*'s anger lasted only until I told her she has another grandchild."

"Your parents believing you're already married complicates matters. It's another lie to untangle, but it doesn't make marriage impossible."

"Marriage to you has never been impossible, Martim. It's just another path. But I see it as the most difficult path, the one most destructive for you. I can survive as the wife of a traveling salesman."

He rubbed the back of his neck and said, "I'm not giving up, Henri. Still, I'll help you establish yourself as Mrs. Rollado before our baby comes."

"The sooner the better, Martim. I'm desperate to have Angelica in my life full time." Her eyes softened. "Thank you for understanding. I love you even more because of it."

A gust of wind whistled across the prairie, swaying the wild grass and ruffling her hair. He put an arm around her and pulled her close. "My worst torment is knowing I'll never be a proper father to my children if we don't marry."

She leaned her head on his shoulder. "I'm glad you're their father. That you are part of them."

He shook away his grief and lightened his tone. "How was your side trip to visit Angelica?"

Henri's face lightened. "The extra cost to travel to Helena was so worthwhile. Our little girl is more lovable than ever. She babbles all the time, scoots everywhere, and loves being with the other babies. The Crittenton home is such a blessing." She took a deep breath and let it go. "I wish I could have taken her with me to meet her grandparents."

He ran his hand over their rocky perch, brushing away the loose grains of sand. "I've never met my daughter either, or held her in my arms, or sang the songs *minha mãe* sang to me, and it breaks my heart."

"I'm sorry, Martim. It isn't fair." She stared into the distance, biting her lip until her frown turned to half a smile. "I hope she inherited your amazing voice. She claps her hands and sways to the music whenever someone sings to her. She even responds to my croaky voice."

His heart settled into wistfulness as he pictured Angelica responding to her mother's singing. "I'd love if she has my passion for music, even if she never knows it comes from me." Wanting to keep the smile on Henri's face, Martim pulled an envelope from his pocket and handed it to her. "This came for you while you visited your family. It's from someone you traveled with last summer on your way to the Crittenton Home."

"Dottie?" she asked, reaching for it.

"No. Check the return address."

"Oh my. It's from Harry Eismann," she said, sliding a finger under the envelope flap and pulling out a letter. "Do you mind if I read it now?"

"Go ahead. It looks as if he had a lot to say. And don't feel obligated to share if you don't want to."

"You knew him too," she said, skimming the first page. "He's settled into a good job, bought a car, and is ready to buy a home." She turned to the next page and gasped. She finished reading to the end without a word, folded the letter, and held it in her hands. Martim gave her a puzzled look and waited. Clouds covered the sun, and the wind turned chilly. She buttoned her sweater and opened the letter again. "It's a marriage proposal, Martim."

He tensed, appalled at the envy creeping in.

She flipped back to the third page. "Listen to what he wrote. 'If you need any advice, dear, show this to Father Ferrera and ask him for his thoughts. He will give you the best advice there is, and I fear no prejudice.'"

Martim struggled to dismiss the stab in his heart. "Harry is right. I can't let my feelings for you affect my counsel." His voice cracked. "I love you enough to let you go if that's what you want. And it might be best. Harry is a good man. You could have a normal life with him. And he could be the father to your children I can never be."

She looked at him in horror. "They are our children, Martim. Not just mine."

"Yes, our children." He avoided her eyes. "I want to claim them. Let the world know they are mine. But you see disaster if I do. So, I'll do my best to show 'no prejudice.'" He steeled himself. It had to be said. "Harry might be the best solution."

Henri pulled away and scowled. "Even if I wanted to marry him. And I don't," she said fiercely. "He wouldn't want to marry me. Not with two children from another man, one I'm not even married to."

Martim's eyes lingered on the prairie. In the distance, a solitary antelope with two young calves grazed on the wild grasses. Just the three of them. No male around to help her raise her young. But that wasn't what God intended for humans. He caught her eye again. "Having two children doesn't have to be a problem. Tell him about the marriage you created and your reason for its secrecy. The marriage certificate Father Cornelius and Greta fabricated is proof enough. You could say your traveling salesman died recently from tuberculosis or influenza."

She laughed. "Someday I might have to do that. But not now." Her voice turned somber. "Though we aren't together as man and wife, it's you I want, Martim Ferrera, complications and all."

Her words were a salve to a terrible wound. "Whatever you decide, I won't stop loving you. Not ever." He helped her stand. Her hand in his, he led her back to the Buick. Neither said another word until they entered Sage Prairie and passed the new parsonage, now under construction.

"Martim," she gasped. "Your rectory is going to be huge."

"Ten rooms, full basement, and all the modern conveniences. The builders should finish it by the end of the year. The sad part is my little family can never share it with me."

Her voice caught when she answered. "You have another family, Martim, all the faithful in your many parish missions. They will share it with you."

He stopped the car at the church. "You're an extraordinary woman, Henri. One not easily convinced. But I warn you, I'm not giving up."

She nodded. Did her eyes suggest he might have a chance?

Three dogs rounded the corner of the church, barking in welcome, interrupting the moment. Henri laughed. "Two more dogs, Martim? When I left in August, you only had one."

He grinned. "What could I do? Their owner left for a job in Oregon and couldn't take them with him."

"You have a big heart, Father Ferrera."

"I must confess. I have an ulterior motive. Their owner trained them for hunting. And I have plans to hunt in Black Coulee this winter." The dogs swirled around, jumping and sniffing, their tails wagging when they got out of the car.

Etta appeared on the rectory steps and called, "Henri, you're back." She rushed towards them with a camera. Caddy was right behind with her usual shy smile.

"It's good to see you, Caddy. And Etta, what a surprise you're here to meet me."

"I couldn't wait," Etta answered. "Pa's been giving me driving lessons this summer. He let me drive Caddy back with the clean laundry. I was hoping you'd arrive while I was here." She held up her camera. "Father Ferrera, would you and Henri, stand by the Buick. I want a picture of Henri's homecoming."

Martim and Henri tried to calm the dogs as they milled around their feet. The task was impossible. Etta snapped a picture anyway.

Martim picked up Henri's suitcase. "Let's get your bags inside, Miss Hoffmann. It'll be easier to visit without the dogs begging for attention."

On their way inside, Etta said, "Henri, come spend a few days with me on the farm. We can catch up. We can bring you back Sunday when the family comes to church."

Martim tensed. He and Henri had so much to discuss in order to decide how to handle her pregnancy and the birth of their second child. After Sunday services, he had to leave for Great Falls to update the bishop on the new rectory's progress. From there he'd go to Havre for building supplies, and when he returned, he had to supervise the electrical installation. That left little time for weeks to have a serious conversation with Henri. And decisions had to be made soon. Despite Henri's refusal to marry him, he'd do everything in his power to help her become Mrs. Jack Rollado.

Caddy sputtered. "But Henri, I cooked you a welcome home dinner. Could you and Etta get together after Sunday services?"

Henri's hand flew to her chest. "A welcome home dinner. How thoughtful, Caddy." She turned to Etta. "I have so much to share, Etta, but it can wait until Sunday if that works for you."

Relief spread through Martim when Etta said, "I'm anxious to hear about your trip home, but Sunday is fine."

Ten minutes later, Martim watched Etta drive away, grateful that Henri had such a good friend with whom she could share her troubles.

Chapter Twenty-Seven

Sunday, September 16, 1928,
The Kroft Farm
Henrietta

Dinner dishes done, and the chickens fed, Henri and Etta walked to the top of a rise on the Kroft homestead and settled on a flat space on the hillside. A herd of cattle grazed on the plains below. Henri shivered as the wind whistled around them. She huddled deep into her coat. "It's like a sea of grass with a sky that stretches forever."

"That's why they call Montana the 'Big Sky Country.'"

"It lives up to its reputation," Henri said, tying her scarf tighter.

They basked in the rugged beauty until Etta broke their silence. "Did you tell your family about Jack and Angelica when you were in Wisconsin?"

"It was hard, but I did. It turned out about how I expected. *Moeder* was shocked and angry but forgave me the instant I told her about Angelica. *Vader* was a different story. He wouldn't talk to me when I left. Still, he'll eventually accept the idea of my marriage. Now that they know, I can take Angelica with me the next time I visit."

"What happens now, Henri?"

She hated to lie again, especially to a friend like Etta. But there was no way around it. She put on a smile and wove a new tale. "On my way to visit my family, I stopped in Minneapolis to see Jack. We spent a few days together."

Etta's face lit up. "That's fantastic."

Henri pulled her knees to her chest and wrapped her arms around them. By now the sun touched the horizon and streaked the sky with brilliant reds, purples, and golden orange. She took a deep breath and let it go. "I loved being with Jack, but I'm not sure it was wise. I'm pregnant again."

Etta's hand flew to her mouth, and then she grinned. "Well, I guess that's not surprising. But you don't seem happy about it."

"It complicates things. Except for a few people, our marriage must remain a secret a while longer. Right now, we can't settle down like a normal family."

Etta gave her a worried look. "Has Jack had any close calls with the revolutionaries who might be searching for him?"

Another lie coming back to haunt her. Henri sighed. "No, but he still watches his back."

Etta nodded. "He's in my prayers every night."

"You're a good friend, Etta."

"If you still have to keep your marriage secret, what are you going to do about this new baby?"

"I hate leaving Sage Prairie, but I have to. Father is sure I can join a group of his friends who plan to tour parts of western Montana in a few weeks. I've wanted to see Glacier Park for a long time, and we may even travel as far west as Coeur d'Alene, Idaho. Then I'll spend the rest of my pregnancy with the friends who are caring for Angelica. While I'm gone, Father will do his best to keep gossip at bay." The tour wouldn't be just a lark. She'd use the trip to find a small town to have the baby where no one knew her or Father Ferrera, a place where Martim could show up as Jack Rollado and seal the illusion of her marriage.

Etta linked her arm with Henri's. "Father's help must be a blessing."

Henri almost blurted he was more than a blessing but caught herself. "I don't know what I'd do without him. The baby is due in late April. Before then, he promised to help me find a loving home where my babies can be cared for, so I can get a job and help with our expenses. Right now, most of Jack's salary goes for travel and living costs when he's on the road. There's never much left for our babies and me."

Etta's eyes filled with sympathy. "Businesses are always looking for secretaries. I graduate high school in May. I still plan to take those business classes in Great Falls. By then your baby will be born. Hopefully, you can join me."

"I desperately want to," Henri said. "But it'll take some doing. If I find someone to care for my babies, I still need a cheap place to live."

"Can you afford the tuition?" Etta asked rubbing her arms against the chill.

"We'll find a way," Henri said, relieved that Martim promised to help pay for her courses. "As much as it costs, it'll be worth it. And it won't be long before I'm earning a paycheck."

Etta's voice brightened. "Hey, we could save money if we room together while we go to school." She giggled. "And since your kids will be close by and their papa can't see them very often, I'll be their 'Pa.'"

Henri laughed; her spirits lifted. "Okay, Pa, I'll count on that."

Chapter Twenty-Eight

Wednesday, April 3, 1929
Martim

Martim's Buick bumped along the road to Great Falls, flinging mud onto the patches of snow melting in the ditches. He marveled at Henri sitting beside him, eight and a half months pregnant and as lovely as ever. Her hands rubbed her swelling belly as she stared out at the rain. It was as if in this moment they were a conventional family preparing for life ahead.

Henri sucked in her breath and grimaced. She pushed her hand against her side.

"Our *bebe*?" he asked.

She half laughed with a groan. "It's kicking hard today as if it's tired of being cooped up."

He arched his brow and grinned. "This new little one seems extra feisty. A bit like you, perhaps?"

"Feisty, for sure," she giggled. "It kicks and stretches so much; I suspect this one will be a challenge growing up." A slow smile spread over her lips. "I'm relieved to be heading to a place where I can finally be Mrs. Rollado."

"I hope it works, Henri," he said, his remorse rising again.

"I'm sure it will." She closed her eyes and relaxed back into her seat.

Martim dodged a pothole. His role as her pastor and family friend was far from satisfactory. But it's what Henri wanted. There were risks even in this role. As careful as they had been, there were whispers about his close connection to her, especially now that she was gaining weight again. He had helped her stay out of sight, touring with friends across northern Montana, through Glacier Park, and as far as Lake Crescent in Washington State. He was sure none of her traveling companions had guessed she was pregnant. These last few months, she'd spent most of her time with Angelica at the Crittenton Home, away from prying eyes. Still, he sensed an undertow of suspicion among the residents of Sage Prairie. Occasionally, he posted a tidbit or two in the *Sage Prairie Weekly* social column and the *Havre Daily News* about her comings and goings; some truths, some falsehoods to counter the gossip.

The baby was due in two weeks. If Henri was going to attend the Business College in Great Falls after the baby was born, the sooner she established herself in town as Mrs. Rollado the better. This morning he'd picked her up in Havre to take her to meet the Kesslers, a Seventh Day Adventist family he'd met last summer. They seemed the perfect people to care for their babies, while Henri attended school.

"Martim?" Her eyes were closed, her voice soft and thoughtful.

"Yes?"

"Tell me again. How did you meet the Kesslers?"

"Last August when you were visiting your family, I was on my way to visit the bishop. I noticed a man and his wife trying to push their car from a ditch just outside of Great Falls. I stopped to help. It took two hours, but we got the car free."

She smiled, her eyes still closed. "Just like you to help the stranded."

"They were grateful, so they invited me to stop by their home for dinner after I saw the bishop. Mrs. Kessler's vegetable and dumpling soup was the best I've ever had. When I raved about it, she encouraged me to come for dinner whenever I was in town. I've taken her up on her offer several times."

Henri's eyes opened, and she frowned. "Just because she's an excellent cook doesn't make her perfect to care for our babies."

He grinned. She was acting like a mother bear. "I watched the couple interact with their two teenaged daughters and their adult son. They were firm but loving."

Henri gave him a doubtful look. "But they're not Catholic."

"No, they're not. But, they're kind, caring, and moral. In some ways they're more Christian than a few Catholics I know."

Her face brightened. "Actually, it might work in our favor if the Kesslers aren't Catholic."

"That's what I've been thinking. Seventh Day Adventists are less likely to hear rumors running through Catholic circles. If they don't hear the gossip, they're less likely to be suspicious when I visit our children."

"Makes sense." She squirmed, getting comfortable, resting her head against the window, and closed her eyes again.

When he'd talked with the Kesslers about caring for the babies while Henri attended school, he'd told them he was Henri's pastor and family friend. The deception ate at him. He was a minister with huge sins on his soul. Every time he preached honor, integrity, and virtue, he felt a hypocrite. Telling the truth and leaving the priesthood would ease his conscience. But he'd pay the price.

The car vibrated through a rocky puddle. Mud splashed onto the windshield as Henri bolted up, wide-eyed. "Sorry, Henri. I didn't mean to wake you." The blades swished through the muck, leaving streaks across the glass.

"It's okay, Martim. I wasn't asleep. I've been thinking about Angelica. When I have to leave her for a while and then return to the Home, she fusses when I first pick her up and is bashful for a few days. Though I'm grateful that she has so many wonderful people caring for her, I'm not sure she knows I'm her mother."

Martim peered through the swish of the windshield wipers. "Soon she'll realize you're her *mamãe*, and she'll know for a lifetime." His chest tightened. "But she might never know me as her *papai*. I'll only be a family friend."

Henri stroked his cheek with the back of her hand. As always, her touch calmed him. "I'm so sorry, Martim. This is best for our babies. But I promise, no matter what happens, they'll know their Portuguese heritage. Mr. Rollado will become you, except without the Roman collar."

"I'm grateful for that," Martim said. But her promise did little to ease his angst. He bit his lip and said, "We're almost there. Time to put on your ring."

From the corner of his eye, he watched her untie the silk ribbon from around her neck and slipped the ring on her finger. She gazed at it and said, "I love that this was your grandmother's."

"It suits you. My grandmother was as unconventional as you. When my grandfather died, she took control of his estate and refused all offers of marriage, not wanting to give up her independence. You two would have gotten along famously."

"I've never put much weight in the supernatural, but I can almost sense her strength." She squared her shoulders, her eyes still on the ring. "From this point on, Martim, I'm officially Mrs. Rollado."

He flinched. Hopefully not forever. Someday, he still wanted her to be Mrs. Ferrera. Half an hour later they pulled up beside a clapboard house on the outskirts of Great Falls. Charlie Kessler and his adult son came out of a nearby shed. As usual, both wore paint-spattered overalls. Ada Kessler walked down the porch steps, wiping her hands on her apron, her two teenaged daughters trailing behind her.

Martim helped Henri from the car. "Come, I'll introduce you." He resisted the urge to take her arm as they walked to the house. The twinkle in Charles' blue eyes and Ada's smile put him at ease.

"Charles, Ada, this is Henrietta Rollado."

Charles took off his hat. "Please to meet you, ma'am. This is my son Glenn, and my daughters Frieda and Dottie."

Glenn grinned, with his hat in his hands. The two girls merely said, "Hi."

Ada pressed Henri's hand between her own. "Father Ferrera has told us about you and your husband." Her voice was sweet and trusting. She eyed Henri. "I see your baby will be here soon."

"In about two weeks." Henri's hesitation to hire the Kesslers seemed to melt away.

"Come in," Ada said. "Father said you need a home for your babies while you attend school. Let's discuss it over supper." She smiled at Martim. "I made your favorite, vegetable soup with dumplings."

Martim sniffed as he and Henri followed the Kesslers into their homey kitchen. "Dinner smells wonderful."

Supper was over before the conversation became serious. Charles put his napkin beside his bowl and said, "Dottie, Frieda, please do the cleanup while Mama and I talk with Henrietta." He sat back in his chair and nodded at his wife.

Ada's kind eyes turned to Henri. "Father Ferrera told us about your husband's work. It's a shame he has to be gone so often."

Henri's hesitation was almost imperceptible. Then she plunged in with the smile that charmed everyone. "As a traveling salesman, my husband is on the road much more than at home. I miss him tremendously. We're grateful for Father Ferrera's help in finding us a caring family for our little ones."

Charles frowned. "It can't be easy having your husband away all the time." He shook his head, rubbing the back of his neck. "Father Ferrera said we would get the children this coming winter."

"Although winter is far off, I want to be prepared."

Charles nodded. "Seems wise." He turned to his wife. "What do you think, Ada? You've wanted more children. This would be your chance."

Ada tucked a strand of hair back into her bun and then put her hands on her lap, contemplating. Finally she said, "As Seventh Day

Adventists, we are called to give of ourselves in loving service. It would be a pleasure to serve your family, Henrietta."

It wasn't the perfect solution, but under the circumstances, it was the best option. Martim shook hands with Charles and Ada. "Thank you for your kindness and understanding." He glanced at Henri. Her smile told him she knew the Kesslers would love their children.

***

An hour later, Martim sat with Henri at the Great Falls train depot, a ticket to Hamilton, Montana in her hand. After considering the options Henri had found in her travels last October, he and Henri had decided Hamilton was the best place to have their baby. The little hamlet was far from Sage Prairie and Great Falls. No one there was likely to know anything about him or Henri except for the stories they wove.

Footsteps and murmured conversations echoed through the station. An enormous clock was mounted above the ticket booth where passengers waited in line. A uniformed porter loaded trunks and baggage onto a handcart.

Henri patted the bulging satchel resting on the bench beside her. "It was thoughtful of Ada to give me her secondhand baby clothes. I had a few items, but definitely not enough."

Martim forced himself not to take her hand and touch the ring, now circling her finger. He clasped his hands together and said, "Ada is a blessing. She and Charles already regard you as Mrs. Rollado." That was good for Henri, but one more step that weakened his case for marriage. He tried to hide his bitterness as he said, "As time goes by, the illusion will become stronger, especially now that you have the marriage certificate. Do you have it ready for our baby's birth?"

"Of course. It's in my handbag. As much as I hate the lie, I can't face the thought of having another child labeled illegitimate."

Martim gritted his teeth, wanting to say, "If we got married, we wouldn't have bastard children." But this wasn't the time or place for argument.

A voice called from across the train station. "Father Ferrera." The bishop's housekeeper plodded to him. "Imagine seeing you here."

He braced himself, faked a smile, and stood. "Mrs. Harman. What a delight to see you. I'd like you to meet Mrs. Rollado, one of my parishioners. Her husband is away on business, and she needs to catch the train to Hamilton." Thinking quickly, he added, "Since I was on my way to visit the bishop anyway, I offered her a ride." He searched the plump woman's eyes for suspicion, but they didn't seem to hold any. Now he'd have to visit the Cathedral rectory, but that wasn't a problem. He could use more communion hosts and a few more bottles of altar wine.

Mrs. Harman nodded at Henri. "I'm on my way to Billings to be with my daughter. She just gave birth to my third grandchild." Her eyes widening, she grinned at Henri. "I notice you're expecting yourself. Your first?" she asked.

Martim stiffened with a quick answer. "Yes, her first." He sensed Henri's questioning look. But if he told the truth, Mrs. Harmon would ask where her first child was and why it wasn't with her. That would have started a whole new line of lies. Better to end it with a single bit of deceit.

The bishop's housekeeper said to Henri. "Good luck to you, dearie. I'd love to stay and chat about babies, but my train will be here soon. Father Ferrera, I'm sure I'll see you at the rectory sometime soon."

Henri stood and offered her hand to the older woman. "It was nice to meet you, Mrs. Harmon. Enjoy your time with your daughter's family."

The older woman took Henri's hand, flushing with pleasure. "Thank you. I most definitely will." She plodded back to a bench on the other side of the station.

Henri pressed her hands to her chest. "That was close, Martim."

"It was," he said, as the throbbing in his ears faded. "Now I have to stop and visit the bishop."

Henri laughed. "Don't stay too long. You're needed back in Sage Prairie by Friday afternoon. I didn't want to tell you, but your parishioners are planning a surprise celebration for your thirty-sixth birthday. You'll have to pretend you know nothing when it happens."

Martim chuckled. "I've already put it out of my mind."

Henri became serious. "Seeing Mrs. Harmon makes me realize how wise it is to have our baby so far away."

He put his head in his hands, his fingers raking his hair as he muttered. "Having a baby shouldn't require so much deception."

She inched closer to him. "Deception or not, Martim, it'll feel good to settle down with my babies and be a true mother."

Her eyes filled with gratitude and disarmed his frustration. "You already are a good mother, Henri. When you arrive in Hamilton, check into the Hamilton Hotel. It's on the left as soon as you get off the train."

Moments later, "All aboard to Hamilton, Montana," echoed through the station.

Martim handed Henri an envelope. "Money to live on until I see you again. I'll visit in a week or two, so I can meet Hamilton's doctor as Mr. Rollado. I'm positive no one in Hamilton can identify me as a priest. So when our baby is born, there won't be questions about its legitimacy." He frowned. "I probably can't be with you for the birth. It's too unpredictable, and I'll be too far away. But when the baby finally comes, send me a telegram, and I promise to be at the baptism."

Tears welled in her eyes. "Thank you, Martim. It's hard to believe I soon will be officially established as a married woman with two children."

He forced a smile. They were parting again. He wanted to kiss her goodbye, like any good husband. Instead, he watched her board the train and wondered if playing the part of an ordinary husband and father for a few days when their baby was born would convince Henri to marry him. Was it foolish to hope?

Chapter Twenty-Nine

April 3–April 19, 1929,
Hamilton, Montana.
Henrietta

Exhausted from the long train trip, Henri hung her coat in the hotel's wardrobe and surveyed the room where she would stay until after the baby was born. An electric fixture with a custard-colored shade hung from the ceiling. The light cast a warm glow over a double bed covered with a rosy chenille spread. Though Henri shared a bathroom down the hall with other female guests, she was pleased to see a large china washbasin with a pitcher of water on the dressing table. The entire room was very opulent, considering Hamilton was a town of a few thousand people.

Henri dropped her shoes on the hooked rug and curled up on the bed. She'd rest a few minutes before heading to the hotel dining room for dinner. She awoke hours later with the baby kicking and an urgent need to use the bathroom. Nighttime silence reigned as she padded down the dimly lit hall to the toilet. Dinner was now out of the question.

In the morning, Henri woke to the sun seeping through the curtains. An hour later she was dressed and ready for her first public appearance as Mrs. Rollado in Hamilton. She checked her profile in the armoire's full-length mirror and ran her palms over her rounded belly. She no longer had to hide her pregnancy in public.

Passing through the hotel lobby to the dining room where they had just begun serving breakfast, the clerk, an elderly gentleman, nodded from the desk. "Good morning, Mrs. Rollado. Did you sleep well?"

Henri flushed with pleasure at being addressed as 'Mrs. Rollado'. She put a hand on her baby and smiled. "Between bouts of activity, my little one gave me a few good hours of sleep." She kept silent about the multiple trips she'd made to the bathroom.

The clerk nodded knowingly. "My wife and I have five children and seven grandchildren, so I understand." He glanced at his logbook. "When do you expect your husband to arrive?"

Despite the heat rising to her cheeks, Henri kept her voice casual. "His business and travel schedule are never certain, but he'll arrive sometime within the next two weeks. I'll let you know as soon as I hear."

"Thank you, Mrs. Rollado. We aim to take good care of our guests."

Henri nodded and toddled to the dining room. The pleasure of being known as a married woman faded and deception ate at her. The baby kneed her insides, squirming and stretching, reminding her of its life ahead. She pushed away her guilt. She had to be seen as a caring mother and wife to an absent father.

***

Two weeks later, Thursday, April 18

When Henri returned from an evening stroll, she checked the lobby's clock. Almost six-thirty. Martim should have been here hours ago. That's what the telegram had said. Had he gotten a flat? Or been chased by bandits, as had happened last October? Even worse, the mountain roads were treacherous this time of year. Had he been in an accident?

Upstairs she stopped in the lavatory and then trudged to the room she and Martim would share the next few days as husband and wife. Days she would cherish, but she better not get used to them.

She propped herself up on the bed and settled in with a book of short stories by Agatha Christie, checked out from the Hamilton Library. Though Agatha's plots were clever, Henri found it difficult to concentrate. Not only was she worried about Martim; she was having a few mild labor pains. Adding to it all, the book smelled like a horse barn, which was understandable since the Hamilton library shared a building with the fire department and its horse stable. She rose and opened the window for some fresh air and to see if Martim's Buick had driven up.

A little after nine o'clock, she closed the book and dozed. Hours later, a soft rap on the door broke into her dream. Her mind held images of her nightmare with horse-riding bandits chasing Martim in his car. He'd sped up and down steep mountain roads, around massive boulders and through washouts. When it seemed he'd gotten away from his pursuers, his car had careened over a cliff. She bolted up and checked the clock. After midnight! Another rap followed with a hushed, "Henri."

She opened the door to her traveling salesman husband dressed in a mud spattered white shirt, a bow tie, and a jacket. Dirt caked the cuffs of his pants, but other than looking tired, he seemed fine. Her worry melted away. She wiped a smudge from his face and fell into his arms.

His lips caressed her ear as he whispered, "You are my strength, Henrietta Marie Rollado. And my weakness. You're the half that makes me whole." He undressed and pulled her onto the bed beside him. She snuggled her back into the curve of his body and fell asleep with his arm nestled around their baby.

In the dimness of early morning, she awoke to Martim lying at her side, his eyes melting into hers. His hand lingered on the roundness of her belly and then slipped over the swell of her hip. "You are not a dream," he murmured. "You're here beside me. No worry. No hiding. No rushing away."

She gave him an impish grin. "If I'm not mistaken, Mr. Rollado, this is how we got into this predicament."

His soft whispers stirred through her hair. "So true, Mrs. Rollado. And now that we're together, with no way to change the circumstances, let's take advantage of it." His touch left her breathless. Love intoxicated her and erased her guilt, capturing her in a swell of bliss. Somewhere in the haze of euphoria, she remembered hearing that making love could start labor. She'd be overjoyed if the baby came while he was here.

An hour later, they strolled down the stairs and into the hotel lobby. Henri's contentment at being seen as Martim's wife mingled with remorse. She reached for her traveling salesman's hand. "How can this feel so wonderful and so wrong at the same time?"

Martim locked his fingers in hers and said, "I have a tortured conscience too. But my heart tells me God forgives our deception. He knows it's the way to keep our babies safe. It's not their fault their parents have sinned."

"Knowing that doesn't make it easier. It only makes it possible," she muttered as they approached the hotel desk.

The clerk looked up from his paperwork. "Good morning. I see you made it in last night, Mr. Rollado."

Martim offered his hand to the clerk and said, "Call me Jack."

The clerk shook Martim's hand. "Did you have problems on the road?"

Martim nodded with a friendly expression. "Three flat tires. I had patches for two but had to find a gas station open late to get supplies for the third."

The clerk frowned. "I imagine as a traveling salesman you're used to frequent blowouts. But three flats in one day seem a bit much."

"True, but I'm used to the perils of the road." He put his arm around

Henri. "Traveling so much makes it difficult for my wife, especially now that she's nearing her delivering date. She'll stay in Hamilton until the baby is born, and for a few months until the baby is old enough to travel. Hopefully, my sales company will allow me to arrange my route so I can visit occasionally."

His eyes met Henri's. The love on his face triggered her guilt for refusing to marry him.

Martim turned to the clerk. "Could you tell us where to find Hamilton's doctor?"

"Dr. Grayson is down the street, second floor in the same building as the City Bakery and Toggery's clothing store."

"Thank you, sir," Martim said, and paraded with Henri to the street where puddles from last night's downpour steamed in the morning sunshine. It didn't take long to find the doctor in his office. Martim waited on the other side of the privacy screen as Dr. Grayson examined Henri. Though the doctor for Angelica's birth had been skilled, he'd worn an aura of judgment. Now, posing as a married woman with a husband accompanying her, the doctor was competent and kind. After the exam she dressed, listening to Dr. Grayson and Martim discuss her condition on the other side of the screen.

"Henrietta and the baby are both healthy," the doctor said. "The baby has positioned itself correctly for birth. It looks as if it will arrive in about a week."

"Could you send word when she goes into labor? I'll come as quickly as I can, but probably won't be here in time for the birth."

The doctor said, "Your wife doesn't have family nearby?"

"No. They're all in Wisconsin," Martim said. Henri knew the casualness in his voice hid his wariness.

The Doctor continued without a hint of suspicion. "Where should I send the telegram?"

"To Father Ferrera in Sage Prairie. He's a close family friend and will know how to reach me."

Henri tied the dress sash at her hips. She slipped into her shoes and joined Martim and Dr. Grayson. Martim helped her settle into the chair and continued his conversation with the Doctor. "Henrietta wants to stay in Hamilton until the baby is old enough to travel. Is there a place nearby where they could get room and board?"

Dr. Grayson smoothed his mustache as he considered the request.

"You might check with the Wilkins. They're a caring older couple that live at the edge of town. Their children are grown, married, and have moved away. I imagine they'd welcome a young woman with a baby." The doctor gave more details and drew a map to the Wilkins' place.

As they walked out of the office, another kick jolted Henri's ribs. She gasped. "This little one is coming soon." She lifted her chin, took in a deep breath, and let it go. "And it will have a father."

Martim grasped her hand. His voice choked when he said, "Angelica has a father, too. The world just doesn't know who he is."

Early the next morning, Henri stood at the window of her hotel room watching Martim's car disappear. Rain poured, and the wind howled, whipping the little trees lining the street to a frenzy. She'd be alone when the baby was born. No Mimi, no Toots, no help from the Crittenton Home. No *Moeder*, no Greta. And no Martim. This was the result of her stubborn independence.

Chapter Thirty

Wednesday, April 24, 1929
Hamilton, Montana.
Henrietta

Henri marveled at her new baby girl's tiny hand curling around her finger. She studied Ernestine's features. So beautiful. So perfect. So like Martim. And so like Angelica, except with darker hair and hazel eyes instead of blue. She kissed her daughter's forehead, amazed at how quick the birth had been. She'd refused the Twilight Sleep the doctor had offered and had been alert through the entire process. The pain was immense, but so was the joy. Best of all, now only seven hours later, she didn't have the horrible, groggy feeling she'd experienced with Angelica. She ached. But she'd been plenty sore with Angelica too, after the Twilight Sleep had worn away. And this time her wrists and ankles didn't have the ugly bruises she'd gotten when they'd tied her to the bed.

Her eyes wandered through the little hospital room, counting twenty beds, most unoccupied. A matronly woman dressed in a well-starched uniform appeared at her bedside. Doctor Grayson's nurse smiled as she ran her hand over the baby's head. "Such a lovely baby, Mrs. Rollado. How are you doing?"

Henri kissed her daughter again, breathing in her sweet scent. "Perfectly wonderful. So different from…" she stopped. It would be a mistake to mention Angelica's birth. She shook her head and continued. "Different from what I heard about Twilight Sleep. Here I am, very sore, but full of joy and completely awake." She smiled at Ernestine. "And my baby has her tiny eyes open exploring the world."

The nurse snorted. "Twilight Sleep. Women have given birth without drugs for thousands of years. I'm in the minority. I think you did it the best way." She sat in the chair beside the bed, pulled a pencil and notebook from the deep pocket in her skirt and said, "Time to get information for your baby's birth certificate."

Henri heard her heart pulsing in her ears. She'd have to lie. Hopefully not a lot.

The nurse started. "Baby's official name."

"Ernestine Marie Rollado." True.

"Legitimate?" Henri didn't have to lie. The nurse answered her own question. "Of course, she's legitimate." And then went on. "Father's name?"

Her baby had an official father. The throbbing in her ears intensified as she answered. "Jack Rollado."

"His residence?"

"Great Falls." Okay, a little lie, but Martim was there often enough.

"Occupation?"

"He's a traveling man." Again, mostly true. Martim traveled all the time between his parishes.

Simple questions followed until the nurse asked, "Number of children born alive and now living?"

Henri bit her lip. This was a lie that would betray Angelica, but there was no escaping it. She closed her eyes and said, "One." If she admitted she had another child, she'd have to explain where Angelica was and why she wasn't with her. That would require even more lies.

The nurse nodded and went on with her questions. Everything else was true.

Finishing, the nurse closed her notebook. "I'll get this typed up, have Dr. Grayson sign it, and send it off to the registrar."

Henri's heart slowed. She'd done it. No condemnation, no disapproval, no suspicion. So different from a year ago with Angelica.

As the nurse left, Doctor Grayson walked in and handed Henri a telegram. "You've gotten news from Father Ferrera. He contacted your husband. Mr. Rollado should be here by late Saturday or early Sunday morning."

"Thank you," Henri said, taking the telegram. It was all working so smoothly. Martim had hosted a conference in Sage Prairie earlier in the week for many of the Catholic clergy in his section of the state. Somehow, he must have arranged for one of them to take over his Sunday services.

He would meet their new daughter, show this little corner of the world he was her father, and be a part of her baptism. She'd already sent a message to Reverend English, the pastor of Hamilton's Catholic Church, asking him to perform the baptism on Sunday after Mass, and she'd gotten an affirmative response. The best part of giving birth to Ernestine in Hamilton was that Reverend English didn't know Father Ferrera. She could introduce Martim as Jack Rollado.

Her heart was back to a remorseful beat. The plans she made were full of deceit. She gazed at Ernestine's lovely face, so pure and innocent. "I'm sorry for my lies, baby girl. I hope you never get caught in their tangle. They're meant to protect you. I pray they don't ensnare you instead."

***

Martim
Sunday, April 28, 1929
On the road to Hamilton
7:00 a.m.

Martim woke stiff and sore. He stretched in the morning sun blazing through his car's window letting the warmth ease the chill in his bones. The night had been cold, even wrapped in his woolen blanket. Yesterday he'd left Sage Prairie as early as possible, traveled to Willow Grove, down to Great Falls, and then headed southwest. He'd driven along the Blackfoot River and almost made it to Missoula before exhaustion took over. He'd pulled off the road and parked under a railroad trestle in a cluster of trees.

The trip had gone well, only one flat. April's rains had eased, so the roads were relatively dry. Sixty more miles, two hours, and he'd be in Hamilton with Henri for his daughter's baptism. He was grateful he could be at the ceremony, but the price for his gratitude was guilt. In order to convince a fellow priest to take over his Sunday services, he'd lied about needing a spiritual retreat.

He grabbed his satchel. Outside, he took a deep breath of the woodsy air and slipped into a thicket of budding willows. After changing into civilian clothes, he replenished his gas tank from the can he kept stowed in his trunk and was back on the road. As the car sped along, an ache tightened his throat. Would this be the only time he would hold his daughter as her *papai*? God willing, Henri would finally agree they should become a proper family. He pushed aside his frustration and sang, 'My Wild Irish Rose', a song Henri loved. Maybe his little girl would love it too.

***

Martim sat on the hotel bed beside Henri, gazing at Ernestine's hazel eyes. "Hello, *minha bebê*," he said, caressing her cheek. "I am your *papai*. You look so much like *sua avo* with her dark wavy hair and creamy skin." He kissed the baby's tiny fingers. "If your Portuguese grandmother were alive, she'd fall in love with you." He brought Henri to his side. "If Angelica were here, our family would be complete."

"I know," she whispered. She took Ernestine and kissed her forehead. "Hey little one, even though your *papai* can't live with us, soon you, your big sister, and I will be together."

Martim got up and paced. The tight control he'd kept on his angst vanished, unleashing his long-suppressed frustration. "It doesn't have to be this way, Henri," he said, shocked by the anger in his voice. "My God, I'm a father twice over. I should be able to take care of my children and the woman I love without having to lie, to hide, to skulk around like a common criminal." His breath came in shaky gulps. "This double life is agonizing. Part of me feels I should never have joined the priesthood." He stopped and met the skepticism in her eyes.

She patted the bed. Tenderness filtered through the doubt on her face. "Sit, my love."

Barely containing his anger, he settled beside her. "I know, Henri. You've said it before. If I hadn't entered the priesthood, we would never have met."

Henri's eyes held his. "And that's why I know our love and our children are meant to be. That's not to say I don't have enormous guilt myself. But I'd have just as much guilt if you left the priesthood. Maybe even more. There are hundreds of people who are better because of your ministry. I can't take you from them. Or them from you. You love me, but you also deeply care for your congregations." She bit her lip and looked down. "I believe our sins help you understand and heal the darkness in others."

Her words softened his anger. "I want to believe what you say is true, Henri. But my heart and my conscience can't come to a truce." He took her hand, locking his fingers into hers. "Sometimes as hard as it is on you, I think you relish the independence of not being married."

She pulled away and scowled. "I don't relish having to lie to maintain my respectability. I don't relish the perilous situation our love has brought our children. And I don't relish the fact that our daughters will grow without a father in their everyday lives." She played with a strand of loose hair and peered at him through tears. "Maybe you're right, Martim. Though I love you more than I ever thought possible, it's true. I have an independent streak. It's my curse. And my blessing."

"Independent," he muttered. "It's one thing I love about you. It brought us together and keeps us apart." He wrestled with a sense of rejection. Knowing that further argument was futile, he forced a smile. "Time to get the baby ready for Mass and her baptism."

Henri's frown faded. "The day is beautiful. After the ceremony, let's celebrate with a picnic."

His mood lifted. "I can't think of a better way to spend the day. While you dress Ernestine, I'll run to the grocer and get things for a picnic." He grabbed his jacket and hurried out the door.

When he returned, he found Henri and the baby waiting in the lobby. "Our lunch is ready in the car," he said, taking Ernestine into his arms. He gazed at Henri. The soft pink of her dress against her creamy skin magnified her allure. He caught his breath and reached for her hand. "You've just given birth and still you're ravishing."

"Pish posh," she said, taking his arm with a flirtatious smile. "Shall we go, Mr. Rollado?"

He grinned, caught up in the moment's joy, feeling as if he was acting in a play he'd written. "Yes, time for church, Mrs. Rollado." Out in the sunshine, they strolled like an ordinary family to his car parked at the hotel's side. When they reached the Buick, an elderly couple stopped them and cooed over Ernestine. His pleasure at being seen as Ernestine's father was tarnished, knowing it might never happen again. Determined to make the best of the day, he shoved his grief aside and helped Henri and the baby settle into the car.

As he tucked himself behind the wheel, Henri touched his hand. "It's wonderful to show off our baby." She frowned. "It's something I couldn't do with Angelica."

He started the engine. "Soon, you'll live in Great Falls as Mrs. Rollado, a married woman and mother. Then you can parade Angelica in public all you want." He couldn't be a part of that parade or share the ups and downs of being a proper family. He watched her lips curl into a smile as he started the engine. Her happiness eased his pain.

Hours later, the little family sat on Martim's blanket in a meadow nestled in a forest of firs. Martim cuddled Ernestine on his shoulder, trying to sooth her fussiness as Henri put the lunch away. The baby had slept through the baptism and the picnic and had awakened just as they'd finished their lunch. "Shh, shh," Martim said and sang "My Wild Irish Rose". She quieted for a moment, but then her fussiness turned to a squall. "I think she's hungry, Henri."

A breeze whispered through the trees and sent clouds of pollen curling through the air. Martim watched as Henri covered herself with a knitted blanket and nursed Ernestine.

Henri gazed at their daughter, rocking her as she nursed. She wiped the milk puddling on the baby's chin and sighed. "Nursing was another thing I couldn't do with Angelica, and I can't do it with Ernestine for very long. I have to spend time with Angelica, or she'll forget me. If I brought her here, it would undo the story we told to make Ernestine's birth legitimate." She shifted her weight and picked fuzz from the baby's blanket. "Thankfully, the Wilkins promised to care for our little girl while I'm gone, and they have a cow for the milk she needs."

Martim sat in silence, absorbing Henri's concerns. Was there anything left to say to convince her none of these complications would be necessary if they married?

Her face brightened as she put the baby at her shoulder and patted her back. "I heard from Etta. She's valedictorian. I told her I'd do my best to make it to her graduation."

"Etta deserves the honor. I'll be there to give the invocation and benediction, and to sing with the Sage Prairie Quartet." A sense of futility soured his stomach. "I'm happy you'll be there, *meu amor*, but it'll be hellishly difficult pretending we are nothing more than priest and former housekeeper." He moved closer to Henri and watched the baby nuzzle Henri's neck. "Do you really feel it necessary to leave Ernestine with the Wilkins when you visit Angelica and go for Etta's graduation?"

She blinked. "Of course. It's too soon to take Ernestine on long trips. Even if she were old enough, I couldn't take her to Sage Prairie. Sure, I have a marriage certificate, a ring, and a story about a pretend husband. It doesn't matter. Some will wonder why I kept my husband and my babies' secret. There'd be whispers, knowing looks, and some would put you in the middle of their gossip."

The agony of their secret shattered his lingering joy. He had no argument left. "You're right, Henri. When you go, you'll tell the Wilkins you're visiting your traveling salesman?"

Henri held Ernestine close and rocked her back and forth. "I have to, Martim. God forgive another lie."

Martim stared through the shadows forming in the forest. Let Henri find peace in her choice. He could not.

Chapter Thirty-One

Six months later
Thursday, November 14, 1929
The Commercial College of Great Falls
Henrietta

Henri and Etta walked into class to the clacking of typewriter keys. Many of the women had come early to practice their skills. Competition for jobs in the business world had gotten tough with the fall of the Stock Market a few weeks ago. Instructor Swartz sat at his desk, scowling over *The Great Falls Tribune*. The two friends perched on their stools at their typing stations. Henri leaned into Etta, nodded at their instructor, and said, "The news mustn't be good."

Etta shook her head. "It's been bleak for weeks. I keep hoping things will get better."

"My prayers exactly. I have to get a job to help support my girls." One more step, she thought, to becoming an independent woman.

The two ladies rolled sheets of paper into their typewriters and worked on building their speed. Ten minutes later, the instructor pinged a bell on his desk; the official signal for the class to begin. The students readied their steno pads for dictation, the first lesson of the day.

Mr. Swartz folded the newspaper and stood, his brow wrinkling as he began. "Ladies, today's dictation will be a summary of the *Tribune's* news on the Stock Market. What's happening on Wall Street will have a direct impact on whether you can find employment."

Henri and Etta grimaced at each other.

Mr. Swartz cleared his throat and paced as he gave the dictation. "The Stock Market dropped again yesterday. In the past few weeks, it's fallen from a peak of 381 in September to 198 at closing last evening. It's lost half its value in two months. The big banks are buying up vast blocks of stock to hold the market steady. But I have doubts it will work. For years, those same banks invested their deposits in stocks. People across the country have lost those deposits as the market continues to plummet."

Usually, the instructor paused for a moment, giving the ladies time to catch up. Not today. He paced faster and his dictation rushed along with him. "People are withdrawing their savings at record numbers. Banks are becoming insolvent, adding more fuel to the huge decline in the market." He continued for five more minutes, grinding out details that filled Henri with dread. When he stopped, it was mid-sentence explaining the cause of the market's fall. He sucked in a breath and let it go. "That's enough for now, ladies. Go ahead, type up the dictation. At ten o'clock, we start our bookkeeping lesson." He returned to his desk, rested his chin on his hands, and pored over the newspaper again.

Henri's mind roiled over the news Mr. Swartz had shared, making it difficult to concentrate on the assignment. Etta elbowed her. "You must be worried about Jack's job. Do you have any idea if the market downturn affects sugar sales?"

"I imagine it does," Henri answered, twisting the silver band around her finger. Of course she'd have to act the worried wife, and keeping up the pretense would be exhausting. Reality hinted of an ominous future with her two babies boarding at the Kesslers while she lived with Etta in a tiny room a few blocks away. She shook her head, clearing her thoughts, and went back to typing the dictation. If jobs for stenographers existed, the competition would be fierce.

Mr. Swartz dismissed class an hour early and hurried out the door ahead of his students. The young ladies plodded out of the building, engrossed in their own thoughts. Outside, leaves swirled in the brisk autumn wind. Henri wrapped her coat around herself and turned to Etta. "When you get to the boarding house, tell Mrs. O'Neal I'm stopping by the bank to pick up money Jack wired me, and I'll be there as soon as I can to help with dinner."

"I'll let her know," Etta said, holding on to her hat as the wind threatened to swish it away. "We're lucky she allows us to work for her to reduce our rent."

"I'm grateful for that, Etta, but I'm not sure how much longer I can stay in school. With Jack sending less money, the cost of rent, the tuition for our courses, and what I have to pay the Kesslers to keep Angelica and Ernestine, I don't have enough to cover my expenses. I'm hoping something changes."

Etta squeezed Henri's hand as they came to an intersection. "You're the strongest person I know, Henri. You'll find a way." Her brows lifted as she grinned. "Tomorrow is Friday. When class is over, we can spend the next few days with your girls."

"I'm fortunate my daughters are close by, so I can be with them on weekends. And I love that you join us, Etta. You've become part of my family."

The wind picked up speed, whipping Etta's hair around her face. She tucked it back under her hat and said, "Remember, I promised to be their 'Pa' since their real dad is away so much."

"You definitely fill a void, Pa," Henri said, laughing.

Etta giggled. "You'd better get to the bank before it closes, Ma."

"Okay, Pa. See you at the O'Neal's in half an hour."

As Henri stood in line waiting her turn at the bank, she pulled out a letter Martim had sent a few days ago. Their method of communication was complicated. Martim signed his letters 'Jack' and sent them to Father Cornelius and Greta, who then put 'Jack's' letters in a new envelope and mailed them to Henri with a Glade Harbor postmark. Henri told everyone that was where her husband was based. Money was wired that way, too.

She read Martim's letter for the third time. As always, he professed his longing to be with her and the babies. His news that the collection plate offerings had fallen dramatically dampened her mood. Even with his everyday expenses and the mortgage payments on the new rectory, he found ways to send money. Despite her decision to become Mrs. Rollado, he hadn't abandoned her and the girls.

***

Christmas Day
Wednesday, December 25, 1929
Great Falls, Montana

Henri walked down 3rd Avenue North to Saint Ann's Cathedral with Ernestine nestled in one arm, and Angelica's mittened-hand wrapped around her mother's gloved fingers. Clouds threatened snow. Henri didn't mind. A white Christmas would be perfect, but she hoped the flakes waited until Mass was over and she got her girls back to the Kessler's.

She entered the cathedral, admiring its elegance. Three stained glass windows arched in the dome above the altar, gold-capped columns rose to a vaulted ceiling, and the polished wooden pews reflected the colored lights glowing in the Christmas stable set up in an alcove near the altar. Though St. Ann's was not as opulent as St. Helena's Cathedral, she felt welcome here. She was Mrs. Rollado, with no need to hide her babies and no worry of judgment as she took them to view the Baby Jesus. Her girls, dressed in outfits Ada Kessler had made, looked perfectly proper and lovely as they stared at the manger.

Henri gave Angelica a penny and pointed to a silver dish at the foot of the crèche. "Put the money there," she whispered. "It's for Baby Jesus."

Angelica bounced gleefully as she dropped her offering onto the plate. The penny clinked against the other coins piled there. She looked up at her mother and asked, "Ernie have penny, too?"

Henri chuckled. "Not yet, little one. Next year she'll be old enough." As she found a place for herself and her babies in a pew near the manger, a lump grew in her throat. The magic of Christmas had waned as she had gotten older. But today, celebrating the birth of Christ with Angelica and Ernestine, her sense of joy had returned.

As the service unfolded, with Ernestine in her arms and Angelica sitting on her knee, her mind was on Martim. He'd been here at St. Ann's often to visit the bishop, sometimes to say Mass, and for a variety of other ceremonies. She could almost hear his rich voice soar to the rafters. At this very moment, he was probably singing for services in Sage Prairie. She wondered how he'd spend the day after he'd made his rounds to his other churches. Most likely, he'd enjoy dinner and the evening with Etta's folks. Her heart ached knowing that if she stuck to her decision not to marry him, they would never spend Christmas together.

She fingered the lacey trim on Angelica's stockings. Martim had sent a pair for both of his daughters. The letter he'd sent with the package had more upsetting news. The collection plate offerings were smaller than ever. She prayed she could manage the lean times that loomed ahead.

As usual at Christmas Mass, the line for Communion seemed to go on forever. And so did her guilt. She couldn't receive Communion, as the mortal sin she and Martim had committed in conceiving Ernestine was still on her soul. As much as it weighed on her conscience, she hadn't been in a confessional since she'd confessed to Father Cornelius back home in White Water after Angelica was born. The confessional was supposed to be confidential, but what if her confessor broke his vow? Or asked the man's name who was her accomplice in sin? Maybe her fear was irrational, and she should have faith. But she couldn't take the chance. Her web of lies was becoming complicated. If she ever changed her mind and married Martim, it would be difficult to undo the tangle.

Her thoughts jumped to the future. In six or seven years, her daughters would receive their first communion. What kind of example would she set if she never took part in the Holy Sacrament? What would her girls think? She shoved the worry away. A more pressing issue weighed on her. How was she supposed to support her family if she couldn't find a job?

The issue haunted her as the magic of Christmas unfolded at the Kesslers. By noon the clouds opened and flakes spilled from the sky. Ada's two teenaged daughters, Dottie and Frieda, waited by the door as Henri bundled Angelica into her snowsuit. They were taking her out for a romp in the snow. As Henri buttoned her coat, Angelica said, "Mudder, me miss Pa. Where she is?"

Henri smiled, thinking of how close she and Etta had become and how their 'Pa' had lovingly taken on a role in her children's lives. She slipped mittens on Angel's hands. "I miss Pa too. But she's spending Christmas with her own ma and pa. When she returns, you can tell her how much fun you had playing in the snow."

Angelica sighed. "Okay." She brightened, grabbing Frieda's and Dottie's hands, and the three scooted out the door.

Henri pulled the curtains back so she and Ernestine could watch them frolic as the flakes fell heavier and heavier. Ernestine's eyes followed Angelica everywhere. And when Angelica fell backwards in the fluffy piles to make a snow angel, Ernestine clapped her hands and giggled. Henri caught the giggles, too. "Next year little lady, you'll be old enough to have sled rides and make snow angels too."

After a dinner of savory shepherd's pie and pumpkin custard, Henri sat in a rocker feeding Ernestine. Angelica stood at a lamp table, mesmerized by Ada's manger scene. Her hand crept towards the Baby Jesus figurine lying in a straw stuffed matchbox.

"Angelica," Henri warned, trying to keep amusement from her voice. "Look with your eyes, not your hands."

Angelica snatched her hand back and sighed. She turned to Ada and said, "Mama Kessler, tell Mudder the Baby Jesus story." Henri flinched every time Angelica called Ada 'Mama', but she let it go. She was teaching her daughters to call her 'mother'. She and her girls were lucky to have a loving person care for them when she could not.

Ada laughed and put Angelica on her lap. "Your mother knows the story very well, Angel, but I'll tell it, anyway." Angelica cuddled into Ada's arms as she embellished the story of Mary riding on a donkey to Bethlehem, of the angels and the shepherds, of the shining star and of the three kings. By the time she finished, Angelica was asleep.

With her girls settled in bed, Henri and Ada sat in rockers near the coal stove sipping eggnog. The back door creaked open and a blast of frigid air rushed in. Boots stomped on the entryway rug. Charles appeared carrying a broken step stool spattered with paint that he needed for his upcoming job. He set to work replacing the bottom rung. Ada looked up from her knitting and frowned. "You've been extra quiet all day, Henri. Something bothering you?"

Henri swallowed. "I have to quit school, Ada, and find a job. My husband spends every moment he can on the road trying to make sales. Banks are failing and the country is going to pieces. No one has any money. With so few customers, he can't make enough to support us. I hoped to finish my business courses and find work as a stenographer. But what's the point? No one is hiring. And the women with jobs are being dismissed."

Charles sat and worked on the step stool. "The Anaconda Copper Mining Company is as skittish as every other business in the country, but the rich folks who run the business and live on Smelter Hill have money. In fact, Mr. Monroe, one of the headmen in the company, is the gentleman who hired me to paint the inside of his house. I heard his wife is looking for a live-in maid to cook and clean." He glanced at Henri. "Is that something you can do?" Henri stopped the rocker and straightened. She didn't relish the idea of being someone's domestic, but what choice did she have? "Well, I'm definitely qualified. I worked as a servant at St. Albert's College in Glade Harbor for a year and a half. And as you know, I was Reverend Ferrera's housekeeper for a while."

Charles nodded as he bolted a brace to the stool's rung. "I imagine you'd get the job if the Reverend gave you a recommendation."

She could almost hear Martim remind her that if they were married, she wouldn't need a job. But he wouldn't deny her the recommendation. She managed a smile and said, "I'm sure he'll give me one. I'll send a telegram tomorrow and ask. Would a recommendation from you help too?"

"My paint job starts the day after the New Year. I'll put in a good word for you then."

"Thank you so much, Charles," Henri said, feeling grateful to have such caring people in her life. "Do they have children?"

"Two young lads were under foot when Mrs. Monroe showed me what she wanted done. But they're school age, so they wouldn't always be around. And she didn't mention wanting help with their care."

Henri sighed. Even if caring for her employer's kids weren't part of the job and the Monroes hired her as a live-in maid, she'd be spending more time around someone else's children than her own. But right now, there was no alternative.

Chapter Thirty-Two

Thursday, March 6, 1930
Sage Prairie, Montana.
Martim

Martim checked the time. Almost eight o'clock. The young couple seated before him had shown up unexpectedly at the rectory office two hours ago wanting counseling for a troubled marriage. They'd lingered longer than he expected. Henri had sent an urgent telegram this afternoon asking him to call her at the Kesslers' at seven this evening. He knew Henri could stay with the Kesslers only so late before she had to return to her room at the Monroes, where she'd boarded ever since they hired her as their maid.

Hoping to end the counseling session with the beleaguered couple, he said, "Remember your wedding vows to love each other through good times and bad. Your life together is difficult now, but prayer and determination can help your marriage thrive. Keep in mind the advice I've just given. Every day, find one way to make your spouse happy. Recognize those thoughtful acts as expressions of love and show your appreciation."

The young man took his wife's hand. She looked at her husband for the first time since they had arrived and said, "We'll try, Father."

As the couple knelt for his blessing, Martim thought of the trials in his relationship with Henri. Right now, things were tough. She was far away with an unfair share of parental burdens. He carried a different burden: the agony of not being able to be a normal father. And worse: not being able to send Henri enough money so his daughters could live with their mother. If she weren't so stubborn, they'd struggle together, living in one household as a regular family.

When the couple left, he phoned the Kessler's. The line was busy. Not surprising, since the Kesslers had four other parties who shared the line. He tried several more times. Finally, his call went through. Henri answered with, "Kessler residence. Henrietta speaking."

"It's me, Henri. Sorry, it's so late."

"Thank God you could call, Jack." Hearing her say 'Jack' sent a stab through his heart. Of course, if the Kesslers were nearby, she had to pretend it was her non-existent husband calling.

Henri's words rushed through the phone. "Our little Ernestine is in the hospital with pneumonia again."

The worry in her voice caught in his chest as she explained their baby's precarious condition. "They've taken x-rays, and the doctor says it may be worse than the bout she had when she was four months old. The Monroes gave me yesterday and today off so I could stay with her. We've tried everything; menthol rub, pots of water on the stove steaming up the kitchen, cold cloths for her fever, a bottle of warm lemon and honey water for the cough. I spent last night in the Kessler's rocker with her head on my shoulder so she could breathe easier. It helped, but not enough."

"Henri. Slow down. Breathe," he said, barely breathing himself. "It won't do our baby any good if her mother is worried to death."

He could hear her inhale and let it go before she continued. "The last two days she's barely eaten. She's beyond crying, though I suppose that's good because crying congests her even more. This afternoon her fever spiked to 103. She was gasping for air and had turned blue. That's when Mr. Kessler drove us to the hospital."

He choked back his own panic "Is Angelica sick, too?"

"She's fighting a cold, but she's okay. She tried to comfort her little sister. Sweet thing. It hurt Angelica's feelings when Ernie wouldn't play with Angel's doll. She thought it'd make her little sister feel better. Of course, it didn't, but Angelica didn't understand. When I put our Angel to bed, she kept asking where her little sister was. When I explained Ernie was in the hospital, she said, 'I want to go too.'"

"It's sweet she cares so much," Martim said, hearing the catch in his voice.

"Angelica is a bright spot through all of this. I wish you were here to share in the sweet things she says and does."

His throat tightened. A sense of helplessness dug at his conscience. He couldn't be with his children to enjoy the pleasures of watching them grow. Now he wasn't there to help with a crisis. He cleared his throat. "I'll be in Great Falls as soon as I can. Tomorrow I must officiate at a funeral, but I'll be there Saturday."

"You will?" A bit of hesitation mixed with the relief in her voice.

"Don't worry. I'll present myself as a caring pastor and friend."

Henri heaved a sigh. "Thank you so much."

The phone beeped. Someone on the Kessler's party line was

listening or wanted to use the line. Henri muttered. "We'd better hang up. I'll see you soon."

"Okay. If she takes a turn for the worse, you'll call right away. I'll drive through the night if I have to."

***

Henrietta
Friday, March 7, 1930

Henri stood at the nursery window, nibbling her lip as she watched Sister Eleanor place Ernestine over a pillow on her lap, thumping the baby's back and kneading her ribs. It was part of the physiotherapy prescribed by the doctor, along with doses of an anti-pneumonia serum. Her baby was still listless, and her chubby cheeks had turned hollow. Though she hadn't improved much, at least she wasn't worse, and her chances under Sister Eleanor's care were far better than if she were home. Thank God Martim was coming tomorrow.

Sister Eleanor noticed Henri at the window and beckoned her in. She gave Henri an update as she continued working on Ernestine. "Your little sweetheart is slowly responding to the therapy, but it'll take several more weeks, perhaps even a month, before she's out of the woods."

"I'm grateful for everything you're doing," Henri said, studying the way Sister massaged her baby's tiny body.

A few minutes later, Ernestine began coughing. "That's my girl," Sister said as she continued the massage. "Let's get it out." As Ernestine choked up greenish phlegm, her breathing became easier. Finally, Sister turned the baby over and handed Henri a jar of ointment. "Here, Mama, rub her chest with this salve. It'll help her breathe."

Henri opened the jar. The smell of menthol and camphor mingled with the odors of alcohol and lye saturating the room. "Hey little dumpling," she said as she spread the rub on Ernestine's chest. "Mother is here to help you feel better." At the sound of Henri's voice, Ernestine opened her eyes. They lacked their usual spark, but she grew a tiny smile when she saw her mother.

Henri jumped at a voice beside her. "How's she doing, Ma?"

Henri turned to see Etta, dressed in a white uniform and a maid's cap. "Maybe a bit better, Pa. I'm glad you work here so you can keep tabs on our baby."

A few weeks ago, Etta quit her business courses to find a job. Like so many others, her parents could no longer afford the tuition. The only employment she found was the maid's job here at the hospital.

"I check on her whenever I can." Etta frowned. "I'm sorry her real Pa can't come to see her."

For months, Etta had hinted around that she'd love to meet Mr. Rollado. She hated lying to Etta, but bit her lip and lied again. "Her father desperately wants to come. But he can't pass up any opportunity to make a sale. Right now, he barely makes enough to cover expenses. And soon we'll have another hospital bill to pay."

A fierce scowl flooded Etta's face. "This economic situation is horrible."

"And now Ernestine's pneumonia has made our life more difficult." Henri grimaced as she wiped the excess salve from her fingers and put the lid back on the jar. She shrugged and smiled up at Etta. "But there's a silver lining. Father Ferrera is coming tomorrow to give her a blessing and to pray for her recovery."

Etta's face filled with admiration. "That's wonderful. And to think Sage Prairie almost lost him to the church in Willow Grove. I'm glad the Abbot honored the congregation's petition and didn't transfer him as he planned. Father is the best pastor Sage Prairie has ever had."

"So true, Etta." It was more proof it was best for Martim to remain a priest.

Etta kissed Ernestine's sweaty curls. "Get well, little girl. We're rooting for you." She patted Henri's shoulder. "I better get back to work. There are tons of sheets to change." She made a face. "And too many bedpans to empty."

Henri watched her leave the nursery, wondering if her friendship with Etta could survive if she ever told her the truth. It was too risky right now. She needed Etta too much.

***

Martim
Early morning, March 8, 1930
Great Falls

The morning sun had just shown its face when Martim parked his Buick near the Columbus Hospital in Great Falls. Ernestine weighed on his heart, but his thoughts were on the phone call he'd gotten from the bishop last night. His Excellency hinted something serious was afoot and required Martim to meet him today to discuss the issue. Was it a financial matter, or something to do with his role in planning the new Sage Prairie high school? Could it be a problem with one of his congregations? Usually, the bishop discussed those topics at their regular monthly meetings. Having to meet in person before their scheduled consultation meant the issue was big. What if rumors concerning his relationship with Henri had reached His Excellency? His mind roiled with the possibilities as he entered the hospital and walked to the main desk.

A nun in a white habit looked up from a stack of papers. “What can I do for you, Father?”

He held his hat in his hands. “I’m Reverend Ferrera, here to give baby Ernestine Rollado a blessing at her family’s request.”

The nun smiled. “Come, I’ll take you to the children’s ward.” The nun’s hard-soled shoes clacked on the polished floor as they walked through the hallway.

When they entered the doors to the second-floor hallway, Martim stopped and asked, “How is the baby doing?”

The nun made a wry face. “She’s very ill. Pneumonia takes a long time to cure. Sometimes up to six weeks. But she’s a fighter and in the very best of care. Perhaps your blessing will speed her recovery.”

Right now, a blessing was the best he could offer. Ernestine was his child, and he wanted to do more. “Is her mother here with her?”

“We sent her home last night. She didn’t want to go, but we insisted she needed rest. She plans to come as soon as she makes breakfast and does the cleanup where she works. Her employers have been generous giving her time off without cutting her pay.”

“I’m sure she appreciates that immensely.”

The nun put her finger to her lips and led Martim into the dimly lit ward. The smell of antiseptic and camphor permeated the air. They passed several cribs with sleeping children until they reached the crib at the end of the room where a Sister of Charity sat in a rocker feeding Ernestine a bottle of milk. His daughter’s eyes were closed. Her lashes curled on her white cheeks, and dark, damp ringlets swirled around her ears.

The nun whispered, “Sister Eleanor, this is Reverend Ferrera. He’s here to bless the sweetheart you’re feeding. And I imagine while he’s here he’d be willing to bless your other charges as well.”

“Wonderful,” Sister Eleanor said. “We never refuse a blessing for our little ones.” She held up the bottle and grinned. “Look. Two ounces. A good sign.” She wiped a dribble of milk from Ernestine’s chin and handed the baby to Father.

Martim stared at the daughter in his arms. Concern about his meeting with the bishop disappeared, replaced by worry for his baby girl. "She's so tiny and pale. It's as if she weighs nothing."

Sister Eleanor peered fondly at Ernestine. "She's going through a lot. I'm sure your blessing will help. I'll leave her with you. She's had her breakfast. Now it's time for me to feed our other little ones."

Martim settled in the rocker and cradled Ernestine in his arms. Her lips quivered as her green eyes stared up at him. "It's okay, *minha bebê*. It's me, your *papai*." He began a hushed Portuguese lullaby. She relaxed and fixated on his face, snuggling into his arms.

He sang as long as he dared, then placed a hand on her head and whispered his blessing. "Heavenly Father, healer of all who are ill, thank you for the gift of my daughter. Hear my plea. If it be thy Holy Will, I beg Thee to restore her to health. Amen." His eyes misted as he made the sign of the cross over her. Though her breathing was labored and raspy, she drifted into sleep. He checked for Sister Eleanor as he laid her in the crib. The nun's back was to him as she tended another child. He leaned over and kissed his little girl's forehead.

He slowly made his way through the nursery, blessing each child. A few stirred. Most slept. Sister Eleanor hushed one fussy toddler, soothing him as he lay against her shoulder. With each prayer, Father asked God to help the parents of those ill children through their tough times.

When Martim finished praying over the babies, he stood in the doorway and surveyed the ward. Sister Eleanor was still busy with the sick child. When he caught her eye, she nodded with a smile. His daughter was in the best of care.

As he turned to go, he bumped into a maid mopping the floor. The women looked up and grinned. "Father Ferrera. Henri told me you'd be here."

Martim blinked. "Etta. She didn't tell me you worked here."

Etta gave half a laugh. "It's only been a week. My parents couldn't afford tuition anymore. And as you know, stenographer jobs are scarcer than hen's teeth."

"Everything is scarce these days. Do you live nearby?"

She laughed again. "Very close. I live here at the hospital. Except for a few dollars, my pay is room and board." Her smile turned to a frown. "It's sad Ernestine's papa can't come to visit. It'd be wonderful if Ernie could see him for once. Henri says there's no chance he can come. That he spends every waking moment trying to make enough to pay the hospital bill he knows is coming." She gave a disgusted snort. "I imagine it's going to be enormous."

Martim's guilt erupted again. He had to do more to help with Henri's financial burdens. God knows. She was doing her part, earning room and board, working for the Monroes, using most of her salary to pay the Kesslers for Angelica and Ernestine's care with only fifteen dollars left each month. If she saved every cent of those fifteen dollars, it would take a month of Sundays to pay the hospital bill.

He asked Etta, "When will Henri be back at the hospital?"

Etta glanced at the clock at the end of the hallway. "Probably soon. She was relieved when you told her you'd come and give the baby a blessing."

"I wish I could do more. When you see Henri, let her know I'm in the hospital chapel."

"I will," Etta said and took off with her mop and bucket.

Alone in the hospital's small chapel, Martim's fingers moved around his rosary. As he prayed, his mind swirled with concern for Ernestine, with worry about Henri's money matters, and with anxiety about his impending discussion with the bishop. What did he want?

Footsteps padded near, and then Henri knelt beside him. "Thank you for coming."

He kept his eyes on his rosary and nodded. "You're right. Our baby is being well cared for." He touched her hand. "I'll come as often as I can to give her a blessing until she's out of the hospital. When the bill comes, let me know. I'll take care of it."

She pressed her hand to her heart and sank back into the pew. "That's a relief, Martim."

He sat beside her. "How are you settling in as Mrs. Rollado?"

"Everyone I've met since I moved here sees me as a married woman. No one questions my husband's absence. They know traveling salesmen are rarely home, especially with times so hard."

He swallowed. "I'm happy for you, Henri." God forgive me, he thought. He almost wished her ruse wasn't working. "I can't stay long, *meu amor*. The bishop wants to meet with me this morning."

"The usual business?"

He nodded. She had so much on her mind. No sense worrying her more. And whatever the bishop had to say might have nothing to do with her.

***

Martim stood in the doorway of the bishop's outer office, knots tangling in his stomach. The bishop's chancellor stooped over a typewriter, punching at the keys, a letter unrolling from the machine. Martim knocked. The chancellor's hands froze. He turned. "Ah, it's you, Father Ferrera. Go ahead, the bishop is waiting." He turned back to his typing.

Martim steeled himself and opened the door to the bishop's inner office. His superior stood looking out the window. He wasn't dressed in official attire. A good sign. The meeting would be informal. Martim cleared his throat. "Your Excellency, you asked to see me."

"Yes. Please come in. Sit down." Was there a hint of steeliness in his voice? Martim wasn't sure.

He made himself relax and settled in a chair in front of the bishop's desk. His heart calmed when he saw an account book open on the desk. Was the ledger a sign his superior only wanted to talk over money matters?

"Tea?" his Excellency asked, pouring a cup from a pot sitting on a serving cart.

"Please."

The bishop handed Martim a steaming drink and said, "I'm meeting with all the diocesan pastors to discuss their financial situations. This abominable depression has left many parishes short of funds. Not just for charitable works, but also for their regular expenses." He settled at his desk and stirred sugar into his tea.

Martim took a sip, pleased to find it peppermint. "You're right, Your Excellency. Many are forced to seek help these days. It's been especially hard on those who value their independence," Like Henri, he thought, and the growing hospital bill she'd never be able to pay on her own. He watched the tea leaves swirl before returning his gaze to the bishop. "I've cut my own expenses to the bone, leaving what I can for those in greater need."

"So, you're making do?"

"Mostly. I do my own auto repairs and help others with theirs. I hunt and fish for my table and for parishioners who need food. In return, they share the bounty of their gardens." He grimaced. "But it's never enough."

The bishop peered at him with solemn eyes. "I know. The Lord asks us to do what is possible and to save the miracles for Him."

"I pray for miracles every day," Martim said, thinking of Ernestine and Henri's financial situation.

The bishop's casual demeanor disappeared as he removed a small stack of letters from a drawer and placed them on his desk. He faced Martim with a steely gaze. "There is another matter we must discuss, Father Ferrera."

Martim's chest tightened as he watched the bishop slip a letter from an envelope and study it. A knock came on the door. His Excellency scowled and said, "Yes, what is it?"

The chancellor appeared in the door. "I hate to interrupt, Your Excellency, but you have an urgent call. May I put it through?"

The bishop laid the letter on his desk, his brow wrinkling as he nodded.

The chancellor disappeared, and the phone rang. The bishop picked up and listened. He turned pale and placed his hand over the mouthpiece. "Father Ferrera, we'll have to continue this conversation at another time."

Martim left. Momentary escape did nothing to ease his fear or his conscience.

Chapter Thirty-Three

Five weeks later,
Saturday, April 19, 1930
Martim's Birthday

Martim let his car speed down the hill, braking slightly as the Buick moved around a curve. When the phone call came this morning, he thought it might be Henri with news about Ernestine. Instead, it had been an urgent request from the Wickham family. Their old grandmother had taken an unexpected turn for the worse. Her daughter hoped he could come and give the ailing woman the last rites before she passed away.

The car ahead of him picked up speed, racing at a dangerous pace. Had the brakes failed? The vehicle careened off the road, over the embankment, and out of sight.

"Lord Jesus, help them." He pulled onto the narrow shoulder, grabbed his black satchel, and scrambled down the steep hill making his way over boulders and jagged rocks as dust swirled around the wreck below. By the time he got to the vehicle, powdery sand coated the mangled remains. Shards of glass littered the bodies of a young man and woman crushed against the dashboard. Blood splattered the windshield and soaked their clothes. He checked their pulse. His hand came away slick with blood. Both had faint pulses that told him they were leaving the world. With an anguished heart, he took his stole from the bag, kissed it, and placed it around his neck. He reached through the shattered windows and anointed each of them with Holy Oil and prayed.

"Father, I ask you to have mercy on the souls of these two young people who are struggling in their final agony. May this holy anointing comfort and aid them in body and soul. Forgive their sins and welcome them into your Kingdom. Amen."

As he put his stole away, he heard moans coming from the back seat. God, no. Not another one. He pried the door open and found a young boy heaped on the floor. His eyes were open, full of pain and terror. Blood gushed from the gash on his forehead and mixed with tears. Two front teeth dangled from his mouth in a grizzled mess.

Martim ran his hand over the little guy's head. "It's okay, buddy. I'll get you free."

"Momma? Poppa?" Fear filled his voice.

Oh God, he couldn't tell him. The child should be with loved ones when he learned the truth about his mother and father. He choked back his own tears. "I've taken care of your momma and poppa. Let me help you." When he found no further injuries, he lifted the youngster from the car. Shielding him from the sight of his parents, he struggled up the embankment and carried the boy to his car. He wrapped the little guy in his woolen blanket and began cleaning the blood around his mouth.

"What's your name, lad?"

The boy's lips quivered as he tried to speak. His dangling teeth got in the way. It was impossible to save them. They had to come out. Martim gazed into the boy's eyes and asked, "Are you about six?"

Sniffling, the child shook his head no.

"Five?"

The boy nodded through tears.

"You know six-year-old boys always loose those top two baby teeth."

He nodded again.

"You're a big lad and five is almost six. Seems like your two front teeth will come out early. Close your eyes and hang on." A simple yank, a groan of pain, and he showed the youngster his two bloody teeth. "Now you're ready for your grown-up teeth to come in."

The lad managed a weak smile as tears continued their trek down his face. Martim dampened his hankie with water from his canteen, wiped the blood from the boy's mouth, and offered him a drink. The little guy whimpered, took a few sips, and returned the flask.

"What's your name, lad?" Martim asked as he began cleaning the lacerations on the youngster's forehead.

"Simon."

"You're very brave, Simon. Can you tell me your last name?"

"Bauer."

Martim pressed a swatch of gauze on the wound, wrapped a strip of cloth around Simon's head and tied it. "Where were your mamma and poppa going?"

"Willow Grove. Grand poppa is gonna to teach me how to ride a pony."

"Ride a horse. Well, you are a big boy."

The squeal of brakes broke the air. An old Ford pulled up. A young man hurried to Martim. "I see there's been an accident, Father. Can I help?"

Martim handed Simon his canteen. "Drink a little more. I'll be right back." He walked with the Good Samaritan to the edge of the road and nodded at the wreck below. "I gave the boy's parents the Last Rites. He told me they were on their way to Willow Grove to visit his grandparents. Could you notify the authorities about the bodies down there while I get their son to his loved ones?"

The chap stared at the wreckage, took off his cap, and bowed his head. His voice quivered as he prayed. "God, welcome those poor folks into heaven and help their little guy. Amen." He put on his hat and said, "They were lucky you were here to send them to heaven, Father. Go ahead. Tend to the boy. I'll get the sheriff."

Back at the car, Martim found Simon had grown very pale. Sweat beaded his forehead, and his eyes closed. "He's going into shock," Martim muttered to himself, checked the boy's pulse, and found it slower than normal. He laid Simon across the back seat, propped the kid's feet on his black bag, and tucked the blanket around him. "Simon," Martim said, gently shaking the boy. His eyes flickered open. "When we get to Willow Grove, how do we get to your grand poppa's place?"

"It's by that fence on the hill."

"What hill?"

"Ask Papa. He knows." His eyes closed again.

Martim climbed back into the car and headed to Willow Grove. He stopped at several places in town before someone could give him directions to the Bauer's. After he got Simon settled with his grandparents and gave them the heartbreaking news, he instructed them on how to help Simon recover from his shock. He wanted to stay and console the grieving couple. But the Wickham family and their grandmother were waiting with their own critical need.

When he reached the Wickhams, he found that the old woman had died an hour earlier. Her family's grief was magnified when he'd told them her soul had left her body, meaning he couldn't administer the Last Rites. But he could pray, asking God to forgive the woman her sins and to receive her into heaven. He stayed to comfort the family as long as he could and left with a heavy heart.

As he drove back to Sage Prairie, he agonized over his longing to marry Henri. If he'd come upon today's wreck as a layman, he could have helped little Simon and taken him to his grandparents. But he couldn't have performed the Last Rites. The young couple would have died with unforgiven sins on their souls. Despite their grief, Simon's grandparents were consoled, knowing their son and their daughter-in-law had received the Holy Anointing.

And then there were the Wickhams. Though they were heartbroken he was unable to give their grandmother the Last Rites, his presence as a man of God had comforted them. Was God trying to tell him to remain in the priesthood and stop pursuing the idea of marrying Henri?

***

The sun had long since set when Martim picked up the phone in his rectory office and dialed the operator. He waited anxiously to be put through to the Kessler's. Another busy signal. He placed the phone back on the hook and stared at the slice of birthday cake Miss Fletcher had made. His stomach rebelled at the thought of eating. He rehashed the day over and over, remembering the treacherous roads he and Henri had often traveled. He hadn't confessed the sin he committed when Ernestine had been conceived, and neither had Henri. What if they were killed with those terrible sins on their souls? Would a priest be available to anoint them in the Last Rites and keep them from Hell. He was desperate to rush to Henri, to find a path back to grace. To be with her, with Angelica and Ernestine before a split second ended their lives. He forked up a piece of cake, but returned it to the plate, and dialed the operator again.

This time, Henri picked up. The joy in her voice said she had good news. The Kesslers must be nearby because she answered, saying, "Jack?" The joy in her voice said she had good news.

"Yes, it's me, *meu amor*."

Her words raced over the phone. "You're getting the best birthday present ever. The hospital discharged our baby girl today. She's on my lap this very moment."

Martim took a deep breath and let it go. "Yes, the perfect gift. Put her ear to the phone for me. I'd like to sing to her." As he sang a lively tune from his childhood, he heard Ernestine giggle. Her innocent joy eased the anguish that had amassed all day.

When he finished, Henri came back on the phone. "You should see her face, Mart…." She caught herself and continued. "Jack. I think she recognizes your voice. The charges for the call will be horrendous, but Angelica wants to talk to her father, too."

This was his first daughter, the child he'd never seen, the one he'd never held, or heard her voice. "I'd love to talk with her. And don't worry. I'll pay for the call."

Angelica's voice bubbled over the line. "Heh woe," she said. "Are you my fodder?"

"I am," he answered, glad he could acknowledge who he was.

Angelica babbled on. "I help Mudder with my widdle sister."

"I'll bet you are a big help, Angel, like your Tia Angelica in Portugal." He wondered if she'd remember this conversation when she was older. His sadness returned, knowing it would be impossible to be a part of his daughters' existence as their *papai* if he remained a priest. Their father would always be Jack Rollado, a traveling salesman who would never be in their lives, except as a myth.

When the conversation ended and the phone was back on the hook, memories of the conversation with the bishop a few weeks ago mixed with his turmoil. Had God kept His Excellency from requesting a new meeting to discuss the issue concerning his relationship with Henri? Was God keeping him from scandal so he would remain in the priesthood?

Or was he meant to approach the bishop on his own before his superior summoned him? Get it all out? Ask for forgiveness and leave his ministry, hoping Henri would marry him? What was it God wanted?

Chapter Thirty-Four

Two years later,
Thursday, May 8, 1931
Buffalo Springs, Montana,
Henrietta

Three-year-old Angelica stood on the floor in the train's coach, dressed in her Sunday best. Her chin barely reached the window's ledge as she stared at the mountains and prairies rolling by. Henri shook her head in exasperation as she watched her daughter absentmindedly slip out of her shiny black shoes. As always, it didn't matter how nice the shoes were or how well they fit, Angelica loved bare feet.

Henri stood Ernestine on her lap, so her youngest had a view of the scenery like her sister. Ernie clapped in delight and pointed to the animals grazing on the hillside. "Cows says moo," she said.

"Those aren't cows, Ernestine. They're antelope," Henri said, tugging her daughter's dress down so her panties didn't show.

Angelica gazed at the herd stretched across the prairie and asked, "Mother, what do antelopes say?"

Henri laughed. "I don't remember ever hearing an antelope, sweetheart, but hunters have told me they make snorting noises." At least that's what Martim had explained several years ago.

Martim! Anticipation and excitement had built ever since she and her girls had boarded the Great Falls train to Buffalo Springs. Martim would be at the station to pick them up. The closer she got, the headier she became. Though she and Martim frequently exchanged letters and occasionally talked on the phone, they hadn't seen each other for almost a year.

She'd been ecstatic when Martim had sent ticket money with a note saying he ached to see her and his two daughters. He'd signed it, 'Love, Jack'. She'd hidden her alarm when Etta said she hoped she could come and meet the elusive Jack Rollado. Thankfully, Etta realized it wouldn't be right to intrude on such a special occasion.

With Etta's help, she was making it work in Great Falls as Mrs. Rollado. She scraped by on the pittance she earned as a maid and from a few other odd jobs. They weren't jobs she would have chosen. But at least she had employment. And with the money Martim sent, she managed. It wasn't easy, but life wasn't easy for most folks these days. Her girls had the basics, sufficient food, decent secondhand clothes, and the best of care from the Kesslers since she still lived with the Monroes. Despite how hard it was to raise them alone, she relished her independence. Sometimes she'd ask for advice from Martim, the Kesslers, Etta, and Greta. But she was free to decide what was best for her daughters and herself.

Her heart faltered. There was a downside to her quasi freedom. The girls didn't have a father in their lives. Except for the one she'd created, the one they'd never see. To be honest, sometimes it would be helpful to have a husband around. If she were married, her children would be living with her. She and Martim could have a place of their own, however humble, to raise their girls together. He could do the heavy lifting, keep the wood box full, and do repairs and outside chores. But as wonderful as a life with Martim would be, she'd manage without him, relying on the help of friends and neighbors. It was difficult but was the price of freedom.

Living as Mrs. Rollado allowed Martim to pursue his calling. She still believed he was best in that role. She'd carry whatever burden she must to keep him free to serve his far-flung flocks. He'd broken his vow of celibacy because of her. She loved him too much to be the reason he broke the vow that made him a priest. Martim cared deeply for her. But over time, if they married, would his love turn to resentment because she'd taken him from the ministry he cherished as well?

Angelica squealed from the window, startling Henri. "Look," she cried. "Two baby antelopes. They so cute."

"They are cute," Henri answered, turning Ernestine so she could see them, too. "It's spring. And lots of animals are having babies right now."

The little girl sitting across from them hopped from her mother's lap and joined Angelica at the window. Soon the two girls chatted like magpies. The woman, whom Henri had learned was Irene, smiled. "I hope my daughter gets along this well with her cousins. She's meeting them for the first time today."

"She seems so sweet. I'm sure they'll love her."

Irene shook her head and frowned. "I don't know. She needs a nap. And when Eliza is overly tired, she's cranky. My brother, who lives in Casper, said he'd pick us up at the station. But his car is unreliable. It's likely he'll show up late, maybe very late. By the time Eliza meets her cousins, it'll be well past her naptime. That will set her off on the wrong foot."

Irene's problem was an answer to Henri's dilemma. Ever since they'd boarded the train, she'd fretted about the impression others would have when Martim met her and the girls at the depot. Having Irene and Eliza with her would dispel suspicion.

She bit her lip and smiled. "A longtime family friend is meeting me at the station. He's a priest, and he's volunteered to drive us to Havre, where my husband is working. I'm sure Father Ferrera would be happy to take you and Eliza to your brother's place." Falsehoods moved off her lips easier now, but they still slashed at her conscience.

"But Casper is out of your way."

Henri shrugged. "Only a few miles. Father has a big heart and is always willing to help."

The worry left Irene's face. "That so kind, Henri. It takes a load off my mind."

An hour later, they stepped from the train. The sight of Martim waiting on the passenger platform sent her heart racing. His eyes, his handsome face, the masculine lines of his body were as alluring as ever. It didn't help that emotion flashed across his face when he saw her. It would be so easy to give in and marry him. She steeled herself against the temptation.

"It's good to see you, Mrs. Rollado," he said, his voice neutral. He stooped and faced his daughters. Henri wondered if Irene could read the love in his eyes when he spoke to the girls. "I'm Father Ferrera. You must be Angelica and Ernestine."

Ernestine's grin flirted behind the thumb in her mouth. Henri removed the thumb and whispered, "You're not a baby anymore, Ernestine."

Angelica tucked her head to her shoulder and looked up shyly. "Mother said we get to ride in your Boo-ik."

He laughed. "Indeed, you do. My Buick is waiting." He smiled at Eliza. "And young lady, who are you?"

Henri broke in. "This is Eliza and her mother, Irene. We met on the train. I told her you might drive her to her brother's home near Casper."

Martim nodded. "It would be my pleasure. Come ladies," he said, picking up each of their satchels. "I'm parked behind the station."

Henri took her daughters' hands and followed Martim. She'd wanted a photo of the girls with their father for a long time. If she couldn't share the truth, at least she'd have a picture of them together. She pulled her camera from her handbag. "Father, would you take a picture of Angel and Ernestine with me?"

"A fine idea, Mrs. Rollado," he said, his voice warm with a hint of emotion. He snapped a few poses, including a group picture with Eliza and Irene, and handed the camera back to Henri.

Henri kept her tone light as she said, "How about a photo with you and my daughters, Father?"

Martim's eyes widened. He grinned. "I'd be delighted to have my picture with them." He gathered Angelica and Ernestine around him. Love and pain brewed on his face as Henri clicked the shutter.

***

Dust flew around the Buick as he drove from the farm where they'd left Irene and Eliza. Henri sat beside Martim with Ernestine on her lap, and Angelica stood on the back seat staring out the window, bracing herself against the bumps in the driveway. By the time they reached the main road, a sense of well-being swelled in Henri. It was as if they were a real family. A short-lived illusion she'd revel in as long as she could.

Martim smiled at her as he shifted into third gear, a smile of affection so deep it triggered a longing to become the family he wanted. Feelings that contradicted her need to be independent. He reached over and caressed her hand. The desire she'd been holding at bay swept through her. She took her hand from his and tucked it in her pocket. Best not let passion take over. Today she had to be a virtuous mother.

She returned his smile and asked, "What are the plans for today?"

"How about a picnic? There's a perfect place on Cottonwood Creek." He tucked a curling strand of hair behind Ernestine's ear, glanced back at Angelica, and then returned his eyes to the road. "It's for our girls, Henri. How often will I be able to spend time with them as their *papai*? They're so young, they may not remember today. But if they do, I hope it's with fondness, even if they believe I'm only a family friend."

Henri swallowed. The day's possibilities flashed through her conscience. Even with her girls present, being with Martim in an idyllic place away from judgmental eyes could make her vow to be virtuous hard to keep. Though he wore his clerical collar, today she had to think of him as the father of her children, Jack Rollado. That made keeping her vow even more difficult, but she owed him this special time with his daughters. She took a deep breath and let it go. "Okay, Mr. Rollado, let's do it."

He hummed, his fingers strumming the steering wheel as he turned onto a path that led to a stand of willows and cottonwoods. Henri rolled down her window and breathed in the sweet smell of new grass, of budding trees, and the freshness of the day. Soon the tangy scent of a creek tickled her nose. Martim parked the car under trees bordering the stream. The serenity of the woodland and Martim's presence filled her with peace.

Martim lifted Angelica from the auto, spun her around, and put her on the ground. She giggled. "Do it again, Fodder Ferrera." He twirled her several more times until she toppled over with dizziness. Dust covered her dress when she finally righted herself, laughing.

Henri pushed aside her irritation at the dirt on Angelica's outfit and brushed it away. She shouldn't be mad at Martim for wanting to enjoy his daughters, but she could remedy the situation. She took Angel's hand. "No more fun and games, Father Ferrera, until I get our daughters into play clothes."

"I'm sorry," Martim said, looking abashed. "While you change the girls, I'll find a nice place for our picnic."

The spot he chose added perfection to the day. A thicket of chokecherries bordered the creek. Their lowest branches swept the ground and, in some places, dipped into the stream. Bees buzzed through their dense white blossoms. A red-winged blackbird perched on a cattail gone to fluff and called to its mate, and somewhere high in the trees a magpie squawked and swooped across the water.

"Birds say peep, peep," Ernie said when Henri sat her on the ground and spread out Martim's familiar woolen blanket.

"Yes, birds say peep, peep," she said absently. Memories rushed in of another time four years ago when she and Martim had soaked her sprained ankle in a creek and how desire had built even then. She clenched her fists, her nails digging into her palms. "Mother of Jesus," she prayed silently. "Give me strength to keep my vow. This day is for our children, not for us."

"Henri? Are you all right?" Martim's hand rested on her shoulder, his touch burning through her skin.

"I am," she said, calming herself. When she looked up, she saw him standing in the sunlight, gold flecking the tips of his dark hair. He'd changed into outdoor clothes, wore fisherman rubbers, and held a pole.

She averted her eyes and opened the picnic basket. "You scout the creek for a fishing spot while I lay out the lunch."

"There's a great pool downstream, but I need bait first. I can catch a lot of fish with the insect larvae hiding under the rocks. That's what I'm after."

Her heart danced as she watched him scour the creek bed for bait. Would the thrill of being with him ever leave? She busied herself unpacking the picnic basket, trying to bury her desire. As she laid out slices of ham, cheese, bread, pickles, butter, and chokecherry jelly, she kept an eye on Ernestine. Her little girl had followed her father to the stream's edge and threw pebbles into the lazy shallows. Angelica busied herself collecting dandelions. Henri reminded herself, her girls were the purpose of the day.

She opened a thermos of lemonade and called, "Martim, come have lunch before the ants carry it away."

Martim closed his bait can and swung Ernestine onto his shoulder. "Come little maiden, your mother says our picnic is ready." He set her on the blanket, grabbed a slice of bread and spread it with jelly. "For you, my sweetheart." He folded the bread in half and gave it to Ernestine. "Tank you," she said, batting her eyes and grinning.

Angelica pranced up. "Fodder Ferrera, I picked you some flowers." She handed him a fistful of dandelions, the milk from their stems oozing through her fingers.

"They're beautiful, Angelica," he said, and slipped one into the buttonhole of his flannel shirt. He took a pint jar meant for the lemonade and filled it with water at the creek. Moments later, a sunny bouquet sat in the center of the picnic blanket. And then he fixed Angelica a jelly sandwich like Ernestine's. The love he showered on their daughters made Henri love him even more. Was she a fool for refusing to marry him?

As they ate, bees invited themselves to lunch, drawn to the dandelions and to a dollop of jelly that had dropped on the blanket. "Bee say buzz, buzz," Ernestine announced, reaching for an insect mining a dandelion for pollen.

"No, Ernestine," Henri cried.

Too late. Ernestine howled. Her mother gathered her in her arms, trying to calm her. Through sobs Ernie announced, "Bee bad girl. Bee bite me."

Suddenly Martim loomed above Henri, holding the black bag he always carried. She hadn't realized he'd been gone. He crushed an aspirin in a spoon and added water to make a paste. "Let me have her, Henri. This poultice will ease the pain."

Five minutes later, Ernestine sat in Martim's lap, her head against his chest, her sobs fading, and her eyes drooping. "You're a magician, Martim. I didn't know an aspirin poultice would help a bee sting."

He kissed Ernestine's curly hair and shrugged. "Something I learned along the way. Look, she's relaxed enough to fall asleep."

Henri nodded at Angelica who lay on her side on the blanket watching with sleepy eyes. "There's another one long overdue for a nap. They've been up since five."

Martim stood with Ernie, now sleeping soundly on his shoulder. "Henri, bring Angelica. My car is in the shade. We'll crack the windows and lay them both on the back seat so they can sleep without the bother of bees."

Henri was about to protest, thinking how lovely it would be for the girls to sleep outdoors, with the creek bubbling a melody and the wind fluttering through their hair. But an abundance of bees hummed around the dandelions, the jelly jar, and the profusion of chokecherry blossoms hanging near the blanket. She picked up Angelica, tucked her into the car's backseat opposite her little sister, and kissed her forehead goodnight.

Henri sat in the shade on the blanket as a breeze rustled through the trees, sending ripples across the water. She watched Martim bait his hook and drop a line into a shaded pool on the other side of the creek. He worked the pool for a while, but having no luck, moved further downstream. When he disappeared around a bend, she pulled *Anne of Green Gables* from her handbag. With no distractions, maybe she could finally get past chapter three.

As interesting as Anne's antics were, the creek's gentle gurgle lulled Henri until she gave in and closed her eyes. She tucked the book under her head for a pillow, drifted into sleep, and into erotic dreams. A hand caressed her hips. Lips touched her ear and murmured, "Henri."

She jumped and opened her eyes. Martim knelt beside her. "I thought you were fishing."

He shrugged. "It's wonderful having you here, Henri. I don't want to waste it looking for trout." He drew in a deep breath and slowly let it go. “I haven’t slept much lately, and this moment is so peaceful. I’m finding sleep hard to resist. May I join you?” Trembling, afraid of what she might do, she sat up. “You’re the one hard to resist, Martim. You’re what I want but shouldn’t have.”

His voice filled with sadness as he said, “I’m tortured too, *meu amor*. I hope today will convince you we could share moments like this for a lifetime without hiding, skulking about, and lying. Today we’re an ordinary family, with our girls napping, and we two enjoying each other’s company.”

She took a deep breath and brushed away a ladybug crawling on his shoulder. There it was again, a not-so-subtle hint for marriage. The desire in his eyes told her there were more to his words than just the need for ‘company’. Would sharing their love intimately one more time convince her marriage was the best path? Did her love for him owe them that chance?

He lay down and pulled her close to him. As wonderful as it was to be folded in his arms, she should get up and walk away, but his touch was so intoxicating, it was impossible to leave. Her guilt dissolved in a flood of passion. Desire swept away the vow she’d made, transporting her and Martim into the truth of their love. They might pay dearly for it later, but now, in this moment, whatever the price levied was worth it. And there always was God’s forgiveness in the time to come.

Later, as Martim slept beside her, she lay awake in his arms, the day now more brilliant, the song of the creek more lovely, and the flowers more fragrant. Time seemed eternal until Angelica’s sleepy voice called from the car. “Mother, I’s awake.”

Ernestine whimpered, “Mudder, Mudder.” Martim’s eyes opened. He smiled and kissed Henri. “Stay here. I’ll get them.” She watched as he helped his daughters out of the car, walked them to the stream, dampened his hankie, and wiped the sleep from their eyes.

By now, remorse skirmished the edge of her happiness. She battled back the invader. There was plenty of time for guilt later. Right now, she let love keep her doubts at bay. God had brought the two of them together as a test. Whether or not they had done the right thing, they had followed their hearts. Their love had created Angelica and Ernestine and had brought them to this moment.

Sunlight filtered through the trees, more beautiful than any cathedral. Two truths flowed into Henri’s heart. Though the love she and Martim shared would last a lifetime, there would never be another intimate moment like this. Her hand went to her belly. She knew without a doubt they had just created another soul.

Chapter Thirty-Five

Nine months later
Thursday, January 28, 1932
Billings, Montana
Martim

Martim sat in a fog of anxiety and anticipation as the train to Billings labored up a hill past grimy drifts of snow. He forced his attention to the passing forest. The trees seemed to groan under the weight of their heavy white coats. The train topped the Bull Mountains and rumbled down the other side. He'd left his assistant pastor in charge for a few days when Henri had sent a coded telegram telling him their third child would arrive soon. The weather had made it too dangerous to travel by car.

Henri was now well known in Great Falls as Mrs. Rollado, and she could have birthed the baby there in the Columbus hospital. But she and Martim decided their new little one should be born in Billings so her traveling salesman husband could appear. He would rather have waited for the baby's baptism as he had for Ernestine. That date could be fixed ahead of time. But he'd given up the idea when Etta was named the baby's godmother. She'd be in Billings for the baptism, making it impossible for him to appear as Jack Rollado.

When the train pulled into the station, he slipped into the Pullman's lavatory and changed into civilian clothes. Fifteen minutes later he trudged through the snow to the McCabe home, where Henri had rented a small room for herself and Jack at a bargain price. As the Great Depression deepened, folks often rented spare rooms giving them money to help them scrape by.

By the time he reached the small clapboard house nestled among a few ghostly elms, the cold had seeped to his bones and his feet prickled with icy numbness. Dozens of dead hollyhock stalks poked through the snow piled next to the house. Thankfully, someone had shoveled a path to the porch.

He knocked on the door, his heart singing at the thought of seeing Henri. A spry white-haired woman in a worn dress, with elbows poking through the holes in her sweater, opened the door. An elderly man in suspenders and baggy trousers stood behind her. The old woman smiled. "You Mr. Rollado?"

He took off his hat and nodded. "Indeed, I am, ma'am."

"Well, Henrietta ain't here," she said, almost shouting. She nodded at the old timer who'd inched closer to her. "My old man took her to the hospital last night. Your little lady hoped your train would make it through the snow. And looks like her prayers was answered. Come in, warm up, and have a bite to eat before you traipse off to see that wife of yours."

The smell of boiled ham, potatoes and cabbage drifted through the house. Though he was hungry, and a meal was tempting, he said, "No thanks, ma'am. If I hurry, I might get to the hospital before the baby arrives."

The old woman frowned and cupped a hand to her ear. "You'll have to speak up, mister. We ain't too good at hearin' these days."

He grinned and repeated himself.

Her gray, wispy brows rose in surprise. "Most men don't want to be around until the hard part of birthin is over," she said, the old man cackling beside her. "But good on you for wantin to be with her. Still, ain't likely you'll be there on time. Her contractions was comin fast and furious when she left."

"You may be right, ma'am, but if there's a chance, I have to hurry," he said, raising his voice to ask directions to the hospital.

Minutes later, he slipped and slid down the icy streets, his mind on the future. As much as he loved his children, this baby had to be their last. Henri lived and worked as a single parent, and three children would stretch her to the limit. God knows he'd done everything possible to persuade her to marry him. He'd sent money and other necessities whenever he could, but it was never enough. It bothered him she still worked as a servant at the Monroes and that their children couldn't live with her. He hoped to find a remedy for the situation soon. But with this depression paralyzing the country, collection plate donations had seriously dwindled, and the new bishop scrutinized every expense, making it almost impossible to come up with discretionary funds.

As he walked into the warmth of the hospital, he wondered again if he should stop this dreadful ruse and resign from the priesthood. Be a man who helped to raise his children. One who was present in their everyday lives, a man who put food on the table and clothes on their back, a father who was around to guide his children through their troubles just as his own *papai* had. He had to try one more time to convince Henri marriage was the honorable path.

The nurse at the desk interrupted his thoughts. "May I help you, sir?"

"Yes. My wife, Henrietta Rollado, was admitted to the hospital last night."

"She was. And your baby arrived at 4:20 this morning."

Martim drew in a long breath. He'd almost made it in time. "A boy or a girl?"

The nurse grinned. "I'll let your wife tell you. Come, I'll take you to the maternity ward. She's resting with the baby right now."

Halfway up the flight of stairs with the nurse, Martim stopped for a moment, remembering the trauma Henri had when Angelica was born.

The nurse stopped beside him. "Is something wrong, Mr. Rollado?"

"No, I just want to be prepared. Did they use Twilight Sleep for the delivery?"

The nurse laughed. "No. Your wife was very insistent, to the point of being completely stubborn. She wanted to be aware during the entire process. And she was a real trooper."

Martim started back up the stairs. "Sounds just like her."

Martim poked his head around the privacy screen and stood watching Henri sleep. A tiny head of fuzzy blond hair was all he could see in the swaddled bundle resting on her chest. He crept in and sat on the bedside chair.

Henri opened her eyes. "Martim, you made it," she smiled, her face still red from the strain of childbirth, her blue eyes full of tenderness. She beamed down at the baby and uncovered its face.

He took the baby into his arms and gave Henri a questioning look.

"It's a boy, Martim. We have a son. And he looks just like you."

He studied his son's tiny features. "I don't see it, Henri. Even his hair and his eyes are the wrong color."

Henri harrumphed. "It may be blond, but it will darken in time and the fuzziness tells me it'll curl like yours. His mouth, his eyes, chin, nose, even the color of his skin, they're all you."

Martim looked closer at his son and frowned, "I still don't see it."

She rolled her eyes and laughed. "Just like a father. Don't worry. You'll see it when he gets older."

Martim gave her a skeptical look. "Did you decide on a name?"

"How does Robert John Rollado sound?"

"A strong masculine name." He gazed at his son; his pride dampened with sadness. "Well, Robert John, I wish I had more to give you than my looks. I'll pray every day you grow strong and honorable and good. May you develop a passion for learning and have an open mind." His throat tightened. "And that you are always a comfort to your *mamãe*."

Henri propped herself up on her pillows and reached for her pocketbook on the bedside table. "I have photos of our girls," she said, and handed him an envelope. "Angelica is wearing the snow outfit you sent for her birthday. And Ernestine is in Angelica's outfit from last winter."

Martim kissed his son's head, amazed at his sweet smell. He returned Robert John to his mother and took the pictures.

"My little girls," he said. "They're adorable. Angelica seems sweet and innocent. Ah, but Ernestine. The look on her face tells me she has a streak of mischief."

Henri gave an exasperated sigh. "Oh boy, does she ever. Sometimes she can be downright willful."

Martim laughed. "Willful, huh? I'm pretty sure she gets that from her *mamae*."

It was Henri's turn to laugh. "True. But right now, we have skirmishes way too often." She handed him another picture. "Here are the girls wearing dresses Ada made."

Martim scowled at the photo. "What were you thinking, Henri? They're standing in the snow without coats or boots. Was that wise? You know how vulnerable Ernestine is to pneumonia."

"It was only for a moment, Martim. And you know photos don't turn out well when they're taken indoors. The sun was out. I had the girls wear their hats. And as soon as the pictures were taken, I rushed them back inside."

Martim scowled. "If their *papai* had been around, he might not have approved."

"Well, he wasn't," Henri snapped. "You just said you wanted our son to grow strong. Do you want me to protect him from a little freezing weather as well?"

"That's different."

"No, it's not." The edge in her voice grew sharper. "I've always admired your support of equal rights for women. That means what's good for our son, is good for our daughters."

"I'm sorry, Henri. You have a point. Besides, you give me no choice but to trust you."

Henri gave him a crooked smile. "I understand how hard that is. I don't always agree with Mama Kessler's methods of raising our daughters either. Sometimes she's softer than I would be. But I have to trust her." She grimaced and adjusted her pillows before she spoke again. "Truth be known, sometimes I'm jealous of her relationship with them. But in the end the important thing is they know they're loved and they're developing into wonderful human beings."

Martim curled his son's fingers around his own and marveled. "So tiny." He leaned over and kissed Henri's forehead. "All three of our children are blessed with a strong and caring *Mamãe*."

"Mr. Rollado?" He jumped. A nurse stood beside him. "Why don't you get something to eat while I tend to your wife and son? The cafeteria is downstairs and serves a decent meal."

Not wanting to miss even a moment with Henri and the baby, he almost said he'd like to stay. But the look in the nurse's eye told him argument was futile. Instead, he asked, "How long before they can be discharged?"

"We scheduled your son's circumcision for Saturday morning. Since your wife didn't depend on Twilight Sleep for delivery, the doctor can discharge them early Sunday."

He squeezed Henri's hand. "You hear that, Henri? You'll be free for Mass with me on Sunday," he said, knowing he would be the one performing the service in their little rented room. It wouldn't be wise to attend Mass at St. Patrick's Cathedral, where Robert would be baptized. As far as he knew, none of the priests there would recognize him. But he couldn't take the chance.

"Service with you will be wonderful," Henri said. "And afterwards we have our future to talk about." He noticed a shadow of sadness in her voice.

An hour later, he left the hospital with the years ahead weighing on him. The meeting with the bishop two years ago twisted into his thoughts. What serious issue had the bishop wanted to discuss when their conversation was interrupted by that phone call? His superior had never brought it up again. A new bishop had been appointed a month later. Apparently, whatever had been worrying the old bishop hadn't been passed to the new one. But rumors could crop up again.

***

Sunday afternoon, January 31, 1932

In their small, rented room, the door closed, Martim draped his stole for Mass around his neck and made the sign of the cross. He smiled at his exclusive congregation of two. Henri sat on the edge of the bed, holding their son swaddled in a blanket. She wore the same hat she'd worn for years, just as if they were in church. He was glad the old couple that owned the home were nearly deaf. Still, he softened his voice to a whisper, said the opening prayer, and sang the *Kyrie*.

As he continued through the rhythm of the mass's liturgical prayers, his mind turned to the ever-present clash between his heart and his conscience. His love for Henri and for his children conflicted with the holy vow he'd taken. He well remembered the day he was ordained and laid prostate on the altar at the Abbot's feet. He'd promised to discharge the office of the Priesthood without fail and to consecrate himself to God. That promise had been kept in all ways but one. His broken vow of celibacy had brought a moral responsibility to Henri and his children. His heart told him his obligation to be a part of their lives outweighed his vow to remain a priest. The process of leaving the priesthood was long and grueling, but it would be worth it if Henri agreed to marry him. He made the decision to ask her once more as he said the Mass's final prayer.

When the service ended, he removed his stole, walked to the window, and stared out at the deep gray clouds hugging the landscape. Darkness overwhelmed his conscience. What words would convince her? As he watched the snow fall, he muttered a passage from the Book of John: *God is light; in Him there is no darkness. If we claim to have fellowship with Him and yet walk in the darkness, we lie and do not live out the truth. But if we walk in His light, we are purified from all sin.*

He jumped when Henri touched his hand. "Something's on your mind, Martim."

He nodded. By now the baby had become fussy. Martim took him from Henri and rocked him as he prayed. "Dear Father, Take my children, their mother, and me into your light."

Twisting the ring on her finger, Henri looked at him through tears. "I've made a decision about our future."

Martim's heart tightened as he shushed his son now in a full squall. The possible paths they could take were all filled with troubling consequences. What choice had she made?

Henri got up to fix the baby's bottle, grimacing as she poured canned milk into the glass container.

He asked, "Your breasts?"

She bit her lip and nodded. "For once I, wish I could nurse, but working and living at the Monroe's makes it impossible."

One more agonizing failure added to the heap already on his conscience. "I'm sorry, Henri. I feel I've abandoned you." His voice cracked. "You deserve better," he said, trying to comfort his son.

"You haven't abandoned me," she said, half snapping. "I'm as much to blame as you. Perhaps even more." She dropped a dollop of cane syrup into the bottle and shook it vigorously. Her voice became fierce. "As difficult as our lives are, I don't regret our children. Or the path I freely chose. Not for an instant. Besides, I know you do everything you can." Her sudden ferocity gave way to half a smile. She handed him the bottle. "Right now, you can feed your son as this will be the only time."

He gazed into his son's deep blue eyes as he fed him and broke into his familiar Portuguese lullaby. When the baby drifted to sleep, Martim laid him beside his *mamãe*, who had propped herself up on the bed. By now her tears were gone, replaced with calmness and a look of determination. She patted the bed. "Come sit, Martim. We need to talk."

"Agreed, *meu amor*," he said. Fear fluttered in his stomach as he waited for her to begin.

Her eyes avoided his as she rolled the edges of the baby's blanket between her fingers. Finally, she spoke. "I've struggled to open my heart to do what is right. But I haven't been able to. The conflict between my love for you and my conscience is relentless. Today, for the first time, my burdens seem bearable." She looked up, her eyes moist. "Martim, your words about living in the light have given me the courage to be honest with myself and with you."

He settled on the bed beside her and put his finger on her lips. "Shh. Henri, please. Let's talk about this later. Today, let's just celebrate our son's birth." He looked down, afraid of what she might say.

She took his hand and rubbed the callouses on his palm. "It has to be now, Martim. Before my courage fails."

He braced himself for what she'd say next.

"You've been so patient as I've tried to decide. The truth is I've done things that make what you want impossible."

"You're wrong, Henri. There are ways to make a marriage work."

"To undo my fake marriage? To just be out with the truth and damn the consequences? I can't Martim. It would ruin you. My heart tells me our love should be the deciding factor. But sometimes love means making tough decisions, especially when reality tells me the pitfalls of marriage are too great."

His heart faltered. He had no words to dissuade her.

She got up, careful not to disturb the baby, and stood by the window, her profile silhouetted against the dark clouds. "Sometimes I believe God has already forgiven me, but then the fact that I've betrayed my faith storms in. We've had three children out of wedlock. What we've done is called…." She hesitated. "I'll be out with it, Martim. It's called fornication. And I haven't found the grace or the courage to confess, fearing that another person knowing would bring you and our babies danger, even if I revealed my terrible sins in the confidentiality of confession."

The word 'fornication' ripped through his heart. He swallowed. "To call it 'fornication', Henri, makes it sound as if we did something ugly. Nothing could be further from the truth." That she could connect that horrible word with his love deepened his grief. He wrapped his arms around her. She pulled away. His grief burned deeper.

She turned to him with pained eyes. "I'm sorry, Martim. I can't let you hold me. Even that simple gesture drains my courage to do what I know is right."

He ran his hands down his face before he could look at her. "Okay, so what must we do, *meu amor*?"

Tears welled in her eyes again. "First, no more calling me your *amor*."

He bowed his head. "If it helps, I won't say it again. But it doesn't change the fact you will always be my love. I'm a man of deep passion and loyalty, to my *mamãe,* my *papai*, to my country, my king, and most of all to you and my children. It's part of who I am, and I can't separate myself from it. My heart and my conscience tell me to resign from the priesthood."

She turned and faced him. "Don't go there, Martim. What about your loyalty to God, to the Church, to all the people you administer to, and to the vow you took when you became a priest? Shouldn't they come before your loyalty to me?"

Barely breathing, he closed his eyes.

When he didn't answer, she went on, her voice cracking.

"You may think of me as your wife, and I of you as my husband. The truth is we're not married. And I'm not Mrs. Jack Rollado. I'm not a Mrs. Anybody. I'm a concubine, a mistress. And I can't go on with all the lies and deceit. If I don't end it now, it will be impossible."

"Henri, don't say that." His voice filled with anguish. He grabbed her, holding her close, kissing her face. "The Lord understands. He forgives."

"Not yet, Martim. To be truly forgiven, we must repent and do everything we can to avoid the near occasion of sin. You are my love, my life, but you are also my deepest temptation. We must be what we claim to be. Merely family friends."

"You wouldn't need me as a family friend if I left the priesthood and married you."

She looked at him with alarm. "No, Martim. It would never work. If you renounced your vows, would we be allowed to marry in the Church? No. Don't you see? Even if the Church sanctioned our marriage, the scandal of what we've done would leave our children vulnerable to a label worse than bastard. And it would kill me if our three little ones were shunned. The scandal, the shunning, and that label would be far more difficult for me to bear than raising our children alone and facing a lifetime without you." She swallowed and squared her jaw. "Being a single mother won't be easy, Martim, but I will manage."

He stared out the window. Snow now fell more heavily. The roads had a new coating of white. Though her reaction was what he'd expected, the pain was so great he could barely breathe. She was right. He had to accept her decision and support her as much as he could. He turned to her, listening to the blood rushing in and out of his heart. "What about this mysterious husband your family and friends have never met? If they don't yet harbor suspicion, they will soon."

"It's on my mind all the time." She frowned. "It sounds terrible, but he has to…" She hesitated. "He has to die. Maybe from influenza or tuberculosis. It's one more big lie, but then it's done."

He paced, fighting his anguish, trying to come to grips with this new reality. He turned and faced her, swallowing. "Perhaps having Jack Rollado pass away would be best. You're a desirable woman, Henri. With him gone, you'd be free to have an actual marriage. There are many honorable men who would be thrilled to call you wife and help raise our children."

"No, Martim. No one will ever replace you in my heart. If I can't be your wife, I will be no one's wife. Of that, I am sure. No matter the struggle. I'll do it on my own."

Feeling as if life had drained from his heart, he reached for her hand but caught himself. "Without a doubt, Henrietta Hoffmann Rollado, you are a strong, determined woman." He got up, packed his stole into his bag, and put on his coat.

"Where are you going?" she asked, lifting Robert and holding him to her chest.

"I can't stay, *meu amor*." He shook his head. "Sorry for those words. They're so natural to my lips. There's too much temptation if I stay. I'll find a hotel and catch the train back to Havre in the morning. I promise, I won't abandon you. And I'll continue to send whatever I can to support my secret family." He paused for a moment, forcing the words off his tongue. "But as you wish, only as a family friend."

***

In the morning he sat in the depot deep in contemplation, waiting for his train. Suddenly, his thoughts were interrupted.

"Reverend Ferrera?"

He froze and looked up. The bishop's housekeeper gazed down on him. "Mrs. Harman, what are you doing in Billings?" he asked, fighting panic.

She looked at him with a puzzled expression. "I was visiting my daughter and grandchildren. What are you doing here? Yesterday, I saw you pass my daughter's house and enter the McCabe home."

"You saw me?" he asked, hoping she didn't hear the fear in his voice.

"I'm sure that was you. You wore civilian clothes, and you were with that woman. The lady you introduced me to a few years ago in the Great Falls Depot. You said she was a family friend. You know, the woman who was pregnant? Yesterday, she was carrying another baby."

He faked a smile and swallowed. "Ah yes. It was my old friend, Henrietta Rollado. And she had another baby." Sweat beaded on his brow. "Sad situation. Her husband wasn't able to be with her."

"Why not?" she asked, her voice thick with suspicion.

He took a deep breath. "He couldn't get away from his job. I came to give her support."

"Oh. I see," she murmured.

The sound of her voice and the expression on her face clearly said she didn't.

Chapter Thirty-Six

Sunday, February 7, 1932,
Billings, Montana
Henrietta

The sun flickered off the snow, belying the cold crisp air. Henri shaded her eyes and picked her way down the icy steps of St. Patrick's Cathedral where her son had just been baptized. The grief she'd felt when she'd banished Martim from her life lingered raw and deep. She doubted the pain would ever heal.

Etta plodded beside her, carrying little Rob. A gust of wind whipped the baby's blanket from his face. Etta tucked it back and cooed, "Can't have you catching cold little guy."

Henri gave half a laugh, trying to lift her spirits. "I can see right now you're going to spoil him, Etta."

"Of course, I am. That's what Godmothers do," Etta giggled. "Besides, remember I'm also his 'Pa' and that's all the more reason to spoil him."

Henri's mind drifted to the irony of Etta playing the role of her children's 'Pa' while their real *papai* had been relegated to the status of family friend. The contradiction jolted her as she slipped on an icy stair. She grabbed the rail before she fell.

"Careful, Henri." Etta warned. "You've been in a fog all morning, even during the baptism."

"There's a lot on my mind," Henri said, limping down the last few steps.

"You're missing Jack, aren't you?"

She nodded.

"I'm glad he could spend time with you and the baby, if only for a few days. But it breaks my heart he couldn't be here for the baptism."

Henri chided herself as tears pooled in her eyes. The emptiness inside her was torture. She almost regretted having banished the only person who could take the pain away. All week she ached to have him back, to be in his arms, to share the joy of their new son. They say, 'love conquers all'. And maybe it does. Unfortunately, the price of her love was disaster. She would never impose that burden on her children. Hot tears trickled down her cold cheeks. "It's hard, Etta. I'm glad you're here to help."

Etta scowled. "It's not right. The sugar company should've given Jack more time with you. You two have hardly been together since you married. A meeting here, a meeting there. What kind of life is that for a family?"

The thought of more lies to turn her mythical husband into someone believable added to Henri's misery. But if the plan was going to work, she had to continue spinning the story. She stepped down the last stair and stopped to wipe her eyes. When she spoke, her voice sounded tiny in her own ears. "I didn't tell you, Etta. Jack can't go back to work for a while. He has tuberculosis."

"Oh my God, Henri. That's awful."

"It is." At least the sadness in her voice was honest. It came from the remorse for her lie and from the loss of Martim. "He stayed with me and the baby for a few days. But even though he was careful not to come too close to the baby, we both worried."

Etta asked, "What's he going to do?"

"He took a train to Deer Lodge and checked himself into the sanitarium at Galen."

Etta brightened. "I know. Let's go see him. Instead of going straight to Great Falls, we can detour through Deer Lodge. It's the long way around, but it'd be worth it. He must be lonely, and I'll bet he misses you and little Rob like crazy."

Henri froze. She hadn't expected this kind of suggestion. "They'd never let us in, especially with a baby."

Etta frowned, and then a grin spread across her face. "That's okay. I heard that the TB patients in Galen spend almost every moment outside in the fresh air. We could stand at the fence, try to get his attention, and wave."

Henri did not know what to say.

Etta didn't wait. "Come on, Henri. At least we should try. I bet seeing us with the baby would lift his spirits. Besides, it'd be a grand adventure."

Henri struggled for an answer. "I only have ticket money to go straight to Great Falls, and I told the Kesslers I'd be back this evening. If we go to Galen, we won't be home until late tomorrow."

Etta didn't seem to care. "Tell you what. I'll use my birthday money to pay the extra expense. Call the Kesslers from the station. If you explain, they'll understand."

Henri sighed, "I don't know, Etta. What if we go through all this trouble and Jack doesn't see us?"

"Then at least we tried. And when you write him, tell him what we did. He'll love you for it."

Still seeing all the ways the plan could go sideways, Henri realized it had to be done, if only to dispel any doubt Etta might develop about Jack's existence. She sighed. "Okay. We'll do it."

Etta peered at the baby. "You hear that, little guy? We're going to see your real pa," she said as she and Henri crossed the street to Mr. McCabe's waiting car. The old man had promised to take them to the train station after the baptism.

By the time they arrived in Deer Lodge eight hours later, Henri was exhausted. She almost wished she hadn't agreed to Etta's adventure but knew the necessity of it. She sat on a bench in the train station rocking with the baby sleeping on her shoulder and watched Etta talk with the porter. They hoped he could give them information about an inexpensive place to spend the night.

A few minutes later, Etta was back and grabbed both of their bags. "We're in luck, Henri. There's a home a few blocks away. They serve a simple breakfast. Even better, the porter thinks the man of the house will drive us as far as sanitarium's gate."

***

By nine the next morning, Henri and Etta stood with the baby at the foot of a snow dusted hill. An expansive one-story building sprawled in the distance. Its spotless white paint set against the deep blue sky seemed to tell the world of its immaculate accommodations.

"My gosh," Etta said as they peered through a massive iron gate. "The building is mostly windows. And it looks like they're all screened and open."

"You've got good eyes, Etta. I didn't notice the windows so much. I was focusing on the rows of patients lying in lounge chairs out in the sun wondering which one is Jack," she said, trying to hide her anxiety. Here's where the plan would succeed or fail. She had to get the attention of some man and get him to wave.

Frigid air swirled around them. Etta shivered as she said, "Notice some patients are in beds. But bed or chair, their arms and faces are all uncovered and exposed to the sun. I'll bet they're freezing."

Henri wrapped the blanket tighter around the baby and snuggled him closer. "I never guessed there were so many people with tuberculosis," she said, frowning. "Isn't that a group of children near the entryway?"

"They're kids all right, and some of them are quite young. But it doesn't surprise me." Etta clouded up. "Working at the Columbus Hospital, I see people of all ages coming in for x-rays. Too many of them end up here. It's nice to know what the place looks like." She smiled. "Now I won't feel so bad when I see paperwork come through that assigns them to the sanitarium."

Henri placed Robert at her shoulder and shaded her eyes. "It seems a pleasant place; bright, clean, and very sanitary. Still, the idea of always sleeping outdoors when it's this cold sounds dreadful."

Etta nodded. "The doctors say constant exposure to sunshine and fresh air along with plenty of nutritious food are the best cure." She turned to Henri. "Did the doctors tell Jack how long he'd have to stay?"

This was a question Henri was prepared to answer. "The average stay is about three hundred days. But it depends on how well his body reacts to the treatment."

Etta scowled. "That's a long time not to be able to work. I know he couldn't send much money. Now you can't even count on that piddly bit."

Henri nodded. The amount of money Martim had sent the last two years had dwindled considerably, but she'd scraped by. She was grateful the Kesslers made sure her girls had enough to eat even when she couldn't pay all they charged. Though Martim had promised to keep sending money when he could, she'd rather not count on him. She bit her lip. "With Jack in the sanitarium, I'll have to be an independent woman for a while." Another lie. It wasn't a while. It was a lifetime.

Etta put an arm around Henri and laid her head on her friend's shoulder. "I admire you so much, Ma."

"The feeling is mutual, Pa," Henri said, standing on tiptoe squinting into the sun. She wondered if there was any man up there she'd be able to point out as Jack.

Etta asked. "Do you see him?"

"I can't tell. They're all too far away."

Etta reached for the baby. "Let me hold my godson. You might get a better look if you stand on the gate rung."

She took Etta's advice and stood on the crossbar. There had to be someone she could claim was Jack.

A man folded his newspaper and slipped out of his blanket. The patient next to him put down a book. Both slowly rose from their chairs. "Look, Henri, those two men getting up. Is one of them Jack?"

Henri shaded her eyes and squinted. "The sun is in my eyes, and they're too far away to be sure. But maybe." She began waving, praying for a friendly gesture in return. Etta stretched and flapped an arm. Miraculously, both men waved back.

"Oh my gosh, Henri. They see us. Which one is Jack?"

Henri waved again. "The tallest one. I recognize his shirt." Thank heavens for friendly people.

"I'm so glad we came, and that Jack saw us. I can tell even from here, he's a good man." Her eyes flashed. "And he seems quite handsome."

"Yes, a very good man and very handsome."

A nurse came out and shepherded the men to their lounge chairs. Sadness banished Henri's relief. Soon Jack might have to die. And she'd have to lie again.

Chapter Thirty-Seven

May 29, 1932
Monroe home on Smelter Hill
Great Falls, Montana
Henrietta

Henri scoured the kitchen floor on her hands and knees, her back aching and her fingers turned to prunes. She stopped, caught her breath, and tucked a loose strand of hair behind her ear. Back to scrubbing, she tackled a grimy splotch by the back door as she searched for a way to ward off pending disaster. The memories of last night's conversation with Martim sent shivers through her. The bishop called him yesterday to set up a meeting at his cathedral office. Martim was required to defend himself and Henri against allegations that had come to the bishop's attention. Thankfully, Martim had managed to delay the session. They had two weeks to prepare.

The house was quieter than usual. The Monroes had gone to the neighbors for the evening, and their boys went with them. Finished scrubbing, she emptied the bucket and put a kettle on for tea. She'd make it mint, as her stomach had churned all day. Martim's news had forced her to find a plausible way for her make-believe husband to die, and it had to happen fast.

A knock tapped the back door as she set two cups and a jar of honey on the table. Etta was here. Tonight, she had to tell her dear friend another bald-faced lie, a lie necessary in order to keep the bishop's investigation from becoming a nightmare. She couldn't chance His Excellency requesting Jack Rollado appear before him to prove Martim's innocence. She drew a deep breath and invited Etta in.

Etta hung her coat on the chair and turned a worried face to Henri. "When you called this morning, you sounded frantic. Are you alright?"

Henri shook her head, felt her cheeks grow pale, and nodded at the chair. Etta sat. Feeling her friend's eyes on her, Henri removed the kettle from the stove, turned off the gas, and poured boiling water into their cups.

The two friends doused their tea bags and added honey, their spoons tinkling in their cups as they stirred. Henri stared into space as she held the tea to her lips and blew into the steam. Etta waited. Henri took a sip, burning her tongue, and put the cup down, forcing words past the tightness in her throat. "It's Jack," she said. "I got news last night he passed away."

"Oh Henri, I'm so sorry," Etta gasped, tears welling in her eyes. She got up, folded her friend in her arms, and held her for a long time.

Though she knew she didn't deserve Etta's comfort, Henri let it soak in until her racing heart slowed.

"My goodness, what happened?" Etta asked and settled back into her chair. "The last you heard, Jack was making good progress."

Guilt swelled in Henri as she braced for the next lie. "He caught influenza, and his lungs couldn't take it because of the tuberculosis." By now, sorrowful tears flooded down her cheeks. Sorrow for deceiving Etta. Sorrow for needing to. Sorrow because she couldn't share with the world or even her closest friend the love she felt for a man who was truly alive.

Etta handed Henri her hankie. "What are you going to do?"

As she wiped away her tears, Henri focused on the information she'd learned when a friend of the Kesslers had died from tuberculosis. "The Sanitarium Director told me I have to go to Galen and arrange for his service."

Etta touched Henri's hand. "At least he'll be buried just a train ride away. We'll be able to take the kids to visit his grave someday."

Henri felt the blood drain from her face. She couldn't take her children to a non-existent grave. His fake burial had to be far away. She swallowed. "I'm having him buried in Minneapolis."

"Minneapolis? That'll cost a fortune."

"I know. But he asked to be buried there. It's where we married. He had a small life insurance policy that will cover most of the cost. I can't refuse his request."

Etta's eyes filled with understanding. "I couldn't refuse a request like that either if there was a way to make it happen." She added more honey to her tea. "I know Jack came from Portugal, but does he have family nearby or maybe friends from his sugar company who could help make arrangements?"

The sympathy in Etta's voice jabbed Henri's conscience. She

shook her head. "There's no one."

"Then I'll go with you."

Henri had expected Etta's offer and was prepared with an excuse. She squeezed Etta's. "You've already done so much for me, Pa. I can't ask you to come. You'll miss work and won't get paid. And I can't afford to pay your way."

Etta scowled. "I'll find a way to cover my expenses. That's what friends are for."

With tears threatening again, Henri said, "Please Etta, no. Though I'll only be gone a few days, I'm away from my kids too often as it is. I'd love if you'd stay, give the Kesslers a break, and spent time with my little ones when you're off work. They adore you. You're their pa and you're Robert's godmother."

"If that's what you want, that's what I'll do." Etta frowned. "But how will you pay for your trip to Galen and the expenses the insurance doesn't cover?"

Henri's mind eased. Finally, she could give an answer that didn't stretch the truth too much. "I'll cash in the government bonds Jack bought for Angelica and Ernestine after Ernie was born. I'd planned to do that anyway. There's a little house near the Kesslers I can afford to rent. If I'm frugal, after my expenses, there'll be bond money left to get a place of my own. And finally, my children can live with me." She ran her finger around the edge of her cup, thinking how much easier it was to pepper lies with truth. Martim had indeed bought bonds for his daughters. Of course, there was no insurance money, but there'd be no funeral or burial plot, just a train ticket, and a brief stay in Galen. Most of the money from the bond could be spent setting up her own household. She gave Etta a hopeful smile. "It'd be easier if someone shared the rent."

Etta brightened. "I'd love to do that." Her face turned all business. "Do the Kesslers and the Monroes know about Jack's passing?"

"I'll tell them tomorrow. I wanted to tell you first." Etta was her test case. If her close friend believed the story, others would too.

Etta's voice saddened. "What will you tell Angel and Ernie about their pa's death? Will they even understand?"

Henri swallowed, happy to be truthful. "The few times they spent with their father were wonderful, but not enough for them to form a deep bond. And they're so young. They probably won't even remember those rare occasions they spent with him or how kind and caring he was. The best I can do is wait until they ask about him. Then I'll tell them what I can."

"It's so sad. They'll never really know him."

That was the bitterest pill of all. Her children would only know the man who was their true father as a kindly priest and family friend. Etta put her arms around Henri and pulled her close. Henri listened to the rhythm of Etta's heart as her tears freely fell, easing her fear and giving her strength. She straightened, wiped her eyes with the corner of her apron, and said, "I've cried enough, Etta."

Etta sat back, her own eyes wet. She sighed and gave Henri a half grin. "You think you'll ever marry again? Kids, especially boys, need a real pa in their lives."

"You're their pa, Etta. They don't need another."

Etta scowled. "Not the same thing, Henri."

Henri brushed away a stray tear. "I know Etta." She heard the crack in her own voice.

As they sat in silence, Henri reflected on the hardships and the tough choices she'd been forced to make ever since she'd discovered herself pregnant with Angelica. Without a doubt, more difficult years were ahead. But she'd come through these harrowing times stronger and more independent than she'd ever imagined possible. Feeling the significance of it all, she finally spoke. "Life with Jack always on the road was hard and sometimes pure hell." She stood with her tea, leaned against the sink, and took a sip. "But to be honest, Etta, I liked the freedom I had when he wasn't around. Don't get me wrong. I loved him. But I've always hated the idea of a man controlling my life, telling me what to do and how to raise my children."

Etta's eyes widened. "You say that now, but you never know who you'll meet, and who will find a way to your heart."

Henri shrugged. "I can't imagine ever falling in love again or being someone else's wife." The impact of her own words had shocked her. She hadn't realized how deeply she'd felt about her independence until the words spilled off her tongue. As she fixed herself another cup of tea, Henri steeled herself for the next bit of shocking news she had to share. How would Etta react when she found out about the sword hanging above Martim, above herself, and above their children? Would she believe the twisted truth? Barely breathing, she finally unlocked the words. "There's one more thing, Etta."

"What is it?"

"Father Ferrera is being investigated by the new bishop."

Etta's hand flew to her mouth. "Oh my God!" She sat back with a scowl. "Is it that old rumor about you and Father?"

On the verge of breaking down again, Henri scolded herself. No more tears. If emotions got the best of her, she might contradict her own lies. Everything she told Etta had to go along with the myth she'd already created. She took a deep breath and answered with a nod.

Etta's face grew darker. "Damn gossipers." A disgusted breath escaped across her lips. "Sorry about swearing, Henri. But I hate it when people jump to conclusions and spread tall tales instead of minding their own business."

"The bishop is taking the rumors seriously," Henri said, rubbing the ache in her temples.

Indignation built in Etta's voice. "To think priests as wonderful as Father Ferrera would have done the horrible things some people say. Sure, you were his housekeeper, and he's been a good friend to you, but that doesn't give them the right to conjure up such wicked stories. They forget how kind he is to everyone, not just you." She took a deep breath and let it go. "If only it hadn't been necessary to keep your marriage a secret for so long."

Henri nodded, cringing at the thought of how bad it would be if the bishop discovered the truth.

Etta's face flipped from anger to concern as she settled back in her chair. "At least the Kesslers, the Monroes, and pretty much everyone in Great Falls know you're married, not some kept woman. They can vouch for you and so can my family." She stared at Henri. "You have a marriage certificate to prove his innocence, don't you?"

Comforted by Etta's loyalty, Henri nodded. "I do. And I know you'll stand by me, Etta. So will others. Naturally, the bishop is demanding proof. I'll show him my marriage certificate, the children's birth, and their baptismal certificates." She had no intention of showing the bishop or anyone else Angelica's birth certificate with its glaring "NO" declaring her illegitimate. Her baptismal certificate naming Jack Rollado as her father would have to do.

"Once you prove your innocence and Father's too, you'll have to keep those documents handy in case the rumors crop up again."

Henri nodded. She couldn't look Etta in the eye. She'd keep the baptismal certificates and the two birth certificates. But eventually she'd have to destroy the marriage certificate. Most children, especially girls, were curious about affairs like weddings and often asked aunts and uncles and grandparents for details. The marriage certificate, with Father Cornelius and Greta's signatures, contradicted the story she'd told *Vader* and *Moeder* and the rest of her family about a wedding performed by a Justice of the Peace. If the contradictions were discovered, all hell would break loose.

Chapter Thirty-Eight

June 10, 1932
St. Anne's Cathedral, Great Falls, Montana.
Martim

Martim sat in the waiting room outside the bishop's office, his eyes closed, his head bowed, praying silently. Sensing someone near, he opened his eyes to the bishop's housekeeper glaring down on him. He forced a smile and nodded. "Good afternoon, Mrs. Harman."

She sneered at him as she knocked on the bishop's door. Not waiting for an answer, she poked her head into the office. "Would you like your afternoon tea, Your Excellency?"

The bishop's "Yes" hinted at irritation.

Her nose remained in the air as she passed Martim and plodded into the hall.

Martim continued to pray for forgiveness for the lies he was about to tell. Falsehoods were his only option. Credible rumors about Henri's relationship with him had finally reached His Excellency. Uncertainty gnawed at his conscience and added to the sour rumbling in his stomach. He'd eaten sparingly since the phone call two weeks ago as penance for the sins on his soul and for those he was about to commit.

Actually, there was that other alternative. Complete honesty. God had arranged for this dilemma and put him at crossroads. Should he confess? No. Henri had made it clear when their son had been born that marriage was not the path she believed was best. He had to protect her and his children at all costs. Right now, in Great Falls, Henri was Mrs. Rollado, a socially accepted woman. Her husband had supposedly died recently. Many knew Jack Rollado as the father of her children, a normal and proper state of affairs. Unfortunately, telling the bishop the truth would destroy Henri's honorable reputation as a wife and mother. He couldn't do that to the woman he loved. And Henri was right. The fallout from the truth could have terrible social consequences for their children.

He had called Henri right after the bishop had given him orders to appear. He wanted to spare her from humiliation, but without her help, he couldn't clear their names. They'd discussed what had to be done, and she'd set about getting her fictional husband out of the picture so Mr. Rollado couldn't be called before the bishop to dispel the rumors. He'd spoken with Henri again last night. She was frightened but prepared with the important documents.

He stared at the pattern on the carpet, thinking about the skirmishes he'd experienced with rumors over the years. Until now, his charitable works, his excellent reputation, and the loyalty of so many parishioners had held gossip at bay. He assumed that his chance encounter with the bishop's housekeeper in the train station several weeks ago had added to the gossip and had tipped the scales. He could have gotten away with that first encounter in the Great Falls Train Depot when he'd been seen with a very pregnant Henri. He imagined the old woman's suspicions had emerged when she saw him in Billings, dressed in civilian clothes with Henri and his newborn son.

His deliberations were interrupted when the bishop's chancellor appeared in the doorway. "His Excellency is ready to see you, Reverend Ferrera."

As soon as Martim stepped into the bishop's chamber, he knew this would not be one of the casual conversations he usually had when he visited His Excellency. The bishop sat back from his desk dressed in official attire, his hands clasped in front of him. Sunlight blinked on the cross hanging on his chest, and a red skullcap hid his balding head. The black cape around his shoulders and the deep red sash around his waist confirmed the authoritative purpose of this meeting.

When the Chancellor left, Martim took a deep breath and made a slight bow. "Your Excellency," he said, feeling unnerved as the bishop's penetrating gaze cut into his soul.

In keeping with proper protocol, the bishop stood and offered his ruby ring for Martim to kiss. Martim knelt for the ritual, the ring smooth and cold on his lips. The bishop signaled for him to take the wooden chair stationed in front of his desk. Martim sat formally, with his feet planted on the floor. He kept his eyes on the bishop as he folded his hands on his lap and waited for his superior to begin.

His Excellency sighed deeply, returned to his desk chair, and began skimming through a pile of papers in front of him. Were those notes and letters filled with the accusations? What did they say? Who sent them? And would they convince the bishop of his guilt?

Martim's head pounded as he waited. He'd been in this office many times, hashing over the problems and the progress of his parishes and discussing theological issues. The atmosphere on those occasions had always been friendly and collegial. Today, an ominous aura hung in the air, much like another time when his life had dangled in a precarious balance.

Today his anxiety was far deeper than it had been twenty years ago when he'd stood before the Republican Tribunal in Portugal. He'd suffered torture and been sentenced to fourteen years of hard labor for a noble cause, a cause he would have died for. He'd been blessed and escaped to Brazil.

There was nothing noble about what had brought him before the bishop today. In fact, the Catholic Church considered his relationship with Henri reprehensible. There might be no escape this time. Though the bishop was quite liberal and much more humane than that Republican General, His Excellency's ruling might end up being more difficult to bear than banishment from Portugal or even death would have been. This time the woman he loved and his three innocent children could suffer the consequences of his sins.

Rebellion against those who had overthrown his king had brought him before the Tribunal in Lisbon; a rebellion he was sure God looked favorably upon. Had his relationship with Henri been an act of rebellion as well? Rebellion against the Church's teaching of celibacy? No. It was love that had drawn them together, a love he'd felt powerless to suppress. In so many ways, she'd helped him be a better minister. Because of her, he better understood the relationship between husbands and wives and fathers and their children. His understanding helped him counsel those with troubled souls. He was more compassionate with the poor, the sick, and with those who had lost their way. Henri breathed love into everything he did and called him to task when he was arrogant. However, those arguments for his relationship with Henri were between himself and God and couldn't be shared with anyone other than Henri.

A soft rap and Mrs. Harman's voice came from the other side of the door. "Your Excellency, tea is ready."

The bishop frowned with annoyance. "Bring it in."

The housekeeper's eyes avoided Martim as she rolled a cart with a tea service for two into the office. She stationed the cart beside His Excellency's desk, bowed to him, and headed back to the door. On her way out, she glanced at Martim. Accusation brewed in her eyes.

When the door closed, the bishop pushed the stack of papers aside, served himself and Martim a cup of tea, and said, "You've sat there long enough, Father. And I'm sure it's been pure torture." He leaned forward and steepled his hands on the desk. "Let's begin. Are you familiar with the rumors about you and a young lady who was your housekeeper at one time?"

Martim nodded, gripping his cup and saucer to keep them from rattling.

The bishop continued. "I haven't wanted to believe such scuttlebutt." He patted the pile of papers. "These are reports collected when my predecessor held this office. Other bits of gossip have appeared since I became bishop, all of which I've been inclined to dismiss. But the reports of your appearance with a very pregnant Mrs. Rollado in the Great Falls train depot in 1929, and now of your recent appearance in Billings with the same woman carrying a newborn baby, have raised concerns. Your layman's attire when you were with her added to mounting suspicion and has given validity to the accusations whispered about you."

Martim swallowed. God help me, he begged and began. "The woman you speak of is Henrietta Hoffmann, now Mrs. Jack Rollado. She was my first housekeeper in Sage Prairie. She and her extended family have been friends for many years."

The bishop continued with a steady gaze. "How did you meet Henrietta?"

"She was a servant at St. Albert's Abbey and College where I taught until I was assigned to my parishes. And I've known her cousin, Father Cornelius Hoffmann, pastor of St. Bernard's in White Water, Wisconsin, since I entered the Abbey."

"Why did you hire her?"

Thankfully he could answer with the truth. "She is spirited, kind, and excelled as a servant at the Abbey, especially in the kitchen. Equally important, she is deeply faithful to her Catholic upbringing. I felt she was a woman the young ladies in my parishes could relate to and aspire to emulate."

"She sounds like a lovely, competent woman. The question is, are your feelings for her deeper than friendship?"

Martim shrugged as he fought to keep blood from rising in his cheeks. "Admittedly, she is an attractive woman, but I always strived to keep my vow." This was the truth, though his endeavors had failed.

The bishop shook his head and frowned. "Tell me, Father Ferrera. What were you doing with her in the Great Falls train depot?"

"It was a mission of mercy, Your Excellency. The baby's father wanted to be with Mrs. Rollado for the birth of their second child. She desperately wanted that as well." He caught himself blanching as the truth turned to lies. "Mr. Rollado traveled as a sugar salesman to make his living. As it happened, his route had him in the area around Hamilton at the time the baby was due. I took Mrs. Rollado to catch the train so they could be together when the baby was born."

The bishop nodded. "Did he make it for the birth?"

"No. But he was there for the baptism."

"Completely understandable. Was it the same type of mission that took you to Billings earlier this year?" His voice sounded skeptical.

Martim answered, hoping a simple answer would be enough. "It was, Your Excellency. She needed support, so I was there."

"I'm a bit confused. I thought Mrs. Rollado lived here in Great Falls."

"She does." He braced himself, realizing the bishop's next few questions would be difficult.

"Why didn't she have the baby here in the Columbus Hospital?"

"This time her husband's sales route had him in the Billings area."

"For the love of God, couldn't he have spent a few days here? After all, Billings is an easy train ride away." He shook his head as doubt built in his voice. "Or, if he was working in Billings and couldn't get away, why wasn't she with him instead of with you?"

Martim forced his hands to remain folded on his lap. "It's a sad situation, Your Excellency. Mr. Rollado was committed to the tuberculosis sanitarium in Galen. She needed support, so I went."

The bishop nodded, but suspicion lingered in his eyes. "Couldn't a close female friend or a family member have given her the help she needed?"

"She had friends caring for her two daughters, and her closest friend couldn't get away from her job at the Columbus Hospital. Unfortunately, Henrietta's family lives in Wisconsin, so they looked to me to give her support."

"So, what you did was part of your clerical mission. That I understand. But you were seen in civilian clothing with Mrs. Rollado and her baby entering a home known to rent rooms. If you'd been wearing your clerical collar and the clothes of your office, your appearance with her wouldn't have caused so much suspicion. You gave the impression you were hiding your identity. The question is, why?"

By now, the fire in his stomach had reached his throat. Yes. He was hiding his true identity. God forgive him. And that identity had to remain buried. He studied his clasped hands and then raised his eyes to the bishop. "Admittedly, it was a breach of good judgment, Your Excellency," he said, stalling for time, looking for a truthful answer. He sighed. "There really isn't a great explanation, except that the weather was unmercifully cold and treacherous. I left my car in Havre and the snow hampered public transportation in Billings. I changed into my hunting clothes for warmth when I arrived, as I had to walk everywhere. However, I can see how this could cause suspicion. Perhaps I acted unwisely in my attempt to stay warm."

Did the expression on the bishop's face mean he doubted the explanation? It seemed he was rummaging through Martim's soul, searching for the truth. Gradually the stern look softened, and the bishop said, "I can see how the weather would have informed your decision."

The bishop sorted through the stack of papers on his desk again. "In looking through notes the previous bishop left in your file, there are several rumors that hinted of an illicit relationship with Mrs. Rollado when she was your housekeeper. But there are also examples of your exceptional ministry and the loyalty of your parishioners." He held up a copy of the *Sage Prairie Newspaper*. "Here's an example. When the Abbey assigned you to a different town, the citizens of Sage Prairie petitioned the Abbey requesting that you remain with them." He nodded and smiled. "It's good to know their testimony persuaded the Abbot to grant their wish."

Martim's face warmed as his guilt overrode the praise.

The bishop's somber look returned. "God has blessed you with many talents, Father. The article you wrote for the Catholic Review was inspiring. When I attended your men's study club, the number of men engaged in the meeting impressed me. Your ladies' organization is thriving under your direction. You've done a remarkable job giving farmers in your area ideas for better farming techniques and animal husbandry.

With his eyes steady on his Superior's, Martim remained silent, agonizing over his hidden life, one that seemed to invalidate all the good he'd ever done. God knew he was a fraud. He swallowed the vile taste in his mouth and promised to spend the rest of his life atoning for his deceit, if only he could save Henri and his children from the fallout of gossip.

Martim's gaze almost faltered when the bishop's eyes turned to steel. "It would be most unfortunate if I had to remove you and send you back to the Abbey for rehabilitation if the accusations are true." The bishop placed his folded hands under his chin. "Is Mrs. Rollado aware of the allegations?"

"She is, Your Excellency. And they devastate her."

"Does she have documents to prove her marriage and the legitimacy of her children?"

"She does," he said, thinking for the thousandth time how fortunate it was he'd been present as Jack Rollado when Ernestine and Robert were born making their births legitimate. It was ironic his presence had also helped cause this investigation. Angelica's birth was another matter. The label of illegitimacy on her birth certificate would haunt him for the rest of his life.

The bishop's brows rose. "Your accusers won't be satisfied until I have proof that negates the rumors. Would Mrs. Rollado be willing to share her documents?"

"She would, Your Excellency. In fact, she is praying in the Cathedral at this very moment in case you needed to speak with her."

"Excellent. And what about Mr. Rollado?"

Martim ran his sweaty hand over his pants and folded them back onto his lap. "Unfortunately, Mr. Rollado passed away recently from influenza complicated by his tuberculosis."

"Interesting." Martim flinched at the doubt in the bishop's voices. He became more uneasy as the seconds ticked by and the bishop studied him. Finally, His Excellency said, "I suppose there's nothing to be done about that. Mrs. Rollado and her documents will have to do." He rang the bell on his desk.

The Chancellor appeared in the doorway and bowed. "Your Excellency?"

"A Mrs. Rollado is in the cathedral. Please tell her I'd like to speak with her and bring her to my office."

Martim turned to the Chancellor. "She's a small woman and often wears a dark grey Cloche hat. She will be with a friend and her friend's mother."

When the Chancellor left, the bishop said, "We'll pray while we wait." As the bishop prayed, Martim's mind turned to the old treatise written by Diogo Feijó, a Brazilian bishop and senator, who argued against the forced celibacy of priests.

In his treatise, Diogo pointed out that the Sacrament of matrimony was also civil law and could be performed legitimately by someone other than a priest. The Church recognized these civil marriages and would bless them at the couple's request. The document argued that because marriage was a civil law, governments had the right to declare who was eligible for marriage, including priests.

Further, Matrimony was the only Sacrament priests could not take part in. Why were priest excluded from this most human relationship? In fact, required celibacy was a doctrine of the Church, not dogma, and thus could be changed.

Guilt meddled with his reasoning. Whether the doctrine of celibacy was right or wrong, it didn't excuse his failure to keep his vow of celibacy. That broken vow marred his soul and threatened those he loved. The pain of this failure dug deeper than any of the physical pain he'd suffered when he'd been imprisoned so long ago.

Martim shut down his inner arguments and prayed for Henri, for himself, and for his children. He was on the second round of his rosary when the Chancellor escorted her into the bishop's chambers. As they entered, he glimpsed Etta and Etta's mother seated outside in the waiting room. Thank God Henri had two people she loved with her to give their support. He was especially grateful neither of them knew the truth.

Henri carried herself with dignity, but her ashen face told him her show of strength was bravado. She was terrified. He ached to take her in his arms and comfort her. But a friendly nod was all he could give.

The bishop stood. Henri bent on one knee and kissed his ring. He dismissed the Chancellor, arranged a chair for Henri, and said, "Thank you for coming, Mrs. Rollado."

Henri responded with a confidence he knew was feigned. "I'm glad I can help," she said, gripping her missal.

"I appreciate you being available for my investigation." The bishop's tone was kind and supportive.

Henri managed her charming smile. "Thank you, Your Excellency."

The bishop returned to his desk, his eyes full of compassion. "My condolences on the death of your husband, Mrs. Rollado. I imagine it must be very difficult."

Henri looked down, twisting the silver ring on her wedding finger. "It is, Your Excellency."

"And your children, how are they managing his passing?"

Henri lifted her head and squared her shoulders. Martim could tell she'd expected the bishop's question and had practiced a response. "They're quite young and not really aware. Jack was a traveling salesman for a sugar company and was away a great deal. Unfortunately, he contracted tuberculosis and was confined to the sanitarium in Galen. Our children rarely saw him. His frequent absences and his illness were difficult for me, but I had help from many people." She swallowed. An imperceptible hint of pink tinged her cheeks as she added, "Father Ferrera was among them."

The bishop glanced at Martim, his face wrinkling in a frown. "Reverend Ferrera has a fine reputation for ministering to those in need. Unfortunately, there are those who believe his charitable deeds extended much further than they should in your case."

Martim glanced at Henri. The pink in her cheeks flooded into a deep blush. He quickly averted his eyes; worried the bishop could read his feelings.

The bishop continued. "I can see you know what I'm talking about, Mrs. Rollado."

"I do." Though her voice cracked, she kept her gaze steady on His Excellency.

The bishop leaned forward. "Father Ferrera said you have documents to disprove the allegations."

"Everything is right here, Your Excellency. A marriage certificate, baptismal certificates, and birth certificates." She bit her lip as she took an envelope from her missal and handed it to him.

Perspiration beaded on Martim's forehead as he watched the bishop study the documents. He prayed the evidence would exonerate Henri. He might suffer a long time in purgatory for the falsehoods he continued to fabricate, but he wanted the woman he loved and his children free from social condemnation.

The bishop took his time scrutinizing the documents and then looked up. "Your marriage certificate and the baptismal documents seem in order. But you're missing a birth certificate."

Martim prayed the bishop would keep his eyes on Henri so he wouldn't notice the shame burning on his cheeks.

Though pink still glowed on Henri's face, her voice was calm. "My first child was born in Helena and delivered by a mid-wife. The mid-wife didn't fill out a document, and as you know they aren't required to do so. In hindsight, I wish I'd insisted, but at the time it didn't seem important."

The bishop shrugged with a smile. "Her baptismal certificate is sufficient. I'm sorry to put you through this, Mrs. Rollado, but it was necessary. Fortunately, the evidence you've shared definitely clears up the situation." He handed the documents back to Henri. "Keep these in a safe place where they will be available should more questions arise."

"I will," she said, her voice choked with relief. "Several people have advised me to do the same."

The bishop's words became stern. "Though you and your family have a friendship with Reverend Ferrera, Mrs. Rollado, from this moment on, you must avoid being seen with him alone. Your contact should only be as any church member." He turned his gaze to Martim and then back to her. "If he gives you support as a widow with three children, which I know you may desperately need, his help must come through indirect channels."

Henri looked at her hands, her fingers white against the black missal. Her voice soft, she said, "I will do as you say, Your Excellency."

Martim's heart faltered. Though he knew the wisdom of the bishop's advice, a lifetime of distant, casual friendship would be torture. But, as Henri had said, it was for the best.

The bishop stood, a caring look in his eyes. "Before you go, Mrs. Rollado, I'd like to give you my blessing." Henri let out a long breath, removed her hat, and knelt. The bishop put a hand on her head and prayed, "May the peace of Christ be with you and your children as you mourn the loss of your husband. May you continue to walk in the way of the Lord." He helped her to her feet. "Your friends are waiting. They will be happy to know you and Father Ferrera have been cleared."

She stood and bowed. "Thank you, Your Excellency," she said, and moved to the door.

Martim sent her a silent message of love, knowing it would be a long time before he'd be this close to her again. She must have heard because she turned. A smile hid the sorrow in her eyes. Twisting the ring on her finger, she glanced at Martim and said, "Good day, Father Ferrera."

He watched her walk into the waiting room and hug Etta and Etta's mother. The door closed. He was alone with the bishop and his desolation. His Excellency returned to his desk and signaled for Martim to be seated.

"For your sake and for Mrs. Rollado's, you must follow the same advice I've given her. The way you chose to support her put you both in a precarious situation. Your effectiveness with your parishioners depends on your utmost discretion. I will continue to expect great things from you, Father."

"Thank you for your gracious understanding."

The bishop broke into a smile. "I heard you and Father Walters plan a special service in Sage Prairie for the Feast of Corpus Christi. I'd like to attend."

The anxiety that had plagued Martim for weeks evaporated. "We'd be pleased to have you as our honored guest."

"Then I shall be there. Now, let me give you my blessing, and then join me for dinner before you take to the road. You have a long drive back to Sage Prairie."

Martim knelt as humble as he'd ever felt. The bishop's hand rested on his head, and his blessing softened the grief. "May the Lord be with you in your ministry, and may He help you remain focused on His work. Go in peace, my son, and walk with Christ."

He followed the bishop to the rectory's dining room. God had protected his secret family. From this moment on, he promised to do everything in his power to atone for his broken vow and his sins of deceit. It comforted him to know that Christ worked through him and recognized the Sacraments he performed despite his terrible wrongdoings. As soon as possible, he'd make a trip to White Water and confess his latest sins to Father Hoffmann, his friend who knew the truth.

Truth. Would his children ever know the truth? Who he was? How much he loved them and their mother? He and Henri had vowed from this point on to perpetuate the myth of Jack Rollado to protect their children. It was an oath he would never break, and he doubted Henri would either.

Chapter Thirty-Nine

Three years later
Saturday, May 18, 1935
Great Falls, Montana
Henrietta

Henri set up her ironing board and rubbed her fingers across her brow. The load she carried as a widowed mother had her weary to the bone. The emotional battle raging in her conscience took a toll as well. Angelica's first communion was coming next week, an important milestone for a Catholic child. Right now, her relationship with Martim still weighed on her soul and barred her from the Holy Sacrament. There was no doubt, Angelica's special day would be marred if her mother didn't join her in communion.

It was Henri's day off, but she'd been up since five, scrambling with too many chores to do. Climbing a chair, she plugged the iron into the light fixture's electric socket and set to work, sprinkling the clothes with water. Wrinkles came out easier when the pieces were damp. A lot of work, but at least now electricity heated the iron instead of the wood stove.

Her mood lightened when six-year-old Ernestine began singing as she dried the dishes. Her voice held promise, a gift she'd inherited from Martim. Ernie began the second verse, belting out "My Wild Irish Rose," Henri hadn't told her it was the song her father had sung to her after she was born. If she knew, Ernie would ask too many questions.

Angelica trudged into the kitchen with a basket piled high with the laundry she'd taken off the clothesline. Henri noticed it was already folded. Not perfectly, but well done for a seven-year-old. Angel's friend Marianne bounced in behind her, full of excitement. "Hello Mrs. Rollado" she bubbled. "My mum said I could come over and see Angelica's First Communion dress."

Angelica added, "May I show it to her Mother? Please."

"Of course," she said, cheered by her daughter's enthusiasm. "But first, you need to finish your chores."

Angelica put an arm around her friend. "They're all done. Marianne helped."

Once again, Henri noted how Angelica gathered loyal friends around her, much like her father. She smiled at the two girls. "I just ironed your dress, Angel. It's lying on my bed with your veil. But be extra quiet. Rob is in there taking a nap."

The girls slept in a small room upstairs in the tiny two-story house, and three-year-old Robert slept on a cot in her bedroom next to the kitchen. He'd begun asking for his own room, and she'd promised to move him upstairs to a little alcove when he turned four. Rent for the old house was manageable when Etta had lived with them and shared the cost. But now that Etta had married and moved out, it was difficult to scrape together money for the rent. Despite the struggle, Henri vowed to do everything in her power to keep her children living under the same roof with her.

Ernestine hurried to dry the last pot and stashed it in the curtained cupboard below the sink. "Hey, wait for me." She scrambled after the two girls. Usually, Henri didn't allow the girls in her bedroom. She considered it her sanctuary, although she shared it with Rob.

As Henri ironed, she watched her oldest daughter through the doorway try on her communion veil and primp in the dressing-table mirror. Angel's reflection included Ernestine standing behind her. Ernie's face puckered in a scowl when her sister handed the veil to Marianne and let her put it on.

"It's beautiful on you," Angelica gushed softly.

Ernie reached for the veil. "Let me see what it looks like on me." She batted her lashes as she turned her scowl to a coy smile.

Angel nodded at their sleeping brother and put her finger to her lips. "Shh."

Ernie rolled her eyes and whispered, "Come on, Angel. Pretty please."

"No. It's your turn next year."

Ernie pouted and edged to the doorway. "Mother. Angelica is being selfish."

Henri stood the iron on its edge and crossed her arms. "Angelica is right. You'll have your turn next year. Now hush or you'll wake your brother."

Ernie sulked back into the room, sank to the floor, and wrapped her arms around her knees. She glanced at her mother with a dark scowl, let her head sag, and picked at a scab on her leg. Her sulk morphed into a puzzled look. She straightened, got up, and sat on the edge of Henri's bed. "Angel, I've been wondering."

"What?" Angel asked, fluffing the veil on Marianne's head.

"Do you think Mother ever had her First Communion?"

Henri blanched. The iron bumped her fingers. Gasping, she set the iron on end, took a dollop of butter, and spread it over the burn. Ernie was quite young, but she seemed to know the chinks in her mother's armor. Maybe her comment was unintentional, but Henri could have sworn sometimes Ernie jabbed at her mother's sore spots on purpose. Henri blew on her burned fingers as she waited for Angel's response.

Angelica sputtered. "Of course she has. She's a grownup."

"Then why doesn't she receive Communion like all the other grownups?"

"Not all grownups go to Communion." Angelica sounded defensive.

Marianne piped up. "Your mum never goes to Communion?"

"I've never seen her go," Ernestine went on.

"Really?" Marianne asked in disbelief.

"Not once."

"How come?"

Ernestine shrugged. "I don't know. Do you, Angel?"

Angelica blinked in silence.

Henri returned to her ironing, her heart racing, her fingers blistered. From the corner of her eye, she watched Angelica's perplexed expression in the mirror. She finally shrugged. "I don't know either."

Henri finished the blouse, slipped it on a hanger, and hung it on the doorknob. She wanted to storm to the bedroom, send Marianne home, and the girls to their room. Leave it to Ernie to be the one to notice and asked the question. But it was a legitimate one. A show of anger would only confuse the girls. In Ernie's case, confusion could lead to suspicion. She grabbed her Sunday skirt and slipped it on the ironing board. Her eyes still on the girls, she moved the iron slowly across the dark blue fabric.

Angel bit her lip and turned to Marianne. "I'm kind of nervous about my first confession. Do you think priests can figure out who we are?"

A look of horror flashed across Marianne's face. "Oh, my gosh. I hope not."

Angel's cheeks turned pink. "I'd be embarrassed if he did. But Sister says it's dark in the confessional. And there's a screen. So, I think it'll be okay."

As the girls' conversation continued, Henri sprinkled water on a stubborn wrinkle and mulled over Ernie's question. She couldn't receive communion. If she did, another sin would be heaped on top of the other sins already there. The only priest she felt comfortable hearing her confession was her cousin, Father Cornelius, who knew about her relationship with Martim. Unfortunately, she hadn't been able to afford a trip back home to that safe confessional.

Confessing to any other priest scared her. Her heart raced at the possibility that her confessor could figure out who she was. And what if he insisted she reveal the name of her children's father? She hadn't found the courage to face either of those possibilities. How could she raise her children as good Catholics if she didn't partake in the Sacraments herself?

She jumped when Angel spoke beside her. "Mother, may I go to Marianne's and see her communion dress?"

"Of course, sweetheart," she said, noticing little Rob standing in the doorway, rubbing his eyes. "Take Rob with you. I told him he could play with Marianne's little brother after his nap."

"Okay," Angel said, grabbing Rob's hand.

"May I go too, Mother?" Ernie asked sweetly, her eyelashes fluttering as usual when she wanted something.

"No." Henri spoke more sharply than she intended. "I need your help with dinner." More importantly, she had to squelch the ideas she knew were fomenting in Ernie's head.

Ernie sighed but didn't argue. Henri had taught her children protest was futile.

Angel and Marianne scampered out the door with Rob, the girls bubbling about their upcoming special event. Henri swallowed her displeasure with Ernie and said, "Get the big pot and clear the leftovers from the icebox. We'll make goulash for dinner. If necessary, we can stretch the mix with macaroni and a jar of tomatoes."

Ernie's scowl disappeared. She loved to cook. Henri went back to ironing with an eye on her daughter. She hoped cooking would distract Ernie and erase the questions she was sure still lurked in Ernie's head. Her second daughter was not the type to drop a topic that interested her.

Just as Henri suspected, a curious expression grew on Ernie's face as she measured a cup of dry pasta and dumped it with a jar of tomatoes into the goulash. "Mother?" Ernestine finally said.

Henri braced herself. "Yes, Ernestine?"

"Why don't you ever go to Communion?" Ernie asked, sounding sincere.

Though Henri had expected the question, it ripped through her, unleashing regret and her ever-present guilt. She swallowed, calming herself. "Ernestine, that's none of your business. And it never will be!" She whipped a spoon through the goulash and snapped, "Now go play. I'll finish making dinner myself."

Ernie backed away with a shrug and went out the door.

Henri turned off the stove, slogged to her room, and lay on her bed staring at the ceiling. As a lump grew in her throat, she scolded herself. No more pussyfooting. She had to face her fear and clean up her soul.

***

Six days later.

Friday, Henri stared at her typewriter in the third-floor office of the Strain Brothers Department Store. She prided herself on finally being hired as a stenographer for the two owners. Unfortunately, the job only paid thirty dollars a week. Prices were going through the roof and since Etta left, there was the added cost of rent. She'd been mulling over a return to work as a maid. Though it was demeaning, it paid more. But today, none of that mattered. The turmoil brought up by Ernie's questions on Saturday had overridden everything else.

"Mrs. Rollado?"

She jumped, wondering how long Mr. Strain had been standing beside her. "Yes, sir?"

"Have you finished typing the letter to our clothing supplier?"

"Not yet, sir, but I'll be finished soon," she said, keeping her voice professional. She shifted the lever of her typewriter, moved the half-finished letter to the next line, and returned her focus to the dictation on her stenographer's pad.

Arthur Strain stood a while longer and finally said, "It's not like you, Mrs. Rollado. But you seem rather distracted lately."

"I am, sir, and I'm sorry. My mind has been on my daughter's upcoming First Communion."

Mr. Strain nodded with an understanding glint in his eye. "Ah. The pressure of a big day ahead."

"Definitely," she said, hiding her turmoil with a smile. She'd agonized all week, praying for the courage to go to confession. As Mr.

Strain left, she checked her shorthand notes, put her troubles on hold, and began typing again.

After putting the letter in the outgoing mail, she tackled a pile of invoices that needed filing, a mindless task that let her thoughts wander back to her quandary. Ernestine's inquisitiveness had prodded her relentlessly these last few days to do what she should have done years ago. Get right with the church and do it soon. An elderly priest had recently been assigned to St. Anne's Cathedral. Henri had studied him from afar as he interacted with the parishioners. He seemed a sympathetic listener, never prying, letting people speak whatever was on their mind without judgment. She avoided contact with him. If she ever found the courage to enter his confessional, she didn't want him to recognize her voice.

Despite his qualities, it troubled her he might insist on knowing who had fathered her children out of wedlock. She had to risk it. Besides, she scolded herself for the hundredth time, the confessional was supposed to be confidential. Priest weren't allowed to reveal anything they heard in confession.

She'd always known that. What held her back? Was it really fear that the priest might recognize her or that her confession would bring Martim before the bishop again? Or was it something more? The Church said her relationship with Martim was morally wrong. But admitting this out loud was like saying her love for Martim was wrong, and that creating the children she loved was immoral. In the confessional, she'd have to say she was heartily sorry for her sin. She wasn't. She could never be sorry for having created her children.

Wasn't God all knowing? He saw the quandary in her heart. Wouldn't He forgive her? Did she really need to confess to a priest if she confessed to God? He knew and understood why her sorrow for her sins could never be complete.

She moved to the window and stared at the Cathedral spires in the distance. All this rationalization was futile and would never bring her peace. She'd defied Church law. The only way back into the Church's good grace was to find the courage, humble herself, and walk into the confessional.

***

Saturday morning, Henri waited in line with Angelica in the hallway outside of St. Anne's Cathedral reception room. The Church's

Lady Society had paid a photographer to take formal portraits of every First Communicant.

She studied Angelica; so beautiful in the dress and veil Ada had made. Did her daughter resemble Martim's sister for whom she was named? She'd send Martim one of the portraits and ask about her daughter's Aunt Angelica.

Her mind drifted in a muddle of anxiety. She barely noticed Angelica's quiet chatter, or that of the other children and their parents around her. If she was going to receive communion on Angel's special day, she had to confess this afternoon. It would take every ounce of strength she could muster to walk into that dark place of repentance.

As the minutes ticked by, the volume of chitchat and excitement built. "Shh," one mother hissed, pulling her daughter to her side. "Where are your manners?"

Some parents frowned at the woman's harshness. Others quietly admonished their own children. On any other day, Henri might have approved of the woman's admonition, but today she had her own problems to work on. Besides, Angelica and Marianne were quietly talking about Angelica's First Communion missal.

"Father Ferrera sent it to me," Angel whispered proudly.

"I've never heard of Father Ferrera," Marianne said.

"He's a family friend, but not from around here. Mother said Ernie and I met him when we were little. She has a picture of Ernie and me with him beside his car." She paused with a giggle. "I don't remember much about him except he swung me around until I got dizzy, and Ernie got stung by a bee. He even sent me a rosary and picture of himself." She handed Marianne a photo she'd pulled from her pocket. "I'm going to put it in my album."

Marianne studied the picture. "He must be really nice to send you all this stuff," she said and handed the photo back. She pulled her own little missal from her pocket. "Here is mine. My dad bought it for me."

Angelica flipped through the pages and sighed. "My father died a long time ago, but I don't remember him."

Before Marianne could say anything, she was called into the reception room for her portrait, leaving Angel looking wistful. Henri's heart faltered. Angelica's day would absolutely be more special if her father were here to share it. He would sing to her, take her hand, and tell her how lovely she looked. All the things a good father did.

But if she had agreed to marry him, they wouldn't be here at St.

Anne's. They'd be living in some quiet town where no one knew their unorthodox past. But that didn't guarantee safety. There were many ways their secret could be uncovered and cause grief for their children.

What she had done was right. Because of her refusal, he still served the people of Sage Prairie as their priest, their counselor, and even as their doctor. As difficult as it was to stay apart and to pretend they were nothing more than family friends, she didn't regret her decision. As hard as it was to live without Martim, being considered a widow was better for her children. They would never face being outcasts because of their unconventional parentage.

She wrapped an arm around her daughter, the familiar sadness stinging her heart. The downside of her decision meant her children would never know their father. The only consolation was the fact they wouldn't exist except for the love she had promised to never reveal. That would never change. Apart from the sins on her soul, she regretted none of it. She prayed again for the courage to do the one thing she had to change. This afternoon she would remove the dark stains on her soul.

***

Her children visiting the Kesslers, Henri slipped into St. Anne's Cathedral a few minutes before confessions were scheduled to begin. She knelt in the shadows of an alcove occupied by a statue of the Blessed Mother. The votive lights beneath Mary's feet sent soft rays fluttering over the Virgin's sorrowful face. The smell of beeswax permeated the air.

The elderly priest Henri hoped would hear today's confessions entered the cathedral. He knelt at the altar, made the sign of the cross, and bowed his head in prayer. After several minutes, he kissed his purple stole and draped it around his neck. He pushed himself up, limped back to the confessional stalls, and disappeared into the middle section. The door clicked shut.

Henri waited, her heart racing, wanting to be the last person to enter the darkened booth of forgiveness. She didn't want others waiting to confess, wondering why she was taking so long. After confessing her years of sins, there would be the priest's counsel. She was sure there'd be plenty of it. Then he would assign her penance and give absolution.

Biding her time, her fingers flew around her rosary, beginning and ending, over and over. The last person in line disappeared into the confessional. A few minutes later, the old woman hobbled from the stall, smiling. She nodded at Henri.

As she entered the confessional, her pulse pounded in her ears and added to a terrible headache. The velvet curtain fluttered as it closed behind her. Her knees pressed on the hard, wooden riser in the darkness. The priest's panel slid open, exposing his shadowy profile. He leaned in close to the grill. The smell of incense crept through the screen.

Her hands met in prayer, fingers folded and tightly locked together. Shaking, Henri took a deep breath and began the words she'd been rehearsing for days. "Bless me, Father, for I have sinned. It has been seven years since my last confession." The next part of her prepared recitation froze in her throat.

"That's a long time, my daughter. Remember, you are God's child, and His compassion and forgiveness are here for the asking."

Tears welled in her eyes. It was true. She'd always believed God's forgiveness was abundant and eternal. Her soul opened. The grace she had longed for flooded in, her tongue set free. "I have sinned, Father. I conceived my three children out of wedlock. I have lied about having a husband who never existed. And I led others to lie on my behalf."

The priest's shadowy profile nodded. "Does this man with whom you have sinned live with you?"

"No, we have little contact any more, except to keep him informed of our children's development."

"Do they know who he is?"

"No. Like most people, my children think their father died when they were very young. The man I told them was their father never existed. I didn't want them to suffer the shame of my sins."

"I see. Why haven't you married this man?"

God help me, she begged. What if her confessor insisted on a name? She took a deep breath and choked out an answer. "He's not available to marry."

"I see. So, he's already taken. How unfortunate. Does he send support?"

Henri's fear subsided. Her confessor thought Martim was already married. And in a way, he was. To the Church. "He helps as much as he can."

The priest paused and then asked, "Are you raising your children in the Faith?"

"I am. In fact, my oldest receives her first communion in a few days." A glitch rose in her growing sense of wellbeing. Maybe she shouldn't have shared this bit of information. Next Thursday, during the Mass for the first communicants, the priest might look over the parents wondering if he could identify her. She consoled herself. Even if her confessor figured out who she was, she sensed he was a priest who would never betray her.

The shadowed profile nodded on the other side of the grill. "Our Lord is pleased. You are endeavoring to be a good mother despite your sins."

A sense of liberation eased the lump in her throat. She had done it. It didn't matter what penance he gave. Whatever was imposed, it would be a small price to free her from guilt.

Her Confessor continued. "You have sinned gravely, my daughter, but I believe God sees the goodness in your heart. First, you must avoid any occasion that could lead you to rekindle your intimate relationship with the father of your children."

"I have for three years, and I vow to continue doing so."

"Your penance will help you with this vow. For three months, you must pray the "Memorare" in the morning when you rise and each night before you sleep. Let it be on your lips as a guide throughout your life. Is it a prayer you know?"

"It is, Father," she answered, thinking how the words would help her with temptation.

"Let's recite them together as you return to God's grace."

As they whispered the prayer together, the long-forgotten sense of peace grew in Henri. "O most gracious Virgin Mary, never was it known that anyone who fled to thy protection, implored thy help or sought thy intercession, was left unaided. Inspired by this confidence, I fly unto thee, O Virgin of virgins my Mother; to thee do I come, before thee I stand, sinful and sorrowful. O Mother of the Word Incarnate, despise not my petition, but in thy mercy hear and answer me, Amen."

The priest blessed her with the sign of the cross and began the absolution. "Dominus noster Jesus Christus te absolvo…" Henri broke into the Act of Contrition. Finished, the priest said, "Go in peace, my child."

Henri walked from the Cathedral free from the weight on her soul. She could join Angelica at her First Communion.

Chapter Forty

Thursday, May 30, 1935.
Great Falls, Montana
Angelica

Angelica knelt at the altar rail in Saint Anne's Cathedral, the ruffles of her dress dusting the step. She folded her hands, pointing them to heaven, closed her eyes, and lifted her face to receive her First Communion. As the host flattened on her tongue, a sense of wellbeing swelled through her. The crisp wafer dissolved, tasting like dry, bland bread.

She followed her classmates back to the pew, feeling as if she were floating on clouds. As she knelt again, her veil brushed her cheeks. Marianne knelt beside her, intent on her missal. Angel opened her own missal and read the message written on the inside cover.

"Dear Angelica, Today, on your First Communion, you are forever connected to Jesus's love, peace, and blessings. Father Martim Ferrera."

She shivered happily at his beautiful words.

Time drifted. When the last of her classmates returned to their pews from the altar rail, other churchgoers drifted up to receive communion.

Angelica knew she should keep her mind on her prayers. But she couldn't help noticing her classmates' mothers and fathers, aunts and uncles, and grandparents follow one another to the communion rail. Her friends had so many relatives. Her aunts and uncles lived too far away to come. And her father died a long time ago. Still, she had her mother. Angelica sighed. If only Mother would… Her hand flew to her mouth, holding back a gasp. There she was, in line on her way to the altar.

Barely believing, she watched her mother kneel, receive communion, and then stroll down the aisle towards her seat somewhere in the back of the Cathedral. Angelica caught her mother's eye as she passed. Mother flashed her a spunky smile that disappeared so quickly Angelica wasn't sure she'd actually seen it. Mother was usually the serious type of grownup. But once in a while, she'd do something playful, and Angelica never figured out what caused the perky episodes.

As hard as she tried, Angelica couldn't stay focused on the rest of the Mass. Before she knew it, Marianne nudged her, whispering, "It's time to go, Angelica." Usually, she felt guilty if her mind wandered on such holy occasions. Not today. She'd been thrilled when Mother showed up at the altar.

She followed her classmates down the main aisle as the children reunited with their families. Passing row after row, her eyes searched for Mother. There she was, waiting in one of the last pews, looking dignified, dressed up in her church hat, her gloves, and her dark blue suit. A man leaned over the pew behind Mother and talked to her. Mother nodded at something he said, as if she knew him. Angel squinted. Who was he? It was hard to tell. Things had become blurry lately. She suspected she needed glasses, but they cost an arm and a leg so she hadn't told Mother.

Marianne hissed behind her. "Angel, we're lagging behind."

Angel realized there was a gap between herself and the boy ahead. As she picked up the pace, she kept her eyes on Mother. The man stood, touched Mother's arm, and moved down a side aisle. She watched the man disappear out a side entrance. And then she caught Mother's eye. The smile on her face seemed happier than Angel had ever seen, as if everything in the world was now perfect.

She slipped beside Mother, eager to see the bishop who waited on the Cathedral steps to give each child his personal blessing. For some reason, Mother held her back, so they were last in line. Mother's hand rested on her shoulder as they plodded behind her classmates.

Outside, altar boys, dressed in white and black frocks, stood on either side of the bishop as he blessed her classmates. The gold cross on his fancy hat and the golden embroidery on his white robes glittered in the sun as if he were the guardian at the gates of Heaven.

When her turn came, the bishop smiled at Mother. "Mrs. Rollado, it's good to see you again. So, this young lady is one of your children."

The bishop knew Mother?

Mother's face lost its happy glow and turned red. A tight smile spread across her lips. "Yes, Your Excellency. This is my oldest, Angelica."

Angel sensed herself blushing when he looked at her. "Angelica, what a lovely name." He turned to Mother again. "How are your other children?"

Mother's face softened. "Angelica's younger sister just finished first grade at St. Mary's. Right now, she and her three-year-old brother are with family friends."

"You're blessed to have so many caring people in your life, Mrs. Rollado." There was something in the bishop's voice Angelica didn't understand.

Mother merely nodded. And then the bishop rested his hand on Angelica's head and gave her a blessing. She wasn't sure what the Latin words meant, but they sounded very holy.

Her feet barely touched the ground as she walked with Mother down the Cathedral steps, chattering about the glorious service, about her happiness at the communion rail, and the procession out of the cathedral, and on to the question on her mind. "Mother, who was that man I saw you talking to in church?"

Mother stiffened. "Just an old acquaintance," she said with an expression that meant more questions were futile.

Angel sighed. Her stomach grumbled. As required, she'd fasted from dinnertime last night until now. But the sharp hunger was okay. It made her worthy to receive communion. Now the breakfast waiting at home would be extra special. She took her mother's hand, sure Mother thought so too.

***

Henrietta

As Angel pranced down the Cathedral steps beside her, Henri felt more peaceful than she had in years. She'd erased the terrible sin on her soul and joined her daughter for Communion. Her biggest burden no longer pressed on her.

Now she could focus on other problems. Yesterday, the owner of the house she rented told her she must move out by the end of June. The landlord's son was back in town with his wife and three kids. They needed a place to stay. It wouldn't be easy to find a rental that didn't take half her salary, and she might have to share a home with another family like so many people were forced to do these days. No doubt, she'd have to take a second job cleaning other people's homes. And there were other challenges ahead. Rob needed his tonsils out, and Ernie's abscess needed a dentist soon before it got worse.

On top of everything else, Henri hadn't been able to afford the glasses Angel needed. Today, that had been a blessing. Her poor eyesight kept her from recognizing Father Ferrera. But one of her biggest problems had nothing to do with money. Ernestine kept pestering her for information about her father. She'd told her children what she could about Jack Rollado, but it was never enough to satisfy daughter number two.

Henri's mood lightened, thinking about Martim. Her heart had leaped when she'd seen him slip through a side door into the shadows of the Cathedral. He'd settled into the pew behind her, wearing a coat that hid his clerical clothes. His forbidden presence had been nerve-wracking and euphoric at the same time.

In their quick conversation after Mass, he told her why he risked coming. He hadn't been present for Angel's birth or her baptism, for her first day of school, or for her birthdays. And he'd miss many more important occasions in the years to come. He'd decided, no matter the possible fallout, he couldn't miss his daughter's First Communion.

Henri smiled, thinking of the love she'd seen in his eyes when he'd spoken of their first child. She couldn't tell Angel about Father Ferrera's presence. She'd be disappointed he hadn't stopped to talk to her and would want to know why her mother hadn't invited him to dinner so she could thank him in person for the gifts he'd sent.

She put an arm around her daughter and pulled her close. Tonight, she'd have Angel write him a thank-you letter. She'd write him too and enclose pictures of this special day.

Her heart filled with gratitude. God had forgiven her, and she'd forgiven herself. The worse thing she'd ever done led to this beautiful moment. Good had come from her sin.

The End

ACKNOWLEDGMENTS:

A profound thank you to my husband Frank who has supported my writing efforts for years; to my sister Marian, whose fabulous research brought me amazing information about our grandparents; to my other sisters, Monica and Margaret, for the memories they shared of our grandmother; to my brother Peter who was a Beta reader; to my cousins Roland, Bernice, and Matt for their fabulous input, and to Kathy, and Rose for their support; to my Uncle Shorty Rob, who shared details of his life growing up with his mother Henrietta and his sisters Angelica and Ernestine.

I am grateful to Anjali Banerjee, whose conceptual input was invaluable; to Dianne Gardner, whose ideas and encouragement from the very beginning gave me focus. She formatted my book for publication and painted the portrait on the front cover. Thank you to Stephen Gardner for my final edits.

I appreciate my critique group, Jan Symonds, Carol Caldwell, and Janice Snyder. Finally, I'm thankful for my Aunt Ernestine. Without her determination to uncover the truth about her father, I could never have written the story of my grandparents.

Trish Mastel Stricklin

Trish Mastel Stricklin lived in Montana until she was 15 when her family moved to the Puget Sound area where she currently lives with her husband and her Boykin Spaniel. She earned a Bachelor of Education from Seattle University and a Masters of Education from Western Washington University. Having taught elementary school for many years, she became a consultant for parents, students, and teachers. After retirement, she wrote several middle grade and YA novels. Recently, she has focused on researching the lives of her grandparents, finding facts that are the basis of this novel, WHAT LIES IN TRUTH.

If you enjoyed reading WHAT LIES IN TRUTH, please consider giving it a review.

I invite you to check out my Website at https://tmstricklin.com and visit Trish Mastel Stricklin on Facebook where I share facts that informed the writing of WHAT LIES IN TRUTH. These two sites will also keep you updated as I write a sequel; the story of how Henrietta's and Martim's secret relationship affected the lives of their three children.

Thank you,

Trish Mastel Stricklin

Made in the USA
Middletown, DE
17 September 2023

38664357R00163